SYMBOL OF TREASON

Book 1 : Symbols Series

Natalya Orekhov

COPYRIGHT AND LICENSE INFORMATION

Acknowledgements

To my husband—thank you for loving me, encouraging me, inspiring me—always.

To my children—thank you for my never-ending education of life and all that matters most within it.

To my family—thank you for all the memories I treasure, and always being eager to make new ones.

To my faith—thank you for never leaving me.

To Designs by Anais—thank you for the remarkable cover, for listening, creating, and providing valuable insights.

To all the Bloggers—thank you for taking on a debut author without judgement, and showed me that "The Symbols Duet" was truly something extraordinary. Ralou with www.collectorofbookboyfriends.com; Texxie with www.prufreads.blogspot.com; Amy with www.writeramyshannon.wix.com; and so many more!

Prologue

Nadia Rumikov

December 2005

My mother's cries were no longer audible as I tried to barricade the poor excuse for a door with anything and everything I could find: a box, the slice of foam rubber we called our bed, and lastly but most promisingly the six foot long 2x4.

My make-shift barrier earned me a few seconds which I used to continue my digging, my desperate scraping of walls, wishing the cinderblocks that trapped me in this suffocating square room would disappear in a puff of smoke, releasing me into the possibility of freedom just beyond.

Magic was a lie. As was justice, along with everything I'd ever heard about the philosophy of ethics. All lies, tales of a life I'd never witnessed and never would. If my makeshift barricade did anything—none of it was for my benefit.

The rickety wood swung back towards me. The force with which my great uncle Boris made his entrance, reduced the paint chipped door to nothing more than a heap of paper-thin scraps atop a cracked concrete floor.

Boris stalked in without a moment's pause, hardly bothered by the jagged splinter protruding from his left fist. The first punch was clear, the pain instant. It had me sprawled across the floor and after that, everything lost its clarity.

Boris kicked my gasping torso, effectively robbing my lungs of the little breath they clung to. My arms wound themselves around my stomach, trying in vain to shield the assault that followed. I heard the definitive cracking of bone, each break fabricating a weapon within me. With each forced move the jagged edge of my own rib stabbed me from within and the pain—I couldn't begin to describe its malice.

I was gasping, crying perhaps, the only certainty I had was the presence of blood. Everything was out of focus; my entire existence was out of focus. In that moment, facing death and the brutality by which I would pass from this life, I no longer believed in anything good. Kindness was but a fairytale

Mama whispered into my ear only to give me hope in a world that had none.

My shaking hands grappled at the wall for balance only I wasn't sure why. Instinct I suppose, a biological decision void of any conscious involvement. Why fight the inevitable? Why fight when death was imminent?

The sharp blade caught the light, sparkling before it cut me. Swiftly, efficiently; it ascended just as quickly as it descended. The random jerking of my limbs had little to no effect on the blades target as it met my flesh each time; once, three times, nine. I'd lost count.

At some point I must've lost consciousness because I awoke lying in a pool of my own blood. The pool grew, the pain matching its determined acceleration. I was hot and cold all at once, my skin burning the fire of a thousand flames with each shift I made. The pain crashing in waves, ready to swallow me, drown me. I was screaming hysterically, desperate for someone—anyone to hear me, only to soon realize the sounds never left my throat. My desperation was trapped, just like me.

The echo of Boris's sinister whistling told me how far or close he'd wandered as my blurred vision was no longer of use, yet even in their broken and worthless state my eyes stared at her. The small hallway to the closet we claimed as our room was her final resting place. Her hands were stretched towards me, aching to protect me with her dying breath, the final sacrifice in *a life of sacrifices for the cancer she called her most treasured gift.*

Her once soft and hopeful eyes were now lifeless. They would never again glimmer with love as we lay down to sleep. Never shine in the most brilliant shade of amber with adoration as she searched out my father in my features. They would never squint with humor when I attempted to be funny with little success. They were empty, and so was I.

I listened to Boris's grumbling voice as he instructed Konstantine to mark and position her body while he finished up with me. I tried to remain indifferent to my fate; to steal myself against the venom I would be bitten with. I tried, only to fail in feigning these last moments; the cruelest and most terrifying moments I could've fathomed.

"When I'm finished, every Blood will know what happens to a traitor whore and her bastard spawn. Honor will be restored."

Boris shoved me to lie flat on the floor and moved to pull down my pants and panties in one rough swoop. The pain from the movements he forced upon my tattered body was enough to make me plead for death. Knowing Boris was about to rape and mutilate me was something else altogether.

I begged for death to whisk me away, save me from these last moments of terror. It was clear I'd lost a significant amount of blood, surely death was near, yet no matter how desperately I waited, it eluded me.

Boris removed his trousers swiftly only to then slow his movements as he stroked himself at a devastatingly laggard pace. His otherwise icy expression held a morbid gleam, as though he were savoring the moment, savoring his success in restoring the family's honor. The sight was like an electric jolt to my damaged mind. It was almost enough to make me go mad and I would've welcomed that veil of crazy.

I shut my eyes, yet it only accentuated the sounds of his approach. My body revolted without warning as I began to vomit uncontrollably. My gut heaved of its own accord over and over, and just as I couldn't control its beginning I was equally unable to influence its end.

It suddenly became too loud. Boris was shouting but I tried to protect my mind from making sense of his words. I heard Konstantine then, and concentrated harder to block it all out. Boris gripped my neck with vengeance and I almost cried out with gratitude for his mercy; welcoming the tightness of his grasp, the darkness, for in this moment I wanted nothing more than to part with the life I was never meant to live.

Mama, I'll be with you soon.

Chapter One

Allison Red

Present Day

"Alice. Alice! Breathe, damn it! Wake up!"

With a gasp I shot upright, shaking, covered in sweat, and my heart pounding so hard I was sure it would rip right through my ribcage. I blinked rapidly, taking in my surroundings hesitantly before realizing that I was thousands of miles from that night.

"Shhhh, it's okay. Just a dream, Alice. Just a dream."

Sitting down he propped his back against the upholstered headboard and held out his hands. I was quick to accept as his arms closed in around me.

"Alice it's been years since your last episode. Why now?"

"I don't know."

And I didn't. What's worse, I was afraid to find out.

Sniffling pathetically I wiped at my face, ridding myself of the tears not yet absorbed by Seth's white tee. I looked up to see Seth's face set in firm lines, stone-like. Anyone who didn't know better would assume the man lacked any feeling at all; but I knew him better than that.

"Alice—"

"Don't. Please. "

Boris's phantom hands still clung to my neck, his thick fingers getting tighter by the second. There was no need for such confessions. Seth had his own demons to overcome without battling mine too.

Seth stared intently, his thumb brushing away a few strands of hair, dampened by the sweat that still laid thick on pale skin. He cupped my shoulders with a gentle squeeze.

"You're stronger than anyone I know. Just don't be so strong that you don't ask me for help."

I closed my eyes and exhaled, releasing memories of a past not too far behind.

"Thank you."

We sat silent for a while; no doubt our thoughts running parallel, though neither of us wanted to give such shadows a voice.

My alarm rang its agonizing tone, so obnoxious it was probably used as a form of torture by the military; effectively breaking the silence.

"You're going to go deaf if you don't chuck that thing."

"It's a love/hate relationship."

Seth grinned, alleviating only but a third of the concern etched in his features. He got to his feet and pulled me in for a tight hug before heading for his own room. I fiddled with making my bed, watching as Seth opened my door, a half smile pinching my cheek in assurance that all was now well until the door clicked.

Alone, I sank to the floor with a pillow to my face, trying to muffle my cries. I breathed deep, then deeper, yet no matter how much oxygen I gasped in, it was inadequate.

Remembering was something I consciously avoided. Commanding my mind to forget; for I would otherwise dissolve in misery. Though it was while asleep that following such laws was most difficult, where there were neither boundaries nor filters. Sleep: my enemy.

My condition had been labeled Insomnia, as though giving it a name somehow made it less invasive. An ailment easily dealt with by a little pill, or so I'd been told. How could they know that sound sleep would only instigate the source of my insomnia? It was a mess, so I kept the stupid alarm clock to make myself feel normal; whatever normal was. It was a laughable appliance; stupid in every way and yet I kept the damn thing.

I needed the shower, desperate to scrub my crawling skin, and it was in that desperate rush that I finally acknowledged the chill which had the hair on my neck stand to attention. Intuition, sixth sense…migraine inducing feeling. I loathed it no matter the name. An ailment I'd coped with since as far back as I allowed my memory to reach. It came and went as it pleased, hitting me unexpectedly one moment yet staying dormant at other times. It was a useless trait that brought trepidation and nothing more. But despite my hatred for the serpent-like sixth sense, I'd learned long ago, if it reared its head—life was about to change in volumes. The prickling sensation announced that today marked—something. For years I'd been telling myself that I was strong and resilient; but as with everything else, it was a lie. I wasn't prepared, never was, and this time would be no different. So I crossed the suddenly monumental threshold to the shower I so desperately needed, knowing whatever awaited me would come to pass malevolently.

The washroom was cold. I liked it that way. Perhaps it was just a preference; yet when I allowed myself to reach deeper, into places I ran away from, I knew preference had little to do with it.

"You take the wall tonight, Mama. Please. Just this once?"

Despite her weathered skin and tired eyes, my mother smiled at me with the same warmth as the sun in the garden. Seventeen years I'd slept by the wall and no matter how many times I'd asked Mama to take a turn, she always found a way to convince me otherwise.

"My Nadia, my dear girl. You know an old body like mine has to be up and down all night. It makes no sense for me to wake you in the process."

"I'll be fine. You know I'll sleep right through it. You have a cough again and you won't get over it if you don't keep warm. Just one night that's all."

Mama was always sick with a cough or fever or something of the sort. The black circles were a permanent fixture under her eyes and had I never seen anyone from upstairs or some of the more privileged slaves, I would've thought it was normal. Based on the little information Sergey and Olga shared with me; I knew my mother was malnourished.

Sergey was my age, Olga was a bit younger. They were here to pay off their fathers gambling debt, a debt they knew would never be paid off. Sergey was kind; as kind as he could be given his circumstances, and mine. When the risks were small he'd sneak Mama and me fresh food, hiding it in the folds of our aprons. But that would only happen when security was slack—a rarity. Sergey would never risk his life for me and I never blamed him for that. He had Olga to look after and no act of kindness was worth jeopardizing their welfare. We knew that. We respected each other's priorities.

Mama always saved her smuggled food. When we were left alone in our quarters she'd unwrap the slice of fresh bread and say "I'd already eaten my portion, this half's for you", it didn't take long before I learned she lied—every time, just as with the sleeping arrangement. She'd look at me with the kindest eyes I'd ever seen, lovingly requesting that I concede, and I would; every time. Just like tonight.

"Don't pout, my sweet girl. Caring for you provides me ten times the warmth the wall ever could."

With a sigh I met her eyes and couldn't stop the ache in my heart at the sincerity I saw.

"I love you, Mama. So much. I worry about you."

"Shh—I'm not going anywhere. I'll be here to protect you and you needn't worry about the rest. That's my job. Now let's get some rest."

There was nothing new to the conversation we'd shared. It'd almost become a routine, albeit a genuine one. But the outcome of the subject was always the same, and it's odd how I found both comfort and sadness in that.

We laid down on the threadbare mattress we shared. I took my spot against the wall which radiated a small amount of heat. Somehow the inner workings of the concrete channeled warmth from the open oven in the kitchen, something we were mindful never to mention.

We raised our thin cotton sheet and pulled it up as far as it would go. Without thought I turned to face the wall just like I always did and Mama wrapped her thin and battered arms around my shaking body, infusing the little warmth she had into me.

Often, as on this night, I found it difficult to surrender my renegade thoughts to the stillness of sleep. The older I became the more the reality of our life disturbed me. The simplicity of my childish mind could no longer shield me from the bitter truth.

The other slaves had cots with wool blankets and pillows filled with cotton. They had access to a toilet and a shower with a curtain for privacy; allowed to eat twice a day and drink clean water.

I envied them. Sometimes I hated them, more so on the bitter days when my masters were particularly angry, looking for any error in my behavior to earn me a beating. Often they didn't need a mistake at all, and without warning I'd be led to the room beyond the wine cellar where I'd be tied up, beaten, humiliated and tossed aside when their egos were satisfied. Those days I was filled with venomous hate.

My mama tightened her hold on me and I released the rising anger. Sergey and Olga may've had privileges I didn't, but they would never see their mother again. Even if they did, I knew she didn't them the way mine loved me. I took solace in that. It was the only thing that quenched my burning desire to revolt. My mama loved me without condition and even I knew that had to be something special, something worth fighting for, so I slept and never heard Mama get up. Not once.

As the water poured over my body I scrubbed vigorously, ignoring the sting; needing to wash away far more than perspiration. As I stood in a luxurious shower you'd imagine it would be easy to forget the open stall I showered in for seventeen years, the hose that hung loosely from a hook, seeping icy water barely strong enough to call a trickle. Bathing was now a spa-like experience. Though, I rarely found much pleasure in it. Most of my idle time was spent fighting the dark, the pain, and the omnipresent grief.

I headed to my closet to sift through my wardrobe. Not that there was too much to sift. Almost everything was multipurpose and lackluster. Clothing had to blend in, just like me. I settled on a pair of faded jeans with a long-sleeved cotton top. Simple. My dark honey-colored locks were parted off-center, swaying over my shoulder's as I swiped on some lip balm.

I stared at my reflection; seeing the ruins of what was once a child who saw the world in a different light, a light no longer there. I saw tragedy and grief, pain and a hunger for justice that I was too weak to pursue. I still counted the days, a ritual which had become a contradiction I found myself unable to overcome. I feared a new day's approach and yet remained afraid that it might never reach me.

Don't worry, I whispered to myself, for I'd become fluent in the art of deception; no other would ever see the true fabric of my being and with that, I could face the day.

Chapter Two

Logan Wallace

September 2002

"Logan!"

"Did you miss me?"

My mother's smile welcomed me at the door. I opened my arms to hug her as she kissed my cheeks with a gentleness that was hers and hers alone. Her affection's used to embarrass me, though she never seemed to catch on when I would dodge her hugs and kisses like a mine-field. Not anymore. The older I became, the more I cherished her love, her devotion—her.

"Something's different about you. Everything okay?" I asked, sensing something off.

"You worry too much. Now get washed up, I made you your favorite. Ten minutes! I want to hear all the latest."

I headed to my room to drop my bag and shower quickly. It was good to be home. California was beautiful, but home…home was a place I never tired of.

"Shit!"

"Hey, Logan. Sorry, I didn't mean to startle you."

"No, it's fine. I'm fine. What are you doing here?"

Lily was beautiful. The most beautiful girl I'd ever met and the way she was looking at me made keeping myself in check a thousand times harder.

"Sal and your dad had some urgent stuff. I heard you were coming home today for break and I wanted to welcome you back."

"Does Sal know you're here?" I asked, hoping he did. Last thing I needed was another 'reminder' of how Lily was off limits.

"Of course."

I sensed a lie.

"All right. Well, I need to shower so I'll meet you downstairs. We can catch up over dinner."

Lily smiled; her cherry lips as seductive as they came.

Make that a cold shower.

Lily was attending our home college: Michigan State. It wasn't here dream but she was all the old man had left and despite getting accepted to Cornell, Lily loved her grandfather enough to stay near him. Sal had his reasons, some real heavy shit with Lily's mother. But mostly the old man worried. He loved Lily more than life itself and having her near him was all that mattered.

I respected her for it. She loved Sal, he was all she had too and truthfully, I didn't believe Lily was ready to leave the comfort of Sal's wings.

I showered quickly, eager to wash away the itching sensation that something was different at home this visit. Throwing on some jeans and a t-shirt I rushed towards the scent of homemade food.

"I've missed your cooking."

I took my seat, Lily followed, choosing to sit next to me rather than across. I could tell my mother enjoyed the sight, no doubt planning our wedding that very moment.

My father and Sal had been business partners since I was seventeen and Lily fourteen, yet even with that age gap I could never keep my eyes off of her. She dated against Sal's wishes, but nobody was ever good enough in Sal's eyes. Lily rebelled often, but eventually tired of the game, breaking the saps heart to smithereens.

Lily was into me, and I sure as hell was into her. But Sal's law applied to everyone; so out of respect, I kept my distance.

"I've missed that handsome grin." Mom said, pinching my cheek as though I was three. I grinned brighter.

With our mouths full, my mother looked happy; smiling in-between the small talk. Yet despite the easiness she'd built around the table, there was something behind that veil of innocence. I couldn't put my finger on it but it was there and it made me tense for some reason.

"What's Dad got going with Sal that he'd miss dinner?"

"He'll be back shortly, Logan. No need to worry."

Only I sensed there was.

*

"You can't! Mom!" I couldn't believe my ears.

"Do you hear me? You can't!!!"

My father wouldn't look at me.

"They're your father's only family, Logan. We're their last hope. How can we turn our backs on them?"

Easy. Just turn around and walk away!

"Dad! Dad, listen to me. You can't do this. Mom cannot heal every wounded animal in the woods. You left, remember. You left because it's too dangerous. Isn't that what you've told me? There's no one there to protect you!"

My father finally looked at me then, and I knew. I wouldn't stop them, they were leaving. I'd always known my father felt a sense of guilt for abandoning his family back in Russia. But to do this? It was insane! They weren't even supposed to know where he was.

"We fly out tomorrow and back Thursday. We'll be okay. It's good to have you home, Son. I booked us at the Dunes for the weekend. We'll have plenty of fun before you head back to California."

I was rendered speechless in disbelief.

My father reached for me but I stood and left. I couldn't wrap my head around this insanity.

"Jake, hey you home?"

"Well if it isn't Mr. Logan Wallace. You in town already?"

"Let's go grab drinks. I need to unwind. You in?"

"Yup. Pick me up."

"Two minutes, asshole." Jakes laughter was cut off as I ended the call. I wanted this mess out of my head and I knew just how to make that happen.

*

I awoke to a splitting headache, groaning as the sunlight invaded my room, forcing me to acknowledge it was morning. I smelled something foul and my stomach churned in revolt.

Upon returning to my bed I notice a note on the floor. I almost didn't bother with picking it up, it was seeing my name scrawled across the stationary in my mother's hand that caused me to reach for it.

Logan,

Please understand. Life is precious, surly you wouldn't turn your back if someone reached out to you for help in their darkest hour. It's the right thing to do. There's food in the fridge and cash in the desk drawer. We'll see you on Thursday.
Love,
Mom

They were gone.

Chapter Three

Allison Red

Located in the Foothills of Lakewood, my café sat between a theater and a mod furniture boutique. The building had large windows and a sign that bore the name Chai Café in bold midnight blue.

I scanned my surroundings while parking simply by habit and headed inside to the welcoming scent of tea leaf and coffee. I loved my time at the café, it was an escape. A place where good memories drifted through scents of apple and spice.

I powered up anything with an 'On' button, walking around on auto-pilot, lost in my thoughts until I found myself staring out the front doors watching the first signs of sunrise and feeling helpless, unable to shake the nagging alarm within. I was careful. Seth was careful. We covered all our tracks and even made false ones. So why did I feel like l was walking the edge of a cliff moments away from plunging?

"Good morning, Sweets."

Marina walked up to give me our hug and cheek kiss combo. I returned this gesture while planting a smile on my face at the sight of my best friend.

"I saw what you did to Andrew's locker."

"What makes you think it was me?"

Marina's grin confirmed what I'd already knew.

"Aside from intuition, your face has *guilty* stamped on it." We both laughed and it felt good.

"Wait till you see the inside."

Having over a dozen pictures of bondage toys plastered onto his locker with clear acrylic glue was bad enough. Whatever awaited inside made me feel sorry for him already.

"I can see where this is headed and it's making me nervous." Though, that didn't keep me from grinning like a teenage fool beside her.

We heard Andrew enter through the back door. We stood like statues with our ears honed and our eyes twinkling with mischief when Andrew strode towards us chin held high.

"The pictures are one thing," Andrew announced while pointing his index finger at us one at a time "The mutilation to my apron, shirt and pants are entirely different."

He held up his now hot pink apron with the slogan; *Submissive for Your Pleasure* accompanied with an image of Andrew wearing a spiked collar.

"Would you've been happier with *Domination Nation?*"

We both erupted in laughter.

"You realize this could be grounds for war, right?"

Andrew attempted to sound harsh but his own humor echoed as he spoke. Seemingly ignoring his threat, Marina approached; giving his midsection a squeeze as he patted her head in the same manner you would an adorable pup.

"We'll find out once and for all if chicks are attracted to men who submit,"

Andrew turned to me with pleading green eyes at the sound of Marina's glee.

"Don't look at me. I told you not to argue with her. The uniform shipment should only take a few more days. In the meantime just flip the apron inside out. It won't fix the pink, but at least it'll hide the picture."

Andrew blew out a breath while making his way towards the front counter. At over six feet tall and very athletic Andrew was like our very own firefighter. Many of our female regulars requested Andrew by name, often tipping him as though he'd serviced them far more intimately than handing them a coffee with cake. Yet despite his ever growing fan base he remained the kind and humble man I'd met nearly a year ago.

Andrew came from money, and though I'd never met any of his estranged family, I knew they disapproved. As much as I agreed that his talents and potential were well above the café, I was certainly in no hurry to have him leave.

As the clock displayed lucky number seven I unlocked the glass doors. The streets were sparse this time of morning. A few vehicles scattered here and there, but I noted one block down sat a black Porsche Cayenne. I wasn't sure why that particular vehicle caught my attention; but something in me sparked, and given my nightmare, the feeling unnerved me— warned me. I retreated, hoping my world wasn't on the brink of collapse.

"Marina I need to finish payroll so just holler if I'm needed, 'kay?"

"Sure. Oh wait, isn't Jenna scheduled this morning?"

"She's probably just running late. If anything, I'll fill in."

"You sure? I could call Stace. Her morning class ends at about ten."

"Nah, its fine. Thursday's her laundry slash cleaning day. I'm not terribly behind on my stuff, we'll be fine." With a nod Marina proceeded to the front carrying with her a fresh batch of our best seller: the Red Elephant.

The cool leather elicited a chill as I sank into my chair; cradling my Earl Grey closer in response. The hot and cold contrast mimicked my emotions as I fought to maintain control over the tornado I kept telling myself wasn't there. My hands trembled against my will and in the stillness of isolation, another tear escaped without permission. If nothing else I decided I must not panic. At the very least memories kept my instincts intact. Panic however led to mistakes, to miscalculations, and potentially to complete destruction.

Resigned, I allowed Boris's phantom hands to press into my throat. The smell of his aftershave assaulting my senses while his whistling rang through me as though a serrated blade. My flesh felt raw, as though the wounds of my past had suddenly been ripped open; only I was too afraid to look. Coward.

The mail consisted mostly of junk with a heavy dose of bills. My email sang a similar tune and before long I'd tied up payroll and entered all the bills into QuickBooks for payment. Nearing lunch hour, I was wrapping up inventory order charts before deciding I was due for a meal.

Stepping through the commons area, I tidied up the remnants from patrons departed, straightening chairs and picking up scattered napkins that cluttered the table tops.

Both Marina and Andrew were occupied so I looked to Jenna who did indeed show up this morning. "I'm headed out to run a few errands. You guys good?"

She graced me with a nod of her head as she filled a cup with boiling water, and I knew enough not to expect more. Jenna was—frustrating. I couldn't say she was completely intolerable; however, 'pleasant' wouldn't be a term I'd ascribe to her either. Sadly I'd been desperate and hired her without my typical protocol—a mistake I atoned for almost daily.

With a nod in return I headed for the door, eager to walk off the snappy string of words which laid heavy on my tongue whenever in her company. But I knew better than to make a scene. Most believed that to show strength was to scream louder, uglier, and throw in a hard punch for good measure. But if I'd learned anything from my life among vipers, it was that patience and calculation delivered superior results. Jenna was simply a nuisance. Nothing more.

I headed east, craving a SmashBurger with all the extras, and just as I hit the corner, not thirty feet from the café, a woman came out of nowhere and crashed right into me; sending us both flying to the ground. I broke my fall before reaching for my holstered gun, only to quickly conceal it when I realized my supposed assailant wasn't actually attacking. I rushed to the woman's side, no longer concerned for my own safety but for the slumped and trembling body before me.

"Are you all right?" Adrenaline caused me to speak faster and louder than I'd intended.

"I'll call an ambulan—"

"No!"

Her head shot back to look straight at me and I felt instant sadness for this stranger. Confusion, shock, and shame showed clearly in her face all at once, and the sight pulled at me so deeply I couldn't look away. She gripped me tighter as she used my weight to stand with the posture of a scared child.

She was larger than I, well over five feet to my barely five; yet somehow I could see how delicately fragile she was.

She wore a thick apron with smudges—remnants of dirt it seemed, and beneath the messy pony tail, shapeless sweatpants, and sweatshirt, this strange woman was really quite pretty. But her eyes spoke only of sadness and loss. She seemed distant, almost as if she wasn't even there at all. With a solid grip I led her to the wrought iron bench a few feet from the café.

"I'm Alice, and this is my café behind us."

I raised my hand and waved back towards the double doors. I waited for a response but she remained silent aside from her heavy breathing. Several bystanders who'd witnessed the collision loitered around until it seemed clear enough we were going to be okay.

"How about we go to the ladies room and get you cleaned up a bit? Then perhaps you can call someone to come and get you?"

"I'm—I—I was supposed to be in my garden. I heard the children but I couldn't find them."

There was little to be said so I stuck to what I could make sense of. There were lots of residential communities around here. She probably lived nearby.

"Do you have an I.D.?"

She handed me her wrist, bearing a sterling silver Figaro link I.D. bracelet that read *Daniel Mills ~ 303-164-1444 ~*. Ignoring my own curiosity at this particularly odd incident, I decided to forge on.

"Alright. Let's get you cleaned up and make that call, okay?"

When I turned towards the café, Andrew was standing with the door already open; his expression unusually hard.

I mouthed "Thank you" as I led the injured women towards the restroom. The dizziness from being upright had me reaching back to touch a throbbing spot on my head. I was bleeding. I hadn't realized I'd hit my head in the fall.

I led her to the sink as though she were a small child. Once satisfied that she was capable of washing up on her own I went to get a first aid kit. I had them everywhere, one of my many quirks as Andrew put it, though, he never complained when I came running with my cornucopia of healing serums and ointments for his various cuts and burns of endless mishaps.

"Would it be all right if I asked your name?"

"Sarah." Was all she offered.

"Okay, Sarah, I have some saline fluid, antibacterial ointment, and bandages. You should clean your cuts and scrapes if you don't want to visit the ER."

I waited for a response that never came. It was difficult to know whether she was even coherent most of the time when she seemed a million miles away.

"If at any time you want to do this yourself or change your mind about the ER visit just let me know. I'm no doctor but I'll try to be thorough."

Sarah looked resigned, never giving me indication one way or another. I chose to proceed with caution and hoped I was doing the right thing.

Sarah's physical injuries were superficial mostly, with the exception of one cut on her right temple which needed a butterfly bandage. The injury I was most concerned about was the one not visible on skin. It was also the injury I had no way of tending to.

Exiting the washroom Sarah swayed unsteadily and I made a mental note to tell this Daniel Mills character that she needed to be checked for a concussion. I wrapped her arm around my shoulder while placing mine around her waist; that's when her legs gave out completely. The sudden shift in balance took us both down, and for the second time in the last twenty minutes I found myself shuffling to get back on my feet. I'd barely had one foot stable when I felt a firm arm wrap around my own waist. I imagine I should've felt relief, but the connection was like electricity shooting straight through me.

It was only when I turned to face the source of the assistance did I realize how unprepared I was. This time, my own feet gave out.

Chapter Four

Allison Red

Without warning the laws of physics ceased their rule. Nothing moved, time was no longer in session; my breath— fleeting.

Lightning was all I could see and thunder was the only sound I heard. I should've ran, left everything behind without a moment's pause and disappeared in search of refuge from what revealed itself in this man's stare. I should've ignored the velvet heat which transcended my being wholly, and masked every effect this man had with my wall of indifference. *He's a stranger*, I reminded myself. Yet I couldn't shake the ominous feeling that…I wasn't sure.

My legs now held me upright, though, I had no recollection of when that occurred. I felt unsteady, disoriented somehow. His touch disarmed me and despite great effort, I failed to convince myself that I didn't want his touch to return. What seemed like an eternity must've only been mere seconds.

I watched this man help Sarah to her feet yet I couldn't identify any detail about his appearance. I saw him and yet I didn't see him. His presence was *inside* me: my pulse, my mind, my skin, and somehow the flesh of his body remained blurred to me. I was losing my grip on reality; and on the verge of panic before his voice broke through the noise inside my head.

"Allow me to help. Why don't we settle her in that chair?" His voice flowed through me, heavy and warm. I moved aside as he now held Sarah by the hand, leading her towards said chair.

As though a fog was lifting, I began to see more of his physical characteristics. Tall, fit…sharp. He moved with confidence but more so with a presence; unseen, untouched, yet undeniably felt.

I stood motionless, unable or unwilling to escape this strange waltz, when the man turned his attention back to me. With both hands his fingers trailed their way down my arms, the heat so powerful I felt it through the cotton of my shirt. He took both my hands in his, gently turning them over.

"You seemed to go down pretty hard back there, are you hurt?" He spoke gently, with genuine concern, a caring unlike that of a stranger as he scanned the scrapes on the palms of my hands.

"I—I'm all right. Thank you—and thanks for helping Sarah."

"It was but my civic duty Ms—"

"Red. Allison Red." My voice lacked ease and I hated it.

"Of course; Allison. The name suits you." His eyes flamed just like moments before, its heat radiating through the small space between us.

"That's very kind, Mr.—?"

"Logan Snow." His eyes looked back expectantly, was I to know him?

Mr. Snow pulled out a chair and ushered me to sit before taking a seat opposite me. He hadn't bothered to request permission for his company. He had a confidence, an aura that drew me in and demanded submission—compliance in all things.

"Allow me to get you a drink and something to eat. What'll it be?"

"As it turns out, Mr. Snow the café belongs to me. Allow me to get you something instead."

"You just took a serious fall, Allison. I insist you sit."

Mr. Snow began to stand. Perhaps the polite thing to do would've been to let him. The sensible thing any normal person in my situation would've done.

"Though your regard for my well-being is much appreciated, Mr. Snow, I insist: my café, my rules. I assure you I'm okay, hands included. What may I get you? Or would you prefer I guess?"

I stood, eager to distance myself; for every moment I remained in his presence the more I was questioning my own sanity.

With visible reluctance Mr. Snow reclaimed his seat.

"Surprise me."

It was a challenge. One I too eagerly accepted.

As the fog thinned, my assessment of Mr. Snow sharpened. To say he was handsome would be to say the Milky Way was merely a cluster of stars. A fact of which he was well aware. A chair I found spacious for my frame hardly contained his. His clothes: tailored. Physique: sculpted. Mouth: sinful. Reason after reason on why I should stay the hell away.

Though I refused to look, I felt his scorching gaze all the same. My pulse raced and my skin still tingled from his touch. How could a complete stranger affect me in such an intimate way? It was ridiculous, what the hell was wrong with me!

I'd never been one to notice attractive men. Why bother when I was busy trying to stay alive? This was different, raw and invasive. Logan Snow didn't request my attention—he demanded it and I obliged.

I needed distance.

"Hello. Earth to Alice."

I turned from the display box to see Marina staring at me bewildered.

"I'll explain later."

"Oh no you don't. You'll tell me right now or so help me I'll have Andrew tackle you right here right now."

Through the sarcasm Marina's concern was palpable. I grabbed both her hands while looking her in the eyes, pleading for her to understand.

"I'm all right. I'll explain later, okay?"

With a side glance I could see Andrew staring at me with a coldness I'd never experienced from him before. Marina squeezed my hands before getting back to her duties. I sighed, though, I wasn't sure for what.

My hands made quick work in preparing the beverages. I remained undecided in whether I was returning to the table out of duty to ensure Sarah's safe return to loved ones or the prickling possibility that my 'duty' was second to what was really drawing me back; like a stupid moth to a damn flame.

I set the hot beverage before Mr. Snow with false confidence. Internally the seconds dragged as I waited for him to take his first sip to either celebrate victory or admit defeat. In show of indifference I took my time setting the remaining two drinks and box of cupcakes on the table.

As Mr. Snow raised the cup to his lips I couldn't refrain from staring in open anticipation.

"Irish Crème. I concede to your victory, Allison. Well done."

Despite his words of praise he radiated anger.

"Do you serve liquor to all your customers?"

"No."

He raised a brow as if to say—was that all?

"You're my first, Mr. Snow, and my last."

"I'm honored."

Every word spoken was code. Nothing was as it seemed.

"Sarah, I brought you some cider and Ibuprofen for your head. This box is for you to take home; my business card is inside so if you ever find yourself in this area again needing help, please come in and get me okay? Anytime, I mean it."

Sarah sat silently with her sight cast toward the outdoors. She gave no indication that she'd heard or understood anything I'd just said to her and I began seeing her as nothing more than a frightened child masquerading as an adult. Mr. Snow watched me intently, almost quizzically, as though trying to figure something out. I both desired his attention and wanted it to dissipate.

"How about we call Daniel? Would you mind if I glance at the bracelet?"

Sarah seemed frozen as she continued staring at the world outside the café windows but placed her wrist gently on the table palm up.

"You sure you want to do that?"

"Excuse me?"

"You know nothing of this Daniel Mills. For all we know he could be her kidnapper or abuser. He could be the reason she appears to be—" Mr. Snow moved his hand in a wave like motion towards Sarah; the insinuation clear.

"He's not."

"And you're certain how?"

Because she didn't tremble upon hearing his name, or fold into herself when she'd heard you insinuate that he was her abuser; because when she gently placed her wrist to expose his contact information, she didn't fidget with the bracelet like it was a poison-laced-leash.

"Call it instinct." I pushed call and pressed the phone to my ear.

After brief pleasantries and a consolidated explanation of how Sarah was currently sitting in my café, Daniel was on his way.

Seemed that intelligent conversation had become a challenge as I fidgeted helplessly in Logan Snow's presence.

The longer we sat in silence the more anxious I became; worrying that if I couldn't keep my voice level, my accent might surface and just the thought—

"Tell me about your café. You've been open since early this year, is that right?"

"Yes, since February."

"Whatever you're doing seems to be working." Mr. Snow's gaze wandered about the busy café before settling back on me.

"How do you compete with a monster like Starbucks a mere five minutes from here?" With a raised brow he sipped his coffee and I relaxed at the neutral topic.

"Thorough marketing prior to launch, double that in free coffee and cake after launch, followed by endless customer appreciation."

Pleased that my voice was level and my accent contained, I reclined into the chair with a bit more confidence.

"I would have to agree." His words carried a chuckle as he raised his coffee cup.

"It seems plausible it'll soon be you with locations on every block."

"It's never been my intension to have more than one location."

"Oh? Might I ask why?"

He was looking straight through me; lifting the curtains one by one. I felt exposed to his gaze—and I almost liked it. God help me.

"Why did you choose to come to Chai Café as opposed to the Monster, Mr. Snow?"

His eyes darkened, the air between us suddenly cooler. Perhaps I'd offended him? Before I could contemplate, a man entered the café, walking quickly towards us.

"Allison? I'm Daniel, Sarah's brother. Thank you so much for calling me."

I acknowledged his introduction with a wave of my hand and pointed to the remaining vacant chair.

"I can't begin to tell you how grateful I am for your kindness."

"It was nothing. I'm sure anyone else would've done the same."

Daniels gaze dropped. It occurred to me that this had happened before; rendering my comment thoughtless. Of course I knew not *everyone* was kind. I knew better than most.

"I gave Sarah my business card in case she should ever be in this area again. I want you to know you're both welcome here anytime."

Daniel smiled a genuine smile, transforming his face. He appeared younger than Sarah, perhaps in his mid-thirties. He was handsome by anyone's standards; blonde hair cut short and slightly spiked, brown eyes with pale skin, taller than I, but so was ninety percent of the population.

His eyes wandered to Mr. Snow and it registered.

"Please forgive my poor manners. Daniel, this is Mr. Snow. He was kind enough to assist me, trouble with footing and all that."

"Daniel Mills, pleasure to meet you, Mr. Snow."

I sensed a moment's pause before Mr. Snow reciprocated the greeting.

"*Mrs.* Red, flatters me. I played a minor role in Sarah's guardianship. Right place, right time."

The punctuation to my marital status didn't go unnoticed. The possible meaning I reasoned was better left unexplored.

Sarah wandered towards the windows, Daniel said nothing so neither did I. He watched her, sadness taking over his features.

"Daniel, I mentioned most of what happened over the phone, however, I also wanted to point out that I offered to have her injuries examined by medical professionals but Sarah refused. I could be out of line but it seems as though she isn't really listening? I'm not deliberately trying to offend—"

"Please. You have nothing to apologize for." There was an extended indecisive pause. Daniel contemplated as I watched him visibly struggle.

"I don't normally share Sarah's condition with strangers but oddly I have a feeling it might be helpful if this should happen in the future, and you really have been generous."

He shifted in his seat, still hesitant.

"Sarah suffered an emotional collapse in the spring when her husband, son, and daughter were killed in a collision on their way home. A flash flood eroded the roadside and it caved just as they were passing. Their car rolled down the cliff side before hitting a boulder. Sarah's doctor says she's unable to cope. The Sarah we see is rarely coherent or aware of her surroundings. Mostly she's lost in her memories and either unable or unwilling to rejoin reality."

I suddenly recalled Sarah saying she'd heard children laughing but couldn't find them. My heart filled with sympathy.

"Our parents—are unavailable. I took Sarah into my care, but I have a family of my own. Keeping track of her whereabouts has proven more difficult than I ever expected. I feel terrible."

Mr. Snow watched me with increased intensity. Why he stayed throughout this encounter, I didn't know. I chose not to ask.

"Sarah has *you*," I offered.

"Such love is a rare commodity. You shouldn't be so hard on yourself."

Daniel looked stricken, as though my words took him completely by surprise.

"Thank you for that. You, Mrs. Red, have been an invigorating experience, truly. Thank you."

After exchanging a few more words, Daniel led Sarah by the arm to his Volkswagen just outside. I followed, carrying the box of cupcakes, which seemed so little now given my new knowledge. With Sarah secure in the backseat Daniel stood before me with a solemn smile of gratitude.

"Thank you again. If you need your injuries looked at please allow me to compensate you for the care—"

"That won't be necessary. Take this home to your family. It's not much, but sugar's always been a good friend of mine."

Daniel surprised me with a heartfelt hug. There was nothing inappropriate in his embrace, and I had no desire to pull back.

Watching the retreating sedan I waved contently. However tragic her situation, Sarah had a brother who loved her unconditionally, and I'd learned long ago, *that* was something worth holding onto.

Upon returning I found Mr. Snow exactly where I'd left him, eliciting attention from nearby patrons; sitting poised and full of demand. I half expected him to have left, and if I'd said I felt nothing upon seeing him still there, my nose would've been nearly three meters long. So while I listed reason after reason in alphabetical order of why I should quietly disappear into my office, my disobedient feet continued their route toward him as though answering a silent siren call I couldn't drown out.

Without comment I took my seat and handed Mr. Snow my phone; the article already on display.

"Storm Claims Three Lives Saturday. Is this your way of saying I told you so?" He asked.

"Perhaps."

"How *were* you so sure?"

"I'm a good judge of character."

"And what judgment have you made about me, Allison?"

"Mr. Snow-"

"Call me Logan. I insist."

I couldn't. I needed the formality, even in form of name.

"Mr. Snow—thank you again for your help and your company. Is there anything else I can get you before I head back to my office?"

The sound of his formal name spilling over my lips felt like a punch to the gut, but I swallowed back my own desires. I stood, both hoping and dreading Mr. Snow following my lead.

Logan Snow appeared upset. Maybe disappointed; or perhaps that was wishful thinking on my part. He gave a curt nod to someone out the window and I turned to find a gorilla of a man dressed in black slacks and a trench coat; like a modern version of Batman sans the mask and cape, standing before a black Porsche Cayenne that I would deem a downgrade from the Batmobile. Turning, I nearly stumbled backward as Mr. Snow now stood mere inches from me with that familiar heat in his stare.

"*Allison,* it has been a rare pleasure to have been in such exquisite company today. I see I've taken up a good deal of your time and I myself must regretfully depart. How much for the coffee?" His voice was hypnotic; his lips wicked.

"That won't be necessary, Mr. Snow. Consider it a token of thanks." My voice wavered against all command, and trapped beneath his piercing gaze, I had little resolve.

Every limb fidgeted, my poker face collapsed, and all that remained was the desire to be swallowed whole. I found no comfort as I continued to shift my weight; my injuries long forgotten until I was stupid enough to rub the back of my neck, accidentally pulling the wound on my scalp. I winced despite myself and in such seconds of my idiocy, Mr. Snow became ice cold.

His hand stretched out towards me and I should've said something; *stop* or *no,* or perhaps stepped aside to distance myself. Only I did no such things. I stood anxiously awaiting his touch, the touch of a complete stranger, the touch that awoke things inside I never knew I harbored.

"You're bleeding."

I heard rather than saw his clenched teeth, the strain in each syllable.

"I'm all right." I whispered the words, wondering if he saw the depth of the lie; how not all right I truly was.

"My physician will examine your wound."

Mr. Snow moved to grab his phone and I surprised us both at how quickly I stopped the device from reaching his ear. He stared icily at my hand, then my eyes; but said nothing.

"I must get back." I whispered.

My hand pulled back, and for the first time since we met, Mr. Snow appeared uncollected—unable to school his features; even if only for a moment.

With a nod Logan Snow left my café, striding quickly, only to get in the back seat of the very SUV I was curious about this morning.

His departure felt unfinished somehow, as though our encounter was the most beautiful tapestry; only ours was left with the threads still swaying to the breath of its weaver, in waiting, and incomplete.

As the SUV became but a dark spot in the distance I felt a longing to be within his company again; a dangerous wish. So I forced myself to let it go; I had no place for such desires.

Turning towards the office I faced the stares.

Marina looked gleeful, about ready to bring out the pom-poms. Her excitement came as little surprise when she'd been counting the days to see me react to a man in any way other than 'yes you're very nice, let's be acquaintances'.

I bypassed Jenna's point blank glare; a mere degree short of a sneer. I cared more about the dirt lining my shoes than about her misguided judgment.

But it was when I looked at Andrew that I faltered. His usual boyish cheer was gone, replaced with a hardness not suited for his handsome face. He stared at me as though it was some face-off, announcing me the loser as I cast my eyes to the floor and making quick steps to reach seclusion. But I wasn't fast enough.

"Alice, you really should have your head examined."

Thinking he was teasing my less than stellar performance with Mr. Snow, I turned to fire back in playful banter. But my retort lodged in my throat at the sight of him.

Andrew's expression held no trace of humor, something I never realized meant so much until it wasn't there. Caught off guard I momentarily drew a blank, standing with my mouth agape. Andrew reached out to touch my hair where blood had blackened it, and I realized he was referring to my head wound.

"Thanks, Andrew. I'm really all right though. Looks worse than it is."

"No. No it's not all right, though, arguing with you is pointless; just come get me if you need anything."

Though his voice rang lighter, his expression was as sorrowful as before. God, it hurt to see him like that.

"You're the first call I'll make, Doc." My attempt at humor bore no fruit, and my heavy handed smile stood alone in the space between us.

"Andrew, wait."

He paused without turning to look at me.

"Is everything all right? I mean, you're—I just—are you okay?" My speech fumbled more than a two year old with a football.

"I'm serious, Alice; watch for dizziness, nausea, sleepiness or even spontaneous laughing. If any of those occur, come get me and we'll visit the ER. Concussions can be dangerous so just play it safe, for me at least."

I took the hint and let my question go unanswered.

"I will."

I watched him retreat through the swinging doors before shutting the door to my office. With my eyes shut tight, my hands over my mouth, I screamed; but found no relief.

*

Hours had elapsed and the café doors stood closed. The tables and chairs were empty and the staff; gone.

A few taps on the door indicated I had a visitor and although I was happy to see Marina, I knew I wasn't ready to face the questions she was dying to ask.

"You didn't have to stay you know."

"Of course I know. I also know that you need to spill what happened today. I've let you stay holed up in here long enough. Start talking." Marina's voice was firm but she looked at me with that prodding softness only she could pull off.

Marina had become a pillar in my life. We met in a Wilton cake decorating class over four years ago and though I kept to myself throughout the course, Marina found a way to sprout a friendship. A friendship so strong I would come to think of her as my sister, her father; my dad and her brother; mine as well. She opened up her family to me and I took it with greed. A debt I could never repay.

Seeing me yield, Marina held up her index finger. She returned holding two paper cups for my impending confession and I gladly took the tea.

Occupying the seat opposite my desk she made herself comfortable; watching me stall as long as I could.

"Has everyone left?"

"Yup."

"Are the doors locked?"

"Yup."

"Did the Martin's pick up their order?"

"Oh come on! Really? Yes, for goodness sake yes, yes, yes!"

And there it was, the threshold where Marina would no longer entertain my reluctance to open up.

"I had a nightmare last night."

I glanced up from my tea to see Marina's smile fade.

"I knew—when I woke up I knew. I could feel it in the air. I don't know what, but something is happening. I haven't had to look over my shoulder for so long. But now it's back to the beginning. I took note of everything. Even became curious about some random SUV parked down the block. I couldn't focus, obsessing over every detail of our escape."

I took a steadying breath.

"I had to get some air and maybe some food, so I walked outside and not three minutes later got body slammed into the sidewalk. You saw the rest."

"I can see your hair's still bloody. How is it? How are your hands?"

My injuries were minor on the grand scale. Reflexively I reached up to finger the crusty hair strands and winced upon contact. There was a lump; sore and tender, but the bandage glue I globbed onto the cut worked decent enough. My hands and elbows had scrapes all over but nothing that wouldn't heal.

"I'm all right. Honestly I even forgot I hit my head at all."

I gave Marina a wry smile, shrugging a shoulder.

"Since you're clearly avoiding stating the obvious I suppose I'll be blunter. Who was the walking billboard for Trojan who had trouble keeping more than four inches of space between you two?"

Oh, that. Of course she wouldn't let this go.

"His name's Logan Snow. He helped when I couldn't handle Sarah's weight on my own. He stayed of his own accord and then left. I know nothing of him."

"You have ten seconds to amend your poor excuse for an explanation."

I loved her.

"He saw me." I swallowed the lump forming at the back of my throat.

"I mean really saw me. He looked into my eyes and opened the door to my soul. His eyes—they were the most expressive eyes I've ever seen. I felt connected to him, some invisible thread that bound me to him. It's stupid I know; diary worthy! Either way it doesn't matter. He couldn't possibly be interested in me. You saw him. He's completely out of my league. Hell, he's three leagues out of my league. And even if by some miracle he was attracted to me I couldn't entertain the idea anyway. How do you explain to someone that you're in a mutually beneficial marriage façade for survival? Besides, I doubt we'll see him again."

By the time I finished convincing myself more than Marina, my voice was nearly a whisper.

Marina sat thoughtful, guilty even—though for what I hadn't a clue. She'd always believed that one day things would fall into place for me. That some mysterious plague would eradicate my assassins, granting me the peace and security I couldn't bring myself to even dream of. Soon after I would find love; true and passionate, which would undoubtedly lead to a white picket fence and tiny feet running about the large green lawn. Trampling all the flowers I would've just planted. And I would be whole.

I loved her optimism, loyalty, and desire to see me happy. But even Marina couldn't argue with logic. Some things just didn't happen. That's why we craved fiction. Each searching for that escape, that fantasy we desired when our reality wasn't enough.

"You're not crazy. I saw it, there was static in the air, Andrew saw it too. Jenna—well she just couldn't keep the disgust off her face. She thinks you're a two-timing-bimbo you know. I swear I thought she was going to tackle you to get thirty seconds of face time with Mr. I'm too sexy for my shirt, too sexy for my shirt sooo sexy yeah!"

I broke out laughing, spilling tea in the process, thus justifying the wad of paper I threw at her head. It was her fault after all.

"Hey!"

Marina grabbed the wad off the floor and chucked it right back at me, hitting me square in the nose.

"I can still remember the first time I showed you that video. I thought it was exactly what Queen Elizabeth would have looked like if she was plucked from the fifteenth century and dropped center stage next to Lady Gaga."

I was clutching my side, unable to stop the laughter.

"I just remember staring at his one hoop earring, fishnet shirt, and wondering why he didn't have a hoop in both ears. At least then it'd be symmetric. Don't even ask! I still don't know!" I could barely speak between the laughter.

Marina was right, I was at a complete loss when she played me that music video on YouTube.

"The odds may be stacked against you, true. But look at how far you've come, Alice. If I'd told you four years ago you'd own your own café and lead a semi-normal life, would you've believed me? No. You would've said to me what you're saying to me now. Logic and reason has its place and time but you can't rule out luck, chance, and spontaneous order to that which seems impossible. Besides, you know me. I'm a sucker for the underdog. And you, Alice are the underdog of all underdogs. One day you'll make all the other underdogs proud and maybe even start an exclusive club. Maybe you'll call it—Rising Hounds!"

"Why an underdog? Why not Underlions, Underbears, or any other ferocious animal? Wouldn't that make for a better climax when we come out on top roaring and throwing around our beastly weight?"

The laughter returned obnoxiously loud, and then I hiccoughed. Marina clutched her side in an attempt to ease the pain while we both wiped tears from our eyes.

We had a true friendship, the kind without bounds or limits. We were entirely honest with each other without worrying whether the other would still be there the next day.

I never intended to drag Marina into my web of chaos, though, that didn't keep her from building a place for herself in my heart from afar; and by the time I realized how attached I'd become, it was too late. That was her weapon. She lit up the room and you couldn't help being drawn towards her.

"Was it that obvious?"

"Oh, you mean did anyone notice that suddenly earth halted in its orbit? Um—yeah. You'd have to be a vegetable to have missed it."

"It was reckless. I can't believe how quickly I became such a fool. Oh God I actually strained to hide my accent. Can you believe that! I haven't had to do that in years!"

I was laughing a frustrated laugh. I wasn't a fan of anyone having such a powerful and controlling effect on me, but at the same time I'd be lying if I'd said I didn't feel electrified by it.

"Don't be such a snob. You handled the encounter with class in my opinion. Who else could be bleeding—with a possible concussion mind you—and still help the woman who knocked you down find her way home, all the while facing the spokesman for edible testosterone, and still make coffee? I would say you passed your first lesson of chemistry on steroids with flying colors!"

"You're seriously delusional."

Our laughter lingered from behind our half empty cups of now lukewarm tea, enjoying these moments for what they were; moments.

"Thanks, Sunshine. I'm not sure where I'd be without you; and we both know the truth in that."

"Then I suggest we don't waste time pondering the 'what if's'. I'm here and you're here. That's all that matters."

"Aye, Aye, Captain!"

"All humor aside, Alice; I won't stop believing that happiness will find you even if logic says it won't. Logic can take a hike. Sometimes—sometimes hope prevails."

I wanted to believe her. It was a nice sentiment, the kind you'd read on a Hallmark card. But this was reality. I wasn't a cat with nine lives nor did I have a get-out-of-jail-free card to whip out when I hit a rough patch. I had one life, one chance, and logic had kept me alive. Sometimes no matter how much we hoped, logic won.

"I'll see you tomorrow."

"Goodnight, Alice."

Chapter Five

Logan Snow

February 2004

"Close the door, Logan."

Sal was pale. Translucent almost. The monitors, I.V., the oxygen; it all spoke of death.

"Sit, Logan. We need to talk."

"If you'd stop this lazy nonsense and got your ass up already we could have a multitude of conversations back at the office." I quipped, needing him to just get up and keep living.

He smiled, but it was weak. Too weak.

Sal reached for my hand. He'd aged decades in these short weeks. I took a seat in the vinyl chair and placed Sal's hand in mine. It was cold and slim, and I knew he'd come to the end.

"I know what you've been doing, Logan." Sal paused, looking me straight in the eyes.

"I'm not judging you. I understand, Son. Your mom and Matthew, they—" An ugly cough cut through Sal as his body shook to get through it. "—they deserve justice. I understand. But I fear you don't. Some things are just beyond our abilities."

I gripped Sal's fragile hand. He was giving me his damn going away speech and I didn't want to hear it. I wanted him to get his shit together, get out of the damn hospital bed, and force his body back into submission.

"Tom's drawn up some documents. Everything, all my assets have been allocated for Lily. Except the company. Logan, the company, I'm leaving you my shares. Lily never wanted any part of it, her heart was always someplace else. I want you to have the company."

I couldn't speak. With Sal's shares I would become sole owner.

I respected Sal. After my parents deaths Sal took me under his wing. I was an adult but he wouldn't take no for an answer. Had me adopt his name as an added security measure. He was a stubborn man but no fool, by any measure. I understood why his relationship with my father started out rough. They were too much alike.

"Look at me, Son."

I looked up to see his eyes boring into mine.

"I need you to promise me something."

I didn't hesitate. "Name it."

"Take care of Lily—I'm not asking you to marry her. Just care for her. Keep her safe, happy, whatever that might mean. I want her to be happy, Logan. She's going to be alone. Like you. You'll understand what she's going through. Help her."

Sal's eyes stared intently, desperate for assurance. Lily meant the world to the old man. How could I deny him such a request?

"You have my word."

Sal squeezed my hand. A handshake.

"I need something from you too."

I had his attention.

"I need the Phantom's name."

Sal visibly shuddered.

"You don't know what you're asking. I beg you to reconsider, Logan. *Please*."

Reconsider? It was too late for that.

"His name, Sal."

Sal schooled his features. *There* he was; the old man I knew. The one who did what had to be done. No matter the cost.

"Gabriel Lorenzo."

I nodded my gratitude and stood to go find Tom. Sal wouldn't judge me, but that certainly didn't mean he was happy with the direction I was headed. Unfortunately for him, my mind was made. I'd come to care for him a great deal. Perhaps I would go as far as to say I'd come to love the old man. But I couldn't be sure I was capable of love. The man I *was*, well, he was gone.

"You're a good man, Salvatore Snow—" I couldn't finish the rest.

"God help you, my boy."

I wouldn't bet on it. If God stood by as my mother's life was ripped from her, surely he wouldn't give a damn for the likes of me.

Bending down, I kissed the old man's forehead. This was goodbye.

Exiting Sal's room I spotted Lily in the corridor. She looked tired, fatigued. Her blonde hair not in its usual pristine style and her lips, missing the shade of red that was distinctly hers. She was a true blonde beauty, you'd never know she had any Italian in her at all.

"Logan! Is he awake? Is he talking? Tell me. How is he? The nurse said I couldn't go in. Is he all right?"

I wrapped my arms around her, wanting to ease some of the anxiety. Provide her some comfort for what was happening in that room to the only family she had left.

"Shh. He's awake. He wants to see you."

Lily's shoulders shook; her tears touching my skin as they soaked through my shirt. The image of Lily vulnerable and scared; it reminded me of that Thursday I awaited my parent's return flight. Standing at the gate, desperate to spot them within the large crowd. I remembered the disbelief as the last passenger made his way past me, the gate; empty. I wasn't ready to face that reality then. Just as Lily wasn't ready to face hers now. But there was nothing to be done. I'd made a promise to Sal and so I held her, for as long as she would need me to.

Chapter Six

Allison Red

I dropped my things on my nightstand, not bothering to change before I headed to Seth's room; needing to discuss security in the hopes that it would alleviate the weight pressing down on me. I tapped on his door which was already open just a crack.

"Yeah, come in."

Seeing Seth sitting on the edge of his bed with his head in his hands, said the night was far from over.

"Hey there, Brother Bear. No need to worry, I've got pots of honey downstairs."

I was never good at being witty, but I was usually rewarded with something for my efforts. Tonight the reward never came and my blood began to cool to match the mood.

"I see honey won't fix what you've got. But my mind is racing so please tell me what's upset you." My voice was calm and even, unlike my racing pulse. Seth still hadn't looked at me. I could see the hard set of his jaw as he clenched his teeth. My fatigue now long forgotten.

Seth reached for my hands nudging me to sit beside him. The air hung heavy around us, a pregnant silence bidding its time. Once Seth met my eyes; *that* look, the look I knew would come one day and I *knew* before he spoke the words.

"I want you to have your own life, Alice." He paused and I couldn't be sure if it was for his needs or my own.

"You deserve happiness and a real marriage someday, one built on love between two people who want to be together; *not* out of necessity or fear."

He tried to appear confident, unaffected, but once you'd lived through tragedy the way I had with Seth, I knew him well enough to see he was struggling.

"You're my family. The only family I've ever really known. But we can't live in fear the rest of our lives. We both want more from this life. It's a risk, I know—damn it I know." Seth's grip tightened and mine responded in kind.

"But it's a risk I'm willing to take. If I make it to old age, I don't want to regret passing up my chance at true happiness."

Over the years I'd built myself a sturdy shelter in Seth, a place of refuge I'd run to anytime I needed safety and reassurance. My shelter never faltered, needed no maintenance, no updating of any kind. It remained steadfast without vacation or sick days, always giving me it's all.

But my shelter never bluffed or debated either. If Seth requested *anything*, his mind was already made; he never gave in to whims. Seth was thorough and calculated and I knew better than to believe anything less.

"I want a divorce, Alice."

I couldn't hold in the tears as Seth pulled me into his arms; holding me for as long as I needed. I'd always known that our arrangement would end eventually. We were both young and had our whole lives ahead of us, *if only we were never found*. But Seth spoke truth: if we reached such an age where we'd reflect on a life lived, it was with certainty we'd wish we risked it all so as to truly live.

I couldn't do that to him. Seth deserved freedom, to take what he desired from life, even if I was not ready to do the same. I couldn't hold him back.

I had to believe that good would come of this; willing the persistent fears which echoed in warning about what could happen to the people we loved most to dissipate. The warnings teetered on the line of inevitability, a dance of torment which robbed me of my own decision to embrace life in all its beauty.

I awoke in my own bed, not remembering how I'd gotten there. A glass of water with two Advil's sat idly on my nightstand. A note tucked neatly beneath the glass revealed the message I would never forget.

The sun will rise and bring us with it.

The sentiment touched home as I remembered the first time Seth spoke the string of nine words.

"Leave me, I'm as good as dead anyway!" I screamed at him, wanting him gone yet fearing he might actually leave.

"Stubbornness has no place here, Nadia. Take the pills, rest, and I'll work out the rest."

Konstantin didn't share much of his inner workings on getting us out of our temporary quarters in Germany. The room was larger than the last place we stayed at in Poland but the additional square footage cost us greatly in sanitation. We had no running water and the toilet past the paper thin wall was merely for aesthetics it would seem. A hole in the ground below served as the septic, reminding me too much of my quarters back at Hell's Mansion. But it wasn't the lack of luxury I found unbearable, it was the dependence.

I felt something deeper than vulnerability each time Konstantin carried me to the prop toilet and sat with me, holding one part or another of my body as I attempted not to whimper and scream from the pain that such fundamental bodily functions inflicted. Each time, he'd clean me up and carry me back without a hint of discomfort or disgust; that was terrible enough, what's worse was his actions forced me to see him as human and not the monster I knew him to be.

Konstantin did his best to maintain my hygiene but we stunk regardless; when only able to wash ourselves down with a rag and semi clean water it was inevitable. The limited clean drinking water too precious to waste on bathing and our appearance reflected as much.

My bandages should've been renewed almost a week ago. Now nearly all the stitches were surrounded with a sickly red and swollen infection. My body was weak with too many injuries to heal. Fourteen nights had passed and yet I still peed blood, the act inflicting such agony I often blacked out, too weak to trudge through it fully conscious. I was no doctor but I couldn't imagine a possible recovery.

Konstantin refused to discuss my condition, but we both knew I was only holding him back. If not for my dead weight he'd be in Colorado already. The Mile High City, he says it's called. America was our best shot and had I been well enough to fly, we could've secured ourselves a spot two days ago.

79

"If you stay, you'll die. Take your chance and go."

Konstantin's features grew hard—a look so familiar to me that I no longer shuddered in response. Then, for the first time, he looked away. The movement caught me off guard and I saw a man, not the weapon my grandfather molded to his will, but a man—perhaps even the remnants of a boy.

"This life bears few certainties. It's overrun with unpredictability ready to highjack you at every turn."

I remained quiet, certain he wasn't looking for any response from me.

"But not the sun. No, the sun remains immune to unpredictability and darkness. The sun will rise, Nadia; and bring us with it."

Konstantin never left, which in truth surprised me more than my body's persistence to heal. It was another seventeen days before I was capable of independent function and another three before we met the elderly couple that would ultimately give us their own identities through their own deaths.

The memory of the real Allison Rosetta Red clinging to her dying husbands hand made me wonder who Seth's mystery lady could be. Seth didn't need to say it but I knew he must've met someone. He would've never made the leap if he didn't have a target and I found myself already deeming this mystery woman unworthy of his heart.

Seth turned his entire life around despite all odds, devoting honor and loyalty to those in need of it most. Such qualities required an equally remarkable individual and sadly I feared his heart's thief would fall tragically short. Not that he required my approval, but it would be nice if she ended up being someone I could grow to love as well.

I wiped at my cheeks and downed the pills, the cool water soothing my aching throat. Robotically I made my way to the washroom to clean myself up; refusing to arrive at the café with puffy eyes and draw unnecessary attention a second day in a row. That thought reminded me of Logan and I immediately chided myself for the slip-up.

His penetrating stare was still as fresh in my mind as it had been that first moment. The heat of his touch, the static, the thunder and its insistent pulse. Instinctually I ran every moment of our encounter through every protocol and found little, if any, rationality in any of it. No matter which way I twisted or flipped the details, the result was equally unfavorable for logic's sake. I fully intended to dispose of all such thoughts, knowing how stupid it was to fantasize about imaginary connections; and stupid I was, because I spent the next hour replaying every second—again and again.

*

I lost the entire morning in a mental fog, my routine; a blur. Unable to recall if I'd even shampooed. I lacked stride and my nerves continued to coil in on themselves as I made my way towards the kitchen.

Seth was sitting at the bar texting profusely on his phone. He stood and wrapped me in a hug that felt sadly strange. I hated it. I didn't want him feeling guilty about pursuing happiness so I did what I was good at, and put on a smile. Although it was forced, once there, it felt oddly genuine. I really wanted nothing more than happiness for him.

"How'd you sleep?"

I shrugged a shoulder.

"As expected I suppose. I did sleep though, so that counts for something, right?"

"I suppose it does."

I could tell Seth was struggling, which made me all the more eager to ease his anxiety about my ability to cope.

I was ready to assure him, equipped with a long winded speech I'd played over and over in my head all morning until his phone rang, excusing us both from the pitiful 'be free' rant that was about to pour out of my mouth.

"You should get that," I eagerly offered, making my way to the kettle to get my morning cup of tea.

"Let me take you to lunch today. We could talk. You busy?" The softness of his voice was a direct contrast to the man I'd faced seven years ago. He was a new person, given a second chance in life. He was going to make someone very happy.

"I always have time for you, Seth. How's one o'clock?"

"Done. I'll pick you up." He winked, answering his phone as he stepped out into the garage. I heard the garage gate open, his Escalade come to life, and drive off.

Both Marina and Andrew beat me to the café this morning; in fact I wondered exactly what time they got there because when I arrived at half past six, nine fresh batches of pastries were already sitting on the cooling rack. It was almost comical.

"Good morning, Sunshine."

"Hey, Alice."

I waited for her glowing smile, the brightness of her green eyes, the laugh that bounced joyously off every wall. I waited, only to hear the oven doors opening and closing in rapid succession as she nearly sprinted past me on her way out front.

"Hey, is everything all right?"

"Yeah, fine. Just busy is all." Marina squeezed out a weak smile before escaping once again.

After another unsuccessful attempt at engaging in conversation I decided to drown myself in work as well.

We had a few large orders to fill for a collection of offices nearby. Fridays tended to be busy as many offices celebrated the end of their work week. Marina was busy baking and assembling while I got the accounting in order.

Normally I let the girls make deliveries because there were usually good tips associated with them, but today Jenna had a mandatory assembly for a class, Andrew was out front tending to his flock of loyal customers, and Marina was clearly in no condition to mingle.

I grabbed the roster and loaded my car accordingly. I saved the new customer for last, a place called L.S. Trade Co. at 7171 Alameda Ave. I recognized the office address because it was the largest building in our zip code. I'd never been inside but on the exterior it was a beautiful monstrosity of a building and looked forward seeing the beast from within.

My first stop was at Shade Technologies, a small but successful family owned commercial window coverings company. I was particularly fond of the Claytons, possibly due to Raymond's ten year old son, Alex.

"Alice! Let me help you with those."

"Thanks, Annette. How was your week?"

"Particularly busy, actually. Jace and Kendal closed on the house so they've been busy moving; and with Jason signing the Marriott account we've been busier than ever. We've had to add a second shift in production three times a week just to stay on schedule."

Annette's cheeks were flushed as she speed-walked to the conference room. The woman was seventy two but had the energy of a twenty seven year-old. She was incredible.

"Where's Alex? I brought a special package for him."

Annette's eyes glassed over and I instantly regretted asking.

"He had a difficult treatment this week so he hasn't been feeling up to leaving the house. Raymond and Pam have been taking turns staying home."

"I'm sorry, Annette, I shouldn't have asked."

"Oh my dear, I'm so glad you did. Alex will be happy to see his special treat. I'll pass it along with a hug." Annette smiled. The lines of her face were evidence of a life lived. Filled with happiness, adventure, and devastating loss. September marked two years since Annette's husband Garrett passed from a sudden stroke. Everyone was finally beginning to get past the loss and then Alex was diagnosed with Leukemia.

None of them talked about the 'what if.' I think they believed if they gave such thoughts a voice it would be like giving in or giving up. It wasn't my place to tell them otherwise so I continued to serve Alex loyally, allowing him to vent all his fears and anger to me when he was afraid to share such emotions with his fragile parents.

"I must get going, Annette. Please pass along a warm hello to everyone. You know if there's anything you need, all you have to do is ask."

"I know, my dear. Now scurry along to your next delivery, there are people waiting on those impossibly good treats of yours."

"Bye, Annette."

The air outside was bitter and stung my skin like a thousand needles. All around me people raced in and out of buildings and cars; eager to get back into warmer spaces, donning their scarves and gloves and heavy wool coats. But not me. I paced my steps leisurely in the frosty air. The cold brought me back to a place where my mama was near and her voice, still clear.

The years had driven an ever widening wedge in my memory of her. It seemed some days it required great effort to picture her vibrant amber eyes; lined with inky long lashes that drew you in and forced you to stare, or the delicate slope of her nose, which seemed to curve a bit to the left but only from certain angles. The feel of her silky hair against my cheek when she'd whisper that everything would be all right; and despite knowing the improbability of such promises, her angelic voice insisted that I believe against all odds.

On days such as this, when uncomfortable and aching somehow, I found it easier to remember her; to smell her distinct citrus scent mixed with eucalyptus, transporting me back into her arms. I could almost feel the brush of her mahogany hair against my skin, and I wanted to smile and weep all at once.

The second and third deliveries were both in the 1st Bank building which gave me an abundance of time to make it to the final stop of the day.

The L.S. Trade Co. building was twenty two stories high and it didn't take a wizard to understand the business opportunities available. The customer was on the twenty second floor; meaning they owned the thing.

If I could display my worth and gain their interest, referrals were sure to follow—which was why I'd made certain their order was perfect; including an extra two dozen pastries on-the-house as a token of thanks.

The underground parking garage had me fingering my sidearm for a multitude of reasons, the most prominent being a lack of escape routes with too many shadows to account for. I approached the service elevator where I stated my name and business into an intercom before the elevator doors opened and I stepped inside. I hated elevators for reasons far too many to count. But twenty-two floors left me no option. The floor was pre-programmed giving me no control once inside and it took great strain not to claw at the doors to let me out.

The doors wouldn't open soon enough and by the time I reached the top I jumped out like a lunatic.

A lovely young woman approached me swiftly and elegantly. She made walking on heels look like an art form and based on appearances I felt one hundred percent out of place.

"You must be from Chai Café. I'm Lisa. Welcome to L.S. Trade Companies."

And just like that, Lisa put me at ease. She was friendly and quick to smile. I liked her.

"I'm Alice." I stuck my hand out to commence the introduction but Lisa swatted it away before leaning in and planting a kiss to both cheeks, Hollywood style. Lisa seemed utterly oblivious to my look of shock and for whatever reason, I liked her more because of it. She was genuine and comfortable and nothing affected that, not even my expression.

"These go to The Summit Conference Room. I'll be glad to escort you."

Lisa grabbed two tiered trays and led the way. The exquisite architecture had me engrossed as we made our way across the impossibly wide space, made even wider by the three hundred and sixty degree views of the Denver skyline to the east and Rocky Mountains to the west.

Every wall, partition, divider; was glass—all transparent and all dedicated to clean lines and minimalism. Even people popped out like art, moving about with grace and purpose; somehow orderly and coordinated, swaying from place to place moment to moment, and it all came together like a dance.

"It's enchanting don't you agree?" Lisa offered.

"Yes, actually that's precisely what it is—enchanting."

"Fitting, given the ownership. Don't you think?"

I looked at her puzzled, not sure what she meant.

"I wouldn't know, I've never met them."

Lisa smiled in response, but the crease between her brows gave view to her confusion.

"The meeting is scheduled in forty minutes. Come by my desk and I'll be sure to give you your payment before you head out. And of course if you need any assistance at all, please don't hesitate to ask."

"Thank you."

Lisa gave me a very pretty smile and stepped out to resume her role in the ever elegant dance.

The high-gloss white conference room table seated twenty-eight comfortably in the center of the room—if it could be called a room. The walls were glass and most of the furniture transparent. Clear tables along the west windows overlooked mountain peaks already covered in snow, which glistened in spite of the fog. It was clear why the space was called The Summit. I felt I was right there, at the peak of the mountain, with snow beneath me—all around me, and I was the accent; the one piece that stood out in contrast to the beauty all around. The feeling was entirely consuming.

Delayed and firm on refocusing, I set about displaying my confections.

I was somewhere between propping up the last display card and folding up the trays when my blood began to run hot and the air crackled like the sound of a burning camp fire. I'd realized too late just where I'd come to.

His presence announced itself and I knew I should turn around, face the ambush; but I was frozen in place. I couldn't bring myself to face the source of such power, so like a coward I looked out at the snow-capped peaks even if no longer able to see their beauty. I was trapped in a transparent box, unaware of what I'd walked into.

I felt him approach, so close I could feel his breath and smell the scent of peppermint that accompanied it.

"Mrs. Red, what a pleasant surprise." The sound of his hypnotizing voice mixed with the effect he held over me was alarming; and I dared to want more.

"Turn around, Allison."

I was afraid. Would he see the thrill in my eyes, the rise and fall of my chest in quick rhythm to my racing pulse? Once I exposed the flush upon my skin would he think less of me? Why did I care?

"My apologies for taking so long, Mr. Snow. I'd hoped to be finished before the conference began. I'm done now. I'll be on my way."

My blood ran in tidal waves, crashing, retreating then crashing again. I was breathing too rapidly. I probably looked like I was having an anxiety attack. Maybe I was. I was starting to shake and the realization that he affected me so completely was terrifying. I didn't understand my inability to faze him out.

At the heart of it was the glaring fact that Logan Snow was a stranger, a mystery I had little means of unraveling, and this truth carried with it genuine fear. I skirted around him quickly towards the door.

"Allison, stop."

I could hardly decipher what he'd said through the roaring in my ears. I needed to get out and get a grip.

"I'm sorry." My words came out desperate and I didn't bother or care as I bolted out the door.

Lisa's earlier confusion increased when I told her the order was complimentary as I caught the elevator in a split second. I never heard her response as the welcoming thud of the elevator sounded, trapping me inside with two people who stared like I had three eye balls. I tapped my foot or maybe stomped, I couldn't tell; while the elevator descended. Both of the other passengers departed on the sixteenth floor with reluctance as I continued to the underground garage.

I'd taken the public elevator down, so I broke out into a run towards my Pilot. I had my car keys in my hand, already pressing the unlock button, when someone put their hand on my shoulder from behind. I reacted instinctively, pulling out my .45, twisting to point the barrel of the gun directly at the assailant's chest.

It was Mr. Bad-Ass-Driver/Bodyguard. His hands were up in show of surrender, though, his expression said such things were never on the menu.

"Mrs. Red, I didn't mean to startle you. I called out once you exited the elevator. You didn't respond. I approached you to get your attention, to speak to you; not to hurt you." His voice was even and showed no sign of distress. He was more than a driver, his confident and almost taunting eyes looking down the barrel of the gun said as much.

By this time we'd attracted the attention of security. They surrounded us like vultures, speaking into their mouthpieces like James Bond impersonators both nervous and excited that today might just end up exciting; a story to share with their buddies about the crazy woman who broke down with a gun. I gathered they were corresponding with their controller as the older man finished with. "Yes, Sir. See you in two."

I was in a foreign building, a basement garage no less; and outnumbered. I questioned every detail, analyzing it, debating whether I was overreacting or under-prepared. I backed up to have all bodies in clear view but kept my gun pointed directly at Logan Snow's driver. He was clearly the most lethal and as I stared into his grey eyes, so grey they almost appeared white, I saw what I'd already knew: he's taken a life and would have no qualms in doing it again.

The service elevator doors opened and Logan Snow approached, stopping two feet from the barrel of the gun.

"Gabe, take security and get out." Mr. Snow barked the order with striking authority.

Bodyguard Gabe ushered the startled security detail to the safety of the elevator. I could feel their stares as they shuffled into the too-small-to-hold-them-all elevator and ascended.

We stood in a warped stand-off for what seemed like hours. In truth I was flooded with relief at the sight of Logan stepping off that elevator and somewhere in those moments I put my gun back into its holster.

"I didn't mean to cause trouble; I wasn't going to hurt anyone." I said this, though, it seemed ridiculous at this point.

"I doubt safety was on their mind while in your company."

I had to laugh at the absurdity of such flattery coming from him. I wasn't a troll, but I wasn't blind either. I saw how many gorgeous women surrounded him in his sky castle.

"Though I thoroughly enjoy that sound, I can't help but wonder what I'd said to deserve it."

I heard the edge of his tone before I saw the heat in his stare.

"They're beautiful. All of them, on the twenty second floor I mean." I paused, battling to camouflage my weakness to him; his presence—his electric current that seemed to be directly connected to my being. I felt utterly vulnerable around him, naked, and I hated being so exposed, but even more I hated that I liked it. I hated that deep down, I hungered to feel his skin on mine again.

"You're kind to flatter me, Mr. Snow; generous even. But let's be realistic; everyone in your building looks like they just came off the cover of Vogue. Hell, even the sixty something year old red head had more class than I do. Whatever game you're playing, whatever bet you made, I assure you that you're wasting your time."

"What I choose to dedicate my time to, Allison, is *never* a waste."

"You're entitled to your perspective as I am mine, Mr. Snow."

"I've asked you to call me Logan and I'd prefer not to repeat myself."

I opened my mouth only to shut it, which he clearly took as a victory if judging by the self-gratified curve of his lips. But more interestingly, his smirk didn't bother me. Instead I felt oddly happy to have pleased him.

"Share a meal with me."

"I can't."

"Can't or won't?"

"Both."

I lowered my gaze, unable to watch the sincerity of his disappointment. It was easier to pretend he was merely being charming.

"You feel it. This pull. This ravaging sensation whenever we're together."

It wasn't a question, so I found no reason to supply an answer.

Logan stepped impossibly close and suddenly there wasn't enough air in the tiny space between us. His palm was warm as it caressed my cheek and against wisdom, I leaned into it. My lungs were heaving, my pulse racing and I felt hyperaware. My eyes shut tight with great strain, yet I sensed his every move; his every breath.

His hands were wound into my hair as they cradled my head. Logan lowered his forehead to touch mine and I could feel the tension rolling off him in waves, each rippling through me in search of release.

"You call to me like a siren." He breathed.

Somehow I understood his meaning, for I felt much the same about him. I sensed his reluctance to fully embrace what seemed to keep pulling us together and somehow that hurt, even though I was doing the same. Logan's breath was hot against my skin and each time his mouth released a breath, my lips trembled with the urge to lift just high enough to touch his.

We stood there, deeply connected and yet still light years apart. I clung to these shared seconds like dreams of the impossible. I memorized the feeling of his warmth; more soothing than the sun…and the ache of it. I wanted to stop time, forget all else, and melt beneath Logan's lips pressed against my forehead. If wishing worked, I would've wished for nothing else.

But as I dreamed from behind my closed lids, I couldn't dismiss my fear. A warning—it was time to go.

"Take care, Logan Snow."

My feet felt heavy with lead, my heart wounded. I made my way to my Pilot and swung open the door, fully aware of every added inch between us. Faintly I imagined Logan sweeping me off my feet, whisking me off to a Happily Ever After; but in real life you couldn't write an alternate ending if unhappy with the way the story was headed. The hero wasn't bulletproof and bombs didn't get disarmed three seconds to detonation. In real life people cried, bled, died, and love couldn't cure evil. I knew this, and paid a high price for the lesson. So when Logan's fairytale rebuttal never came, I slid into my car, closed the door, and drove away without looking back.

Chapter Seven

Allison Red

I was headed to my office when I unintentionally overheard Marina on the phone. "I don't know, but I trust you—me too." She was crying.

I sank into my chair but found no comfort in the soft leather. Something was off with her. Wanting to comfort her and simultaneously demand she tell me what's wrong was pointless—I knew enough to at least know that.

It was the twenty fifth of October and truly I had plenty to do in preparation for end of month reconciliation so I poked and pounded at my laptop keys, running data reports and doing uploads; but I was too bothered by Marina's cool demeanor to fully concentrate on the tasks.

My phone chirped with a text.

Seth Red: Pulling up now.

And that's when it hit me like a stupid brick; and all that was left to wonder was how could I've been so blind and self-absorbed to have not seen it sooner.

Moments later Seth strode in and we were off on foot to The Elephant Bar neighboring the café.

We waited ten minutes for a booth in the corner, a small price to pay for privacy when privacy was priceless. The entire wait we skirted around each other like some insecure newbie roommates freshman year. Even after being seated it felt awkward; so I cut to the chase.

"I know about Marina."

Seth appeared unsurprised.

We sat silent for some time. My emotion displayed openly on my face while Seth contained his.

A young server walked by and I laughed dryly in response to her quizzical expression.

"Why didn't you come to me from the beginning? What made you hide it, Seth? I would've been happy for you."

"No, you wouldn't have. You would've told me I was being a selfish bastard and you would've been right. You would've punched me, thrown nightstands at me, and beaten me with the crowbar in your trunk. That's why I hid it. I'm as selfish as they come, Alice. I wanted Marina. I wanted her and I couldn't allow you to reason with me."

"I could easily do that now."

Seth looked at me dismissively.

"You forget that I know you as well as you do me. It's beyond that now. A fact you're well aware of. Tell me you didn't already know before your head hit your pillow that I had someone in my life."

I remained quiet, in effect telling him just that. He was right of course. Had he told me from the beginning about Marina I would've threatened him with everything I had to have him step away before it was too late.

Seth pulled out a thin stack of legal size paper from his laptop case. I didn't bother looking at the details. I signed off on all the X's marked with yellow arrows, feeling the weight of change and all that came with it.

The server arrived with our drinks and took our orders. We were quiet a long time, alternating between looking at each other and out the window.

"Just promise me one thing."

"Name it."

"Protect her with your dying breath."

Seth's eyes turned to stone, as I knew they would. "Always."

We ate our food robotically. I couldn't tell you how my shrimp cocktail tasted. Halfway in, I gave up; setting my fork aside.

"Would you tell me how it happened?"

Seth took a breath as he focused on nothing in particular.

"Remember the countless hours I'd spent helping renovate her house?"

"Oh, you mean the money pit she called a diamond in the rough?"

Seth's grin gave the impression that those dreadful four months of pain, sweat, and even blood were somehow a pleasant memory. Everything that was cut open, torn out or removed revealed a worse issue than the cosmetic crap that was useless to begin with.

I was ready to set fire to the three-bedroom ranch but Marina claimed it was love at first sight and I quote "For better or worse, richer or poorer, I'll make this neglected jewel beautiful again". I'd thought she was crazy, but truth be told, it ended up quite extraordinary.

"We'd made it down to the basement bar cabinets. When I took off the tops, we found piles of mice feces. I blocked off the end and I began to remove one cabinet at a time, hoping they didn't have a hole in the wall to escape through. By the fifth one, they had no place to go. Three grey balls scurried from one corner to the other only to realize their escape route was blocked. I had every intention of killing the damn things when Marina ran in and jumped on my back."

I was enthralled with his silly story of three little mice, like it was some children's bedtime story.

"She'd asked me what I was doing and I said what had to be obvious; getting rid of pests. She asked if they'd robbed me, knocked up my sister, or kidnapped my firstborn. I laughed but soon realized she was dead serious. When I tried to reason and explain that they'd only come back if we let them go, you know what she said?"

I shook my head, too invested to let my voice intrude on this compelling story.

"'Can you blame them for wanting a better life?' she'd told me. Seems ridiculous to find such depth in something so adolescent, but her words and care for three insignificant rodents changed something in me. I think that's the day I allowed thoughts of a future, a wife; family. Once that happened there was no stopping it. I'd desired her for years and finally reckless enough to take her."

I remembered Marina releasing a shoe box of mice into a wooded area not far from the house. I told her it was only a matter of time before a hungry owl got them, to which she responded "My only goal is to give them a chance. That's all I can do". I laughed at her silliness then.

"I'd made the decision to break our arrangement months ago but Marina kept stalling. She feared you weren't ready to move on; willing to sacrifice her own happiness for the sake of yours. I loved her more for it but last night I couldn't let it go on any longer. Somehow I felt that your nightmare was a sign to come clean. I called her last night, told her we spoke. She freaked, she's been shedding tears and drowning in guilt since."

A large group made their way past us talking obnoxiously loud about Danny wrecking his brother's car or something of the sort, drawing attention from patrons across the restaurant while remaining oblivious to common courtesy. By the time the noise level subsided enough to hear one another speak again, I simply had nothing left to say. Seth took my lead and for some time we were silent.

It took great effort not to think of Logan Snow as I listened to Seth confess his affections for my best friend, and though I mostly failed, I didn't let it show. I idly fingered the simple gold band on my left ring finger, slipped it off, and placed it in my palm. Seth did the same; a silent goodbye to what was.

*

A tear stained face awaited me in my office. Leaping from her chair she flung her arms around, locking me to her.

"I'm so sorry, Alice. I wanted to tell you. It killed me to lie. I just— I was—I didn't want to hurt you. You're my best friend—" Her voice was strained, attempting to speak between her sobs. I hugged her tight and let her release whatever she felt compelled to set free.

"It wasn't planned, it just happened and then we couldn't stop. I know it was wrong, I wanted to confess so many times but I knew you were still struggling and not ready to move on. But at the same time we couldn't stop seeing each other. I know it's a mess, and I understand if you're mad. I'm sorry, I'm just so sorry."

I pulled away enough to meet her blurry eyes.

The strain of her voice, her guilt stricken features, the tight grip of her hands on mine as though she feared I'd pull away while she was ready to hold on with all her strength; was bittersweet. I recognized my own contributions to the convoluted mess. Looking back, it wasn't difficult to understand why she felt the need to hide their relationship. When faced with all of my daunting insecurities, her best option was to keep it secret.

"The only regret I have is making you feel you had to hide. I'm sorry for that."

There was no need to force my smile.

Marina let out a slow and heavy breath recognizing the sincerity in both my words and expression. She took a step back to sink into the chair behind her; her shoulders sagging.

"Don't you feel violated? Don't you want to yell, scream; I dunno, maybe throw something at me?"

Her words could've been humorous if she weren't serious.

Taking a seat next to her I relaxed into the cool leather.

"Shocked? Yes, and sad and anxious and happy and confused and one hundred more emotions, most of which I couldn't find a word to describe."

Marina watched me with strained intensity. She needed this, as did I. So I opened up.

"Change is difficult for me. The fact that you cared enough that it drove you into hiding makes me regret all the more that I put my own needs before yours. I didn't see it. I should've—looking back I can't believe I didn't, but I worried about my own needs more than I cared for yours. You've been supportive, understanding, and patient with me throughout our friendship; sadly I can't say the same about myself. So let us be happy; just happy." My voice broke and we clasped hands before she released and exaggerated breath.

"I had this whole scenario worked out in my head, but you go and take this like a hero, throwing all my practiced responses out the window!"

"No worries, we could always do a re-run; I'll have a complete meltdown and you can debut your speech."

"Ever the thoughtful one, aren't you. Well if you'd like to know, I feel a thousand pounds lighter; I swear the stress alone has claimed at least five years off my life." There was heaviness in her tone.

"Well if I've learned anything from this, it's that I underestimated your ability to evade and *lie*. Wasn't it just a few months ago you gave me reason to believe you had the hots for Jason from School of Mines?"

A flash of guilt passed her beautiful blotchy face.

"I had no choice! After you caught me latched onto Seth for longer-than-just-friends-do at the BBQ I freaked out. Jason was a pawn, a good one at that."

"Oh, you're heartless."

Marina rolled her eyes.

"Desperate actually. Seth wouldn't speak to me for a week after my role play flirting."

"You know what's even worse?"

"What?"

"I never even suspected. You did all that for nothing."

Marina froze before breaking into laughter and I soon followed.

"I guess my intuition meter is rustier than I thought. What kind of friend am I when the two people closest to me are in love and I'm completely oblivious?"

"Don't be too hard on yourself; you forget who Seth is."

Forgetting was an unattainable goal. I never forgot; I managed.

"I'm sorry, I shouldn't have said that."

My face must've given something away.

"No, it's okay, it's just been a whirlwind couple days."

Marina frowned.

"It has, hasn't it?"

"You have no idea." The words were out before I could stop them. I winced, seeing the interest on her face.

"Oh?"

I hadn't actually intended to share my encounter with Logan Snow this morning. I sensed that the less I spoke of it, the easier it would be to put it all behind me.

"The new customer for delivery this morning was for Logan Snow."

Marina's eyes were wide as saucers.

"I told you, Alice! I know what I saw yesterday!"

"Don't get ahead of yourself."

Her smile faded, yet the twinkle in her eye remained.

"He asked me to dinner. I said no. We had an— encounter in the parking garage which didn't change much. Besides he knows I'm a Mrs., what kind of man pursues a married woman?"

Marina could see I was grasping at straws. Shaking her head she looked me square in the eyes.

"I won't push you, but let's not call a circle a square. We both know what happened at the café yesterday. I'm certain today was no exception. Though I can't force you to open yourself up, Alice, I *will* tell you when you're cross-dressing your circle!"

I knew she was right. Admitting it out loud would only intensify the swell of emotions within me. Surely it couldn't be healthy for such inner turmoil.

"My circle isn't ready to be a circle—yet."

I wasn't sure why I insinuated that eventually it would be. Regardless, at this point I was unable to discuss or contemplate the subject further.

"I'll take it. This calls for an ice cream movie night. My house Sunday—let's say 5pm?"

That sounded like just what we needed.

Chapter Eight

Logan Snow

December 2006

"Igor's in."

About damn time!

"What took so long? Did he have some lover's quarrel with Konstantine? This is bullshit! What the hell happened to the timeline, Gabe?"

"Patience. Everything's a test. The way you blink could condemn you on a bad day. Igor bid his time. I fully endorsed his decision. Had he played his hand too soon they would've knocked him and been on their way."

I knew that. That wasn't the point!

"Ily's trip to the specialist was our shot. Ily has *one* wife and she's only going to die from cancer once! Igor was supposed to be at his post by then. It's over now. Another shot like this might take years!"

Gabe remained silent. Over eighteen months of strategic planning for this one moment and the whole blueprint got derailed by a single man, *Konstantine*.

"We may have another viable option."

"Explain."

"The traitor daughter Anastasia and her girl. They've gone missing. Intel says these two women may as well be Ily's undoing. You so much as mention one of them and Ily see's red. The girl's referred to as the Rumikov's symbol of treason among the other gangs. We find them, it'll lure him out."

"Missing? What are the specifics?"

"My money's on the wife, perhaps her impending death brought out some motherly instincts in her. We know none of the other slaves would dare risk their lives for the other; not that it kept Ily from killing off two of them out of pure rage. They'll want to cross borders. The wife has two posts she's related to. I would scout them first before broadening the search. They may just be our golden ticket."

"Do it."

With a nod Gabe left.

I was a fool. This mission; *my* mission, was costing me far more than I'd originally anticipated. Though, I sure as hell wasn't backing out now. Not until Ily Rumikov had taken his last breath, and if I was lucky enough, I would be the one to take it from him.

*

"Update?"

"Seems the wife was wise enough to avoid using someone close. We've broadened the search but I need to send at least six more men if we're going to be efficient."

"Done. Same agreement. They deliver, they get paid."

We pulled up to the construction site where my new building was nearly complete. McCarthy was becoming irritated, digging deeper and *deeper* into my business affairs. The scum was a federal agent, using the bureaus resources to further his own corrupt interests. It was a wonder how any of his *actual* cases got solved. The man was dipping his fingers into the black market more with each passing year.

The new building was by no means modest; precisely what I'd intended. A shiny front to my operations. McCarthy was a thorn but he most certainly wouldn't be my end. The piece of shit was dirty and his agenda in tailing me had nothing to do with his civic duty.

"Mr. Snow. Good to see you sir."

Hank handed me the hardhat and charts.

"Walk me through, Hank I haven't much time today."

"Inspections passed. There was a minor electrical glitch with the security elevator but we're already working to resolve that. The added room we discussed is complete per your specifications. We were set back two days due to delivery delays but the crews have put in good work. March is still a reliable deadline, we're doing everything we can to ensure we meet it."

"Good work, Hank. Show me the room."

The space was perfect.

"This remains off record, Hank." My eyes leveled with Hanks. The burly man was twice my age if not more, and wise enough to know what lines not to cross.

"Yes, Mr. Snow. I assure you, all is per our agreement."

"Good man, Hank. I'll leave you to it then."

Leaving what was to become officially known as L.S. Trade Co., we set off for a building already constructed, abandoned perhaps would best describe its dank and cold offerings. Ideal for my needs.

"McCarthy's not buying the trail, Logan."

"I never expected him to. But he's greedy enough to bid his time. If he highlights me too soon, he gets nothing."

"You really want to be looking over your shoulder for him?"

"Elimination isn't an option. He's FBI. I don't need that shit. The new arrangements and the new building will buy us the time we need."

Chapter Nine

Allison Red

Against my better judgement I detoured my route home, convincing myself I needed to stop by Whole Foods. But when I found myself searching for a certain black Porsche exiting the L.S. Trade Co. building I could no longer deny my true intention.

I arrived to the welcome of an empty house. I went through my usual process of arming the alarm and putting my gun in my night stand drawer before undressing.

Facing the head of the tub, holding the pajamas meant to cover my naked body I realized I hadn't indulged in a hot bath in years, and today called for just that.

Lighting several candles, I poured a generous amount of bubble bath that smelled like lily of the valley, a birthday gift from a few years back.

I hadn't used it yet, saving it I suppose; afraid to waste such extravagance. Today however, it wouldn't be wasted. Today I *needed* the soulful pick-me-up that lily of the valley offered.

The water swallowed me up in the deep tub, the bubbles fizzing and popping playfully.

At first, I thought of nothing beyond the gentle sway of the water. When finally content, I let my toes peek out above the bubbles, idly wondering if I should paint them pink again or move onto something darker like the beautiful pearlescent plum color I recently picked up.

I enjoyed those first moments of simplicity, an easiness that moved like a lazy breeze.

It started innocently, the way it always did, and my thoughts were once again on Logan Snow. The slip-up this time was momentarily wondering if *he'd* prefer my toes decorated in the plum over my usual petal pink. Stupid, yet that seemed to be my trend now.

My curiosity had no particular direction, branching out much like a sunshine-seeking tree. I wondered if he liked dogs, and if he happened to have one would it be named Bullet? What was his favorite season, and why was his car of choice a

Porsche? I wondered how he'd decided to do whatever it was that L.S. Trade Co. did. From what I could find it was a currency exchange floor and involved in various charities. Did he have siblings and loving parents and if so, did they visit often? Finally I wondered about his reasons to hold back, could they be more complicated than my own? Or maybe a much simpler excuse sufficed for him?

When it came to romance my resume was rather unimpressive—a mediocre collection of romance novels, a few dozen romance movies, and an assortment of psychology books. Sprinkle in a third party's view on watching strangers interact and that about summed up my level of expertise.

My relationship with Seth was never romantic. I suppose I could've fallen for Seth; he certainly was handsome—tall and built Ford tough as the popular slogan went. There was nothing that should have kept me from being attracted to him, yet Seth and I never felt anything remotely romantic for one another.

Through our journey of survival we formed a fundamental bond, one we now referred to as *family*. I couldn't explain why that was, the same way I couldn't explain my reaction to Logan—why before knowing something as fundamental as his name, I'd already felt connected to him.

I reasoned that leaving Logan in that garage was the best thing I could've done; a selfless action to save him from harm. If I was honest, there was a list of other things that assisted in that decision; however, inexperience and the need for self-preservation just seemed like sorry excuses to use. So I stuck to what loomed the most dangerous—my past.

Breathing in the lovely scent of the bubble bath I noted that Marina did well; the scent was almost an identical match to the flower itself. And it was while in a state of physical relaxation that I allowed my mind to wander farther than it should.

Mama stepped out and just as I'd suspected, she noticed it instantly.

"Nadia, how—when—you didn't need to, but oh my dear girl, thank you."

I watched while trying not to blink as Mama's face lit up. Her eyes glistened and it made me happy because I knew they were good tears, the kind she cried when remembering happy times.

It was just three tiny little stems but that's all I needed really. The market we walked by usually had them and I snuck two stems on Saturday and the last one yesterday. I kept them hidden in a tin can filled with water. I worried Mama would be mad that I'd snuck them but she wasn't, and I was relieved. I think she needed this, I think we both did.

Mama patted the concrete floor and I knelt down to join her.

"The first time your father gave me Lily of the valley I lied to him; said my flower of choice was tulips. I don't know why? I think I was scared he knew more about me than I wanted, but perhaps that wasn't it at all. Didn't matter though; your father looked me square in the eyes and said my mouth could lie but my eyes would always reveal the truth."

It was a story I'd listened to many times, but each time it felt new somehow. Mama never figured out just how my father knew the delicate flower was dearest to her. I believed she never really wanted to know, somehow the mystery made it more intimate.

"Happy birthday, Mama."

"It is indeed, my sweet girl. It most definitely is."

"Mama?"

"Mmm."

"Can I ask you something?"

It had been just over two weeks since we'd fled, and perhaps it was being out from under the suffocating grasp of Hell's Mansion that I felt somehow empowered to voice something I'd always wondered; but too scared to ask. Not from fear that Mama would get angry, but rather from fear of hurting her.

"You know you can. What's troubling you, Love?"

117

"It's just that—well it's—never mind. Let's just forget I said anything."

"Nadia, tell me. Come on now, no secrets, remember?"

"Well, I don't want you to be hurt—I, well, I'd always wondered if you regretted your decision to run away with Papa and everything. I mean, if you were given a second chance would you do it differently? I mean, I understand if you would, I wouldn't be hurt that is; I've just always wondered is all."

I'd started out mumbling and by the end rushed through it so quickly, I wondered if Mama even understood half of what I'd said. And when I finally gained the courage to look up to see her pained expression, my regret was instantaneous.

"Mama, I'm sorry, I shouldn't have asked. Forget about it, just some silly thoughts bouncing around in my silly head. I'm so sorry, let's just forget it, okay."

Mama flung her arms around me and hugged me incredibly tight; tears falling. I remained quiet, allowing Mama to hang on for as long as she needed while I wondered what her reaction implied.

"I was pushed to my knees as they held your father on his…" Mama paused and I suddenly found myself not wanting to know any of it.

"…I was sobbing and I think I screamed because Uncle Roman punched me then. I shrunk into myself but Roman grabbed my hair and forced me back onto my knees to watch

your father's execution. I was dying inside, willing it all to be a horrible nightmare; pleading for mercy that never came. And right before Uncle Boris passed the blade through your father's throat, your father smiled sadly and told me, 'No regrets, my Love'."

"Mama, please forgive me—I didn't mean—"

"I was taken to the Mansion and beaten, my arm broken, my ribs; no better…my face hardly recognizable. I passed out eventually but awoke the following morning. There was a gathering and I could see Alexander's family was in attendance. I was so confused, I couldn't fathom what your father's family would be doing with your grandfather in the betting warehouse."

A sob ripped through her and Mama was unable to drown it out. I held her, filled with dread and unprepared for such lessons.

"I watched them drag your father's lifeless body to the center of the arena. Your grandfather stood then; proud, confident—evil. He'd said 'This is what happens to traitors, this is what awaits anyone who dares challenge my authority'. The pigs were released, digging straight through bone. There was nothing left to bury. Alexander's parents were forced to watch their son's body disappear before their eyes. Midway through the carnage I was dragged to the stage and dangled by a rope above the animals. It was a presentation; a warning. We were

made examples of and my father made every second count. After I'd endured several piercing bites, they settled me back on stage where my father announced that I would serve as a slave in what I used to call my own home."

"Mama, I—" I couldn't formulate a single thought.

"There's no need for words, Nadia; for there's nothing to say. The answer to your question is yes, I would do things differently."

"Of course you would, Mama, and who could blame you."

"I would've hosted a grand celebration, the kind your grandfather would expect in order to attend. My brother, uncles, and all their son's would be there too. I would spare no cost, hire the most exquisite dancers and lavish food. I would play the role of loyal and happy daughter without a hitch. I would prepare a toast in the family's honor and let them party until the sleep aid in the wine took effect. I would've shoved cyanide into each of their mouths without regret, and run away with your father. We would've lived long lives and raised you in a loving home and you would've had siblings. You would've been such a lovely sister, I know it. And that, my love, is my fatal regret; for being so naïve as to believe your grandfather would let us go…have even a gram of mercy for his own daughter."

Mama went back to caressing the Lily of the valley, in search of happier memories. I held her hand, occasionally *giving it a squeeze if only to reassure her I was still there; that she wasn't alone. We'd missed dinner and I didn't think either of us was bothered by our empty stomachs as much as we were haunted by our fears.*

Our contact was due to meet us in eight days, which was eight days too many. Every minute we stayed here our chance of being spotted and ratted out quadrupled. We were sitting ducks, simmering in a soup of no-where-to-run. The police were a joke. Two thirds of them were corrupt and the other third wished they were offered the higher paying blood-soaked rubles. Politicians were worse than the police, and the common citizen didn't stand a chance. Those who ruled did so with an iron fist. That's how they maintained order. Even the kind-looking couple down the hall could rat us out if only it meant they would secure themselves a meal.

Grandma Nina was probably dead, or nearly there. I wished I'd been nicer to her the day she gave Mama the envelope, but I hadn't been able to see past my anger; past the confusion of how she could allow her own daughter to suffer the way Mama had. Even still, I couldn't help feeling some gratitude; after all, she'd helped us escape knowing the price could be her own life. I think realizing the cancer would kill her within months anyway—this was her chance to clear her guilty conscience.

"Nadia?"

"Yes, Mama."

"Promise me something."

"Mama, don't talk like that; we're making it out together so there is no need for promises."

Mama squeezed my hand and I couldn't stop the hot tears that came down.

"Promise me you'll fight for your life; that no matter what happens you'll find happiness somewhere, find the beauty that still exists somewhere. I was robbed of love and happiness but it exists; I know because you were created, you survived within my beaten and broken body; my miracle, my sun in the darkness. Promise me you'll embrace the good, laugh whenever possible, and never dwell on the past. Form friendships with kind spirits like yours, find passion, find love, and embrace it— grow it. Promise me that you will never give up."

Mama had her hands on my face and they were shaking as she stared at me with desperation. My head continued to shake despite Mama's hold, though, she wouldn't relent.

"Mama, please—."

"I need to hear you say it, understand? You must promise me."

"I promise."

"With conviction, Nadia!"

"I promise!"

I hadn't slept that night, and though it was too dark to see, I knew neither did Mama. I didn't know if Mama knew what awaited her just days ahead. I didn't believe I ever really wanted to.

I wasn't sure how long I was in the tub, but with the water cool and my toes pruned I'd decided it was long enough. I proceeded to the shower, allowing the fresh water to wash away the residue from my trip down memory lane.

Seth wasn't home when I climbed into bed; instinct told me he was spending some much needed time with Marina. I was happy for them, maybe even a bit jealous. But nothing came without consequence, and if being completely honest with myself, I didn't believe I had the guts to fall in love. Mama had to live with the guilt of what happened to my father, and despite my promise to her that night, I didn't know that I ever could.

Chapter Ten

Allison Red

"Good morning."

"Hey, when'd you get home?"

Reaching past me to hit some buttons on the coffee machine, Seth yawned.

"Late. I went to the office after Marina's. Some messenger stuff I'd ordered."

"Guess you're really going to need that coffee then."

Sitting down at the island with coffee in hand, Seth smirked.

"Always."

After a sip of his liquid strength he motioned for me to sit beside him.

"I know about Logan Snow."

Marina.

"Before you say anything just hear me out completely. Let me first say Marina didn't mean to let it slip; second, she seems to be enamored with the guy despite knowing next to nothing about him."

I sensed irritation in his tone and had to admit that I found his territorial behavior positively amusing.

"Furthermore, I was also intrigued by your response to him. I take it you understand why?"

My raised brow told him indeed I did.

"Right. I ran his records. It's apparent that privacy is of high value to him. His business profile was somewhat accessible; however his personal file was not. His records either don't exist or his security team deserves a raise."

"What for?"

"I may lack a PhD in psychology but I'm no fool. You've never so much as batted an eyelash in another man's direction. If it's truly nothing—fine. If not, we need to be covered."

Determined to appear indifferent, I feigned boredom.

"Thanks, Brother Bear. I assure you it's nothing. In the future, the highly unlikely future, ask me first before hunting okay?"

Seth's expression said he saw through my flimsy strategy, but respected me enough to drop it.

"Yeah, you got it."

"Seth?"

"Yeah" He mumble sighed.

"Thanks for having my back."

Standing, Seth wrapped me in an embrace I hadn't realized I needed. We were us again, just upgraded.

Pulling away, Seth appeared content; I imagine he saw the same in me.

"Don't forget about dinner next Sunday at Elway's. Dress up, it's a special occasion."

Special was an understatement. This was already the second time he'd mentioned it.

"Wouldn't miss it. Attire request duly noted."

Seth kissed the top of my head and departed for the day, to chase leads and solve impossible riddles. I headed to the café where sugar was always ready to take me places closer to my mama.

Customers lined the counter and occupied just about every seat in the café, yet I couldn't shake the feeling of emptiness. Around ten o'clock my inner monolog assured me that if I turned to look at the café door once more, I would suffer a neck injury. Turned out my obsession with the door wasn't as inconspicuous as I'd hoped, judging by the pity glances Marina kept casting my way.

I'd decided to confine myself to the back kitchen where I'd baked more volume than any typical projection for a Saturday. Then retreated to my office where I cleaned, organized, reorganized, and cleaned once more before my anxiety finally began to subside.

Stacey peeked into the office looking a bit uncertain, uncomfortable even. I waved her in and gave her a welcoming smile that seemed to melt away some of the apprehension.

Wow, was I that bad today?

"Hey, Alice. I know you're sort of busy today but there's a woman out front who wants to place an order and she'll only speak with you. I offered her my help but she made it clear it had to be you."

"Thanks, Stace. I'll be out in a minute."

I slid my phone into the back pocket of my jeans and went to find the woman. It wasn't uncommon for customers to ask for my by name. I prided myself on that.

The customer was blonde and beautiful and appeared annoyed; almost angry. She looked me up and down; uninhibited in her scrutiny, as though that was the most natural way to greet someone.

"Hello, thank you for waiting. I'm Allison Red."

"I would like six dozen of your most exquisite pastries."

"All right, here are the menus for pastries, sconces, cupcakes—"

"Absolutely no cupcakes! This isn't some pathetic gathering of the Real Housewives of Denver. I want the best you've got; European pastries. Stick to chocolate, vanilla bean, and the like. Absolutely no trailer trash red velvet. The meeting begins at 9 a.m., so the display must be set up no later than 8:30."

"Of course. Where will we be delivering?"

"7171 Alameda Ave. The twenty first floor."

My hand trembled as it typed *his* building's address.

"What day would you like the delivery?"

"Monday the 28th."

"All right, I have you all set. Stacey will be making that delivery on Mon—"

"That won't do. I don't entrust my business dealings to minions. You'll be making the delivery personally."

There was something off-putting about this cherry-lipped bombshell. Besides her serious case of a superiority complex, there was something else. She looked at me with a mixture of envy and repulsion—a strange combination to say the least. Luckily my curiosity helped keep my temper in check during this Beauty Queen's tantrum.

"Okay, I can do that. That will be $347.43. You can either pay now or upon delivery."

"Oh, please. Here." Her sarcasm was thick. She curved her pouty lips in self-approval, as if she were patting herself on the back for each blow she landed.

I took the crisp bills and made change.

"You're new to this, aren't you?"

It wasn't a question but I could tell she was hoping I would answer naively. Instead I slipped the cash into the tip jar while physically biting my tongue.

"Alice, is there a problem here?"

Andrew stopped next to me; his fireman's arms crossed at his chest as he glared Blonde Beauty down.

"No. Thanks for checking. We're all finished up though, so I'll be seeing you Monday then—I'm sorry I didn't catch your name."

"I never offered it."

And with a flick of her tiny wrist she flung back her golden hair and turned to walk out the door. This encounter was rather...I wasn't sure.

"We should spike her order, have her on the toilet for days and laugh hysterically in her face when she comes back to sue us."

"Why, Andrew, didn't you know? That princess had her colon replaced with a magical diamond and now her shit transforms into pixie dust that makes her shine like the black star she is!" It was my best stuck-up voice.

"Ah, but of course. I'll be sure to inform Professor Weston I've solved the mystery of black holes. His class can now rest assured that they do indeed suck, viciously in fact."

We were laughing too loudly by this point, and had Marina been freed from her current batch of Dark Chocolate Forrest, she'd have joined us.

"Don't leave out the pixie dust phenomenon. Scientists must explore its magical properties and cultivate it for world peace you know." I added.

Andrew smiled his thousand kilowatt smile, giving my shoulders a squeeze before answering the call of his ever faithful regular: Red Head Megan.

I watched her for a minute, and sure enough, she did it again! Andrew replied with his usual politeness while busying himself with her order. It was always something; her outfit, necklace, bracelet, earrings; or today, her bright pink four inch heel pumps. She was also complaining about a paper cut on her thumb which she nearly shoved in Andrews's mouth in fear that he might miss the microscopic injury. The girl just got her driver's license a few months ago and was too young for such graphic courting techniques! But then again, what did I know; I grew up in a dungeon.

The café was hit with a late rush and I stayed out front to help push orders through. Between coffee beans, tea leaves, and cake, I'd fulfilled over thirty orders in less than sixty minutes and thanks to that no-good-sitting-on-her-throne-princess I couldn't clear my mind of the anxiety and anticipation of being back in the L.S. Trade Co. building come Monday.

My head had resumed its synchronized movements with the front door while my face fared no better in hiding my disappointment each time the individual walking in, was someone other than the man I was longing for. I knew I'd failed because now Marina had her arm on mine and pulling me out back.

"Want to talk?" Marina's voice was soft, understanding.

I suddenly felt sad and angry, and frustratingly confused. I was hit with the image of Red Head Megan only now it was *I* who stood in her bright pink pumps foolishly fantasizing about someone I had no business romanticizing over— for reasons tragically different from Megan's. The shock of reality jolted me and I suddenly needed space to think, air to breath.

"Alice, hey hold up. Are you all right?"

"Yeah, I just have some things on my mind is all."

"Well, you wanna go grab a late lunch and talk?"

Any other time I would've grabbed her hand and we would head out in search of a meal together, but not today. Today I needed to clear my head. Or dig in it?

"Can I take a rain check? I—well today I just need to handle some things."

I could've shut my mouth at rain check; it was the flash of hurt I saw that made me want to soften the blow. I knew she was trying to help; however, I wasn't at the point where I could decipher my own thoughts, let alone take on someone else's perspective. My eyes pleaded for understanding.

"Sure. I'll be here. Always."

"Thanks. I'm going to head out for an hour or so; if anything comes up, just call, okay?"

"Of course. Take your time."

I grabbed my jacket and before I knew it, I was three blocks from the café. It was warm given the time of year, and the fresh air was as invigorating as it was cleansing.

The café was part of a development meant to replicate the metropolitan vibe of downtown Denver in the suburbs of Lakewood. The businesses all housed dozens of condos above them with spacious balconies for residents to soak in the view of the Denver high-rise to the east or the snowcapped mountains to the west; or if you were lucky and wealthy enough, the penthouse rooftop decks had it all.

My fast pace had taken me much farther and I was no longer looking up at Lakewood's urban oasis; now welcomed cheerily into streets of bright yellow's, green's and blues, all lined with white porch's which stood happily occupied by some version of chair or swing with equally colorful cushions.

I pictured the occupants of these tidy happy homes as wearing bright-colored polo shirts, khakis, and sundresses. I imagined they knew all their neighbors at least four houses down on each side; had block parties as they idly chatted about a new office promotion while their children ran from house to house sharing toys and ice cream.

Rationally I knew I was painting only part of the real picture that existed in these bright homes. But I liked the warm aura this neighborhood projected, so I consciously avoided other less vibrant possibilities.

I suppose while Seth and I shared our agreement, I was content. Our relationship may've never been romantic but he was a companion nonetheless. Could I be content watching him build a life, a family with my best friend, and find enough fulfillment in gazing from the sidelines?

The responsible, sensible answer should've been *yes*. But my agreeing to be a martyr and live a life of solitude was compromised the moment I looked into a particular pair of blue eyes and felt emotions I'd never expected.

"Alice!"

I looked up.

"Daniel, what a surprise! What brings you out here?"

Now smiling he moved towards me wearing what else— but a pair of khakis and polo. I guess I wasn't so far off after all.

"I could ask you the same thing. I live here. Green house on the right."

"Wow. Talk about coincidences. How's Sarah?"

His smile came down a notch.

"We had her observation visit with Dr. Healy this morning, just got back actually. Dr. Healy says there's been no improvement; that we should consider moving her into a facility. Sent me home with a stack of brochures to go through with Emily but just looking at them feels like a betrayal."

"Oh, Daniel I'm so sorry. I don't even know what to say. You think you will?"

"Honestly, I don't know. We're running on intuition I think. I'm always in and out of the office and Emily is overrun with the kids. We share the responsibility, but sometimes we just can't fit it all in. In that sense putting her into a home would probably help us stay sane, and Sarah would likely be safer too; since we've let her go missing more than once."

Daniel kicked at the pavement as he stuck one hand in his pocket and pushed the other through his hair. His struggle was undeniable and I wished I could say something to help, though, I had nothing to offer.

"But we're fearful that if we take Sarah away from familiar surroundings, familiar faces, voices, pictures, friends, then her chance of coming back is almost nonexistent. We've discussed this concern with Dr. Healy and he can't deny that her best chance of recovery is to remain with us. It's a lose/lose situation. We can't afford home-care because the insurance company will only cover her care at the three contracted facilities, and to be quite honest none of them look very welcoming and—ah, I'm sorry I didn't mean to drop all this drama, we just got back and it's sort of the only thing on my mind."

"No please, I'm glad you shared, truly. I only wish there was something I could say to help."

"Lending an ear is all I need I suppose. Thanks for that. Life's just not fair, you know? I don't mean to be judgmental but there are so many terrible people in this world. Why did this happen to Sarah and Tim? They were happy, loving parents. They were high school sweethearts, married right out of college, did everything right, and it's just so damn cruel. Kaylee was supposed to have the lead role in her ballet recital. Joel had just turned six two weeks prior—"

Daniel shut his eyes tight before covering them with his palms as he visibly struggled to regain composure.

"These things happen to other people, you know. You're never prepared to be those other people yourself. I'm not certain it's really hit us yet. We've been so focused on getting Sarah back that I think it's distracted us from dealing with it all and in a way I'm almost grateful for that small reprieve."

We stood in silence for some moments, both thinking things we felt were better left unsaid. It wasn't awkward, and neither I nor Daniel felt rushed to fill the stillness. Daniel would never know just how familiar I was with grief, how well acquainted I was with the overpowering desire to retaliate; and seven years later, very little had changed.

"Don't fight the anger, Daniel. Accept it. Let it claim its part in your grieving. Then when you're ready and you're certain it's what you really want, put down a layer of good soil and plant a tree right on top of the anger's rightful place. And each day you'll be faced with a choice, you either let the tree be swallowed up, or you feed it, nurture it, and with time the tree's roots will spread, grow stronger, and break apart the anger into little fragments. The anger will always be underneath, and that's all right, but with time the tree will absorb it into itself enough that life is livable and still beautiful—though, never quite the same."

Daniel looked at me anew, somehow seeing what he hadn't known was there all along.

"How long ago?"

"Many years."

"Would you share?"

I almost wanted to.

"Perhaps another time."

Daniel nodded in respectful understanding.

"Tell Emily there'll be a box with her name on it. The café is open till nine o'clock."

"I couldn't, Alice. You've done too much already."

"Surly you wouldn't refuse me the fulfillment of goodwill, would you?"

Daniel chuckled but I could see him acquiesce.

"Good, then it's settled. I better get back. This is my lunch break."

"Can I offer you a ride back?"

"No, but thanks. I walked for the fresh air. It'll be nice to fill my lungs before heading back. It was good seeing you. Take care!"

"You too, Alice."

Chapter Eleven

Logan Snow

August 2010

"The press would like a photo op."

"No."

"Mr. Snow, you're the most significant donor, and tonight was in great part for you. This is great publicity, take advantage."

"I said no."

"But you're the guest of honor. The press is expecting it. What am I supposed to tell them?"

"I'm sure you'll think of something, Allen. My decision is final. No press or kiss next year's donation goodbye, understand?"

Reluctantly the lanky man nodded and left. He didn't understand of course; he couldn't. That was however, irrelevant.

Gabe stood from his chair and poured a glass of rum. He held it out to me and I declined.

Prick.

"How long you going to keep up the prohibition?"

I shot him a deathly look and he laughed in response.

"Tell me, employer…" He drew out the damn word like some game.

"…what has you suddenly so invested in all these children's charities?"

Ahh, that's what had his panties in a twist. The beast had feelings after all.

"Must I really explain it, Lorenzo? Legitimism."

"You certain 'bout that?"

"If you're referring to my finding out about your upbringing. I assure you that has nothing to do with it. If you wanted someone to fall in love with you, you picked the wrong employer."

Gabe stared at me a long time, scrutinizing, attempting to smoke out the truth. Tough shit, Lorenzo. He'd become the closest thing to a brother I'd ever had. He sure as shit didn't want to hear it, and I wouldn't give him the satisfaction.

"Good. I would hate to terminate our contract because you became weak and did something as stupid as to pity me."

"You speak as though you don't know me at all, Gabe. I'm offended."

Gabe wasn't convinced but he dropped it. Good.

"Now, if you're finished playing the damned damsel in distress, perhaps we can get back to the task at hand."

Gabe grinned that familiar cold and sinister grin, and I welcomed the topic change.

"The container passed customs. The group's happy with our services. They've decided to sign."

"Good. The price has gone up fifteen percent."

"And the reason?" Gabe inquired, as if he didn't already know.

"Security costs of course. They're more than welcome to return to their previous supplier but we both know they won't."

"You make too many people angry, and they'll take you out from pure spite."

"That's why I don't exist. Logan Snow is a legitimate business man and Monarch, well, he's a ghost. How do you kill a ghost?"

The sounds of music and laughter filtered through the thick doors. Lily was out there; my date, charming the executives with her carefully chosen dress, bright smile, and just the right amount of physical touch to get the imagination going. She loved being desired. Craved it. There was never enough attention to quench that endless thirst of hers. After Sal's death she'd become someone else. As if the only anchor which kept her grounded was Sal himself. His unconditional love for her. Without that, she'd become ravenous and nothing was ever enough.

My drive for revenge paralleled Lily's need for attention in many ways. I wouldn't be fulfilled until I took from Ily what he took from my parents. Truth was, once I'd completed my vendetta I would likely remain empty. But by then, I would no longer care.

Chapter Twelve

Allison Red

I never got to meet Daniel's wife Emily. I'd gone home to meet the SolarCity rep before she'd arrived. The inspection passed. It was simply a security measure. Ensuring another energy source in case one failed.

The house remained empty aside from the soft tap of my feet from one hall to the next, a reality I struggled adjusting to and when "Chopped" on the Food Network channel could no longer hold my half-hearted attention, I retired to my welcoming bed.

I awoke the next morning early, though, I remained in bed well past the morning sun. It was Sunday and sometime around eight o'clock I decided to attend church.

I slipped into a secluded corner where the preacher's voice rang clearly into my ear and though I tried, none of his message registered. It all felt jumbled in my head, so before the service came to a close I left.

On my way to the café I grabbed a takeout burger and ate in silence while sitting at my desk. The order for Blonde Beauty was up first thing tomorrow and despite my primitive urge to lace the pastries, I knew it wasn't all on her. My aversion was as much my fault as it was hers.

She represented everything I wasn't; the perfect match for a man like Logan Snow. It wasn't difficult to imagine Logan looking her way, responding to those cherry lips that just a day ago insulted me openly like I was beneath her; transporting me back into stone walls where the elite ruled without compassion or remorse.

The worst part… I was jealous.

With great effort I rose up and headed towards the kitchen to make the best damn pastries Barbie had ever seen. Within a few hours I'd prepped all the toppers spanning from isomalt sugar to tempered chocolate straws to rice paper origami; I held nothing back. The ganache and icings were tucked away in the fridge and all except two batters were already baking, because they tasted best if rested for twelve hours. Barbie may have looks but I had dignity, and that was worth more in my book; even if it was a book most people didn't care to read.

Three hours after arriving, I locked the doors and headed to Marina's for our ice cream movie night. I picked up two pizzas because instinct told me Seth would be there.

Sure enough, as I walked into the kitchen Seth was poised at the counter nursing a coffee mug with Marina standing at the open fridge.

"Close that fridge, Sunshine, I've got us covered."

"Enough for all?"

I raised my brows at her.

"Call it instinct. Now come on, it's getting cold."

Seth calmly pushed away from the counter and came over to kiss the top of my head. I smiled back.

"You staying long?"

"And intrude on your sappy ice cream movie night? I would love to! But unfortunately for you ladies, I'm needed back at the office. We have a new lead and it's time sensitive."

Marina set several bottles of water in the center of the table before settling in beside Seth. Whether Seth attempted to hide it and failed or perhaps not trying to hide it at all, it didn't matter, his brown eyes burned with adoration each time he aimed his sight toward Sunshine. Such obvious affection once again raised the question of just how on earth I'd missed it before.

"Well, rest assured that we'll be thinking of you while enjoying the wonderful entertainment value *Bedazzled* has to offer. Truly we're sorry for your loss." Marina offered Seth.

"Isn't that where the guy grows up in an underground bunker with his parents and then tries to re-enter the modern world as an adult?"

"Um, no. You're thinking of *Blast from the Past*. Same actor, different movie. *Bedazzled* is about the shy guy Elliot who loves the girl he works with and makes a deal with the devil for seven wishes in exchange for his soul; but none of them work out." Marina dutifully explained while loading her plate with food.

"Ahh."

By the look on Seth's face I got the distinct feeling that it really made no difference to him. He was humoring us.

"Well as much as it pains me to miss such a masterpiece of a motion picture, I'm afraid duty calls."

"Well, since I feel much the same about your choice in films that succeed in depressing me more than entertaining me, you're forgiven!" Marina shot back playfully.

I watched their flirty banter from my familiar spot of third party observation. I found plenty of enjoyment in observing, but with it came a sense of longing; a desire of my own.

"I suppose we'll have to stick to neutral territory then. Watch vintage Mickey Mouse and Winnie the Pooh." Seth offered her.

Marina smiled at his goading.

"Good. I'd always loved that golden bear."

Seth chuckled, I rolled my eyes, and Marina just smiled with gratification. We finished off our meal with an occasional random comment, but mostly we just ate.

"You ladies have fun, lock up, and don't turn the volume up too high."

"Yes, Sir."

Seth wrapped his arms around his spunky love, effectively locking her in place. He just held Marina for a long moment as his lips rested against her forehead. Perhaps it was the lingering mood of my church visit today, but I was certain I saw something ominous in Seth during that embrace.

I cast my sights towards the table for clean-up, not wanting to intrude on such a private exchange.

I was placing the dishes in the dishwasher when Seth walked over to plant a kiss atop my head before heading out the door without a word.

Marina and I settled comfily on the couch, quite possibly the softest couch ever made; an array of snacks, but most importantly we had our ice cream.

Two words: Haagen Dazs.

I held my beloved Cookies 'n' Cream while Sunshine continued her love affair with Dulce de Leche. It was little pleasures like these that really made me miss my mama.

We had reached a critical part of the movie—where the soft-spoken Elliot finally approached his love interest Allison in a bar, only to have her reveal that after four years of working together, she had no idea who he was—when Marina finally said something.

"Don't read too much into this—unless there's more than I'm aware of; then you should read into it all you need—but did you get the sense that something was bothering Seth tonight?"

This was where lines began to blur. Without giving it too long a pause I decided to go with optimism. Perhaps it was the persistent neon-lit desire to protect my best friend and be hopeful for her sake; for whatever reason, optimism won.

"Yeah, probably just fatigue though. He's been working insane hours, he's tired and waiting for the break in the case that has yet to come. Not to mention his I-can-solve-any-case-ego is bruised."

"True. But did you get the sense that he was—I don't know, worried or something? I mean safety has always been a priority for him, but the past several days it seems—well like for instance yesterday he literally had me go outside with him and demonstrate my *process* of getting in and out of the car, then the house, then arming the alarm before proceeding to adjust my *process* where it was weak, so to speak. Things like that—you think he's worried about, you know—"

"I think having your relationship out in the open has put things in a new light for him. Your wellbeing is a top priority, I say get used to it. This will more than likely not be the last time. Plus, it's probably like foreplay to him." I smiled because I could see that last part quite possibly being true.

"Besides, if there was any real danger Seth wouldn't conceal it." Sadly the moment the words left my mouth I was faced with a heavy doubt about the truth of that statement. What made it sad was that I should've had absolute confidence, so why was I suddenly so unsure?

Marina looked relieved and that offered me comfort to my otherwise unsettled nerves.

Elliott had just experienced his first failed wish where he was a wealthy man married to the ever so lovely Allison before everything suddenly went downhill. Elliott found out his loving wife was having an affair with her English tutor Rauel before realizing his wealth was a result of his success as a Mexican drug lord, and lastly got shot at by the Russian's because of a deal gone bad. At this point I was usually laughing or smiling at the comical antics, however as Elliott entered his second wish that was destined to fail, I was lost in my newly discovered distrust in Seth.

I had never doubted his leadership before. Each of us was well seasoned on the reality that you stood better chances of survival if both parties were well prepared and well informed at all times. No secrets.

Could it be his secret relationship with Marina that put a dark spot on our relationship? Or was it simply a side effect from all the monumental changes in the past few weeks, the nightmare, and divorce— meeting Logan Snow? The last thought lingered long past Elliott's experience as the hot shot basketball player who seemed to have it all until he realized in the state of undress that he was tragically lacking girth down south. So as Elliott begrudgingly whipped out his handy devil-calling cell phone and dialed the much guarded code of 666, I begrudgingly requested that my brain filter out any thoughts pertaining to a certain individual.

Elliott's remaining attempts at winning Allison's affections failed and for his final wish he decided to be the selfless man he'd always been and simply wished that Allison have a happy life; with or without him. As Hollywood would have it, Elliott's soul was released for his selfless act and just days later he met another woman. A down to earth, quirky, and clumsy woman who in every way was Elliott's perfect match; right down to looking eerily similar to the soon forgotten Allison. They lived happily ever after and I had to hand it to Hollywood, they sure knew how to bring out that happy ending.

And I was as big a sucker for them as the rest, in fact I was probably worse.

I stretched and grabbed some empty bags of corn nuts, Haagen Daz containers, and bottles of water before heading to the waste bin in the kitchen.

"You need help with the order for her Royal Highness tomorrow?"

"Nah, I finished what I needed today. Usual time tomorrow is just fine."

"I didn't want to say anything and I'm sorry if I'm making things worse instead of better but, you gonna be all right with it being Snow's building an all?"

"Yes and no. But mostly yes, I think. It's the floor beneath his so I might get lucky and sneak by without a scratch."

"I hope so too, Sweets. But just in case, I'll have the Neosporin handy so don't go all Hulk on me and tell me if you're hurting, all right?"

"I will."

Chapter Thirteen

Allison Red

Seven fifty five.

Seven fifty six.

Seven fifty seven.

I was hot, sweaty, and panicking. The predicament was lousy and frankly I was angry—pissed actually, for having allowed myself to be reduced to a clammy-palms-pudding-brain mess. While attempting to stare down the neon digits as though I held the power to freeze time, I continued to battle the siege that was Logan Snow; who now held my self-respect in the palm of his hands as though it were only a noun.

Eight o' two.

I climbed out of the Pilot and slammed the door, grabbed the trays and carriers and nearly growled into the all too familiar intercom before ascending to the twenty first floor.

I was running on anger and I rather enjoyed the mild reprieve my cooled veins offered as I walked to the receptionist who seemed annoyed by my presence. Tabatha, as indicated by her name plaque, effectively shooed me off in the direction of the conference room without actually saying a word, and like a good little delivery girl I scurried to said conference room which resembled The Summit almost identically if not for the colors.

Red seemed to be on the menu and it was served in abundance. Tasteful I thought at first, and yet after mere moments inside the room it began to close in on you while you fought the urge to squirm and searched out the nearest exit for fear of being suffocated by the crimson predator. I idly wondered if the effect was intentional; perhaps a brilliant business tactic.

My movements were calculated, precise, and not fifteen minutes later I folded up my carriers and tentatively breathed a sigh of relief. While passing the public elevators, as though the fates wished it, Blonde Beauty accompanied by an entourage of six stepped off and onto my path; casting the same combination of repulsed-envy as the first time we stood before one another.

"Mrs. Red."

"Hello—" I stopped, realizing she still hadn't introduced herself. A fact she was obviously pleased with and I felt so small standing before her. A feeling which had nothing to do with my actual height.

"I must be going. Do enjoy."

"Indeed, we intend to."

There was an eeriness in her tone. An unsettling shadow which seemed to eclipse her amber irises and for a moment I wanted to let all the anger her heiress-like demeanor elicited to break free and smack her porcelain face. The useless idea dissolved quickly because truly, what did it matter? I wanted off of this floor and out of this building where I sensed I didn't belong, so with my threadbare restraint, I let her pass.

It felt like an eternity waiting for the damn elevator; Tabatha's eyes burning holes into my back, so I gave up and pushed past the heavy doors which led to the stairwell. The moment the crisp air, which distinctly smelled of concrete and steel, hit my senses I felt a heavy dose of relief.

Running on my self-imposed elliptical I wondered why I insisted on putting myself in such situations. My hair was straight and I wore no makeup except my strawberry-scented lip balm. True, I was tempted to give Blonde Beauty a run for her money-tossing-elitist-attitude-high-horse. But then again who was I kidding? I would've lost that race unless undergoing a complete metamorphosis. She was stunning and I was...me.

With a deep breath I pushed open the heavy doors of the stairwell with keys in hand and skirted around the monstrous concrete posts blocking my path. I looked up to find my Pilot, only to be slapped in the faced with my anxieties validation dance. That arrogant sixth sense which warned me not to come here now yelled 'I told you so' through a riot grade bullhorn directly into my ear.

My synchronized movements faltered; my brain distantly analyzing if it wasn't too late to turn around and wait this out behind the concrete behemoth I'd just passed. But analysis showed I would only be donating more of my already suffering backbone and given how little I had left, I wasn't ready to give up any more.

His Porsche sat idly with its engine running alongside the curb near my Pilot and the momentum from my mini-marathon just moments ago took flight for parts unknown; leaving me too vulnerable, too accessible for whatever hold Logan seemed to have over me. I felt his penetrating stare as the thousands of goose-bumps rose to attention along my spine. His effect was more than thought or feeling: it extended to my physical being, the aches real, my breathing rapid, and I knew beyond any doubt that if I gave in, Logan Snow would consume me.

With all the intelligence of a naïve mouse I scurried towards false shelter, somehow believing escape was possible; probable.

"Alice, to what do I owe the pleasure?"

He was leaning against the hood of the Porsche now, more casual than on our previous encounters. He was wearing slacks without a suit jacket, the sleeves of his button down shirt rolled up to his elbows; he seemed—ruffled or rugged or maybe I'd become so delirious that such insignificant details had somehow gained meaning?

"A delivery for—she actually never introduced herself. Twenty first floor, lots of red. My apologies, I—I must be going."

The owl's eyes were telling. He was upset, angry. He stretched out his talons slowly; eager to have my undivided attention and I wondered if mice ever *wanted* to be devoured? If deep down they desired the owl to possess them in a vice grip as they soared across the sky? If in secret they hoped for abduction, to escape a life that seemed so callous?

"I trust you were well received and compensated?" The question was leading and damn me if my inner damsel in distress didn't want to come out and play.

"The transaction's been fulfilled, Mr. Snow."

My response displeased him.

"You took the stairs."

"It's good cardio."

"Tell me, Mrs. Red, is that mouth of yours always so clever? Perhaps I'm going about this all wrong." Logan pushed off the hood, his path set straight for me.

"Perhaps a more intimate conversation would help those lips speak more—uninhibitedly?"

Our current position was certainly more intimate. We were caught in a dance without sound, led only by the cues of our bodies. We never touched, not even a fingertip made contact with the other, and it was weirdly erotic. I was aware of him, all my senses sabotaged solely by his presence and nothing more; leaving me to wonder how much further could I fall if he reached out?

"It's Ms. Red now." My lips betrayed me, revealing secrets best left hidden.

I wouldn't meet Logan's eyes; afraid of his power, afraid of my own weakness, afraid of what I was capable of doing and knowing how much I wanted to do it.

"Alice." The sound of my name upon his lips sounded haunted—pained. I couldn't understand and yet I felt I should.

"Good day, Mr. Snow."

I was careful not to touch Logan as I skirted around him and towards my Pilot. I heard little above my pounding pulse, the radio was playing in the car, but I heard nothing other than the low notes of Logan's last spoken word.

A wild mixture of emotions swelled angrily within me as I felt a void inside me grow.

*

If I'd hoped getting back to the café would help bring my Monday back onto a happier track; that hope was blown to smithereens by the news Andrew gave me upon my return. I investigated and contemplated the remainder of the day only to conclude that it was an utter failure, which left me little to look forward to this morning. As I closed my eyes in an effort to rid the image of my office's unwelcome guest lurking about, instincts both dangerous and too familiar overpowered me.

"I need you to run a Raven profile."

Seth looked up from his phone, his jaw hard, and his stare sharp.

"Who?"

"Jennapher McKenzie, you'll know her as Jenna."

"What happened?"

"Andrew said he noticed her coming out of my office yesterday while I was out on delivery. That's not the issue, my staff is allowed to enter the office on occasion; he'd seen her slip something inside her shirt. From his interpretation he felt something was off in her behavior."

"You scanned your office, nothing was out of place?"

"Nothing that caught my attention. She could've made a copy or a note with something for all I know. I don't keep anything about our history at work but she's been a thorn in my side since the beginning. Something's off here."

"How long has she been employed at the café?"

"Since late February." I saw the glimpse of hope in Seth's reaction. His thoughts mirrored my own. The Brotherhood wouldn't wait so long. If they sent Jenna in for information they would've made their move by now. But things change and we've been out of the world of The Red Brotherhood for nearly eight years; that's ample time for many transformations within the organization.

"I told you from the start to let me run every applicant. You should've listened."

Yeah perhaps I should've. I was a fool to have believed civil rights actually existed to begin with.

"I did what I felt was right at the time. But Jenna picked the wrong day to go sneaking about. All her info is here. I want everything, the entire run."

Seth's gaze leveled.

"Is this serious?"

I hoped not.

"I don't know."

I had every confidence Seth would access what was needed. Between himself, Luke, and Greg they had every talent necessary. It was Seth who initiated the discussion about collaborating and opening their own investigation branch. An endeavor that ultimately earned them respect within the industry, though, Seth was always careful to stay within the shadows.

The café greeted me with warmth wrapped in cinnamon and cocoa. No doubt Marina just whipped up a batch of our popular Snail. Every good café had to have a cinnamon roll on menu, it was almost a prerequisite.

"You're late."

"And you're a godsend."

"That's yesterday's news, Sweets. What's up? You all right?"

I allowed Marina to think my tardiness was due to yesterday's encounter with Logan Snow. Not wanting to worry her about Jenna until I knew what I was dealing with.

"I'm fine. Just a slow morning is all."

Marina gave a half smile before turning to the ovens.

I set off for my office and threw myself into work. Halloween was days away and the deadline for the promotional ad was midnight. The social networking sites also needed updating, a chore if there ever was one. I'd rather be mopping the kitchen floors than logging onto Facebook.

The landline rang and I silently thanked whoever was calling for saving me from all things social media.

"Chai Café, how may I help you?"

"I'm looking for, Alice."

"This is she."

"I'd like to place an order for tomorrow, lunch-time."

I glanced at the calendar.

"We'd be happy to; may we begin with a name, address, and phone number in case we get disconnected, and then we can design your order."

"Steven Reinhart with Reinhart and Associates. 303-882-2424 at 7171 S Alameda 11th Floor Suite 1150."

I wondered if I should just decline the order right then. My hand shook from the mere address, saying all that needed to be said.

"Thank you, Steven. May I ask how you heard of us?"

"Your information was passed through Mr. Snow who owns the building. I've been using the German bakery north of here for several years but if Mr. Snow recommends something, my experience tells me it's good. We're celebrating a birthday of an associate; male. Whatever you'd like to feature I'll trust. We'll need enough to feed approximately sixty."

I'd been in business since February and suddenly the largest and most prestigious building within my café's servicing limits had welcomed me with open arms all because of one man.

"I'm pleased that Mr. Snow felt strongly enough to refer me. I have you set up for delivery on October thirtieth at eleven thirty with Jenna. Is there anything else I can do?"

"Indeed, would you make the delivery personally? It's my business practice to meet those I deal with in person."

Was every order for that building going to veto all delivery personnel other than me? I couldn't enter that building! Every encounter with Logan Snow chipped away at my armor; in truth I feared I would give into his pull if I saw him again. So if this was a deal breaker for Steven and all who occupied the L.S. Trade Co building then I would willingly forfeit any business they had to offer.

"I understand. I share your need to meet those we conclude business with and if I could get you to come visit my café I feel it would give you a more in depth experience of what Chai Café has to offer. Unfortunately I must keep my scheduled commitments that day."

Steven was quiet a moment, more than likely for effect.

"With an offer like that, how could I refuse? I've got a meeting in Highlands Ranch Monday mid-morning. I'll be by around eight."

"Monday around eight it is. Thank you for the business and I look forward to meeting you, Steven."

"Likewise, Alice."

Several key strokes, and the order was set for Steven's associate; as was Alex's package, set to go out with the Shade Technologies order tomorrow. It'd been well over a month and I hadn't heard a word from the child. I was beginning to seriously worry this time.

The cancer blindsided Alex; the whole family. Pam wouldn't stop crying and Raymond continued to say how strong and brave Alex was, that nothing could conquer him so long as he fought. Alex understood his parents' condition. They had to think positively for the alternative was—unthinkable. But Alex needed an outlet, a place where all his hurt and anger and bitterness could be released and understood. How could we ask of a young boy the courage most grown men lacked?

When I visited Alex, I refrained from saying words I knew he'd come to loathe: *brave* and *strong* and *hope* and *chance* and so many others at which, if I paid attention, I'd see him visibly wince. During our rare time together, Alex often cried, sometimes he punched pillows and threw things. I listened faithfully when he spoke angrily, and sometimes with a vocabulary I wished he'd never known.

Sometimes as I told him about my childhood, the childhood of Nadia Rumikov, Alex would grasp my hand and squeeze too tightly. It was our secret. My stories offered him some comfort and perhaps even some implausible hope. He often asked what death was like. I would tell him I never made it past the corridor, and I knew he wished I could say more but truth was, I couldn't. Death passed me by and therefore I was never truly dead. I wasn't resurrected, I simply survived against tremendous odds. Alex said he'll say hello to my mama for me, and I let him say it because he had to voice the thoughts he couldn't escape.

I wanted to show up unannounced but knew better than to press. He'd write when ready, and he appreciated that respect; the ability to still dictate certain parts of his life.

I'd managed to prep most of Stevens order before releasing the tears which seemed inevitable whenever I thought of Alex. My phone chirped and I answered without looking at the screen.

"Hello."

"Hey, Sweets! Did you forget about us or something?"

"I could ask you the same thing. You think just because you've some case, you can take a break from your brotherly duties? At least Seth comes by every few days. You and Dad have been M.I.A. for nearly two weeks, and texts don't count."

"Since when did texting become insufficient?"

I could hear the smile in Luke's voice and it brought one to my face in turn.

"Since you stopped pairing it with a physical visit. Should've asked Seth, he clearly got the memo."

As Marina wove herself deep into my life—and my heart, she brought with her Luke and her father who had become mine and Seth's very own family.

"Well, we both know why Seth comes by, now don't we."

I laughed.

"Umm, yeah. Now that I have my head out from under a radioactive rock, I know exactly why he comes by."

"Well, while Seth sneaks off like Romeo in the middle of a serious case, we're left holding the fort."

Greg was a cop, a good one. When Gwen died he left the force, took his children and moved. Luke served six years for his country, discharged after a nearly fatal wound. Seth, well, he knew the mind of a criminal; Ground Zero, they called it. It didn't take long before the three men realized they each brought to the table a unique set of skills which enabled them to open up a private investigation firm, along with surveillance consulting and management. Each man driven by internal struggles they kept to themselves.

"Yeah, I keep hearing how this case is kicking all your asses; bringing that massive ego of yours down a peg or five."

"It's been brutal, Sweets; just keep those tasty treats coming back with Seth. So long as I have that, I think I'll survive."

"Wow. Thanks."

"Hey, I should be blaming you! If it weren't for your insane baking abilities I wouldn't be addicted to the damn sugar-high. I've become a junkie and do double time at the gym just to upkeep my lady-lovin' bod."

"Oh my, here we go."

We both laughed and it was so nice to hear Luke's voice.

"What's Dad yelling back there?"

"He's blowing you a kiss like some fool; saying something about missing you."

"Well tell him I demand you both visit tomorrow, I won't take excuses and I won't forgive you if you fail to show up."

I listened as Luke relayed my demands to the Captain.

"We'll see you Sunday."

"Not good enough. Besides Sunday is Seth's request. This one's mine and I demand you visit or face the wrath of one monstrosity of a hissy-fit."

"No you won't, you wouldn't know how."

"Try me."

"Sheesh, all right. See you tomorrow."

"Good."

"Before you go, I saw a Raven today. Made four rounds before landing."

Jenna.

"Thanks, Luke. See you tomorrow."

My gut twisted, and whether it was based on Jenna's lack of merit alone or because the memory of her intrusion insisted I remember the void that grew within me that day, it made little difference. If I was wrong, so be it. If right, the game begins.

Chapter Fourteen

Logan Snow

May 2013

"You should eat something."

I pressed pause, meeting Lex's eyes. The woman was kinder to me than I deserved.

"She's special isn't she?"

"What makes you say that?"

"The way you look at her. It's different. I've never seen you look at anyone like that."

I would've preferred to ignore Lex's observation. It drew out thoughts I kept pretending weren't invading my head. I should've made my move by now. But I just couldn't bring myself to make the call. It was as though I was somehow connected to her and I craved it. I loathed it. I couldn't get enough of it.

"Am I capable of such emotions, Lex? Would I even know what it was or how to keep from destroying it?"

"You're capable of far more. And I should know. Now, let's get you some food and go from there."

With that, Lex left me to my thoughts. The surveillance footage streamed live from the building adjacent to her café. I was itching to tap into her own feed but I knew better than to pry too far. Her system wasn't standard, with who knew what alarm triggers. So the grainy stream from Urban Lofts would have to suffice. For now.

*

"You're avoiding me."

"Hardly. I'm running a company, Lily. I haven't time for distractions."

"Ha! That's rich when that's exactly what you've become. Distracted. We have plans tonight. Pick me up at seven and wear your grey suit with the blue tie I gave you. Don't say no to me, Logan. Do it."

Her endlessly long legs held no allure as she disappeared from my office. Lily was the closest to me I'd ever allowed any woman.

That had changed.

I'd changed.

*

"Logan." Lily cooed.

"I knew you'd come tonight."

I wanted to feel *something*. I could've used the release. But nothing within me stirred.

"We'll be dining at Rioja." My voice was cold. Vacant.

"Why the ice, Logan? Have you forgotten who I am?"

My gaze leveled with Lily's. *How could I forget?*

Lily leaned in, seduction ripe within her amber irises but I stopped her coldly, leaving her staring in disbelief. Almost hurt.

"I don't even recognize you anymore, Logan. What the hell is happening to you?"

"Let's just enjoy dinner."

"No! Answer me!"

"Calm yourself, Lily."

"Kiss me then! Prove you haven't changed. Kiss me!"

Lily moved over me, a desperation I'd never seen before etched within her elegant features. I raised my forearm to halt her advance within the small space of the backseat.

Meeting Gabe's stare in the rearview I signaled for him to turn back. We wouldn't be going out into public with Lily unhinged. She wanted more. I was never going to be the man to give her that.

"King will escort you wherever you wish to go tonight."

Lily pulled back, and though I could've stopped her, I didn't. Her hand connected with my cheek and the relief she sought, never came. There was pain in her stare. A mixture of fury and defeat which didn't suit her heiress-like persona.

"Good night, Lily."

Without a word she exited the car where King stood, ready to play caregiver for the night.

Gabe was staring at me in the rearview mirror. A look I had no patience for.

"If you've something to say, say it."

"You've been blinded, Snow."

I wasn't blind.

I was a fool.

Chapter Fifteen

Allison Red

I'd told Andrew not to worry; that everything with Jenna was fine with total ease…as though my gut wasn't twisting in knots. There was a risk Andrew would make a random comment, maybe confront her altogether, but it was a risk I had to take; until I knew what I was dealing with.

"Busy, huh?" Trish's voice chimed, bringing me back. I simply smiled.

"Yep, something about that fog just makes people want to sip hot beverages and settle in." Trish continued.

I remained silent because fog reminded me too much of a time long ago, though, I wouldn't let it show.

Trish was the youngest of the staff. She'd just graduated from Green Mountain High School last summer and was in her first year of Red Rocks Community College. Photography was her dearest passion and she was amazing at it. I'd replaced three of the café's art pieces with her very own works.

"What can I get for you today?"

"Um, Café Bembonn, eh meedeeum." The Russian accent was thick; the woman clearly struggling, using her hands as she spoke, pointing to the menu for assistance.

I gathered she was asking for the Café Bombon which was simply espresso served with condensed milk. Russians loved their fill of condensed milk.

"Of course, is there anything else I can get you?"

"Ah, yis. Dee seenimone." The middle aged woman pointed to the Snail before searching out her wallet, which seemed lost in the massive designer bag.

It amazed me how even now, I had to squash the urge to help and allow her to speak her native tongue. But instead I smiled politely, leaned in ever so slightly as though trying to catch each syllable to solve the puzzle of what she was attempting to say. I looked thoughtfully towards the items she pointed out and gave no indication that I was anyone other than All-American Allison Red.

I returned with her Café Bombon and Snail just as she found her wallet.

"Thank you, have a lovely day."

People kept pouring in and the café remained crowded. The last eight customers I'd served had asked for their items to go when it became evident they wouldn't have a spot to sit. I busied on with order after order when, somewhere between brewing a cup of Earl Grey with lemon and honey, and reaching for a Red Elephant, I saw the men walk in.

I smiled and decided that two weeks was too long for them to not visit. I served guest after guest for the next eleven minutes before Steph arrived to take over.

"I wondered if you'd forgotten how to get here or if you'd been sneaking away to some other sugar shop altogether." Dad bent down for a hug and swung me around before I swayed into Luke's embrace.

"Sit, Sweets, we brought you lunch."

"Oh, you brought a peace offering?"

Dad smirked.

"You're not going to let this go are you?"

I put a finger to my lips, tapping it several times.

"Mmm. Depends."

"On what?"

"On what you brought for lunch."

"Well then, prepare to be amazed for this is a box full of magical ingredients. Once you partake of its goodness you'll no longer be angry at two men who have sadly been working countless hours in an effort to ease another's grief." Luke was waving his arms around the P.F. Chang's to-go boxes while imitating the suspenseful voice of a magician who was about to reveal extraordinary illusions.

Dad took a seat with Luke not far behind when I opened the Chinese food packages to find enough food to feed a small army.

"I rule that as much as I enjoy the theatrics and this very enjoyable special treatment you've provided today, I much prefer seeing you on a weekly basis. In which case you're forgiven, and thanked for a very lovely lunch."

"Done." Dad smiled, Luke followed.

"Have you guys already eaten?"

"Yesss…"

Luke saw where I was headed and therefore was already reaching for a fork and plate.

"Well this is clearly too much food for me so let's dig in."

I grabbed several bottles of sparkling water before seeing Luke with his already full plate; then served each man his soup before reaching for my own.

"The weather is perfect for soup. Thank you."

"I anticipate a very cold and wet winter this year. Are your tires good? Have you had them checked, the brakes, alignment and all?"

"Yes, Dad the tires are good. I don't need anything else right now. By the way didn't Seth walk in with you?"

"Seth and Marina have decided they want some privacy in the back kitchen. Time alone—Marina requested." Luke wiggled his eyebrows suggestively and Dad scowled in response.

I laughed.

Dad cleared his throat.

"I'll have Trenton pick up the Pilot on Wednesday and have the shop run a full diagnostics report, then fix anything that needs fixing."

I knew better than to argue with Dad when the subject matter pertained to safety; simply appreciating the luxury of having someone who cared enough to worry at all.

"Okay then, thank you."

Dad nodded with pleasure and continued to work away at his food.

"So anything new with the case?"

"We've run into some delays, lots of dead ends, and more questions than we started with. We're working, Sweets that's all I can say; we're frustrated too."

I watched Dad as Luke spoke, careful to pretend I didn't see the haunted look in his eyes.

"I hadn't realized it was that bad. I shouldn't have made such a fuss about you not visiting; I'm sorry."

"No, I'm glad you did. It's been good to take a brief reprieve from the office and see you. I'm afraid your fussing was necessary to get us out here, however, we better head back now."

Dad was finished with his bowl and plate of food, as was Luke. They ate with the efficiency of programmed robots, not leaving a single grain of rice behind. My plate laid half full but I kissed them bye before they exited and shut the door behind them.

I forced the remainder of the food into my mouth not tasting much of it. Something about being alone took away the enjoyment and flavor of every spice. I tidied up before walking out to see that Jenna had returned from the deliveries for the day.

"How did the delivery go for Steven?"

"Fine. The payment is in here."

"Well that's great. Thank you."

I smiled at her but received no more than the stare of someone merely tolerating me. Jenna moved on, as did I; without any indication that inside I was seething.

*

Last night had followed the same formula that's now become the norm: a house quiet, dark, and empty and I would've laughed if I'd had the confidence I wouldn't end up in tears. I laid still for hours, afraid that if I'd moved at all, the shadows that terrorized my mind would find me, and that little existence I'd created here in Colorado would vanish, as would I. By sunrise, I'd given up on sleeping all together.

Today children would dress like witches and goblins. Boys will spread generous amounts of red makeup creating an artistic expression of horror to admire before heading to school. The welcoming door stoop has been transformed into the entrance of Hell with no shortage of skeleton bones scattered about; cobwebs ready to immobilize your futile escape. Tunes of the loving heart have been replaced with screams of unbearable pain, echoed only by sounds of chainsaws and soulless heckling.

The theater was featuring its goriest picks for this special Halloween night, a cornucopia of haunted houses filled with demons eager to consume innocent lives, serial killers with pick of the litter to torture endlessly all evening so long as tickets were sold. The entire nation was in celebration of all things horrid tonight, and I found myself hating this calendar day more and more each year.

My ability to rationalize the human motive to celebrate such morbidity fell tragically short and so I chanted the mantra 'who am I to judge' only that's exactly what I found myself doing. I was angry with the Little Red Riding Hood walking into the theater and the Game of Thrones worrier two steps behind. I felt my blood heat at the sight of Freddy Krueger toting around his lifeless victim drenched in blood paint; and the family with three small children all dressed like pirates, the Father, clearly Captain Jack Sparrow; I hated it all. Every reminder, every image dug deep inside my broken soul and forced me to relive what my mind had worked so hard to lock away.

But sitting alone in a dark house on such a night when the moon glowed so amber it appeared to be on fire, simply wasn't in my plans.

The guys were working yet another late night on the same case dissecting the lead they'd uncovered yesterday. Luke mentioned another case from Salt Lake City that had too many similarities so they felt there was a connection. Marina was attending a bridal shower for a good friend from collage. An odd night for such an occasion, though, I supposed that was the point and so I stayed at the café.

Though my staff had kept their costumes G rated, my customers were less kind to my aversion of such festivities; concluding the kitchen as the best place for my trembling mind till closing time.

As though reaching for a first-aid kit, I pulled out every weapon in my arsenal and immersed myself in work. Within minutes the island counter was covered in confectioners' sugar, gum paste, and fondant. The various cutters and molds laid ready for use with isomalt melting in the oven as I reached for the colors and paints. The petals kept forming and the ball tool kept mending their generic state until they appeared almost real, delicate, and full of unique beauty. The sixteen gauge wire worked quickly between my fingers, so efficient that twice my skin paid the price, drawing blood, deeming the need to pull out the real first-aid kit.

The girls had wandered in and out of the kitchen several times, mostly getting replenishment pastries for the front, though, I paid them no mind; too invested in escaping the sound of splintered doors and vomiting.

Time elapsed and I had no indication other than my progress in sugar flowers. The drying rack was nearing at capacity before I decided to move on and experiment with isomalt; test just how far my imagination could go before my creation cracked and crumbled to the countertop.

I felt the familiar gust of chilled air behind me and the sound of Stacey's voice filled the space.

"Alice, there's someone here to see you?"

"Sure send them back."

I'd listened only half-heartedly; too driven to complete the butterfly's wings to be just so, before it cracked between my not-nearly-steady-enough fingers. I'd realized too late that had I listened more closely, I would've caught the intonation in her voice.

The door swooshed open and I felt him claim all space, the way he always did. His presence collided with my relentless anticipation, as my heart battled a war against reason. Suffice it to say, either way I'd lose. The butterfly lay broken in several shards, yet my hand remained poised in the exact position the wings were moments ago. As though the world kept moving forward while I refused to move with it.

"Must you exert such effort to suppress what I do to you, when I've laid bare before you the effect you have over me?"

"You can't, we can't." My lips trembled in sync with the unsteadiness of my feet.

"Turn around, look me in the eyes and if you can say there's nothing here, I'll leave."

Logan Snow knew exactly what he'd asked, and by which terms I was to fail.

My luster-dust-stained fingers gripped the edge of stainless steel which prompted me to visualize my current state of appearance. My apron was a mess and I was fairly certain the powdered sugar had also found its way into my hair even though I'd pulled it back into a messy bun. How fitting, when I was certain I'd turn to find Logan perfectly put together as he always seemed to be, and the image proposed the question of how could I possibly affect him as he says? But more so, how could a man of his valor be susceptible to such effects?

I didn't believe it to be healthy when you must concentrate to the point of near pain just to turn your body without collapsing. I didn't believe it to be natural to feel as though the laws of the universe were no longer in rule. I didn't believe it to be real when you looked into another's eyes and felt as though you were looking at the future yet unraveled. I didn't, only somewhere between meeting Logan Snow and that moment, my understanding regarding such illusions no longer applied.

Every encounter, every glance, every thought had collaborated to bring me to this moment where I was no longer strong enough to deny that which I'd desired all along. To argue against that which wasn't supposed to be real. To battle that which it would seem, I was never meant to overcome.

"You win." I whispered my surrender and looked directly into the eye of the storm set straight for me.

Within three strides Logan Snow had his hands where I'd wanted them all along. Our lips met with a heady combination of passion and anger as his hands unwound my bun before gripping my locks possessively. He roamed my body, leaving every neglected patch of flesh begging for the caress of his hand, the burn of his grip. I arched my back generously as he bent down to bridge the gap in height, and I found a dark pleasure in his dominance.

His lips were hot and smelled distinctly of peppermint and power; its potency matched only by its addictiveness. Logan claimed me from within, leaving nothing spared. My hands wandered blindly and found pleasure in every strand of thick hair that slid between my fingers, every muscle that flexed against my palms and the sharpness of his jaw in contrast to the softness of his mouth. My fingers danced with exploration as Logan Snow continued to fill me with need.

His grip tightened at my nape, immobilizing my movements and opening up my neck for his mouth's taking. I was spiraling into an abyss of nothing and everything, led only by whatever Logan gave; a nip before a kiss or the feel of his hot breath as he slid his lips along my collarbone before reaching my ear where he'd meticulously cater to my pulse point; a particular spot which ensured all senses were heightened.

I moaned openly, filled with emotions which urged me to weep, for I knew I'd never be the same again. Our breathing was labored, the space filled with sounds of need and demand of fulfillment and as I neared the point I couldn't begin to describe—Logan's grip lightened.

"That's exactly it."

I was confused.

"What?"

"Your taste. It's exactly how I'd imagined it, with one exception."

"What's that?" I spoke breathless.

"Its effect. It's more."

There was meaning in his words and whether he deemed it so or by a fault of my own, I was unable to decipher their hidden message. Logan looked at me then, his eyes a portal of unusual clarity which allowed my prying gaze to linger, revealing a bottomless depth; and I shivered.

The portal vanished in response, as though I'd failed a test I hadn't known was coming. The failure ate away at me as though I'd just doused a bath of baking soda with buckets of vinegar.

I said nothing, afraid I suppose, or perhaps too stubborn. Logan pulled away leaving too much space between us, a distance which carried with it a physical ache.

"What were you doing?" Logan's chin directed towards the tables covered in sugar of every medium. His voice was harder, less vulnerable than from moments before—a consequence, I thought.

I shrugged a shoulder.

"I was having a creative streak."

"I can see that. Though, that isn't what I'd asked."

It was unnerving to speak under his penetrating stare, to voice my thoughts rather than hide behind the shield of assumption.

"I've had a lot on my mind and turned to my sugar friend for help. As it turns out, sugar was happy to help."

"What's been on your mind that you had to call in the big guns like sugar?" Logan finished with a light chuckle; the vibration was just another jolt of electricity to my already sensitive skin.

I contemplated continuing our playful banter. I almost wanted to simply play this game, wherever it was. Only I couldn't.

"What's happening here? What are we doing?"

The air crackled, as if the whole universe was on pins and needles; waiting to know the answer. Logan held my gaze and all traces of humor left his striking face.

"It's complicated."

"So un-complicate it." I shot back.

Logan moved his hands further back, threading his fingers through my hair with his palms just under my ears.

"I'm a man of great demand, and that carries with it equal obligations. I can't offer you a traditional relationship or anything of the sort."

I'd imagined him saying a lot of things, but somehow the words leaving his mouth had never made the list. Perhaps my prediction was right; this was just him needing to get me out of his system. I cast my gaze downward in an attempt to conceal my disappointment.

Logan's grip tightened, pressing me to look back up. Reluctantly I let him.

"See me tomorrow." He asked, his voice low. Logan's strong hold wouldn't allow me to look away. He was evading and I was yet again weak and naïve.

"I work."

"I'm a paying customer, Ms. Red. The Summit has a conference at eleven and I expect to have my order an hour before that time."

So weak.

"Tomorrow then."

Logan's lips met mine, soft at first, as though saying thank you before gaining momentum and claiming that which laid deeper than the surface of my mouth. I couldn't help but feel that the pace of the kiss too had meaning. Logan held the power all along to bend me to his will. My willingness merely sped up the inevitable, thus earning me a gentle and intoxicating thanks.

Logan was out the double doors and halfway down the corridor when my eyes shot open with equal parts of anxiety and disbelief. Gabe stepped out of the shadows, loyally following his employer, while Jenna stood staring with one foot inside the double doors.

What felt so intimate and private was suddenly invaded by voyeurs entirely unwelcome in my private affairs. My anger flared, then turned itself on me; for it was my own damn fault. I'd become reckless and clumsy and I hated it, no, I loathed it. I was losing pieces of myself, the new vacancies being replaced with a woman I didn't recognize.

Jenna walked past, proudly wearing a righteous smirk, before grabbing two trays of pastries and leaving me alone to battle my inner monologue.

My poor representation of marriage was just that, poor. A woman with a husband as wonderful as Seth yet said woman threw herself at another man.

But the outside world was blind to my secrets; to them I was merely another statistic in failed matrimony.

By the time I'd wiped the last remnants of sugar off the island I'd concluded I'd forgotten who and what I really was; and for that matter, wasn't.

*

The moon had lost some of its earlier copper glow, now a pale yellow ball sitting high in the night sky. The house was empty, the fridge; the same. I brewed some decaf tea and stepped off onto the patio, a wool throw wrapped around my shoulders to shield me from the bitter cold. The air smelled of impending snowfall, the earth releasing its fermented fragrance, warning all living creatures to secure food and shelter or face the brutality underprepared.

I sipped my hot beverage and listened to the sounds of the night. The rustle of dry grass as creatures caught their meals or avoided becoming one. The breaking of branches followed by high pitched howling that was suited for a night such as this. An owl took to the sky in search of its ideal vantage point, finding it in one of the evergreens bordering the house. It perched itself high above the ground, waiting patiently for its victim to gain courage or simply display sheer stupidity. Every creature played the game, their life on the line and the odds seemingly forever against them. *I understood.*

The moon was now low in the western sky so I turned my back and washed up for bed. I had no shortage of things to think about, and simply lying in a bed without any distractions gave my mind free reign to take me beyond the blood stained curtain; where evil ruled with an iron fist. It was these hours I hated most, for in then I couldn't escape my secrets.

Picking Colorado had proven itself an asset for our aliases as Seth and Allison Red. Seth was right about the low activity here for the Krasnaya Bratva "Red Brotherhood" and we'd reaped those benefits. Still, tonight was no different than any before it—I could boast all I wanted—after all we'd evaded The Brotherhood for seven years—seven years more than any other before us had ever managed. Yet deep down, I knew it was only a matter of time.

The Brotherhood had no shortage of resources both monetary and of the breathing species. Becoming the most powerful mafia in all of Russia wasn't achieved by failure, and my illegitimate existence wasn't immune to their morbid efficiency.

With bitter truth behind my closed eyelids I could no longer ignore the seething glare of my conscience. What was I doing with Logan? His presence had the ability to void everything outside his penetrating gaze, and that ability was the scapegoat I would use for my laps in reason. The right thing to do—the safe thing—was to pretend this was a misunderstanding, chemistry, lust, and whatever else fell under that category.

I was no martyr; my need to sacrifice this "thing" was as much for myself as it was for Logan, because ultimately I was a coward. I could've delivered myself to The Brotherhood at any point over the years. But I was selfish; I wanted to live.

The knowledge that my existence had harmed and killed others closed in on my heart a bit more each day.

Mama.

In truth, the most good I could've done would've been to part with my life. But I couldn't, and so I attempted to cover my true colors with bright yellow's and greens of generosity and kindness, performing deeds of goodwill under the pretense of good citizenship, when in truth it was a poor display of atonement for all the pain my existence had released upon others.

Seth saved me and where was he now? Hiding. Looking over his shoulder every damn day of his life when he could've become my grandfather's right-hand man had he simply done away with me like he was supposed to. Seth would've been wealthy beyond measure, respected, and feared…the predator and not the prey.

Others praised me for all my great qualities and virtues; my drive to lend a helping hand, my monthly donations or politeness and soft smile. Often I was so deep into my role as Allison Red I almost believed them. But when alone in my bed, I had to face the brutal truth; I was nothing more than a disease, a self-gratifying virus which refused to die. No disease deserved praise; certainly not love.

My resolve was clear but it was following through with it which scared me. So I did the only thing I could—I prayed. Pouring my heart out as I asked for wisdom and clarity when it seemed I had so little of both. For peace within, as chaos ruled the world I couldn't control, and for healing wounds that seemed to linger no matter how much I wanted them to disappear.

Chapter Sixteen

Allison Red

I arrived early at the café, needing more time to fiddle with my sugar friends. I'd hardly slept, and my resolve was waning.

My connection to Logan ran deep and I knew I wouldn't be content with a fling or a "thing" without meaning. But to have what I really wanted was even more reckless than last night's kiss; why build a future when you were nearly certain you'd never live to see it?

I envied Seth for pursuing his relationship with Marina, for opening up to love and receiving it in turn. I also hated Seth for adding Marina's name onto his death warrant. If they found Seth, Marina would die with him, and that was a cold hard fact.

"Good morning!"

Marina walked by, putting her things away while I focused on placing my array of batters into the oven.

"Good morning to you too, Sunshine."

Marina just smiled.

"Hey you're coming on Sunday right?"

"You couldn't get rid of me if you tried!" I said moving onto prepping the boxes.

"Dad's relentless calling has no end in sight at this point. He's gushing, actually gushing at the news of Seth and me. Are men even allowed to gush?"

I smiled in response. Dad had called a few times to see how I was holding up. Being my surrogate father meant nothing to Greg. He treated Seth and me as though we were his very own.

I assured him I was great, diverting the conversation from myself to the new couple. Marina was right, Dad was gushing. A six foot four inch, two hundred fifty pound, steel framed detective was reduced to nothing more than a bucket of pink goo.

Jenna walked in, looking as happy to see me as Bill Clinton was to see Monica Lewinsky post scandal.

"How was your night, Alice?" Each word dripped with sarcasm while she barely contained her glare of contempt.

Perhaps it was just the timing, my fatigue, or the rude awakening to the fact that I would never experience what others took for granted—regardless, my temper rose and I physically bit my tongue before I spewed several choice words just itching to jump out of my mouth. My hands coiled into fists eager to connect with a particular flesh and the depth of my anger frightened me, revealing how weakened I'd really become.

The Raven results couldn't come soon enough so I could rid myself of Jenna. Unfortunately for me, I needed the damn documents to know which course of action was necessary, and the wait alone was a feat worthy of a medal.

"Fine. And yours?" My mouth curved politely when inside I felt anything but.

"Jolly." With a final snide glance she departed with a skip in her step like a punch to the face.

"What was that all about?" Marina asked.

"Jenna walked in on me with Logan Snow last night."

"Wait. What? Snow visits you and you don't call me the minute he leaves? What is going on? Why do I feel like I'm always hearing these things from outside sources?"

"Don't read into it like that. You had the party and when Dad called, he mentioned that everyone had gone for the night, but when I pulled into the garage, Seth wasn't home which left only one possibility. You were—busy."

Marina looked at me anew, hardly believing this was truly happening, and the hurt was crystal clear.

"That doesn't mean that I won't answer my phone when you call. We're not kids, Alice. Seth's tongue could be half way down my throat and I'd still answer your call. Don't you dare insult me by denying it."

The anger, unfairness, and pain that seemed omnipresent in my life had thus found an outlet. The past several weeks have boiled dangerously and Marina had fallen victim to it. I wished to deny it, but despite my unconditional love and happiness for Marina's relationship with Seth, I also harbored envy; and I no longer questioned how such conflicting emotions could exist simultaneously, because there was no answer that would ever make sense.

"Look, I—" I had nothing. My emotions continued to swirl; too much of a blurred mess to single out any thought.

"Since Seth's divorced you I feel like you've pulled away, you don't share unless I push, you hardly call me anymore just to chat, you've thrown yourself into work and I can't help but feel like you're slowly shutting down."

I remained silent, leaving Marina to wonder if she should do the same.

"Don't do this, I beg you," she said.

"Let me in, that's all I'm asking. Just talk, even if I don't understand, there is no need to carry the burden alone when I'm standing right here—after all our history don't I deserve that much?"

My vision swelled, matching the storm within. It was impossible to miss the catch in her voice. I was good at pulling away, and for reasons not at all honorable. I moved closer, her hurt and sadness in plain view.

"It's true, all of it. And further proof to how broken and irreparable I am. I pretend, I try, and at points I even have hope, but it's short lived and always followed by a crippling blow of reality. I'm sorry I'm incapable of being a better friend, a better person. I'm sorry I—"

Marina hugged me before the tears leapt toward the stained concrete we stood upon. I remained still, too afraid Marina would realize any moment how one-sided this friendship truly was—that she deserved better, and finally walked away.

"Broken—sadly I'll admit that's true."

My tears fell faster.

"Irreparable—that's only your insecurity."

I pulled back ready to present the case for my failures but Marina took the floor first.

"You have demons, I get that. For someone who's endured the unspeakable since before your own birth, it would be impossible not to. But your mother was right, Alice; your heart is beautiful because despite the constant reminder of all the injustice you were victim to, you still try."

I looked straight through my friend, saying what had to be obvious; trying meant nothing without accomplishment.

"I know what you're thinking, but think on this if nothing else. You praise me for every little thing I do for you, from getting you a birthday present to buying you you're favorite ice cream for movie night, no deed is insignificant in your eyes. You've placed me on a pedestal for doing nothing more than loving you and being a friend, and don't get me wrong, I love being on a pedestal but I can't be up there all alone when you should be up on one too." She looked at me with those eyes that needed to be certain I was still following along.

"You not only buy me gifts on my birthday but you send me something for my half birthday! Along with every other holiday of the year, often times with no occasion at all. You almost never splurge for yourself but when it comes to Dad, Luke, Seth or me, you have no boundaries. You dedicated nearly every spare minute for four straight months helping me remodel my house and when I got you the Aveda spa package as a thank you, you nearly flipped out because you thought it was too much! You refused to have the café open on Sundays, even though everyone advised it would mean you lost a significant amount of revenue. But you wouldn't budge because you felt so strongly that your staff should have a day to unwind and spend with those they love. The list is endless but you've never acknowledged any of it as meaningful. You say nothing you do is ever good enough. And anything I do, is somehow so significant it's worthy of a trophy!"

Several minutes passed and we both stood silently. I sensed Marina working to gather her wits as I worked on keeping mine.

"I've always known you struggled with loving yourself. You believe yourself to be nothing more than a burden, a curse. I wish I could help you with that; I thought I was. You refuse to believe anyone could truly love you because how could they when you don't love yourself? I'm guilty for not seeing the severity of it sooner, wishing so desperately to believe you were getting better, but I think we both know that somehow the turning point was the day you met Snow. He made you feel something you desperately wanted, but instead you punish yourself for wanting it at all."

My head was bent in defeat; in shame.

"I don't know any other way." I wasn't sure Marina heard me when it was barely a whisper, but she moved to wrap her arms around me and I accepted the comfort she offered.

"I don't know what to do either, Alice, but we'll figure it out—together."

I'd read that all living things from soil to plants to animals felt renewed following a heavy rain, I felt the same must be true following the shedding of tears. I'd been a fool to believe my forward journey would be anything but challenging every step of the way, though, I'd never known anything in my life to be different.

"I'm sorry." I whispered just loud enough for her to hear. Marina squeezed me tighter, the scent of jasmine strongly present as her blonde curls caressed my face. She pulled away smiling, before grabbing the next batch on the tray and moved to place them in the ovens.

"Okay then, let's start from the beginning. What happened?"

I followed suit, assembling boxes and inserts while giving a detailed account of all activities beginning with my creative streak to my epic first kiss and that I was headed to see Logan at ten. By the time I was finished I was wiping the same counter for the fifth time, certain it was clean but continuing to wipe back and forth just in case.

"Oh my, Alice. That's—unexpected."

"You're telling me."

I finally gave up on the counter or I'd wear out the stainless steel.

"Does Seth know about this?"

I shrugged a shoulder. "It happened less than twelve hours ago. Besides I was foolish to agree. It's better if I walk away."

Marina looked thoughtful as she silently worked through my news.

"I gotta be honest hun, I've always hoped you'd meet someone and live a little, maybe even for selfish reasons thinking if you moved on with your life, Seth would move on with me."

Marina gave me a sad smile, waiting to see if I was hurt by her admission; I wasn't.

"I never pushed you because you needed to go at your own pace, even though it often infuriated me to no end how you managed to be utterly oblivious to all the guys who'd showed interest in you over the years. Let's not forget that some had been very established and handsome men. Granted none quite as appealing as Snow but handsome nonetheless."

Marina let out a deep sigh and now she was the one working the wash cloth over the spotless counter.

"I guess when I saw your reaction to Logan that day, I was so excited you'd finally showed interest in someone, not only that—it seemed almost electric; the vibe between you two. Even from a distance I could see the atoms exploding. I was so excited, I didn't really even think about how this would affect every miniscule aspect of your life. The adjustments you'd need to make for a relationship of any form."

We stood quiet and I couldn't fill the silence because my throat had a knot lodged so deep it might have required surgical extraction.

"I suppose it was easier for Seth and me in a way. We had years of friendship to build our trust before we pursued our relationship. I also knew his history; we had no secrets. But it seems like this thing you have with Logan is wild, an untamed animal that's been caged up and has finally broken free at the sight of its mate."

I groaned.

"What's with all the animal references?"

"What? They get the point across."

I shook my head at that, but laughed because it sort of did.

"I guess what I'm trying to say is give it a try. You've been hiding for nearly eight years and you'll still be careful, but you need to live, Alice. Actually live. You'll never know unless you try. You've always trusted your instinct and from what I've seen it says Logan is safe. So you don't know much about him— but you feel connected, and that holds weight all on its own. Go with that. And if you need a partner to analyze every detail to death, I'm your gal."

My heart was torn from my brain, each wanting the opposite of the other. My hand trembled as it latched the edge of the countertop for superficial support.

"I'm scared."

I couldn't share with my best friend the rest of my fears. She was happy and I couldn't take that from her.

Looking back at her warm emerald eyes said I didn't have to.

"Seth's guilt for the possibility of death is what kept us from each other for a long time. He tried to make the decision for both of us and that wasn't right. I made the choice that I wanted to be with him and he made the decision to never regret—no matter what happens."

Tears filled my eyes as I listened with strained intensity.

"I only want to see you happy, Alice. Whatever that might be, that's all I want."

Maybe my dream wasn't a sign of my past coming upon us. Maybe subconsciously I was ready to let go and move on. Seth said that's why he'd decided to come clean and break us free of our arrangement. What if he was right? Could I really just do this for myself? The mere thought felt wholly forbidden.

I reached for her and Marina accepted my embrace.

"Hey! No PDA in the kitchen you two. Break it up or let me join."

Andrew had his silly grin and we both opened our hug to let him join.

Despite my attempts at keeping busy I saw Andrew's questioning look once he saw my blotchy face. I noticed his eyes on my empty ring finger and how his brow creased. He busied himself with the bins of coffee beans, but the signs were all there. I felt dirty. For no other reason other than that Andrew's opinion of me mattered—to me. I didn't want him to see me merely as a statistic of failure, though, short of telling him the truth or something too close to it; there was nothing left for him to think.

"So how was last night?" I asked him.

"My folks hosted that event for the Democratic Party I'd told you about. I was responsible for entertaining the McDonnell's: Frederick, Barbara, Keith and the twenty two year old, very suitable, very narrow minded, Brittany." Andrew sighed. His excessive force with the coffee bins said the evening wasn't how he would've spent it.

"Sorry."

"Yep. Me too."

Andrew smiled, though, it never reached his eyes. His disappointment spanned further than his unsuccessful evening with Colorado's elite. He was disappointed in me. He'd left traces of the bitterness in his voice, stolen glances, but mostly in his departure. He thought he was friends with someone full of integrity only to find out I was a liar, a cheat.

The next few hours came and went and I was really starting to feel nervous, anxious, confused, and about five other equally frustrating emotions. I knew what the *right* thing to do was; the problem remained that I wanted something different.

I packaged the pastries and headed out back. The moment my feet hit the parking lot I stopped. Gabe was standing in front of the Porsche with his arms crossed over his chest. Our eyes met as he approached taking the boxes without a word.

"Gabe."

"Ms. Red."

"Is everything all right? I wasn't aware that you'd be here."

"Please get in."

"I don't understand?"

Gabe turned to fully face me after loading the pastries in the trunk.

"Mr. Snow sent me to pick you up. He's awaiting your arrival."

Gabe gave me a pointed look, like this must be obvious, and gestured with one hand to get inside the car. I was weak and reckless when it came to Logan Snow; as proven by my prompt obedience.

During my six minute ride I'd managed to squeeze out one text to Marina only to prevent any worry as to why my car was still parked with no sign of me. The remaining five minutes, forty seconds was spent inside my head as I battled between what I craved and what I feared.

I noticed Gabe entering a private lot with a swipe of a keycard. He parked, grabbed the carriers, and ushered me to the elevator door that looked like it came out of a bomb resistant bunker. The black ridiculously-thick steel doors sealed us in as it ascended and had it not been for my stomach tingling, I wouldn't have known we'd moved at all. I knew Logan had wealth. I was familiar with the signs but more than anything it was Logan himself; the way he carried himself, the way he spoke, how every move was calculated and with purpose. He oozed confidence and power. But there were lots of very wealthy people in Colorado and most of them didn't have secret elevators and full-time bodyguards.

The chime of the elevator announced our arrival and Gabe led us through two doorways both needing the earlier keycard. We entered the lobby where Lisa appeared as if out of thin air, plucked said boxes from Gabe's Hulk-like hands and scurried towards the same conference room I remembered.

Without instruction on where to go, naturally I followed Lisa. I was mere inches from the conference room when I felt goosebumps rise upon my now electrified skin.

"Turn right, at the fork go right, and enter the only door on the left."

Shivers, actual shivers rippled through me. I followed his instructions hyperaware of his presence. The side glances and flat-out glares I received from some women had my earlier uncertainty resurfacing. I was out of my league and stepping into the confines of his office wouldn't change that fact.

As was the case with the rest of the floor, the walls to Logan's private office were glass, different only in their thickness. Though I was no expert, even I could tell it was impenetrable glass. I archived this observation next to 'key card' in my mental Rolodex of all things Logan Snow.

Logan pressed his front to my back. Sweeping my hair to one shoulder his fingers trailed from my earlobe to collarbone. My breathing quickened from his nearness, my skin sparking from his touch.

"You're exquisite."

No. I was ordinary, but the way he breathed the words made me feel like I was Red Carpet worthy.

"Turn around."

I could listen to his voice endlessly, all commanding and confident. Mid turn I noticed the glass walls were now frosted, obstructing us from the rest of the floor. My chest was rising and falling at warp speed. Logan's gaze intensified, striking my veins with that familiar lightning. I trembled at the knowledge of how much he affected me, connected to him by an invisible force I felt but could not name.

"You see me." Logan stated this fact with awe, caressing my cheek with a look of adoration. I'd never felt more treasured than when seduced by his all-consuming gaze.

Without warning Logan crushed his lips to mine, his tongue delving deep and unapologetic as he pressed on with an intensity that would surely mark or bruise. I reveled in his heated need, matched only by my own desperation to be devoured in every way his wicked mouth promised.

Everything outside this moment ceased to matter or even exist as I pulled at his suit jacket, irritated by the fabric separating his skin from mine. Somewhere along the way, I found myself lying on a sofa. The heat from the luminescent fireplace adding to the warmth I felt within.

Logan roamed my body and I welcomed the sensations his touch evoked. Greedily ignoring the roar of my conscience as I slid my hands through his hair, over his shoulders, and down his back feeling his muscles flex with every move he made.

Capturing both my wrists he held them above my head while pressing me deeper into the sofa. I'd never experienced such arousal. To me, sex was tainted. A trauma I could never quite rid myself of. But with Logan I felt…like I was a whole woman.

"Beautiful." Logan breathed the word and despite all my broken ugliness, in that moment, what I saw in his piercing depths made me believe I was just that.

No response was needed, leaving only the intensity of emotion that passed between us; conveying what words could not. My eyelids closed as his lips ghosted my parted sensitive mouth, forcing me to only feel and taste him. His kiss lacked urgency or demand from moments earlier, leaving me in strained anticipation each time his mouth made contact with my skin as I succumbed to his blissfully synchronized torture.

"Do you need me, Alice? Do you ache for me?" His tone was bordering a growl.

I was unable to find my voice, looking to him, searching his eyes in an attempt to understand this; whatever *this* was.

"Yes." The answer barely left my mouth before Logan kissed me with a new found hunger. I welcomed his shift in mood; my hands tugged, aching to touch him only to have him tighten his hold, keeping them captive.

My sweater and camisole rode up high, too damn high and I froze. My muscles tensed and I wanted free from his grip for reasons I couldn't voice. Logan must've seen the horror on my face because he released me instantly.

"I'm sorry. I—I just—I'm sorry." I stuttered.

Logan rested his forehead against mine as we both worked to calm ourselves. He adjusted my camisole placing gentle kisses to my collarbone, the hollow base of my throat, and finally on my lips.

"Are you all right?"

I nodded, wishing he would turn away; not see what I couldn't hide.

"What you do to me—I crave you, Alice."

Logan blew out a slow breath and sat up bringing me with him. His arms wrapping around me as I straddled him, burying my head in his neck. Logan rubbed circles on my back and I was becoming addicted to that gesture. With my head still buried, I breathed him in; smokey with just a hint of spice. The scent was calming and allowed me to get a grip over my tension-filled bones.

"I think I better go set up those pastries and head back to the café."

"I'll walk with you." He offered.

I nodded, suddenly insecure and hating it.

"That door leads to a washroom if you need a mirror."

I decided I did.

The bathroom didn't disappoint in luxury. It had to be the size of my bedroom with a Jacuzzi tub of all things. Really? In an office?

My reflection glared at me through the floating mirror and all I could do was stare back. I'd failed to do the noble thing and walk away. I'd made my choice; however selfish it was.

Conversations halted as we made our way towards the conference room. I saw and felt the stares, silently quenching the urge to glare back. As we stepped into the conference room, Logan flipped a switch that instantly frosted the glass just like his office.

Lisa's capable hands clearly had no need for my assistance as the contents of the boxes laid beautifully displayed, so I picked up a slice of Midnight Madness and brought it to Logan's lips. Taking it in one bite he lightly nipped my fingers with a grin but before I could reach for a napkin he grabbed my wrist. Bringing my fingers to his lips, he sucked on each one in succession, retrieving any remnants of the chocolate ganache with his tongue. His hungry stare erased my unwelcome insecurity and I invaded his mouth, enjoying the sweetness left behind by the pastry mixed with his own taste, and moaned at the pleasure it gave me.

Logan cupped my backside setting me on the conference table, instinctually my legs wrapped his waist and I raked my nails against his back under his suit jacket. The door swung open and I turned to see a wide-eyed Lisa with her mouth hanging open. With his hands still in my hair Logan shot her a look that made me flinch in her defense.

"What?" The demand seeped out from in-between clenched teeth as Lisa looked like a rabbit facing a bear.

"I'm so sorry, Sir. Brooks needed a moment of your time, he said it was urgent and I—I should've knocked. I'm sorry, Sir." Lisa cast her eyes to the floor awaiting instructions.

"Wait for me here, this won't take long."

Without a response from me, Logan stormed out of the room. Casting me a sideways glance Lisa mouthed "sorry" and shut the door behind her. I sat on the table for a few minutes unsure how long 'not long' was before hopping off and making my way to the wall of windows to enjoy the view.

At the sound of the door opening, I turned and felt as though I was just punched in the gut. The sinister gleam in her amber irises giving way to the impending disaster. She was every bit as beautiful as I'd remembered, and every bit as vicious.

"Hello." My voice was small even to my own ears.

"You have no business here. Logan belongs to me and whatever pathetic charity he's bestowing on you won't last. He's *above* you."

"Somehow I think Logan's fully capable of making his own decisions."

If it was possible, her sneer intensified.

The Beauty put a perfectly manicured hand on her hip, arching a perfectly colored brow while flinging back her perfectly silky blonde locks behind her perfectly sloped shoulder revealing a perfectly shaped face, before speaking the perfectly selected words that would be my kryptonite.

"I don't believe we've ever been properly introduced. I'm Lily; Lily *Snow*."

My knees went weak as my hand grasped the table for support.

"Ah, I see this was unexpected for you. You really didn't know. How sad." Her sympathy mocked me as I struggled to gain composure.

Logan opened the door and against my will, my eyes shot to his as my pain morphed to unconcealed anguish. His eyes widened, jaw clenched, and his hands fisted. Long seconds passed, each stabbing me deeper as I watched him battle his current predicament. Lily appeared pleased, as though finding her husband's mistresses was a sport; one she was good at.

"Give us a moment. You may wait for me in my office." Logan addressed Lily, his tone lacking the harshness I'd heard just moments earlier with Lisa, inconsequently confirming my dreadful suspicion.

Lily smiled before departing to her husband's office where he'd just held my heart in his open palm; a palm no longer gentle, a palm no longer safe. Logan reached out to touch me but his gesture was like a slap in the face. I stepped back so quickly you'd think he was poison, and in that moment poisoned was exactly how I felt.

"What did she say?"

Was he seriously asking me what Lily revealed so he could determine how to neutralize the situation? The telltale signs were all there. I should've known. Too bad I threw logic out the window when I started listening to my heart.

"Her name is Lily Snow. Doesn't that say it all? I suppose now I know why you couldn't offer me a relationship." I couldn't keep the bitterness from saturating each word.

"I'll grab a cab."

I turned to leave when his hands shot out and he pushed me against the glass with both hands on my neck, his fingers in my hair, his thumb caressing my jaw. He was trembling.

Consumed by rage visible in his every feature. Despite my own anger, it still pained me to see him so torn. How pathetic I am, I thought. Laughably so.

"Don't. Do. This." His words were strangled. Time elapsed and the reality of the situation began to set in, the pieces all fitting together in a picture of lies and deceit.

"It's done."

In my weakened state I looked over my shoulder to see Logan standing with both palms against the frosted glass, head hung in defeat. It was over; over before it ever began.

I found my departure from Logan's building much like the first, only this time I was broken, and the murmurs surrounding my less than graceful exit barely registered. Gabe tried to talk to me at the elevator and offered to drive me, but he saw the finality in my expression offering me a soft nod in condolence instead. I appreciated it coming from him.

As the elevator doors closed, I fought to maintain control, at least until I was out of the building. Dashing through the main lobby I breathed deep as I pushed my way outside; the frigid air invigorating my constricted lungs. I refused to look up, feeling Logan's eyes on me, far away, yet powerful enough to still reach deep inside me somehow.

The scent of impending snowfall from last night had come to fruition as millions of snowflakes floated from the sky.

The grey gloom above was a mirror image to my aching soul, a heart cut open and bleeding.

I had no jacket, or my gun, and debated calling a cab to take me back. But agony decided I needed the twenty minute walk in solitude to think and collect myself before anyone saw me.

I slid my phone into my back pocket and began my journey; my heart pounding, my breathing a combination of gasps and sobs. The excessive blood flow kept me from feeling the bitter cold fully, and for that small gift I was grateful.

What was I doing? A simple question I had no answer for. I felt hurt, embarrassed, deceived—the list continued much like the need to vomit. How was I so stupid? Was I as vain as I'd painted Jenna to be? Was all of this just a carnal attraction?

Desperate to validate my behavior I racked my brain to find reason in all of this; I found none. The evidence was reviewed and the jury returned the verdict.

Swallowing the pain I forced my feet to keep moving. Anger and confusion bringing on dark memories I would've otherwise suppressed, but given my predicament the punishment fit my crime.

How many women had I seen murdered once their part was played in the saga that was the Rumikov men? Women flocked to their feet as though they held the key to the Gates of Heaven; with their good looks, wealth, and mouths that wove lies so beautiful it could be mistaken for art; each poor girl believed she was the exception to the rule. Her reward for lying, stealing, or providing false alibis—the horror of realizing her life was as expendable as the tissues in a Kleenex box, only they always realized too late.

I used my intuition to navigate the streets of wolves' in sheep's clothing. Logan; confident, wealthy—add in stunning and hypnotic eyes, and I should've seen red flags and sirens blasting "danger, danger" in at least five languages. Yet in my walk of shame, my heart cried for me to turn back. Back to the peacefulness offered in his embrace, the impatient passion his kiss gave birth to, and the connection that gave me a wholeness I'd never known.

My mama's voice broke through my jumbled thoughts, and I let her.

"I saw him, I mean really saw him and my knees gave out when he saw me. I could hear Papa's icy voice instructing me to display my superiority and disdain for such trash, but I felt and displayed no such things. All I felt was an ache."

"Why hadn't fear stopped you, Mama?"

Even as a teenager I struggled to understand why my mother behaved so recklessly.

"I was possessed, consumed entirely, and no amount of fear could quench what connected us. We just were."

Remembering my mama's words; hearing her voice as if she was walking beside me, re-telling the same story that I never tired of hearing, it hit me how eerily similar my experience had been with Logan. The love my parents shared, as potent and imperious as it was, it still failed in keeping them alive.

Perhaps that was the price for something so profound? The higher you fly—and such. Clearly my circumstances with Logan were less than favorable for any relationship. Should I be happy it ended so early before we suffered a harsher fate? The question sent a shiver up my spine, giving me new perspective and even a twisted comfort.

Life was precious, surely even a lonely life of solitude was better than not living at all? Yet here I was, checking off the box marked 'undecided'. I may've not understood why, but I knew what these feelings were all the same. I could say it was stupid and impossible, but in the depths of honesty and revelation, I accepted it for what it was, and what it would never be.

My tears had stopped their steady flow, and though I couldn't feel them, I could see my hands were blue, certain my ears, nose, and feet were no different. I entered the café through the front door and made a beeline for the ladies room. As I took in my reflection, I saw I indeed looked utterly broken. I ran my numb hands under hot water and winced as it stung like thousands of angry needles.

Minutes after I let out a deep breath behind my closed office door a soft knock announced Marina's invasion. Without a word she rushed to my side and hugged me tight, stroking my hair like my mama would've done.

"You want to talk about it?"

In a soft whisper I said all I needed or could.

"The woman from Saturday, there was a reason she never gave me her name. It's Lily Snow...his wife."

Marina clenched her fists, her lips a hard line.

"Logan got called out for something and she walked in. She ambushed me, played me; knowing exactly what Logan was doing."

"Did he see her with you?"

The dagger may as well have materialized as the pain was all the same.

"He asked me not to walk away. It doesn't matter now. He couldn't even bother trying to deny the truth."

"That bastard!" Marina was seething, her fists shaking with fury.

"Let it go. It's over."

"How can you say that? He hunted you like you were some prey; led you into his den of lies. He deserves retribution damn it!"

I blinked back tears, willing my lids to intercept and dispose.

"Life's a sinister game, Marina. I lost—I'll always lose; call it destiny. All that's left is to accept it."

Marina wanted to protest, make sense of this; find hope and light in this endless darkness. But she was a good friend and so she said nothing. Offering me the only condolence I could accept, her compassion.

Chapter Seventeen

Logan Snow

Present Day

The hundred pound punching bag was hardly moving now that my muscles were screaming for mercy, when I had none to give. I continued to pound the leather in an effort to clear my head, only it seemed with each passing day the exact opposite occurred.

What the hell was I thinking?

I'd lost perspective. The finish line was so close I could taste it yet I went and did the most injudicious thing possible— fall for the bait. My actions had run parallel to that of a housewife on a Lifetime movie network binge. Pathetic.

In the beginning watching Alice Red was research, or so that's the bullshit I fed myself. I'd become a trembling schoolboy each time I saw her, wanting to pull her pigtails or simply chase her around like a damn dog.

Then Sarah Mills happened and all I saw was red. When she knocked Alice to the ground I about crawled out of my skin. Sarah should be thanking her lucky stars for being a woman. Had it been a man I wouldn't have managed to stay inside the Porsche until they'd made their way back to the café.

My lungs burned and my panting was deafening to my own ears, but I continued to punish myself for my lack of self-control. I'd compromised the whole mission and for what? Lightning? Damn euphoria? Eleven years of strategic planning, patience, and countless resources spent in setting up my revenge. When Alice all but fell into my lap my plan jumped years ahead of schedule. A damn lottery ticket—until it wasn't.

I should've known my limits from the first time I'd laid eyes on her, should've kept the lid on my heart that died the day my parents did. Yet somehow, even from a distance, Alice had opened the casket and revived what should've remained buried.

I deserved the crisis I'd created and the insistent void I felt, where there wasn't one before.

"I've got news."

I stopped mid-punch and I could practically hear my fists cry out in relief.

"It was Cecilia Whithers."

Well that came as no surprise.

"Her source?"

Gabe cleared his throat, a clear indication I wasn't going to like his answer.

"Cynthia divulged your schedule. Apparently the phrase 'clear my schedule for a delivery' is interpreted for something scandalous based on Ms. Red's first visit and worthy of gossip. Lily was informed by Miss. Whithers the night prior and bid her time accordingly, assuming their predictions proved valid."

So my personal secretary had difficulty staying within her privacy contract. This begged the question of what other crumbs had Cynthia gossiped, and ultimately leaked to Lily.

"What would you like to do with this knowledge?"

"Nothing."

Gabe's eyes sparked with understanding. The best information, was the kind no one knew you had.

Chapter Eighteen

Allison Red

Standing in the middle of my closet I stared at the only three dresses I owned. A sad lot really. It wasn't that I didn't enjoy dressing up, I probably enjoyed it more than I ought to. As a child I often daydreamed of flowing gowns, heels, and lip gloss. To resemble someone of value rather than a stow-away. And yet rather than decorating my body in silk and jewels I remained bound to monotone and multi-purpose, for in too many ways I remained a prisoner. It was the occasional church attendance which was the culprit for the dress inventory; reasoning that most heartless murderers didn't attend the House of God.

Picking the navy blue dress, I grabbed the silver heels, and headed to the car; knowing I was once again, running against the clock.

Stepping to the hostess' post I took a moment to be thankful for arriving in one piece with no unwanted attention from the state patrol.

"I'm here for the Seth Red reservation."

The hostess glanced at her computer before responding with a welcome smile.

"Yes. The rest of your group's already been seated. Please follow me." The pleasant brown eyed girl led me to the far corner of the dining hall.

"Sorry I'm late—the time just got away from me."

Seth exchanged a knowing look with Marina. Dad looked concerned while Luke offered a sympathetic smile.

"Marina, you look gorgeous!"

Dad, Luke, and Seth all chimed in on how Marina seemed to be glowing. Though, it was said as a means of diversion, the statement was no less true.

Within moments we'd all settled and conversations took over as we awaited our drink order.

"Cole called, leads are a dead end."

"What about the landlord on the last known place of residence?"

"Landlord's a drunk five days a week. Hardly remembers what he did thirty minutes ago. Nothing."

The conversation continued as the guys discussed their case. Normally they got a break within the first week. Though, this case was different and seemed to have them running in circles. Marina and I chatted about nothing in particular as we allowed the guys to wrap up their discussion.

"How are things going at the café?" Dad's soft eyes centered on me, scrutinizing as only a seasoned detective could.

"Great, did you enjoy the box of treats Seth brought back Thursday?"

Dad shook his head, knowing exactly what I was doing.

"Trent and Kyle nearly squealed like schoolgirls at the sight of the blue box. Thanks, Precious. We miss not coming by regularly but this case has us all wrapped around its finger."

"Luke, how's Angie?" I asked.

Grabbing his crisp white napkin he brought it to his mouth, wiping away nonexistent crumbs. Uh Oh.

"Wouldn't know. We haven't spoken in weeks."

"So does that mean you've switched gym memberships then?" Marina's voice lacked sorrow.

"Actually, no. I'd be out a good chunk of cash and I've already lost enough on that endeavor, no sense in throwing in my membership to top it off." There was bitterness in his words. I didn't want to pry so I offered my support instead.

"Well if you need a pick-me-up, you know where to call. Sugar's a cure for all you know."

Tonight was just what I needed. As much as I'd wanted to be sitting on my deck bundled in wool and sipping hot tea with only the luminescent glow of the moon—this was better. *This—Family* was what kept my life from becoming a gaping crater.

Seth cleared his throat and once he had everyone's attention a flash of nervousness crossed his face, and it hit me!

"Thank you all for coming tonight." Seth cleared his throat once again, Marina looked confused.

She had no idea. This was perfect!

"Though my commitment and love for Marina only became public recently I confess that I'd fallen for her long before. It only made sense that the most important people in our lives be present tonight."

Turning towards Marina Seth looked at her with such intensity and passion I was defenseless against the swell of my heart. Marina held Seth's gaze, mesmerized, as though the rest of the world was no longer in her peripheral vision. She only saw Seth and the sincerity of what he was doing.

Seth slipped from his seat and stood on a bent knee before my best friend.

"Marina Katherine Meyer, I was unworthy, tainted, and hollow before you entered into my life. I kneel before you a new man, humbled and baring my soul. Will you share a future with me? Will you be my wife?"

You could hear a pin drop at that moment. It seemed the entire restaurant became aware of the intimate exchange in our far corner. Marina tried to speak past her tears, however after a few attempts she nodded her head vigilantly while only broken words escaped.

"Yes— I will—I love you—."

Pulling a ring from the breast pocket of his suit he slipped it on her slim finger as her hand shook.

Elway's erupted in shouts, whistles, and applause as though this was a well-orchestrated scene in a movie. But it wasn't, this was real and my elation for them couldn't have been more sincere.

Dad, Luke, and I gave the newly engaged pair a few moments to regroup, bidding our time to bombard them with congratulatory dues. Dad reached out placing his palm on top of mine; squeezing in support and I responded in kind. We smiled, our eyes saying everything words could not.

"Son, it makes an old man happier than Christmas morning to see his little girl glowing. Knowing the man I've thought of and loved as a son is the reason, that's just pure sweetness. I love you both. Congratulations!"

"Oh, Daddy—thank you. I love you too—"

Marina stood from her chair headed to where Dad stood to accept a loving embrace from his little girl. Luke stood, waiting for the break in their hug. Dad patted Marina's cheek where he'd placed a kiss, then stepped aside for Luke.

"Congratulations, Sis! And thanks for making my job easy. I approve."

Marina's grin mimicked Luke's. As they hugged, Seth made his way to Dad, exchanging the customary handshake/hug combo before Dad whispered something into his ear.

Marina walked back to her seat as Seth moved onto Luke. I intercepted, wanting to offer her my own warm words.

"Congratulations—I'm afraid no words could encompass the depth of happiness I—"

Marina hugged me tight, shortening my speech. It turned out she was at a loss for words.

On his way back to his seat Seth gave my shoulders a squeeze before bending to kiss my cheek. Seth whispered softly "Thank you" in a voice almost too gentle for a man like himself.

Always, Seth; always.

Our food arrived moments later smelling every bit as delicious as it looked. The a la carte menu apparently hadn't hindered our celebratory mood as we'd ordered enough food to feed double the people currently seated at our table. Seth had the honor of saying grace before we all dug in like starved animals.

Conversations were light but mostly we concentrated on working away at our plates.

"I say we get dessert!"

We all looked at Dad as though he'd grown two heads. After such a filling meal we all looked like we were on the verge of a food induced coma.

The four little piggy's groaned but ultimately gave in, requesting dessert be brought out twenty five minutes later to allow us some time to digest or risk exploding.

"I've got a lot of calls to make. Your aunts will have a fit if they hear the news from another source."

"Thanks, Dad, but we have a lot to discuss, so please don't commit to anything okay?"

I'd met two of the three aunts, the term Bridezilla or Auntzilla rather, came to mind.

Three desserts arrived buffet style. Do-it-yourself S'mores, Seriously Chocolate Cake, and Warm Dark Chocolate Brownie. Each decadent, delicious, and I was certain in some countries, illegal.

While in my sugar coma I barely registered Seth's second request for an audience.

"Marina and I would like to ask Luke and Alice to be our Best Man and Maid of Honor. You're the only two that will be in the wedding party but you're the only ones we want."

While Luke appeared to contemplate the offer in mock consideration I sat up straight as an arrow.

"I would've thrown a fit if you'd asked someone else. Of course I will!"

"Well, Jenna did make for a tempting option, but she's taller than me and I can't have that."

Marina shrugged her shoulders as though this was a valid point. Mysteriously my napkin clocked her in the forehead and we broke into a laugh.

"Well damn, now I have to accept. I can't very well let Alice get stuck with Trent or Kyle. They'll maul her at the altar!"

"Wow that's—thoughtful?" I said in lieu of throwing another napkin, because that wouldn't be proper dinner etiquette. I was fairly certain they limited it to one napkin toss per hour. Luke lucked out.

"Of course I'll be your best man—I'm not about to watch my baby sister get married from the sidelines. I want front row seats!"

My eyes settled on Dad as he watched his children, his expression that of a man entirely content.

"Dad, will you walk me down—"

"I would be honored, Baby-girl. Your mother would've been so happy."

Dad rarely spoke of Gwen. Everyone grieved differently. Despite the years passed, the pain of his loss was evident at the mention of his late wife.

"Thanks—just thanks, Dad."

Seth wrapped an arm around Marina's shoulders, pressing her to him. His comfort quickly alleviating her tears, reminding us all to appreciate every moment.

While watching the people who meant the most to me, I willed myself to void any thoughts of Logan. A feat I had yet to conquer for I may as well have asked the sun to cease its shine.

Like a planted seed he'd bloomed, and though I tore the flower out the day I found out about Lily Snow, the roots remained; aching to resurface and bloom once more.

*

I'd passed yet another message to Alex via the order that went out this morning. I'd heard nothing from him in weeks, and my commitment in giving him control over our friendship was threatening to retreat. I'd sensed it was bad, that he was scared and filled with anger and resentment at all of it. But I also feared that my insistence that he attend group therapy with kids such as himself may have pushed him too far too soon. Today's message marked off attempt number four.

I saw a man enter the café with purpose in his step. I seemed to have caught his eye as well because he was headed straight for me.

"Mr. Reinhart, I presume?"

The older gentleman stuck out his right hand as he stepped closer.

"Indeed. And you must be the ever so lovely Allison Red I've heard so much about."

"All good things I hope." Steven's expression told me it was a toss-up and it wasn't difficult to deduce why.

"Gossip, to me, will always remain just that. I like to draw my own conclusions."

"Allow me to impress you then, Mr. Reinhart."

"Please call me Steven. My formal name makes me feel rather old."

The silver peppering his hair and the weathered skin were clearly no match for Steven's sharp eyes, which should've been my first warning.

"Well then, Steven, what is it exactly that dissatisfied you with the German bakery. If I have a better understanding of your needs and expectations I may attend to them more closely."

We had walked towards the far corner near the windows, each taking a seat within brown leather chairs.

"My trial order had more to do with interest than dissatisfaction if I may be frank."

I nodded my consent.

"You see, Allison, Mr. Snow is rather an elusive man. In fact I've never had the liberty of meeting him personally, though not due to a lack of trying."

Things had suddenly become unsettlingly clear.

"I'm a driven man, Allison. And understanding my target will only help me in my aim."

That's what I was now—a plaything. I felt sick.

"I'm sorry to have wasted your time, Steven. My interactions with Mr. Snow are solely business based and to be frank, I don't disclose information pertaining to my clients."

If I'd anticipated disappointment on Stevens end, I would've been the one left disappointed. Steven played his last hand and revealed that my response was of no surprise but rather further proof. Of what—I wasn't sure. He got what he'd came for and therefore no reason remained to keep his company.

"I'll see you out."

"You're very talented. Your merchandise stands out from the rest. How did you come up with such a menu?"

The message was tactless for a man of his position, though, no less grating.

"Trade secret, Mr. Reinhart, you understand I'm sure."

Steven's smile broadened in amusement and I itched to slap the smugness off his snide face.

I watched as Steven disappeared into the back seat of a town car, before entering my office and slamming my fist into the steel wall with force beyond wisdom. Several knuckles split, the pain—a distraction from the agony within my chest.

I stood staring at the trickling blood and refused to shed a single damn tear. The adrenaline subsided almost instantly, so with much reluctance I took my seat and went to work cleaning myself up.

Three days had since passed that fateful morning and every second burned like molten lava, leaving behind nothing but ash. My brutalized fist only highlighted how pathetic I'd become, yet sadly, I hadn't the energy to care.

I pushed my mind to work, though, unsurprisingly the sales reports, expense reports, schedules, charity calendar— everything blurred together and it seemed I couldn't focus long enough to be productive. The last time I'd looked at the mocking clock it was just past ten and now at half past noon my task list had yet to have anything marked as done. I was lost in my head, or maybe just lost. Was there a difference really?

A knock sounded and I answered as cheerfully as I could but my voice deadpanned against my efforts.

"Come in."

"We need to talk."

Seth's urgency kicked at me to wake up; breathe some oxygen and concentrate. He dropped a black folder in front of me and took a seat, patiently waiting while I fingered through the pages.

"Your hand."

Seth stared at the bandages clinging to bruised skin and I simply couldn't bring myself to care about the wound enough to explain.

"It's not The Brotherhood."

Seth's fury at my dismissal was visible, though, he said nothing.

"No. They wouldn't pay Jenna to spy. Especially not for so long. She's working for someone. Does the corporation Trinity Investment mean anything to you?"

"No. Where is it based out of?"

"Cayman Islands."

Of course, why would it be anywhere else?

"What about her phone records, email, GPS, anything?"

"Drop phone. Her laptop has nothing linked to the funds or their meaning, everything is done via phone. As far as we can tell Jenna goes about her life like normal. If we could get her drop phone we'd hit it home. But if we make a wrong move, she tips them off, and we're screwed."

How pleasant.

"So we sit on it. Don't make a move and I'll play it clean. We have a Christmas party planned. She's RSVP'd. I could do a Thanksgiving Party instead, move up the date."

"No, that might tip her off. Leave it and sit tight till then. Can you do that?"

I nodded.

"Good. Whatever she knows, she hasn't used or you'd be dead already. Or perhaps her employer has a different motive all together. Just hang in there."

What option did I have?

Seth hugged me tight before slipping out of the office. I heard his jolly voice carry in the hall, playing his part. The constant role playing remained a necessity for the sake of survival and for the first time—in a long time I wondered at which point I would decide it was no longer worth it?

Chapter Nineteen

Logan Snow

Coward. I'd thought myself many things, though, never that. Yet as I sat slumped at my desk long past the sunset hours, that's exactly what I was. This was when I should've brought out the whisky, saying farewell to my decade of personal prohibition and drank myself into oblivion. But alas, that would've been too cliché; even for this.

The album laid open before me, a photo of my mother and father proudly holding their newborn son stared back at a man no longer recognizable. This vision, this truth, was what brought me to my oblivion; my anger and grief. I willed myself to shut the portal to what once was, and lock it up again; yet I couldn't bring my hands to close the page. A page. That's all that was left. Just a photo on a thick page.

My mother came to me last night, nine years since the last time she'd visited, and I was weak because I couldn't deny how much I'd missed her.

Neither of us spoke as she caressed my cheek with the gentlest palm, while I stood before her but a boy. I felt the weight of ten thousand oceans crash against me as her angelic eyes pierced me—and my façade. I willed my hands to cover my face—my shame—only to have my body betray me.

Her gentle hand rested upon my thundering heart as I braced myself for the moment she'd turn from me, disgusted and repulsed at what I'd become. I waited, only to see her kind features smile before whispering.

"There you are. I thought I'd lost you."

I awoke shaking, my eyes wet and my heart—aching.

These past months I'd done more soul searching than a monk on steroids and though that should've brought me closer to contentment, I couldn't be further from it.

A part of me died the night of my parent's execution and as the details of their senseless deaths surfaced, the rest of me was buried. It wasn't their death alone that caused the shift in my soul but rather what surrounded it; inconsequently setting in motion the last decade of revenge.

Alice was always a means to an end; either to the man I am, or was. Both the question and its answer had been staring me in the face since the first time I laid eyes on her—only to be evaded at every cost, and *that's* what made me the coward that I was.

Chapter Twenty

Allison Red

Several weeks had faded from my timeline into what had become an ever growing sinkhole known as my heart. I lied to myself blatantly if only to get out of self-loathing, but even lies didn't last forever when your pitiable reflection glared back from just about every reflective surface.

"Alice?"

As though awoken from a spell I looked up to see Marina's sorrow-filled eyes.

"Hey, Sunshine. Do you need me out there? I was just finishing up."

"I brought you something to eat. We could chat for a bit."

My eyes blurred and I had to swallow back the knot threatening to render me mute.

Marina set out some burritos while I grabbed the water from the mini fridge.

"Dad's been asking about you. He's worried, you should call him."

"When'd you see him? They haven't been by have they?"

"Nah, I haven't seen him, Seth's been telling me. We're all concerned about you, Sweets."

I smiled with all the conviction I could muster, and hoped it would suffice.

"Have you been sleeping any better?"

No.

"Yeah."

"What about food? You've lost weight."

Some thing's simply didn't exist anymore, among them was my appetite.

"I'm eating fine. It's the working out perhaps? I feel fine."

"That's another concern, Alice. That H2H fighter is twice your size. She could really hurt you. Maybe just stick to the boxing for a bit. You're not thinking straight. Take a break, I could watch the café and you could take a few days off. Maybe go to Pagosa Springs or maybe stay a few nights with me. Like old times."

I chewed away at the food before me; avoiding eye contact for fear that she'd see just how far I'd fallen. Even *I* couldn't face that truth. I'd locked myself in my own purgatory; a place of solitary confinement and no sun. In truth having Marina's company meant more than words. Her presence gave me false hope that I was not yet entirely alone when in reality I always was, by a fault of my own doing.

"Alice?"

I looked up at two teary eyes.

"I'm getting married."

My brows creased. I already knew this?

"In just over two weeks."

"What?"

"Seth doesn't want to wait, neither do I. We've set the date for December eighth."

"But what about all our planning and your aunts and the venue—everything?"

"It doesn't matter. My aunts will have to understand and the details; I really couldn't care. Every day that passes I realize how meaningless everything else is. What matters is we want to be together."

My tears fell freely with the first sense of joy since my heart was torn from my being. I stood without pause and reached out to an open-armed Marina.

"I'm so happy for you." I declared wholeheartedly.

Marina laughed in-between happy tears while holding on tight to a friendship I never deserved.

*

Today seemed brighter as I eagerly vacated the softness of my bed, though, not due to the grey blanket of clouds outside my window. Today I had several tasks due for completion and each one brought me nothing but anticipation.

As Maid of Honor I had been entrusted to secure a photographer, florist, equipment rentals, and lastly the wedding cake. My lips curved and the feeling was like a burst of fresh air. I had something to look forward to, something which effectively off set—if even by a small margin, the omnipresent ache.

I'd reclaimed some life and this small victory fed me. By the time I reached the café I'd already bartered a deal with Lewis Photography; his highest quality package in exchange for one year of free service at the café. Done.

Then in-between baking and boxing this morning's orders, I managed to schedule a meeting with the florist eight blocks from the café before heading to my office for business related affairs. I rushed through my stack of account payables in an effort to make my one o'clock appointment at Frank Floral. Tomorrow was Thanksgiving and if I didn't make it to my appointment in twenty minutes I would be set back until the twenty seventh, an unacceptable timeline.

"Andrew, I gotta run. Mr. Thacker should be by to pick up his cake. Pack up an extra dozen of anything for him. Whatever would fit a sixty year old woman's birthday. He'll argue but don't listen. Thanks!"

I had no time to hear Andrews's response as I zoomed to the florists.

The shop was dated and the uneven gravel served as customer parking. The lime colored wood siding demanded you take notice in all the wrong places, and for a moment I thought about quietly driving away and finding another florist.

"I'm here to meet with Mrs. Frank?"

The young woman barely let me finish before she screamed for her mother so loud I thought my eardrums would pop.

"Ms. Red, I'm glad you could make it. Let's walk the shop so I can show you around."

The silver curly haired woman held youthfulness not suited for her mature years, though, she was lovely; even when hidden beneath a heavy vinyl apron and galoshes big enough to fit an ogre. Mrs. Frank spared little time before pointing out what they had to offer; each bouquet more beautiful than the one before it.

"So the date is a solid December eighth. Is that correct?"

"Yes."

"We have a booking that day but I'm sure we can work it in. What do you like?"

"As I'd said, the wedding is for my good friends Marina and Seth. We're open to your expertise, though, we'd like to keep white prominent in all the arrangements. Perhaps a hint of pale pink for the floor displays but otherwise white."

"Any specific flowers you're drawn towards. If they happen to be out of season I'll advise against it but that doesn't mean it's impossible, simply more risky and expensive."

"She likes tulips; they're her favorite. She also likes peonies and poppies. Truthfully she'll be happy with whatever you create but if you could incorporate tulips that would be wonderful."

Mrs. Frank smiled and I felt calm that the job would surpass all expectation. She held a confidence about her, a whispering certainty that assured you talent wasn't dependent on shiny equipment or pavement, and I believed her.

"All right then, Anna will have you fill out some forms at the counter and I'll be sending you the finalizations within a few days."

"Thank you."

Mrs. Frank smiled again and disappeared to tasks beyond the peeling paint wall.

Anna did as instructed and prepared my order. On my way out the crooked front door Anna handed me a beautiful bouquet of tulips.

"What's this?"

"A thank you for your business. We'll see you on the eighth."

With that, I was certain I'd chosen the right place.

*

Once the last item on my wedding to-do list was completed the reprieve dissipated; thus forcing me to drown in work or drown in despair.

I chose work.

I was certain a visit from Sunshine would fix me right up, rub off some happiness on my withering corps, but I refused to interrupt her day of wedding planning with Seth.

The sun departed hours ago giving darkness claim to the land for longer and longer with each passing day. Much like how I felt inside it seemed.

A light knock sounded, bringing me back to the dim present.

"Hey, what did the rock climber name his son?"

249

"Uh? Pebble?" I guessed, and Andrew scrunched up his face as he shook his head.

"Cliff."

"Ah, right. That makes sense."

Andrew sat down reclining his tall frame into the chair.

"I happen to know for a fact that you've no reason to be here any longer. I also happened to know that you've plans tonight."

I raised a brow.

"Is that so? Those plans would be?"

"I'm taking you out so you can at least pretend to be normal and healthy." Andrew raised a hand to stop my protest.

"We'll have a great time, I promise." He waited seconds before adding.

"At least do it for us."

Crafty. I laughed a bit at his well-played scene.

"Okay. What exactly did you have in mind?"

"We'll eat at P.F. Chang's then head to Lucky Strikes so I can beat you shamelessly."

Andrew knew me well enough to know I didn't do clubs, bars or anything of the sort. My life was as mundane and unexciting as possible. Just like I wanted. A simple and *safe* existence.

"All right, but you're paying." I shot back.

"Get moving we leave in ten minutes."

Eight minutes later I was pulled out the door so fast I only had half my coat on when already getting into his X5. My hand flew to the seat warmer in hopes that at least my butt could retain some feeling in the frigid November cold.

We picked a secluded booth towards the back and ordered our drinks. We laughed light-heartedly about nothing in particular, just simple and generic banter. But soon we settled in enough to allow the mood to deepen and the conversational topics followed.

"Alice, can I ask you something?"

"Sure."

"Where's your wedding ring?"

I never planned to share. It was my business. But with Andrew, I wanted to. If only a small part, for his drop in judgment of my character bothered me.

"If I share, you must understand it will only be a small piece. If that's not enough tell me now and we'll avoid the topic, but if I proceed you must promise to never follow up with more questions. Agreed?"

"Agreed."

Andrew's eyes were deep with interest. I just hoped this would offer him enough to see me as he did before the divorce.

"Seth and I were never really married. Aside from the state issued certificate nothing between us had ever been romantic. Truthfully, Seth is like a brother to me."

"Wait, what?"

Well you see, Andrew, the real Allison and Seth Red died and we took over their identities and the best way to make it work was to keep it as Mr. and Mrs. And—no.

"The arrangement offered us both the circumstances we needed. Since then things have changed. Seth has moved on with his life and I couldn't be happier for him. You can't share any of this with anyone, you understand, right?"

Andrew's curiosity was only superseded by—regret?

"Whatever it was, are you all right now? Are you safe?"

His intuition was better than I gave him credit for.

"Yeah. We're good."

Andrew nodded robotically, his thoughts unreadable.

"What could be so bad that you'd need a fake marriage?"

I should have kept my mouth shut and let him think less of me. This was a bad idea.

"Andrew, you agreed. No follow up questions. Look, thank you for dragging me out but perhaps it's late and—"

"No, don't. You're right. It's just not what I expected. I'm sorry. But just be honest with me, are you safe now?"

How could I lie when he was so sincere? Simple, it wasn't a choice.

"Yes."

The server set down our drinks, giving us a few more minutes to examine our menus thus providing the provisions for a topic change.

"You all set for Maddie's wedding?" I asked.

"Do I have a choice?"

Andrew shrugged a shoulder fingering the glass of his coke.

"Hey, it'll be great. Sure you'll have to put on your game face for a bit but the reception should be fun, right?"

I didn't really know actually but tried to make light of the topic I'd chosen.

"It would be fun if you went with me." Andrew wriggled his eyebrows as he said it.

"Touché."

Andrew grinned and I dropped my attempt at making his sister's wedding a happy event. Andrew furrowed his brow as he stared, seemingly mesmerized by his beverage.

"Maddie's worse than before, trying to outdo everyone else because heaven forbid she has the same flower arrangement that some random heiress used or didn't use last winter. Who keeps track of all that?"

Andrew ran a hand through his wavy hair as he sighed.

"I love my sister, I do. I love my parents but respect is something else entirely. We're so far apart I wonder if we'll ever find common ground or if I'll always be the odd man out? It'll be the usual variety of investment bankers, CEO's, politicians, and family money. The girls are all the same and finding someone to have a normal conversation with is as likely as Jenna being an undercover Mother Teresa."

"You never know when your luck's about to change. The right girl might just appear out of nowhere and you'll be a gonner."

Andrew looked at me with unconcealed intent.

"She already has. Only I wasn't who she wanted."

"Andrew—"

"Wait, that wasn't fair. I'm sorry. I never meant to tell you. But that was when I thought you were a married woman and suddenly I find out you never were and I, I just—"

"Andrew—I—I don't know what to say. I'm sorry— I love our friendship and respect you but I—" Andrew cut me off before I could finish my poor excuse for an effort for—whatever this was.

"You don't have to explain it. I know. I've always known. A part of me held on to some hope because though I didn't know the circumstances of your marriage, you and Seth just never came across as two people in love. More like roommates I suppose and so I thought eventually you two would see you didn't fit together, you'd move on—and I would have my chance."

I was about to say I was sorry again—

"The day when Snow came into the café every bit of hope I'd held on to was swallowed up by what I saw between you two. I knew you'd never look at me like that."

Andrew's green eyes pleaded with such sadness and defeat it broke my heart. I searched for soothing words but no such words existed.

"I'm sorry; please know how sorry I am for hurting you, Andrew."

I'd been blinking back tears for five minutes before admitting defeat.

"Hey, no tears tonight, remember. Tonight was supposed to be healing."

Andrew reached out to wipe away the drops. His thumb lingering just a bit longer than necessary, though, I didn't move away.

"Alice, you don't see yourself like I do. You're humble and kind despite whatever skeletons you harbor. You think you're ordinary, but ordinary people don't send boxes of treats to unsuspecting families or are to blame for the 'Mystery Donation' Stacy received when her scholarship faltered. There's a glow about you. You're rare—so rare."

Nobody was supposed to know. I should've denied his observations but it was a time of truth under no pretenses, so I didn't. We sat for a while. Andrew looked sad but resolved, as if letting the truth out, gave him a sort of closure. I hoped it did.

"Okay, enough of this silence. Back to business, I took you out to have fun and fun we shall have."

Andrew smiled, silently requesting I follow suit and not allow his admission to alter the evening. I wanted to believe it was possible to go back to being friends. I wanted nothing else. But I couldn't be sure we'd pull it off, and Andrew's stolen glances said he feared the same.

The food arrived and we even decided to get the Banana Spring Rolls dessert to share. We walked to the Lucky Strikes Bowling Alley a few blocks south and secured ourselves a lane at the far end. True to his word Andrew beat me both games. And though I didn't fall flat on my butt, my 190 was no match for his 260 in round two.

Our talk was easy and full of humor. I was surprised and abundantly grateful for that. It made room for hope that we could save our friendship.

We were about to start our third game when I felt the air around us electrify. The unfamiliar public venue had my instincts on instant alert.

I scanned the exits and assessed all bodies within sight. There was a wall to the east end of the alley which blocked off the pool tables, restrooms, and some various doorways. I couldn't see behind it and I knew I needed to; quickly.

"Hey I'm going to run to the girl's room real quick. No cheating now. I have a feeling I'll be winning this round."

I pointed my index finger at Andrew with a playful scowl. He looked back in mock horror at the insinuation that he'd cheat.

"Aww, Alice I'll take pity on you. All you had to do was ask!" Andrew half yelled to my retreating back.

I responded with "Never!" and rounded the wall.

Nothing seemed out of order as I made my way to the ladies room. I made a bee line for the handicapped stall, shut the door, and paced; repeating "I'm overreacting" over and over like a mantra. No matter the years or progress I'd made, it still only took milliseconds to hijack my senses.

My hands were clenched into fists and I all but stamped my feet about the large stall. *It would never be public* I told myself and it was this little crumb of truth which facilitated the courage to exit the lavatory.

Passing the pool tables I caught sight of a crisp business card propped up in the middle of the second table. Knowing that upon entering the lavatory the table was void of any objects was only partly why it wound up in my trembling fingers. The logo on the front was what drew me in like a moth to its demise. I stared at it as though unsure if I was suddenly dreaming before finally flipping it over to reveal the hand written words.

I never meant to hurt you. Enjoy your evening.

The note wasn't addressed to anyone, but I knew the intended recipient all the same. Knowing Logan was responsible for my fit of panic did little to ease my nerves. It simply added heartache to the toxic cocktail.

I should've ripped the small cardstock paper to shreds and tossed it in with all the other discarded trash, but I'd come to terms with the knowledge of my dismal weakness and slipped the stationary inside my back pocket.

I returned to find Andrew wearing an awkward half smile as two pretty girls sat opposite him, chatting, and advertising their physical assets. I smiled at his expression when he spotted me; both women following his line of sight, a look of displeasure quickly taking hold of their features.

"Alice, this is April and Christy. Ladies, this is Alice."

"Nice to meet you." I offered, extending my hand towards April then Christy. Both reciprocated while sizing me up.

This ought to be fun, I thought; but lacked the necessary enthusiasm. Within minutes of their company it became evident as to why Andrew showed no interest in carrying a conversation with either blue-eyed beauty.

"So you girls mentioned you go to school. Is it local?"

Christy and April exchanged a snide glance.

"We attend Stanford. You know, in California."

Christy looked pointedly at me as though there was a high chance I wouldn't know what or where California was. Perhaps it was a type of cheese? I was tempted to play along.

"That's interesting, what are you studying?" I asked.

Andrew stood to play his turn and the moment he vacated his spot Christy no longer spoke; merely glaring instead. Once Andrew resumed his post Christy magically carried on as though the last two minutes of awkward silence were but a figment of my imagination.

"I study Political Science and already have several offers for positions on both sides."

"I'm studying International Relations. I want to help those less fortunate than we."

April looked as though she expected us to nominate her for the Nobel Prize. Sadly it was all show. Not an ounce of sincerity in either of them. There was no place for it when their egos were so big it hardly left room for the designer clothing hugging their curves.

I returned after knocking down but four of the pins to find that my seat now belonged to Christy and her very long pair of legs.

Each lane housed a couch for seating with each set of two lanes sharing a small table and both couches facing each other for conversation. A great set up if in a large friendly group split between two lanes; not so great when paired with strangers you wished would just smile politely, but otherwise mind their own game. Naturally I occupied Christy's recently discarded place and witnessed just how far her flirting would travel.

"So, Andrew, is this how you prefer to spend your free time? Bowling with a—friend?"

It wasn't difficult to decode her hidden message when her hand shamelessly found its way to Andrew's jean-clad leg, too high above the knee.

"Sure is. When you've got Alice the venue doesn't matter."

"Perhaps you simply need to broaden your horizons to recognize how much you're missing out."

Andrew politely removed the unwelcome palm atop his leg before heading to take his turn. He was visibly irritated, though, he wouldn't act on it. He'd play the gentlemen to the very end because that's simply who he was.

April took the opportunity and rose to play her turn in the lane next to him. April was undoubtedly the runner up in their entourage. I may've been out of ear shot but my eyes saw perfectly fine as April caressed Andrews arm, probably complimenting him on how strong he was for lifting the twenty pound ball as though it weighed nothing.

My eyes returned to Christy to find her lips twisted, as though disgusted at the mere sight of me. It was too absurd to be real I told myself, we'd just met these people less than an hour ago.

"If you care for Andrew at all you'll leave him alone. Do you even know who his parents are?"

Clearly Christy did. I only knew they were wealthy and well known—obviously.

Obtaining Andrew's personal information wouldn't be difficult; it was out of respect I never ran his profile. He'd share what he wanted when he wanted and as a friend, I owed him that.

"No. Does that matter?"

"You're something. You're definitely something."

"So I've been told."

Andrew returned, coming to stand beside me. Leaning down he whispered low in my ear. "Are you all right?" I smiled my response before he took a seat beside me on the arm rest of the couch.

Reluctantly Christy stood to take her shot and I watched the alluring sway of her hips as she made something as unattractive as bowling shoes somehow appear fashionable. By all accounts Christy was pretty, and going to Stanford—which had to elicit at least some level of intelligence. All this brought me to the puzzling question of why such beautiful and intelligent women would ultimately have so little substance?

"I thought you said you would be winning this one?"

Andrew's smile was wide and full of humor as he asked a pointless question. I laughed in response, because winning at this point with one turn left was about as probable as uncovering the secret to world peace.

"I might be a loser but I'm a loser with dignity."

I approached the machine which dutifully spit back all the bowling balls and found my hefty sized seven pound sphere in the lovely weathered peach tone. I raised the humble sized weapon and began my approach before releasing it into the opposition of pins. I could hear Andrew laughing because even a half blind bat could see I was barely clipping the corner pin before the ball ultimately hit the gutter. I turned and smiled confidently as though I had some trick up my sleeve, when I had nothing of the sort.

I could've shouted something stupid for the benefit of Christy and April who'd made their way closer to Andrew. However, the alley was so noisy my shout would never have reached them clearly, so I simply appeared as confident as an Olympian.

The diligent machine returned my ball and I once again took the pose of a less than seasoned player. The ball was released with plenty of force and to my surprise it claimed three more pins and one more on my third and very last shot. I reclaimed my original seat now that Christy was back on her side, and watched as Andrew effortlessly hit yet another strike and nine more pins for his final shot.

I jumped up and down yelling "Yes! I win!" as loud as I could.

Andrew stared in anticipation, waiting to hear what possible transformation could've taken place to announce me as the winner.

"Oh, didn't you know. Today is opposite day."

We both laughed heartedly as Christy and April looked less than impressed.

"What? Are you like in third grade?"

I looked at Christy point blank.

"Wouldn't know, I'd never been."

We made quick movement in replacing the borrowed bowling shoes with foot-ware of our own, then grabbed our things as we headed to the counter to check out.

"Andrew." Christy cooed.

"Good night, ladies."

"Give it some thought."

Christy slipped something into his front pocket with the look of promise in her eyes. Andrew pushed away before grabbing my hand and nearly sprinting up the stairs where freedom awaited.

We continued our speedy approach towards Andrews SUV which unfortunately for us, was blocks away.

"Sorry about dumb-and-dumber tonight. I tried to switch lanes but the only four lanes left were reserved for a party."

"Seriously—I'm at a loss. It was actually painful to watch." I managed to say in-between my chattering teeth.

Andrew snickered as he shook his head.

"I wish I could say the same. Honestly though, most of the girls that attend my families functions are not far from what you just witnessed. I suppose I've grown immune; and you wonder why I hate those damn things."

"Well I can now say with certainty *and* sincerity, that I'm sorry for you." I frowned before we both broke into a short laugh as we continued the short drive back to the café.

"Here's what I don't get though. They clearly hated the venue and highly over dressed for anything so casual, so why show up at all? What would've brought them there only to be bitter the entire time?" I had my suspicions, though, I wouldn't let it show.

"My father most likely hired them to—woo me into their circle." I looked at him in disbelief. Pretending that his admission was beyond my own imagination. Christy's comments now made complete sense.

"Would he really?" I asked, continuing to play clueless.

"He has in the past. There's no telling what he'd do to get me back into their world."

My mind was turning.

"So you working at the café must be pouring salt into his wounds."

Andrew looked distant.

"Even in this day in age, a male heir is more valued than most would like to admit. My sister doesn't stand a chance as long as I'm alive. My father will do whatever it takes to have me groomed for secession as though we're living in the sixteenth century. Commissioning young women to seduce me is truly mild in comparison to the lengths he'd go to. And if I was still the same person I was two years ago, it would've worked." Andrew paused, collecting himself.

"It's all out of love. He's not an evil man, Alice, just very misguided. He believes he's saving me from throwing my life away when I have the pathways open for so much more. His heart is in the right place even if his methods and ethics aren't."

"Andrew, I hadn't known it was that bad. Are you sure you want to stay at the café? Perhaps some negotiations with your father would provide a better outcome."

Andrew sighed heavily.

"It's easy to get caught up in the world of my father. The opulence and power, the fear and respect your pedigree elicits from those who both envy and despise you. I wasn't always so different from them. Perhaps at some point I surpassed their lack of empathy for all others outside the world of the elite."

Andrew's eyes met mine.

"Several years back I lost someone."

I found his hand in the darkness of the SUV, placing my palm on top of his in reassurance.

"You want to talk about it?"

Andrew shook his head.

We'd been idly parked beside my Pilot for some time, silently working through our separate thoughts before Andrew turned in his seat to face me.

"I would rather be surrounded by people like you in such a humble setting as the café, wearing an apron and serving up beverages than facilitating deals that more often than not are driven by money rather than ethics—and I would rather have you in my life as a friend—than not at all."

Andrew reached out to touch my cheek, the back of his fingers caressing my skin.

"You deserve fireworks, Alice. Snow's an idiot."

I smiled, though, it was weak and filled with too much regret.

"One day, Andrew, you'll make a special girl very happy and she'll fulfill you beyond your expectations, for your heart warrants nothing less. Your family will come around. They must or they'll never experience true goodness in this world."

Andrew's palm twisted to cup my face before he leaned in to touch his lips with mine. I wanted to feel something—

anything, but all I felt was sadness, for I couldn't return his affections.

Andrew's lips pulled back as his thumb caressed my jaw. He looked at me, his heart open, pure and loving. Andrew smiled sadly.

"Happy Thanksgiving, Alice."

"Yeah. Happy Thanksgiving."

I swung open the door.

"Hey, Alice?"

I turned to see a noble man; a man worth loving.

"Thank you."

Without pause I reached over the center console for a hug. Andrew's arms were quick to respond, closing in around me. Before pulling back I turned to place a gentle kiss on Andrew's cheek and for a moment wondered how lovely it would've been if I was but a normal girl who fell in love with a sweet boy. How simple our lives could've been together. Why not Andrew, I asked myself almost bitterly, why? The answer was there, I simply couldn't face it.

Andrew understood that my gentle kiss was a silent goodbye, for I would never reciprocate his feelings. I left the confines of his X5 knowing full well I'd let Andrew go forever—a freedom he deserved.

Chapter Twenty One

Allison Red

Upon arriving at the ever empty house I headed for the office to send Seth a fax. It contained information I wouldn't risk sending by email or text. I hit send and grabbed my phone to text confirmation.

Alice: Fax

Seth: Received

Finding Jenna's employer was taking too damn long and I feared the possible outcome of adding Andrew's parents to the Raven file. If Andrew's father commissioned young women to lure his son back into his circles, well, what would keep him from hiring Jenna to spy on him at the café?

After changing my clothes I donned my apron, turned up the volume on my phone and lost myself in music as I pulled the necessary ingredients to make that which I knew the guys would no doubt expect upon my arrival tomorrow.

My hands worked the dough and filling like a well-oiled machine, which evidently was a good thing since my mind was far from the kitchen.

I glared at Logan's business card from tonight and willed myself to discard the pain-inducing note. But I failed, and with every glance my failure grew more pronounced as if to taunt me in my weakness.

My anger rose and all I could do was scream into the stillness of an empty dwelling. Damn him! Damn him for tonight, for that first day in the café! Damn his eloquently spun web of deceit that I couldn't help but want to fall victim to, but most of all damn *me* for being such a fool! For becoming no better than any other misguided woman, for I couldn't bring myself to stop fantasizing about a monster.

The squishy mess of dough and rice had seeped between my fingers; a casualty to my fit of hopelessness. For a few seconds I just stared at the mess in my hands, attempting to calm the urge to shatter and destroy all that was within my reach.

What happened to me? To the confident and independent being who'd lived through Hell and still walked the streets with a smile on her face? At what point did I become incapable of controlling my own thoughts and the reactions of my body. How did I become—*this*?

I'd lost all sensibility. If there was ever a time I flirted with meeting my end it was now; for I'd lost all self-respect. A lifetime of survival and skill, all for the sake of taking that next breath had effectively become obsolete at the hands of one man.

I'd survived more than most could fathom all to be left pondering if I would ever overcome Logan Snow, just a man, and yet he wasn't simply that.

Conjure One was playing *The Center of the Sun* in deafening volume. I found a dark poetic reminder in the lyrics of a place familiar; a place I feared. The music stilled with a ding of a text, bringing me from my trance and slamming me into another as the screen lit up to display the five word message.

Anonymous: Pick up the incoming call.

The lull of Conjure One singing of violins fell away to an empty echo in my head as I awaited the next call like a prisoner on death row.

I picked up on the first ring in show of mock bravado while my heart raced the hundred meter dash in one second's time.

"Will you see me?" *That* voice, the voice I'd dreamt about too many times to count erased all traces of fear, in its place—emotions threatening to destroy me all together.

"No—." The call cut off.

I wasn't naïve enough to believe he wouldn't be at my door within minutes and all I could do was throw my phone at the wall in response. Damn him and his ability to bend me to his will!

I turned off the stove, washed my hands, removed my apron and debated calling Seth, only to quickly abandon the thought. Instead I channeled my anger and frustration to the surface in hopes that it would aid my faltering reason when in his presence.

Logan bore the ability to consume me, take over all thoughts, desires, demands—*me* as a whole. Logan sucked me into his aura; his empire and I both loathed and yearned to be ruled by him. Even now as I awaited his impending arrival I felt my body electrify at the thoughts of his nearness. I felt my soul call out to him from deep within, an ache I couldn't pinpoint in order to remove; it was here and there and all-consuming at the slightest thought of him. Some invisible entity severed and longing to be whole again; within his arms.

I'd felt his presence long before swinging the door back to find him touching the first porch step. Logan's eyes shot to mine and I burned before him.

Stepping aside I watched hungrily as he dominated the door frame both physically and figuratively. He moved confidently—calculated, overpowering; and he knew it.

Logan stepped closer, close enough that I could feel his breath against my skin. His palm cupped my face and I hated myself for not stepping away.

"You must go." My voice was diminutive. Pathetic.

Without a word Logan removed his shoes and coat and moved into the kitchen as though I'd said nothing.

I stood motionless, faced with a choice or the illusion of one.

Logan grabbed the bowl of apples before moving to the sink for washing. This was ludicrous. Was I to play house with him while his wife plotted against me in return? The mere idea reeked of nothing but insanity; a catastrophe beyond measure.

I remained rooted to my spot beneath the archway as Logan dried each apple and inspected for stickers before placing them back into the bowl. Logan proceeded to grab an apron off the hook before threading it over his head as though it was the most normal thing. The small piece of fabric with a damask pattern and lace trim laid ridiculously small upon his large frame nearly rendering the thing useless, though Logan said nothing, and neither did I.

If I thought his presence would affect me, I was wrong; for his presence consumed me. Choice was an illusion I concluded.

I set a large empty bowl holding a mandolin with the small blade setting in place next to his bowl of washed apples.

"Cup the apple in your palm and with the paring knife cut slits from the stem to the bottom all the way around about a half inch apart. Cut close to the core but not all the way through, so the apple center remains intact. Then dice it on the mandolin in various directions so that the slices come out short in length."

I was filled with rage and my voice reflected as much.

I set the oil, then arranged the red trays lined with paper towels next to the cooktop. Placing the utensils and sugar bowl on the other side I rolled out the balls of dough into flat pancake-like discs. Every insignificant task took deep concentration while in his presence—a force-field set on sucking me in. He was playing and I was none the wiser for I'd joined him in the charade.

Logan moved to my station with his completed task in hand. I didn't bother glancing at it before moving on to prep work.

I assembled the pierogis and began to deep-fry them after a batch of fifteen. Logan mostly watched, his eyes burrowing deep.

I noted he'd not once asked me what the food was called. A small detail perhaps, though, my gut said there was more.

It wasn't long before the last four pierogis were plucked from the hot oil and tossed to the tray with more force than the pastry deserved.

The luminescent hour of make-believe had passed and the weight of reality loomed over us. Tension filled the room, my head—my bones. It was suffocating and yet I was willing to hold out just a bit longer, where I could pretend I didn't have a Red Brotherhood issued death warrant and Logan didn't have a beautiful wife waiting at home. But as with everything, there was always an end.

"Get out."

"Alice—"

"Don't you dare touch me, you selfish bastard. If you have an ounce of decency you'll leave and never come back."

Logan's hand fell away as I retreated to the opposite end of the kitchen.

"I'm not married."

My head spun. This was a trick, another eloquent lie. It had to be for I might lose my mind!

"Liar! Get OUT!"

Logan straightened, tall and confident as if preparing to face-off in battle. Despite myself my breath hitched as he advanced on me, closing in the space around us.

"Lily and I share the Snow name, though, we're not related by blood nor are we bound by any other contract."

I felt—sick. Actually physically sick and I couldn't form thoughts, for all I saw was darkness.

"Why?" The tremble of my voice only illuminated my pain.

"Because—I'm in love with you."

I stumbled back as if he'd struck me.

"Screw you! Love? You're crazier than me! You don't know the first thing about love because if you did you'd never have done what you did to me!" My voice was hoarse as I screamed each venomous word from depth beyond reason.

My head was shaking of its own accord as my feet continued to back step for every forward step he made.

"Did you ever even stop to consider me? Consider the risks I took—you bastard!" I stopped myself, before revealing things better left hidden.

"You're a monster, a heartless beast. How could you do this to me? Huh? Answer me!"

"I was punishing you!" Logan's tone was edged sharp and raw. My back hit a wall as Logan glared, daring me to retreat.

His touch was rough as he thrust his hands into my hair, gripping me at the nape to hold his stare. His mouth ghosted across my needy flesh, teasing, taunting, and angry.

"You revived the person I buried years ago. A person— not meant to come back." Logan's teeth sunk into the tender flesh below my ear and I whimpered against my will.

"I fought against you, your pull, and your purity. The moment I saw the agony in your eyes as you looked from Lily to me, I knew you'd won. You took it all and left me *nothing*. I realized then I wanted nothing more than to fall at your feet and plead for you not to walk away before casting Lily to the streets for manipulating you in her childish games. You made me *weak* and for that, I. Hated. You."

His grip tightened deliciously, pushing my head further back as his mouth trailed on.

"I hated your ability to see past my armor, I hated how your skin could sooth away my desperation or the way the mere sight of you would light the darkest corner of my soul."

Each word scraped his throat, raw and un-apologetic. It seeped inside my body, my bones, mixing his flesh with mine, and I felt every emotion as though it were my own.

"You betrayed me without knowing—stripped me raw. I wanted to punish you. Hurt you in an attempt to prove you hadn't made me weak and pathetic. But God help me—I loved you more."

I was trembling, or perhaps we both were. My eyes were shut tight, unsure if my fists were pushing Logan away or pulling him impossibly closer. I was swallowed by agony, the misery of knowing what I would never have. The worst fate was to know happiness was within reach, to have a taste, to know its touch, and live the rest of your days haunted by the memories.

"—your resilience, bravado—delicious smart mouth. Your kindness, especially when you think nobody's looking. Your simplicity; more beautiful than any shade of makeup. There's no escaping this, Alice."

The pain was every bit physical as it was emotional. I was broken, the remnants of me scattered across the pale wood floor; a puzzle too complicated to ever be made whole again.

Not since the murder of my mama had I felt such utter abhorrence for my blood family. Miles, oceans—continents separated us, yet they still *owned* me, possessed the power to sabotage my deepest desires and needs.

Defeat was bitter and bitterness was abundant.

Logan may've claimed love now—but once he found out the truth? He'd run—and who could blame him. I would be a permanent target on his back.

"You don't know what you're saying. You don't know me!"

"Don't I?"

He was challenging me again; egging me on. Perhaps adrenaline aided me with the will to push back rather than give into our fable. Maybe even some revenge for his punishment, but mostly it was fear. Fear of the horror that lurked in the shadows, bidding it's time to devour me and everything I loved. I shoved at Logan and he moved.

"I'm not pure, far from it actually. Tainted, infected, damaged, plagued, tampered—you name it and I would be listed as its perfect definition. You think you know me? You don't even know my real name! I've lied to you since day one; everything is an illusion. Don't you see? You can't love what isn't real!" My voice wasn't my own, broken and vacant.

"You deserve better. You have promise of a future and no shortage of prospects to share it with. Look at you, you have women falling over themselves for you. Why pick me? I'm nothing, a fraud—I'm not even in the same rank as you!" My words dripped with bitterness.

It was fitting.

I deserved this.

Logan's face hardened with each acid-soaked syllable I spit out. He made no effort to reach out to me as we now stood feet apart. His jaw working hard, his veins bulging at his neck; straining to contain the fire warning to blaze dangerously.

I was intent on his every move, every breath; had a hair fallen from his head I would've noticed, for every second was burned into memory.

"Are you that petty? What is it exactly, Alice, be specific. Is it the money? The body? Is it the handsome face and piercing blue eyes that women can't seem to see past in order to find a human being behind the well sculpted piece of flesh? Say the word and I'll mutilate this curse everyone can't seem to get enough of. I'll carve it up nice and pretty for you so that you're sure to never have doubts as to our *ranks*. Say it, Alice. SAY IT!"

Logan stared me down, his eyes no longer bright with beauty, now dark with rage. My secrets no longer mattered for we long passed that threshold, and I no longer feared his rejection. Some puzzles weren't meant to be put back together.

"Enough! I'm wanted dead, understand? Dead!"

I ripped at my clothing, thrusting the shirt off before shoving my pajama bottoms to the bamboo floor. Panting and growling like that of something other than human. My striptease lacked any sexual appeal as my hands jerked violently to reveal what hid beneath.

"I have enough scars! It's only a matter of time, Logan They'll find me and when they do, no one I love is safe. They'll kill you while I watch, carve you up, burn you, rip you to pieces. All while laughing and enjoying your screams as they bleed you out. They'll save me for last knowing the pain of my own death is nothing compared to watching the one you love suffer!"

I turned in a full circle; ensuring Logan saw the mural of horror upon my skin that hid beneath the shield of fabrics.

"You have a future, Logan. With me, you never will. If you truly love me then *please...go*."

Unable to face off any longer I sank down against the wall, wrapping my arms around my knees as I hit the cool floor.

If there was ever a time I wept, truly wept, it was now; wearing my bra and panties, yet naked and bared to my soul.

*

My arms wound loosely around his neck as he lifted me effortlessly—delicately. Logan held me close as he made his way towards the sofa. The fireplace casting an orange glow across the room as Logan laid me down.

Kneeling, Logan's fingers traced the puckered flesh across my abdomen. I watched transfixed, as he lowered his lips to my past, my pain, and my fear. He caressed and kissed every scar; accepting it—accepting me. Once the last of the imperfections on my stomach were healed, Logan helped me to stand; proceeding to care for every wound which had mutilated my thighs and back from a lifetime of brutal beatings.

Tears fell hot and steady as I watched each piece of my shattered puzzle lifted delicately, lined with Logan's love—acceptance, and put back together; made whole again.

Most people would say sex was the most intimate exchange between two people. But I would bear witness that no sexual act could hold a candle to what we'd just experienced. The gift Logan gave me was a bond deeper than flesh and sensation, it was a covenant.

Logan sat, bringing me with him; securing my trembling body atop of his. My ear listened closely to the heart-beat I now knew as my home; that's what Logan had become—Home. A throw made its way over my scantily clad body before Logan's possessive arms secured me in.

I was ready, ready to tell him who I really was.

"Nadia Rumikova, that's me, or rather who I used to be. I was born a bastard child into Russia's most powerful mafia family. My mother's offence against the honor the family shackled her as a slave, I was one too. To my grandfather, I was nothing more than a reminder of my mother's treason; representing everything he despised and therefore my life as a slave was far different from the others."

I was opening up; releasing demons that stole a little more of me each day.

"It was the fifteenth of December. I can still remember the smell of snow mixed with mud so filthy that even in its frozen state it gave off a scent foul enough to make your stomach churn. It was the night my mama died; the night *I* was meant to die." *Breathe*.

"My grandfather accomplished most of his order that night. Boris brutally murdered his niece as though she was nothing and as he threaded his cold fingers around my neck, his icy eyes held no remorse, no regret—no soul. As I watched my mama's lifeless body on the hallway floor, I wondered how you could take a life and feel—*nothing*. Nadia did die that night I suppose; I'm no longer her. But my grandfather won't rest until Nadia is truly dead. Until my body, which pumps his blood with that of my father's is burned and buried ten feet below the earth's surface."

Logan lifted my chin towards him.

"The Rumikov's will *never* touch you. Do you hear me?"

An eerie certainty settled around him, an uninhibited fury in search of restitution.

"Don't promise such things. Life's nothing if not uncertain."

"Wealth brings power, Alice, and power brings—many things."

"No. You can't waste—"

"Stop!" Logan's fingers touched my lips.

"You'll never question the means by which I will ensure your safety. Make no mistake, my love, there's no going back. I will protect you, even by my dying breath; for there's no length I wouldn't go to and no law I wouldn't break."

There was a finality in his tone.

I nodded hesitantly—knowing a battle would offer me no victory. If my hesitation worried Logan, he said nothing of it. Instead his warmth enveloped me, offering comfort and protection of the highest form. To refuse it would be to turn your back to the sun while naked on the coldest winter day. To accept it was to hand over your right to protest whenever you disagreed. The choice was simple. I basked in the sun.

I laid peacefully for an unknown amount of time. It was late, I knew that, but the details ceased to matter. Logan's fingers danced in delicate patterns I would dream about in his absence, and his breathing lulled me as his heart beat beneath my ear.

"Alice?"

"Hmm."

"Who is Seth?"

My steady pulse was interrupted by Logan's unwelcome question.

"Konstantine—Boris's right-hand man the night—that night."

"Did he hurt you?"

Had I not been in a dark place myself, the ice in Logan's voice might've alarmed me; warned me. The way in which Logan acclimated to my past *and* my present—lacked—something—*everything*. It all spoke of familiarity and much more.

"No."

"I need more than that, Alice."

"I'd seen Konstantine at a few dinners from the corner I always coward in, trying to stay out of sight as much as possible. But mostly I saw him in surveillance footage from jobs. My grandfather was grooming him for a promotion and my mama's and my execution was his golden ticket into the circle."

We were silent a while, though, I felt Logan urging me to continue.

"I heard his voice—his footsteps, but I never saw his face that night. We heard them picking the lock, a split second and we knew death had found us. Mama shoved me in the closet where we slept and told me to be quiet, I tried to protest and she slapped me—there were tears in her eyes and love and gut wrenching fear. I heard them close the door swiftly, Mama tried to make it sound like I'd gone to the market, begged them to let me go, said she wouldn't fight if they would just let me go. Boris laughed—said he liked the fight, that perhaps he'd rape me in front of her just to get more fight—the way he liked." *I couldn't breathe.*

"The sounds of my mama's cries—they haunt me. It's the sound of agony singing its favorite tune. It seeps inside your bones and echoes in the silence. I—I didn't make a sound. I tell myself it was to grant Mama her last request but not really. Truthfully I was a coward and frozen in place. Exhausting every bit of energy into wishing I could shrink, shrink small enough to hide between the thin sheets or inside the crack of a wall and I would never complain being so small; if only it meant I wouldn't be touched by the fate which awaited me." *Breathe.*

"I was bleeding and immobile. Boris stripped me for rape and I vomited. He was strangling me when I passed out and when I awoke, Boris was on the floor with his throat slit. That was the first time I saw Konstantine that night. He saved me. He didn't have to, his decision was too late for my mama, but he saved *me*."

I tightened the throw around me, my legs and arms huddled in a ball.

"Do you trust him?"

I faced Logan's furious oceans without a moment's pause.

"With my life."

Logan crushed me to him, his arms everywhere, pushing and pulling as though he couldn't get me close enough. I'd never seen him so vulnerable and the sight grounded me.

"I'll never let you go, Alice. No one will hurt you. I swear it."

Logan pulled back slightly. His expression—regretful—determined.

"I believe you." I whispered.

Logan kissed me, really kissed me for the first time since his arrival. There was no urgency as his tongue danced with mine, hard then soft, his teeth nipping at my lip. The kiss was gentle, almost reverent, as though being savored.

This evening wasn't about sex or our physical attraction, which was just as powerful if not more so than before. Tonight was about facing what really connected us, drove us—made us. We broke down barriers, lies and fears to build a foundation, and Logan's kiss was evidence that we both understood.

I felt his phone vibrate but Logan made no move to look at it.

"What're your plans tomorrow?"

"I'm having dinner at Marina's with the family."

"I'll be joining you. What time?"

There it was—the control, the commanding ruler bidding his will—and I found a deep forbidden pleasure in it.

"Five o'clock. I'll text you the address."

Logan touched his lips to mine before bidding some more.

"I'll pick you up at four." His eyes were gentle, urging me to understand, accept.

"I'll be ready."

He peppered each eyelid with a chaste kiss before grabbing his coat.

"Sleep well, my love."

Chapter Twenty Two

Logan Snow

"You could've called and made an appointment." Seth's irritation was blatant.

"I find Gabe's more persuasive, don't you think?"

Seth's smirk said it all; and now I had to say mine.

"It's a rather special day. After all these years, I finally get to me the notorious Konstantine Poplov."

Seth pulled out his piece, the barrel directed at my chest. I raised a hand, telling Gabe to stand down. I was gambling, Seth could shoot me any second. It was a shit gamble but one I had to make. Besides, Seth knew if I didn't live, neither would he.

"Who are you?"

I didn't hesitate.

"Monarch."

"YOU!"

The bastard was swift. Landed two punches to my side before I retaliated. He ought to know that to put down a beast you always go for the heart. With a final blow to his side I stepped back, kicking his fallen .45 towards his feet.

He was bleeding from someplace on his face. It was hard to tell with the blood smeared everywhere. I was bleeding too. The taste of copper filling my mouth.

"Why am I still alive?" He was panting.

"Answer me!" Seth was clutching his side, his hand gripping the gun tighter than before.

"I'm proposing we join forces."

He looked at me skeptically.

"I don't trust you."

"Good. Now that we've discussed our feeling perhaps we can get to what's really at stake here."

"Monarch. Ha! I never thought the man actually existed. Tell me Monarch, what's your business with The Brotherhood exactly?"

"Ily's grade C bookie from over a decade ago, Vlady Grishkin got greedy. Vlady reached out to his estranged son Matthew who was then married and lived in the states with his wife. Lindsey had a heart too kind so she convinced Matthew to help. They traveled to Russia with one hundred fifty thousand cash; leaving me behind."

Seth's eyes widened. He knew what happened next.

"The money was paid, but we both know Ily Rumikov doesn't have a forgiving bone in his body."

"Matthew and Lindsey's only son died in a car accident." Seth stated.

"It'd be best if everyone continued to believe that."

Seth's eyes offered me condolences but his mouth refused to speak such weakness.

"How long have you known about Nadia being here?"

"I run files on every business and resident within a ten mile radius of my building. For security purposes, I'm sure you understand. There was a trail, I followed. It only took days to make the connection."

"You planned to use her."

I flinched.

"I did. I needed to validate the information first so I had to see her for myself. The months following, I continued to watch her, telling myself I was gathering Intel— I was a fool. Because the moment I saw her something inside me changed. Watching her these past months elicited a transformation I didn't want, but it happened anyway."

"And what of me."

Indeed.

"We're not friends. I tolerate you only because Alice trusts you and calls you family. I'll admit my gratitude for saving her. That's it."

"That's rich coming from you. Need I remind you what you arranged that fateful night?"

"How about I show you Igor's remains after you left him to hang because you were too much of a coward to stand up and take my deal. He had a kid. You ought to know what it's like growing up without a Father."

I handed Seth the folder, the contents—a plan that might save us, or perhaps only give us false hope. Seth reviewed each page vigilantly, his jaw working to contain his fear of what awaited ahead.

"Of all the people on this planet how is it that you and Alice managed to meet, and not only that, but be insane enough to fall for each other. The planet must have some sick sense of humor or you're just hell bent on getting Alice killed."

"Spare me your moral high ground. What do you think will happen to your fiancé and her family if you're found? You think I haven't thought of that you selfish piece of shit. I didn't choose this, but screw you and the rest because I have it and nothing will take Alice from me. We either join forces or we don't, but don't for one second think I'm seeking your approval. Your opinion means nothing to me so make your move."

We were seething and exhausted. Neither of us wanted to be in this cold cinderblock-walled room in an attempt to try and dig our way out of the graves we'd found ourselves being dragged into.

"Lily, who is she, other than Sal's granddaughter?"

"No one of consequence. As I—"

"Bullshit! No more, not with what's at stake. You're either straight with me on everything or I walk. How long since it ended?"

"Eleven months." I clipped.

Seth pressed his palms to his eyes and I knew he'd made the connection.

"Alice requested I run a file on Jenna, ring any bells?"

"Jenna from the café?"

"She's been having a steady influx of funds deposited bimonthly into a secondary account with a sum doubling the bimonthly amount the day she came to work at the café. We tracked the source of the funds belonging to Trinity Investment."

"Lily."

"She knows you've been infatuated with Alice and it's not difficult to make the timeline line up. How much does she know?"

"Not much. She knows my parents were killed but not of the circumstances. I have no connections to my life before my parents' death. Sal was the only person who knew everything. He adopted me, gave me his name and inheritance of the company with only one request; that I made sure Lily was taken care of."

"Fix it. If she break's it's on your head".

"Done".

Time passed but it didn't register. There were no sounds in the dim-lit room besides our breathing and desperation. With all our skill, determination, and even my wealth; nothing was certain. Only that death was near, and coming out unscathed was only for Disney.

"If Alice comes asking, I won't lie." Seth clipped.

I could live with that.

"Agreed."

"When will your contact give us what we need?"

"Hours, two days at most."

I could see the dread in his eyes and understood the feeling.

"If it's true, we're dead. I'm tired of running like a damn mouse." Seth's words came heavy with dread before he hung his head.

"I would've gone back. Alice was settled several years into our arrival and I would've gone; knowing I would die but take out as many of those blood-thirsty bastards as I could in the process. It was—it was Marina who gave me the will to keep going. They're on to us. I can feel it in my bones and for the first time in my life I'm—"

I could sense he had more to say but his conditioning took over.

"Money buys resources. I'll spend every last dime if that's what it takes."

"Then we have a deal. Should our suspicions materialize I'll make the sacrifice. I have a crescent shaped scar about one and a half inches in diameter on my inner left thigh. Alice will look for it; make sure it's visible."

This merger's significance was beyond my comprehension. And now that Seth had joined me I should've felt relieved.

I should've.

Only I didn't.

Chapter Twenty Three

Allison Red

The weather outside my window begged for me to reconsider and crawl back under the covers. It was foggy and grey and so dark you'd hardly know it was morning short of having a clock to confirm that fact.

The turn of events from hours ago unleashed chaos, a hurricane of change I anxiously awaited with trepidation; the irony was not lost.

As the reflection of my naked body in all its repulsiveness stared back; I no longer listened. The healing of Logan's acceptance spread over me like that of the most potent balm, where I remained cocooned within a love I could not deny myself.

Either Seth came home late and left before I awoke or he simply never showed. I was both upset and relieved because to inform my family of Logan and all that would follow was as easy as sailing the world without a compass.

I wracked my brain to uncover the ideal way to come clean, and after scrapping thousands of unviable options I decided ripping off the bandage was best. Sink or swim; fly or die trying.

The café awaited me with aroma and warmth. The place I never tired of, the space I always yearned to return, the place Mama always felt close in. Our space. We'd close at noon today; though this had little effect on volume. The roster listed eight separate orders for pick-up and with Marina out prepping for tonight's dinner I would have to complete all the orders myself. So I went to work, eager to hear the hum of Mama's voice as the scent of batter filled the space and my mind.

I was behind schedule and the last two orders had yet to bake while their scheduled pick up was up in twenty minutes. I ran from one end of the room to the other like someone who resembled a person on fire.

"It's burning."

Was I on fire?

"Alice, the oven."

"Damn it!"

I opened the oven to find a batch of Bear Paw destroyed and swatted at the smoke in the hopes that the fire alarm wouldn't activate; that would be just perfect right now.

"Sorry, Alice; I would help but we're slammed out front. I came back to tell you we're out of Red Elephant. Any back here?"

"The rack on the left there, top tray. There's only two dozen. Once they're gone you'll have to tell the folk we're out. After this screw up I don't have a single minute to spare."

"Got it." Steph reached for the tray without much effort. She was runway tall and curvy; with dark chocolate hair that hung to her waistline matching her complexion. She was naturally gorgeous; the kind of beauty Cover Girl advertised but couldn't deliver.

"When the eleven o'clock pick-up arrives, offer them a free beverage. They might have to wait a bit."

Steph offered me an apologetic smile before rushing out the stainless steel door.

By some random miracle, I'd collected myself enough to complete the remaining two orders only marginally late.

"Were they upset for having to wait?" I asked, once the last pick up walked out the door.

"Didn't appear to be."

"Good. How'd you girls hold up out here?"

Trish looked up with a grin.

"We're burned out."

I laughed at the reference to my mishap.

"Before you girls go, grab a box of whatever's left."

299

"Hell yeah! You don't have to tell me twice."

Trish jumped before running for the tray of boxes to fill. Steph came up and hugged me before doing the same.

By half past one my pilot was in route home, where I would shower and prep my end of the Thanksgiving bargain.

*

I was wearing a knee length charcoal dress; going as far as adding eye liner to my usual lip balm routine. I'd never be on the cover of Vogue but Logan's hungry eyes said I had no need to be, and that was enough.

He wore a grey pinstriped suit with a cobalt blue button-down shirt; the top two buttons undone. He was utterly delicious and I took great pleasure in the raw way he watched me as I backed up to allow his entry.

Logan's lips locked on mine and I savored every thrust of his wicked tongue in its lustful greeting. My response was equally urgent as I worked to get my fill, his taste far superior to chocolate, and a far more potent aphrodisiac.

"You're a sight to behold, my love".

"Then behold me."

We danced blindly until my back was pinned against the coolness of the wall while the heat of Logan's body pressed ever closer to my front. His hands roamed shamelessly—possessively across my body as his mouth savored mine. Not for the first time I wondered what price I'd have to pay for such happiness.

Logan pressed his lips to my forehead; a gesture I'd come to know as his way of stopping before we spiraled out of control. My hands remained wrapped around his neck, my fingers caressing his skin as I worked to calm myself in turn.

"Are you ready?" He asked.

I wasn't sure I'd ever be.

"Yes."

Logan helped me into my heels and wool coat before stepping outside to see Gabe holding the back door open. Perhaps it was the dim lighting of dusk, but I was almost certain I saw satisfaction as my eyes met those of Gabe.

"Happy Thanksgiving, Gabe."

"To you the same, Ms. Red."

One corner of Gabe's mouth turned up ever so slightly and I would've missed it if not for my scrutiny. I'd come to respect him and I was inclined to believe the feeling was mutual.

"Wait, I've got food on the counter."

"Gabe."

Logan continued to usher me into the car while his right-hand man took care of the rest.

"Does Gabe blindly do whatever you ask?"

"Gabe is many things, my love; blind will never be one of them."

I shivered; sensing utter darkness behind the truth of the statement.

Within minutes we veered onto Sixth Ave. West. Logan held me close; snug in a place made just for me, and in that moment I was nothing if not content.

Logan's hand stroked the length of my arm from shoulder to elbow and my skin thanked him for taking the initiative and removing my coat once I was seated beside him. His constant caresses lulled me, made me believe that I truly had a chance at a future; a future with him.

"Are you all right?"

I turned to face him.

"Tonight might not end well. Be prepared for it." My voice was quiet, almost hoping he wouldn't hear my warning.

Logan turned his torso to face me before grabbing my head in his hands.

"Nothing will stop me from having you, Alice; for even an army would fail against my will to claim you."

My eyelids fluttered close as Logan's lips descended on mine. I was his and my family would have to accept it, for they too no longer had a choice in the matter.

The distance between Marina's home and my own was relatively short so as Logan released me back into the nook of his arm we both remained silent. I spent that time lost in my own thoughts about the man who had captured me so completely, a man I knew little about yet felt like I knew all I needed to. I'd become someone else entirely; a woman who'd thrown logic and reason to the wind as she drove off into a mesmerizing sunset with him who consumed her.

Such knowledge held too many uncertainties so I let myself be cradled by Logan's masculine body and took pleasure in how perfectly we seemed to fit—him hard where I was soft, dominating where I was petite, tan where I was fair—together we had it all.

Pulling in to Marina's driveway I noticed Dad and Luke were already there, no doubt trying to sneak every bite they could while Marina wasn't looking.

I never rang the doorbell when entering Sunshine's home; it was as good as my own, as mine was hers. I led Logan inside were we made quick work of removing our shoes and coats, my pulse racing, for any moment many things could end up broken.

I felt heaviness in my footsteps accompanied by something I could only describe as giddiness. I was all over the place, with only Logan's firm grip on my hand to anchor me, or I'd surly float off to places other than here.

As we entered the kitchen where as I'd suspected everyone was gathered I glanced to Logan one last time before turning to face the shock.

"Alice?"

Marina appeared devastated; the pain so clear it almost spoke on its own behalf and my heart twisted. Seth was entirely unmoved, Dad scowled, though, it was nothing compared to Luke's open look of contempt.

"Logan Snow will be joining us tonight, as my date."

The men stood as though controlled by a single thread and retreated into the study. Logan moved to go with them before I stopped him, searching his eyes.

"I'm certain Marina would enjoy your company." He said.

"Maybe—"

"Shhh. I'll be fine."

Logan's confidence was iron. I half expected to see the cavalry marching behind him, though, as he strode towards the lion's den, no army followed.

I turned to find Marina busy with all things food and in no hurry to look my way.

"Sunshine?"

The angry sounds of chopped cucumbers stilled, though, Marina made no move to turn towards me.

"I'm sorry."

"When? Just tell me when, Alice. How long!"

Marina abandoned the knife, using both hands to grip the counter—her back still to me.

"Last night nearing midnight."

I patiently waited as she'd done for me countless times before. I waited for her to come around and be ready to hear what still remained unspoken. I would've waited tirelessly, in endless shifts if I'd had to.

With her eyes red and jaw firm she finally turned to look at me—I wasn't off the hook.

"What about the *wife?*"

"He's not married."

"Then who the hell is Lily Snow?" The words seeped from between her clenched teeth.

"A woman that's in love with him, and desperate. They share the name, that's it."

Marina's relief was palpable. I understood.

"I don't trust him."

"He *knows*, Sunshine. I told him everything."

Her eyes glossed over as she collided against me, her arms locked tight around my body as mine did hers. She cried and I joined her for no words were welcome in that moment. We stood locked in our embrace for time unaccounted. This wasn't what Marina had always envisioned for me. But she loved me anyway.

"I'm happy and so scared for you." Her voice was small as she wept into my hair.

"Me too."

We pulled back and simply looked at one another.

"I know I should've called; warned you. I was caught between two tides and thought the best option was to announce it to all of you, at once. Please try to understand."

Marina's smile was small.

"I'm sure I'll understand tomorrow, right now I feel hurt."

"I know."

"Then just tell me what happened."

"Well, an asteroid hit and my world is no longer recognizable, and now I think the foxes around my house are robots or hybrids at the very least.

"You're stupid you know that."

"Yeah, I've suspected for some time now."

This time it was Marina who threw the towel at me and we laughed a small but heartfelt laugh. We'd survive.

"I'm in love with him, Sunshine. It happened and I can't go back."

"I know, Sweets. I know."

"Do you think he's still alive in there?" I asked hesitantly.

"From what I saw, he's more than able of keeping his own. They'll surface when they're good 'n' ready so just get your lazy ass over here and help me set the table already."

"Oh crap! I forgot, I have the salads and potatoes in the car."

"Yeah, yeah, always some excuse."

I rolled my eyes as Marina waived her rooster-shaped oven mitt at my head and went to grab my coat.

I was more certain than ever that Gabe had superhuman abilities because I hadn't one foot out the door before he was mere feet from me.

"Ms. Red."

"I'd forgotten the food, Gabe."

"Of course, I'll get what you need. Please go back inside where it's warm."

And that must've been his human side.

"Thank you, Gabe."

He provided me with a curt nod before heading back out the front door.

"Wait! Join us."

"I must decline, Ms. Red."

I wasn't about to back down.

"I insist. You see, I have a feeling we'll be seeing a great deal of one another and I can be quite bratty if I don't get my way. If you decline I'm more than certain you'll be paying a hefty price for it later."

If I was trying to make him laugh, I'd failed. Still, something I'd said must've worked because he silently slipped out of his shoes and heavy coat.

"After you, Ms. Red."

"Oh, one last thing, please call me Alice."

Despite his effort, I saw the grin amidst the firm angles of his features.

"Marina, this is Gabe. Gabe, Marina."

"Ms. Meyer, it's a pleasure."

"Wow. You're one big dude. I guess I'll toss that second batch of dinner rolls into the oven; I was sort of on the fence about it but you just 'bout made the decision for me so thanks."

Marina was pointing her wooden spoon at Gabe as though they'd known each other for years, and I couldn't have been more grateful.

Gabe wandered the house as we began to set the table. The secret to my mashed potatoes was half and half with butter. The guys never got enough. I scooped it into the ceramic bowl and set it atop the blonde maple table adorned with a lavish feast. Perhaps they weren't your traditional Thanksgiving platters but as the years progressed so had our recipes. I'd influenced Marina's palette as she had mine, the result; nothing short of—unique.

"There's my sweet girl."

Dad approached, wrapping me in his warmth, an embrace I didn't believe I'd outgrow.

"Hey, Dad. Happy Thanksgiving."

Dad looked at me in a way he rarely did.

"Is this what you want? That's all I need, to know it's what you want." Concern painted his every word.

Dad held my shoulders steadily and I confessed.

"I'm so happy, Dad; so unreasonably filled up but at the same time I'm so scared. How can I anticipate the future and fear it all at once? I just don't know. Logan somehow became a part of me and it's not fair of me to spring this on you but—I can't go back."

Dad tucked me under his chin and for a while neither of us spoke.

"Fairytales are just that, my sweet girl—fairytales. We can't plan for everything in life, and sometimes, it's the surprises that bring us the most joy."

I pulled back to see Dad's eyes glistening.

"Be happy, Alice. Live—be filled up. Don't give the uncertainty of tomorrow rob you of the promise of today."

No further words were necessary. Dad's unconditional love had no bounds.

"Greg."

Logan stood in the archway appearing more powerful than I remembered. Dad nodded at Logan's one word request and released me.

"I'll gather the others, I'm starving."

Logan approached me as Dad disappeared, summoning them with shouts of "you all have thirty seconds to reach the table or risk going home with empty stomachs". I smiled at his hungry commands.

"How'd it go?" Logan's voice was low—concerned.

"We're good. You?"

Logan pulled me in, locking me flush with him as his lips caressed my ear.

"I have what I want." His words penetrated my skin, bringing with them desire and need; but more so it was the comfort they gave me that mattered most. His strength and love translated to peace; the one true desire I believed I'd never experience, yet here I stood engulfed by it.

"Good to see you, Sweets."

I pulled back from Logan's embrace only to be hugged by my brother.

"You sure know how to make an entrance, don't you?"

"Does this mean I'm forgiven then?"

"I could never be angry with you, Sweets; never you."

Luke's smile evaporated as he looked to Logan, and it wasn't difficult to deduce the sentiment wasn't extended to my date.

The daggers shooting from Luke's eyes were cut short as the remainder of my family infiltrated the dining room.

Chivalry was thick and well delivered as my chair slid out of its resting place without my touch, followed by the napkins delicate decent to my lap without a single touch from me. Logan was bringing out all the stops and I found myself unsure of how to feel.

Headed towards his rightful place at the head of the table Seth bent for a quick kiss to my cheek.

"Happy Thanksgiving, Seth."

"Yes it is, isn't it?"

A territorial palm closed in just above my knee, his fingers biting my skin so deliciously I nearly whimpered when he lightened his hold. Logan knew his rough touch awakened me in ways I wasn't ready to voice, but for now, he was willing to speak for us both.

Seth stood.

"Happy Thanksgiving everyone; I believe each of us has much we're thankful for this year, though, I'll be the first to boast that this year has been the highlight of my life. Let's give thanks—Heavenly Father I bow before you humble and open. In the uncertainty of this universe I ask you give us courage to face our fears and appreciate our times of happiness and peace. We thank you for this meal and for the hands which prepared it. Amen."

Everyone was silent.

To the common ear Seth's prayer might've sounded general or scripted; in truth it couldn't have been more genuine.

Each platter made its way around those seated, offering and tempting each set of hands to scoop up and taste its goodness. From the corn, to cucumber/tomato slaw, to the potatoes, and of course the symbolic golden bird; our plates were full and very busy. I watched Logan's skilled hands dip the turkey into gravy before bringing it to his lips, and wondered how he could make something like eating turkey look so sinfully erotic. I could feel his eyes on me as well from time to time and wondered if he dissected my movements as I did his.

"Marina, congratulations on the wedding. Have you set a date?"

"Thank you. We're mere weeks away actually. December eighth."

Seth's eyes shot to Logan's; a glance exchanged.

"So soon. I was under the impression you'd only been engaged a few weeks."

"Why wait. When you have what you want in front of you the details of shoes and silverware coordinating with plates no longer matters."

"When put like that, how could anyone argue?"

Marina smiled, though, not at Logan.

"Allow me to offer you my mountain retreat as your venue if you're still in need of one. You could tour it if you'd like."

The offer was generous but neither Seth nor Marina would accept.

"We'll tour it immediately then." Seth spoke up.

Wait, what? What was Seth doing?

Marina was clearly thinking the same thought as she looked at her fiancé.

"Done. Gabe will make the necessary arrangements and inform you of the date, Saturday at the latest. I'm certain you'll enjoy it."

Logan's exchange with Seth seemed to only give the illusion that Marina, or anyone else for that matter, was involved.

This unlikely situation spoke volumes, and for my own sake, I chose not to share its tales with anyone else.

As though it were prearranged, the cast in tonight's episode of *My Life* dutifully returned their sights back to food. Seth hardly looked my way while Luke all but stared in disbelief, keeping quiet only because of Dad's not-so-covert request. I stood, grabbing the empty bread roll basket.

Upon returning I stopped under the archway to witness what my momentary absence gave way to.

"Is it customary within your circles of the wealthy and corrupt to manipulate women?"

"Luke that's enough."

Dad's admonishment befell on deaf ears.

"Enough? Hardly. I'm only asking what everyone's thinking. You expect me to just sit across the dinner table from this asshole and discuss what? Salad?"

Logan motioned for Gabe to reclaim his seat and enjoy what was left of his meal.

"You care for her." Logan stated.

"An emotion you must not be familiar with."

Logan ignored Luke's remark.

"Good. Than allow me to say this: there is no length I wouldn't go to ensure Alice's safety. I have many regrets, too many to count, but I will no longer let anything keep Alice from me—including you. You may hate me; I accept that. However if it is Alice's happiness you seek than perhaps we save this conversation for a more private setting."

Logan spoke fluidly, full ownership and control. Luke's face reddened with fury.

I needed some air, some room to breathe and think and maybe even something to hit. I wasn't nearly close enough to the patio door before I heard footsteps closing in.

"Alice, wait up!"

I turned to face my surrogate brother.

"How much do you really know about him?"

"That's not really the question you want to ask. What your asking is do I know what he's hiding."

"Do you?"

"No."

"That's it? You're going to tell me the fact that you know next to nothing about the man who's proclaimed you as *his* is somehow okay?"

"What do you want me to say? I *am* his. I was and have been since our first encounter."

"My God, you've been reading too many damn romance novels."

The moment the words left his mouth I saw his regret, but that didn't ease their sting.

"That was low."

"Alice, look—"

"Stop! Just stop okay? I know you're concerned but let me make this clear. Logan's a part of me now, my lack of ability to explain our whirlwind relationship subtracts nothing from that. I know this is sudden and out of character for me, I get it—I do, but I've finally found a slice of happiness. He makes me happy, Luke and I need it—I'm dying without it." By the end I spoke in nearly a whisper.

Luke's inner struggle played across his features like a montage without humor. He was worried, as was I, but in the end; the decision was made.

"You're right, I don't understand. There's so many holes in this I can't begin to count them!" He stopped, running his hand through his short hair.

"Just so we're clear—I support *you* not him."

"I'll take that." It was small; but enough.

"I'll walk back with you."

"No. You go on, I need the washroom first."

With a sad smile Luke went forward as I headed right. Inside the small room I sunk down against the faux wood door without flipping the lights. I wasn't entirely blinded by the igniting masses of energy whenever Logan was near, I knew something was lurking. If being honest, I almost didn't want to find out.

Luke's concern was valid. Following my passion-fueled heart was new territory; a terrain unfamiliar, and in great need of a navigation system. But I'd learned that very little of my life fit the standards of society, and if moving forward with Logan, despite the looming grey matter of the unknown or untold was questionable…well, I'd never fit the mold anyway.

*

The remainder of dinner ran parallel to the first half; in an abundance of tension. Throughout the evening Logan's self-confidence, conviction, and tone never wavered. Many times I'd find my mind wondering how we got here; how statistically, our relationship would never work. Each time like magic Logan's gaze would find mine, and I'd remember that mathematics wouldn't dictate my future.

Luke's scowl eventually softened and he began to contribute to the conversation. I'd asked Dad about the difficult case a few times but got the feeling he was unwilling to share. I knew it'd been driving them up the wall, I didn't want to push so I moved on. Marina either couldn't or simply didn't care to filter her mouth. Several times asking questions better left to our private gossip than in the present audience. Gabe...I couldn't decipher the man.

Dad retired first, Luke followed mere minutes later; leaving the five of us to finish clean-up before calling it a night as well.

"It's been a long time since I'd experienced a warm and welcoming setting. Thank you for your hospitality."

"You're welcome, Logan Snow." Sunshine spoke curtly, more hostile than warm.

Logan nodded realizing that was all he'd get out of Marina on the first night.

"We'll see one another soon then. Good night." Logan finished before helping me into my heels.

"Soon." Seth confirmed.

He walked us out, where he hugged me with uncertainty. His heavy silence throughout the evening was more than he wanted it to look like. The trouble was, I didn't have enough to confirm my suspicions, and so I left it at that and departed.

Chapter Twenty Four

Allison Red

Fresh snow had covered the metro area while its citizens feasted, so at this late hour the crystal white canvas had hardly been disturbed, letting me admire its beauty as Gabe maneuvered the Porsche without the slightest glitch.

"What's going through that beautiful head of yours?"

"I'm—happy. You've given that to me. But I keep wondering if I'll just wake up one day and realize it was nothing more than a dream."

Logan's fingers tangled in my tresses as he urged me closer to him, our lips but a breath away.

"No smokescreen, Alice."

Logan lifted my hand to touch his handsome face.

"This is real; ours to make of it whatever we so please."

"If only it were so easy."

"Then I won't stop until you're just as hypnotized as I've been by you. Until I own every thought of yours as you own mine. I will consume you and please you, love you and protect you. And nothing; not even the forces of Hell will stand in my way."

My lungs burned as I absorbed every word, every promise, and beautiful threat.

His lips were angry against mine, full of conviction, and I ached to have more. We pulled back, gazing at one another as my heart beat wildly.

"You'll be—"

Our intimate moment slammed into screeching breaks and firearms as Gabe shoved a .45 in Logan's expectant hand. In a split second everything changed. My heart pounded harder for new reasons as my eyes absorbed the sight before me.

"Stay in the car no matter what, understand?"

"I can—"

"No! In the car, Alice; it's not up for debate."

Precious seconds passed and I knew this wasn't the time to take a stand.

"Okay."

Relief flooded Logan's features only to be overcome by un-concealed rage as he joined Gabe on the drive of my no-longer-recognizable home.

My once sanctuary was now nothing more than a cornucopia of choice words and illustrations not suited for innocence. I was still reading the various phrases when my eyes landed on what adorned my oak tree mere feet from my front door. A shiver ran down my spine as I examined the life-size effigy hanging by the neck from a noose. It swayed in the wind; a knife lodged into the figure's chest, centered at the heart.

The knowledge that this wasn't the doing of The Red Brotherhood did little to warm my chilled and shaking body. The Brotherhood wouldn't publicize their presence; or draw unwanted attention to their target for that matter. The display before me was hostile, passionate, and despite my vigorous blinking, very real.

Whoever was responsible had every intention in executing their threat. I had a good idea of who the responsible individual was, and what prompted their message.

I watched from the confines of the back seat as Logan and Gabe exchanged a series of heated words before Logan got in.

"It isn't safe here. We're going back to my place. Meanwhile my people will investigate."

It was neither a question nor an invitation.

"I could stay with Marina, Seth will be there."

"I need to be certain you're safe and that's with me! I have resources he doesn't. You're coming home with me, Alice; if I have to tie you up myself!"

"This'll only provoke her further!"

Logan pulled me into him; tucking my head beneath his chin.

"My team will figure this out." He offered, not even acknowledging what I'd just said.

"Do you love her too?"

I wished I'd kept my mouth shut; but I couldn't disguise the hurt. Logan breathed heavy, running his hand through his hair in an attempt to keep some composure.

"This's neither the time nor the place so let's get you to safety and go from there. All right?"

Nothing about his statement helped ease the ache.

"Yeah, all right." My tone told him so.

The short drive was spent in an uneasy silence. Whatever he'd had with Lily was prior to us I'd told myself; and yet it still stung—however irrational that was.

The property was gated like Fort Knox. A stone gate no less than ten feet, cameras…codes. I half expected to see armed guards at the head of the drive.

The house felt oddly familiar to me. As Logan led us up the floating stairs and down the hall I realized how comfortable I felt; a place I'd never been in yet felt convincingly welcome. We'd reached the south end of the second floor; ten foot double doors ushering us inside. Undoubtedly it was Logan's room.

"The washroom's through there. Use whatever you need."

Whatever hospitality Logan offered, was lost to the fog of his omissions.

"I'd rather stay in a guest room—"

"No."

"And why not?"

"Because I want you in my bed!"

My back stiffened and his hands ran through his hair; a calming mechanism, or simply a sign of frustration.

"I'll feel better knowing you're in here tonight. It's the safest room of the house, understand? I'll be just across the hall."

His explanation offered little comfort, as had every other word spoken since we left my vandalized home.

Nothing would feel right until we moved past what happened tonight, and as I looked into Logan's aquamarines, it was clear the conversation wasn't happening anytime soon.

I turned away towards the washroom and upon my return, I was alone. I found myself yet again caught in a funnel of battles and wars; and though Lily orchestrated this battlefield, it was Logan who'd wounded me.

I wandered about the massive room, with its infinitely high ceilings and custom made furniture, attempting to digest the wealth of information which was Logan's home. Circling the space I'd failed to find a single picture or personal artifact within the estimated thousand square foot suite. Thinking back, the passage through his home was equally lacking in heritage.

A soft knock sounded and my pulse responded.

Logan stepped inside, carrying a tray.

I wasn't hungry.

He set the tray on the nightstand, motioning for me to sit.

I refused.

"Alice, please."

"Unless that tea's capable of speaking on your behalf, you're wasting your time. I'm not doing this, Logan."

"It's to help you relax."

"*Why* do I need to relax?" I goaded.

His jaw was firm, his veins corded and tightening still.

"It was brief."

"Not good enough."

His eyes pleaded for me to reason when my heart had no room.

"I never loved her; I cared for her. For years she was the only one I allowed into my life and I took advantage of it. I broke it off because she wanted forever and I was never going to be the man to give her that."

"How long has it been over?"

"Nearly a year."

"It's not over for her."

"I know."

"Last night you meant for me to believe you were never involved, that it was entirely one sided. Why not tell me the truth then?"

"I planned to—eventually."

There was more to this.

"Eventually? You know my darkest demons, my soul lays bare and open before you and you planned to tell me *eventually*?"

"Yes."

Our tones were eerily calm—the calm before the storm.

"I need more than that. I'm not asking."

Logan's breathing deepened, as did his stare.

"Because I'll stop at nothing to have you."

"That's supposed to somehow make it better? You want what you want and damn anyone who gets in your way? You should've told me! I deserved to know!"

Logan gripped me so tight my skin stung, and I loved it.

"Yes—you deserved to know."

He was staring me down, chipping away at my resolve.

"There are so many obstacles threatening to keep us apart. So many damn threats, and the thought of me without you..."

Logan buried his face in my neck, breathing long and deep, as was I.

Lily wasn't the only secret.

"Lily was a mistake. I had enough to overcome when I came to you last night. I couldn't risk adding yet another hurdle to the list. I planned on telling you. I just needed time; time to convince you to be mine, time to build your trust."

Logan moved to rest his forehead against my own, his hands still in my hair. And there it was: *fear*. The last piece and my suspicions no longer wandered blindly.

I remembered the feeling when seeing his Porsche the morning we met; a feeling familiar to me from a time long before that morning, and it didn't make sense, until now.

"You watched me didn't you?"

"Alice—"

"How long?"

I was trembling, needing to know and at the same time willing to be ignorant of it all. Logan's fists tightened in my hair and I liked it more than he'd ever know.

"Since December."

A battle broke out within me. There was more to this. He watched me for a reason.

"Why?"

"Time, Alice; give me time."

"Trinity Investments; its Lily's isn't it? She knows and blames me, and now I know just how deep her hatred spans, how far she's willing to go."

There was a beast trapped within his depths, a fury begging for release.

"I—"

Logan's lips seized my own, desperate and erratic, coaxing me to lie back as he hovered above me, dark, beautiful, and utterly afraid.

"Logan—I need—I need."

The desperation of his kiss and touch had become my own and I was slipping further from answers; deeper into the all-consuming void that was Logan Snow. I had to stop, I had to pull back and stop. Stop. Stop!

Logan growled as he pulled away; wounded. I realized I must've screamed aloud, and for a moment we just stared at one another.

"You can't keep bending me to your will! There's more to this and I deserve to know!"

My heart was running, I felt as though it would rip right through my chest; unable to control the shaking.

As I stared at Logan I saw he'd locked himself up, refusing to give me what I needed and I couldn't stop the anger.

I laughed bitterly at the memories from mere hours ago, wrapped in his embrace happy and content. But if there was one thing I knew with certainty; life screwed you.

"Marry me."

My ears rang with disbelief.

"How dare you—"

"Marry me and you'll have your answers."

His stare was wild and full of challenge; desperation.

Logan reached for me but I recoiled in response. Not a day ago I believed his history couldn't possibly be darker than my own; I no longer had that luxury.

The joke was on me.

Tension filled the room with a force hell-bent on ripping me open. Logan rose to his feet unsteadily, I tried not to look but my eyes betrayed my every half-hearted command.

"Soon, Alice. Soon you'll see, that every beat of my heart beats to your symphony alone."

He stormed out of the room—only to root deeper into my soul.

I thought back to the day we'd met, replaying every moment. Logan never intended to fall in love with me; his resistance now making perfect sense.

His terms were sabotage; and despite it all, I fought the urge to give in. I remained seated on Logan's bed; occupying the exact position before all my walls came crumbling down, leaving me alone to fend against the brutality outside of his embrace.

Chapter Twenty Five

Allison Red

Memories from last night flooded my coherent mind; every detail imprinting itself upon my heart, and I felt sick.

Slipping out of bed I donned the robe and slippers that I knew weren't there when I fell asleep. My things still sat neatly folded on the chaise, my phone indicating missed texts. I reached for the device and scrolled.

11:13pm - Sunshine: Call me.

11:24pm - Luke: Are you all right?

11:40pm – Dad: You do what feels right knowing my door will always be open. Unconditionally.

11:59pm - Sunshine: I need you to call me.

12:33am - Sunshine: I don't care what Seth says, I need to hear your voice so Call Me Now!

01:05am - Luke: Just be careful, Sweets.

01:19am - Sunshine: I just need to know that you're okay.

01:41am - Sunshine: I will never forgive Seth if something happens to you.

I wiped at my tears, hating how easily they seemed to form lately. There was one person who never reached out: Seth. Nothing was an oversight, not with Seth. He was leaving me a trail, knowing I would follow dutifully.

"Oh My God I Hate You! Unless you've been held prisoner for the last eight hours I won't forgive you."

"I'm sorry." My voice was quiet, too quiet.

Marina calmed audibly. I had no doubt she would.

"What happened?"

"The house was massacred, not one area left untouched. There's an effigy, a dagger lodged in her heart. It was eerie how much of herself she left behind, Sunshine. I felt her presence, in the wind, the trees—the illustrations. She was everywhere."

"He broke her heart didn't he?"

"He did."

"You feel sorry for her, don't you?"

Was I not supposed to? I didn't know.

"She's hurt."

"That may be so but you're the target of her grief. Now's not the time to sympathize with a woman who's gone mad. You won't cure her with kindness, Alice. Do you hear me? I know you well enough to know you're somehow finding a twisted crazy way to blame yourself for all this."

Perhaps.

"Don't. It won't help anyone."

"I'm sorry for not keeping my phone on me. Things got out of control and I just—I—I don't know. I just disappeared."

"Did you come back?" Sunshine understood.

"I did."

"Hey, Alice?"

No response was needed. Marina had my attention.

"There's something more to Logan isn't there?"

It wasn't fair. Marina deserved a better friend, someone who brought more happiness as opposed to—

"It's too late for me, Sunshine. I'll talk to you later. Get some wedding plans done today."

I ended the call with heaviness I couldn't escape.

I slipped into the washroom to find a clean toothbrush with an array of personal products from shampoo, lotion, deodorant, lip balm, and a variety of other items. I showered robotically only half aware of the opulence which surrounded me. None of it carried through without his presence. There were a few bags with brand labels, some familiar but most not, set along the counter with a note.

No arguments. Logan

The clothing fit me better than it should have. I'd chosen a pair of low-rise jeans, the softest cotton camisole with lace trim and a hunter green cashmere sweater with a boat neckline. Logan had gotten me attire I would've picked myself and though I should've felt comforted, I felt exposed.

It was barely past six and the café awaited me like a child awaits its mother. Or perhaps I was the child? It didn't matter. I navigated the grand corridors and vast spaces quickly, eager to reach the front door where a taxi was supposed to be waiting.

"Good morning, Ms. Red. May I assist you with anything?"

I turned to find a woman carrying a stack of towels.

"I'm, Ms. Lexington, though, everyone calls me Lex. I trust you found everything you needed this morning?"

Her face was kind and welcoming. She had a Motherly effect and I rather liked being in her presence.

"Yes, thank you, Ms. Lexington. Forgive my manners, I didn't see you."

"No need to apologize, It's a large space. May I fix you some breakfast?"

"That's very kind of you but I'm rather in a rush. Please forgive me."

"A rush? Is Mr. Snow aware of where you're headed? I'm sure he'd like to help get you to your destination. I'll go get him—"

"No! That won't be necessary. I'm certain he's much too busy. It was such a pleasure meeting you and thank you—for every detail."

Ms. Lexington gave me a weary smile as I made quick of slipping into the coat and Uggs; two items amongst the many within the bags.

I ran for far too many minutes to reach the front gate where I could see a taxi idling at the entrance of the drive. The house was now a shadow in the distance but I knew he was watching. I felt him gazing out the window at my retreating back. His jaw set firm and his hands tucked securely within the pockets of his slacks where he could maintain a pose of casual while his veins burned. I didn't need to turn around to confirm his heart was thundering, I knew because Logan lived within me.

*

Stepping out of my office I headed to the front.

"Jenna, when you finish up come see me in my office."

If she was intimidated by my cold tone she didn't show it. I'd been all over the place since leaving Logan's home just hours ago. He could've stopped me. Several touches was all it would've taken and I would've melted before him as he knew I would. He didn't. It occurred to me sometime after the second bite of my chocolate-mousse-sugar-high that Logan's absence this morning was intentional. He'd anticipated my behavior; I didn't leave—he let me go.

Around my second cup of tea I had to convince myself that agreeing to his terms was weakness; the convincing was still in session.

I was drowning.

"Come in."

Jenna walked in looking confident if not threatening. She took a seat without pause, crossing one leg over the other at the knee.

"Do you enjoy your work, Jenna?"

She looked bored.

"I serve drinks and cake, what's not to like?"

"You must've misunderstood me. I wasn't referring to your employment with me."

Boredom was suddenly replaced with uneasiness. Now we were headed somewhere.

"I'm curious, your disdain—is that merely a role or is such contempt entirely genuine?"

"You have *no idea*." Jenna's tone held menace as her lips thinned to pale pink, matching the tone of her freckled skin.

"Enlighten me then."

"You've everything handed to you on a silver platter and yet you still want more. You're nothing but a selfish gold-digging cow, breaking up happy homes, taking that which isn't yours to take. You *had* a husband and you tossed him aside like leftovers as you lured in a married man, and the poor sap fell for it. If only he knew he was being bled out. You're all the same."

Without saying it, she'd revealed what lied at the core of her hatred towards me.

"Is your father still around?"

Jenna visibly flinched.

"That's none of your damned business." She seethed.

Lily was no idiot, she knew exactly what instrument fit the job. Jenna was commissioned due to her trauma of a broken home. All Lily had to do was fabricate several calculated lies then sit back and allow Jenna's imagination to do the rest.

"You're a bright girl so I'm sure you've gathered that as of this moment you're no longer employed here. In addition, you're to stay away from the café and not within five hundred feet of me. This packet has everything you need to know so I expect you off the property within minutes."

"Wishful thinking if you believe this place is yours. Congrats on figuring me out, Alice. Really, top notch job; word of advice, don't get too comfortable."

I feigned indifference but in truth, her glee was chilling. This plan went deeper than I'd anticipated. That was never a good thing.

Chapter Twenty Six

Logan Snow

Watching Alice sneak away as though I was some meaningless mistake cut deep. Looking in the mirror I saw the Bastard that I was, staring back at me; mocking me. I wanted to put my fist through his pristine face but pulled back to answer the damn phone.

"Snow."

"Lily has arrived."

"I'll be at the car in five. Have security watch her."

"Done."

I could see the L.S. Trade Co. high-rise and shifted my thoughts to the ruble that awaited me. I'd always had a soft spot for Lily, felt guilty for allowing our relationship to ever get intimate. I could justify my actions, after all I wasn't a priest.

Dating was never my forte when most women couldn't see past my sculpted bone structure or bank account. Most men within my circles enjoyed that shit, I had no tolerance for it. Lily knew me better than anyone, we shared a bond. I didn't intend on changing. Never planned on a future beyond my set goal. Lily was simply my companion during that journey and I was hers.

Until Alice.

I headed up in the private elevator to find Lily standing in the middle of reception looking as put together as always. Bypassing pleasantries I headed towards my office knowing she'd follow without invitation. Security stayed behind, minding our privacy; likely walking on eggshells unsure of when I might snap. I needed to finish this before the staff filtered in.

Once settled, Lily worked double time in presentation. Her dress bore the perfect cut to better display her ample cleavage, crossing her legs just enough to show the hint of the garters beneath the ensemble. I'd give her credit for effort. But where Lily presented her qualities with designer attire, salon cared hair that was never out of place, and a body sculpted by a personal trainer; Alice had heart. Her hazel eyes drew you in, her voice; gentle and sincere. I craved her curves, natural and honest. Alice was frightened by my unearned biological attributes, she was terrified by my wealth, and harbored a resilience I lacked. I envied her for it. Alice captivated me in the rawest forms, beyond what met the eye, down to what gripped the soul. Alice had done what I couldn't: see goodness in the world after it had taken what you cared for most—and burned it.

Turning my attention back to Lily left me cold.

"What part of 'it ends' was unclear to you?"

"I did it for you, for us—"

"Stop! It was sex, Lily. There is no *us*."

She looked like I'd just punched her.

"But she doesn't know you the way I do. Nobody does. Don't you see how different you two are? You'll never work. She's a liar and a whore. Whatever she's done to manipulate you—"

I stood, my face inches from hers.

"Watch what you say or I swear you'll rue the day it left your mouth."

Lily threw herself at me, her lips colliding against my own as her tongue sought entrance. My efforts to remove her proved pathetic as her mouth and hands continued their assault. Though I had no intention to physically harm Lily, once her nails dug so deep they pierced the skin, I passed the point of caring.

Prying both her hands from their death grip on my neck I twisted them behind her back, ignoring her cry of pain. I shoved her back and watched in rage as she stumbled to the floor in a look of disbelief.

Wiping away the remnants of her lips from my mouth I moved on, forgoing my attempt to soften the blow.

"I will buy out your shares. You'll take the money, you'll do so without media, and you will never as much as come within a mile of Alice."

I cared for Lily, as much as I'd ever thought I could for another human; until my world was no longer what I always thought it was.

Watching Lily sob while sprawled across my office floor was a sight I would likely never rid myself of.

"*Please.*"

The last time I saw Lily so broken was when Sal died. I winced at the vulnerability both in her voice and pleading eyes as she remained on the floor sobbing. I truly was a bastard. But it was too late now. I couldn't live without Alice, and as much as it pained me to see Lily so devastated, envisioning a life without her held no ache.

"Please don't do this—I—I love you Logan. I've loved you for so long. I can be what you need. I can live with whatever it is you have going on with *Her*, I'll wait until you get it out of your system. We'll be happy together. Please, just please don't do this, give it some time, I'll be patient."

I deserved the bitter pain flowing through my veins like acid as I listened to her plead gracelessly.

There was a special Hell for the likes of me and I'd earned my place inside that burning pit. I didn't deserve Alice, her heart, and purity; but I refused to let her go.

"Alice is my future and the only woman I'll ever love. Our arrangement was a mistake and waiting for what will never be is another. You deserve to find someone who'll love you in return, but that will never be me."

Lily kept her gaze fixated on the floor before her, and I welcomed the reprieve as she broke for a man who didn't return her affections.

"But you promised. You swore your word to Sal that you'd take care of me. After everything he did for you, you're going to betray him? Huh? Answer me!"

Damn her.

"I would have! I would've cared for you just as I always had but you made me chose Lily! YOU! Like a petulant child you threw a temper tantrum to win back your favorite toy! I can't love you the way you want!"

I shook with fury, pacing like a caged beast.

"Our attorneys will conclude the remainder of our business settlement. One day you'll come to understand this was the right thing to do."

Without a second glance I walked out the door, saving her whatever dignity remained. The door hadn't shut fast enough as an agonizing sob reached my ears but I wouldn't turn back.

"Miss. Snow will be a moment, see to it she gets home safely."

"Sir."

Chapter Twenty Seven

Allison Red

"What happened?"

Andrew stared at me with concern and frustration. He'd arrived within twenty minutes after I'd called. I wouldn't say more than that Jenna was no longer employed at the café but evidently that wasn't enough. The moment he walked in the door, I was dragged to the office to 'talk'.

"Nothing, it was time to let her go and I had let it drag on long enough."

"Bullshit! You led me to believe that everything was fine after I saw her sneaking around but I could feel that something was off. Tell me, is she after you? From your past? Was she blackmailing you?"

Andrew may've been my friend, but this was enough.

"Stop! Your concern may very well be coming from a good place, Andrew but its unwelcome here. We had a deal and there are no exceptions to that rule. My past is not a topic for discussion so I will ask you one last time never to mention it again."

Andrew's was angry and his thinning restraint—visible. I'd made a mistake by telling him.

"I'm not made of stone, Alice. I care for you and this entire situation makes me uneasy. You may think you're doing me a favor by keeping me in the dark but you're only hurting me by pushing me away. As though by letting me help you, you're leading me on. I care for all my friends, not just the one I fell in love with."

God, watching his sincerity was torture.

"You're too good a person to help the likes of me, Andrew. I won't share my secrets for the very reason that I care for you. I know you don't understand but it's true."

"And I'll believe you the day you *show* me our friendship. Because playing friends is not the same as *being* friends. As it stands now, our friendship is only a convenient term."

Andrew left the office without waiting for a reply. Which was fine because I had nothing to say. From his perspective he had every right to be angry, I couldn't blame him for that. But that wouldn't change the reality of my life. There was nothing to be done but tell him the truth, and I'd never do that.

Just minutes after posting the job opening online I had two interviews scheduled within the hour. Both failed miserably. So I anxiously awaited Steph's classmate Rachel's arrival, ever the more hopeful that she would be a good fit.

I looked at my traitorous phone for the umpteenth time only to be faced with a blank screen; not a single call or text. It became evident Logan wouldn't coax me. If I went to him, it would be entirely on my own.

I could go back to the kitchen and lose myself in work or call Marina and make more wedding plans, but I wanted none of it. Nothing held any allure, for the only comfort I sought was the safety of his arms, the warmth of his breath upon my skin, and the scent of home while his heartbeat lulled me.

"Alice, Rachel's here."

"Thanks, Steph. Send her in."

I gathered my things before the knock sounded.

"Come in."

"Rachel, hi, please have a seat."

The young woman was hesitant and shy with a sweet smile.

"It's great to meet you, Ms. Red. Steph's always spoken so highly of you."

"That's kind. I feel the same about her. So I noticed your resume said nothing about previous barista work or baking. Do you have any?"

"I've worked in various jobs since I was fourteen years old. I've never worked in a coffee shop specifically but I'm a quick and eager learner. I always show up no matter the weather, I do my work and do it well. I promise I won't disappoint."

There was a vulnerability to Rachel. She attempted to drape over it with will-of-heart but it was there and it spoke volumes.

"Your current employer?"

"Quick Laundromat off Twentieth Avenue."

"And what's the reason you'd like to leave if you don't mind me asking?"

"The café has a vibrancy I'd like to be a part of."

It wasn't so much her words I was hearing, it was her body language. Her mannerisms told me more.

I gave her resume one last glance before concluding the interview.

"I'll need you to fill out these forms. It'll take several days and if everything comes back clear then I look forward to having you join the team."

Rachel held on tightly to the stack of stationary riddled with questions broad and personal, and left.

To my relief Rachel was a viable option; on the condition her file came back clean. I no longer had the luxury of offering my employees civil rights of privacy.

In the solidarity of my office, I waged the battle of wills within me. Once I could no longer lie to myself, I departed. Headed on a journey of surrender.

*

The cab pulled away nearly an hour ago while I continued to stare at wrought iron as though the element had some wisdom to share, some secret on laying my lingering fears to rest. But the dumb metal remained just that.

An endless waging of wars within offered me no reprieve as I battled between the voice of reason and that of a yearning heart. This was not a dilemma of commitment for I was his and his alone. My return would be an exchange, his embrace for my reservation to retreat; the terms non-negotiable and indefinite. It was a question of principle and the recognition of need; which of the two was greater?

I was shaking, my feet moving forward, my skin sensing his nearness. The cold was sharp and stung my skin as I continued my steady steps up the paved drive. The glow of light grew brighter, though, not much else could be seen as the snow continued to fall in rising aggression. I was soaked and shivering; my hair stuck to my neck and face, and my toes numb. I didn't care, I was home.

Logan's shadow appeared in the distance and my knees gave out at the sight of him. I sank to the ground for I knew I would never survive Logan Snow; I never stood a chance. Logan reached me within several strides and took all control; the way I'd secretly wanted him to all along, and if that made me weak, so be it.

My arms wrapped obediently around his neck as he carried my shaking body to the only place I cared to be. Logan wove through doorways and various spaces though I never cared to open my eyes. I was safe in his arms and our surroundings failed to matter. It wasn't until I was being released into the soft cushions of a chaise did I see we were in his bedroom with only the glow of the fireplace mimicking the cobalt flames I loved.

Logan knelt before me and I succumbed to his searching oceans. I dove without hesitation, plummeting to the depths I'd never known. I no longer needed air. I was drowning in my deepest desires, a death I welcomed.

"I kneel at your feet a broken man. A man as cold as he is empty, and in desperate need of your warmth. For within your heart I've found the man I should've been, the man I want to be. I vow to cherish and protect you. To be your advocate, your champion, your friend and your family. In a world without justice I will let nothing harm you. I cherish you; Nadia

Rumikova…Allison Red: my angel who's captivated my heart beyond measure and beyond return. You're mine and I'm yours for I live and breathe for you, and you alone."

I wept in fulfillment. A silent stream dripped steadily down my cheeks and I knew such happiness couldn't last, so I embraced it; for whatever time I had.

"I do."

Logan needed nothing more and neither did I. His lips descended upon mine and I found solace in their power to touch me beyond flesh and into the wounds deep within: scars and nightmares of endless abuse, of rape, and of torture. Such haunting history began to dissipate as Logan's mouth wove healing without words and I succumbed to all he promised.

His hands worked at the last pieces of fabric still covering parts of me I vowed I'd never let another touch, propelling my pulse to quicken with intensity.

"Logan, I—"

His hand glided over my sensitive skin to cup my face, calling me to look at him.

"Shh, it can be beautiful. Let me show you."

I let the cotton pool at my feet as a yearning grew, a need—desire. My hands worked unsteadily at Logan's clothing as he aided me in my efforts. He was beautiful, untamed—somehow forbidden.

Logan swept me into his arms and to the welcoming bed. Our mouths found no time for words as we savored every moment of our connection, every possessive pull and gentle caress. Logan knew where I ached for rule and where I yearned for worship. His ministrations beat harmoniously in tune with my body and I opened to him. I gave him every part of me and he took it without remorse; Logan claimed me, just as promised.

*

Our bodies laid entwined beneath the silk duvet with beautifully stitched patterns; patterns Logan's fingers replicated on my skin and I laid mesmerized by his touch.

I'd read novels where women climaxed endlessly in the arms of their lover. Characters who'd been virgins throughout the story suddenly taking-on roles of sexual vixens with all the know-how of a seasoned escort.

Such novels were full of shit. I hadn't become an orgasm-machine overnight; though here I was, fulfilled beyond measure. I could still feel Logan's every movement and it made my skin electrify at the mere memory of the beauty in its rawest of forms. His palms roaming my needy flesh, pressing hard then soft before releasing me into a place where dreams were born.

Love was more than screams and moans, I think I'd always known that. Novel's rarely brought me enjoyment, and now I understood why.

Love was pain.

*

I awoke to a hazy dawn outside the wall of windows, still wrapped tightly within capable and strong arms. I didn't have to look up to know he was watching me.

"How long have you been awake?"

"Long enough."

Not since I was young had I slept through the night; not since the world lost all color in the eyes of a naïve child who was beaten for the first time and forced to face reality. That's what Logan had gifted me, something beyond monetary value.

"What's going through that beautiful mind of yours?" His voice was dark velvet; I wondered if he knew it.

"I don't know what happens next, where do we go from here?"

Logan lifted my chin to meet his eyes.

"You're my wife now, Alice. Now we build our life together."

"It's not that simple."

"Let me worry about the details."

Is that all it was—details?

"Oh crap, the café—"

I jolted from bed naked, lacking grace in my rapid movements.

"Alice, stop."

Logan laid propped up on his elbow, looking about as edible as vanilla ice cream dipped in Belgian chocolate dipped in sin. My pulse quickened and there was no hiding the flush that broke out upon my skin.

"We have plans today."

The word 'but' sat heavy on my tongue but I swallowed it back. Instead I watched hungrily as Logan pulled back the covers and reached for his jeans.

I remained rooted to my spot; an arbitrary stopping point where I only hungered for his touch and rule. Logan approached me with leisure, stepping behind and sweeping my disheveled tresses to one shoulder as his mouth nipped at the other. My legs were jelly, my mind close behind them while my heart—was something else entirely.

"You—you do things to me and I can't—" I was panting shamelessly as Logan's hand roamed my bare flesh.

"It's what you do to me, Alice. For every breath you take speaks to me—"

I was backed against the chaise now, my back lowered to the soft fabric and I was lost in a haze.

"—your every need I will fulfill, your every desire—"

Logan's voice grew rough and heavy as his touch gained momentum and I, I lost all control.

"—a challenge I will conquer—"

Logan proceeded to bind me with a stray belt.

"—there's nothing hidden from me, Alice; for I see you in your entirety. You belong to me."

Nothing was truer.

Our bodies moved with beauty and I reveled in the love I didn't deserve.

*

Logan carried my tired body to the steam shower and washed every part of me with reverence. I was cherished. When finished Logan dressed me, each artifact placed upon my body with love as his hands continued to caress and his lips—seduce.

I found myself wondering if I was dreaming over and over. Fearing that I'd wake up and Logan would disappear. But when I opened my eyes he stood before me, handsome and powerful as ever.

"You hungry?"

"Famished actually."

Logan grinned and I couldn't help the smile that spread across my face at the memories of the last nine hours.

"Good. Lex has prepared us breakfast, we mustn't keep her waiting."

There was a fondness as he mentioned Ms. Lexington. I found I wanted to know more about the people Logan cared for. I wanted to grow a fondness for them as well.

Logan led me through the home to the kitchen where the slender older woman stood before the stove.

"Good Morning, Mr. and Mrs. Snow. Please have a seat, breakfast is nearly ready. Your tea and coffee is on the table."

She knew.

Ms. Lexington gave a soft smile before turning back to her skillet of savory scents.

"Logan?"

"Lex knows everything about me, Alice; and you as well. There's no need for concern. You'll find she's quite taken by you already."

Taking the seat Logan pulled back for me I noticed the tea, but it was what floated within the tea that drew me back.

"Raspberries." I whispered.

Logan's eyes hid nothing. The darkness within them was open for my intrusion and I shivered at its depth.

"Nothing is hidden from me where you're concerned. I've never denied that."

No, he hadn't. He knew every detail, down to the insignificant berry I liked in my tea.

Ms. Lexington began placing platters of every variety upon the veined marble. Every time her gentle palm would touch my shoulder, I would turn to look at her and she'd offer another kind smile before returning to get something else in the kitchen.

"Enjoy your breakfast, I'll be down the hall if you need me."

"Thank you, Ms. Lexington. Everything looks amazing. Truly."

"Oh my dear, it was my pleasure. And please, call me Lex."

I nodded and Lex disappeared beyond the corridor wall.

"Does nothing about me surprise you?" I asked, once we were alone.

Logan set down his coffee.

"On the contrary; everything about you surprises me. *Everything*."

I felt his every word.

We ate mostly in silence. Occasionally Logan's phone would vibrate and he'd reply accordingly without volunteering the placement of his thoughts, when my own couldn't hide from his all-knowing gaze.

"Where are we going today?"

"My property in Genesee. We're meeting Seth and Marina."

"I can't leave the café understaffed. I'll have to meet you there later."

"Alice." Logan's voice called for submission—trust.

"I've sent two bodies fully capable. You may check in anytime. I'm sure Andrew will fill you in." His tone said it all.

"You *knew*."

Logan took the last bit of his eggs before setting his fork aside.

"I'm certain you're the only one who didn't. He couldn't help himself."

"Did you know about Seth and Marina as well?"

His gaze was daring.

"Indeed."

I laughed coldly.

"How did you find time to run your own company or even catch a breath for that matter?"

Logan stood too quickly and was inches from my mouth before I could suck in any air. His hands wove deep into my hair as he ghosted his lips over my skin.

"You'll find I'm very driven. There are no limits when what I want is within my sight and you, Alice—are what I wanted *more* than my next breath."

His lips coaxed me back into playing nice as I gasped for air beneath his wicked mouth. This was us. And we were a current of beautiful chaos.

"I won't deny that watching you was an addiction. And I'll never apologize for falling in love with you."

I trembled with the knowledge of how much I enjoyed his dominance. We were crazy and destructive and beautiful and passionate and I was a hypocrite, for had anyone else watched me I would've destroyed them. But with Logan, I longed for his voyeurism. So who was the more twisted of us?

"It's time." His tone was matter-of-fact.

Without pause Logan led us to his office where a thin stack of documents laid facing me, my name written in various paragraphs. There was no pre-nup and the small detail pulled at me unexpectedly. I took the pen from his hand and signed my name; forever binding us in print.

Chapter Twenty Eight

Allison Snow

The Porsche was warm, though, the absence of Gabe left behind a creeping chill. He was tending to—something.

Neither of us spoke, as though leaving the cocoon of Logan's home opened us up for harsher realities, and I found it easier to simply pretend we were still in his bedroom with the real world dimensions away.

"Lorenzo." Gabe's voice rang through the dash speakers.

"ETA ten a.m. have everything ready."

Logan released the button on the console and the silence resumed. Logan offered me nothing on his plans so I chose not to ask.

As we wove through the winding highway I stared out the window, watching the endless evergreens heavy with white coats covering the landscape. The sky was sullen and brooding and now that I could ask Logan the questions I should, I no longer wanted to.

More than once he turned to me, silently prompting me to voice my inquiries and in response I kept my eyes fixated on the world passing us by.

"You must ask." His voice was stern. Prompting.

I continued my love affair with the unforgiving rocks littering the roadside.

"It was the deal, Alice. Now ask!"

And now I wanted to wait. Live the dream of our new life just a bit longer. Be naïve; be free of the constant weight of reality dragging me down at every turn. Having to jump through hoops and crawl through trenches just to find the sunlight again. I just wanted a damn break, and live in this fantasy a little longer!

"My father's name was Matthew, only son to Vladimir Grishkin."

Why was that name so familiar?

"Don't."

"They're dead. Sam Snow was my father's business partner but most importantly, a man my father trusted. He took me in though I was an adult, and had me adopt his name. Gave me his company upon his death. Lily was Sal's granddaughter."

Please stop.

"I cut ties with all who knew me, changed the company name and relocated to Colorado. Built it into an empire through marked deals and dark promises, driven solely by revenge and hatred."

"I need to get out, stop the car!"

My fingers tingled and I felt light headed. I should've known, should've seen this coming but this simply wasn't possible. Billions of people populate the earth, this simply wasn't possible. This couldn't be happening. It couldn't!

"When you filed for the café, your profile was ran like everyone else within the area of my building. I dig up every detail of every individual I run a profile on. Everyone has secrets and I make it my business to know them. You would've passed if it wasn't for a report that surfaced in the German records which stated you were eighty two years old. We dug deeper. Within days I'd had enough—"

"Shut up! Stop the damn car. STOP!"

Logan pulled over and I nearly broke open the door, running towards the wall of jagged and merciless boulders blocking my path. Logan approached me from behind and I turned to face his stone-set features while propelled by uncontainable vehemence.

"I'm CRAZY and you're INSANE and this—this is some sick alternate reality! I'm supposed to be your bait right, a pawn? I ran across continents only to serve myself up to you on a silver damn platter? How poetic!!!"

Logan's gaze smoldered yet he refused to answer me.

"Did you know I watched? Huh? Did you? How are you even capable of looking at me without disgust? I was there, Logan, do you hear me? I was THERE!"

"You're mistaken, I've seen the footage, and you weren't in it."

"Because I was three rooms down, freshly beaten and raped for having committed the punishable offence of spilling Vitaliy's rum. I was forced to watch, a prequel to what awaited me so I never forgot my place!"

I felt the earth shake beneath my feet, the trembling of all matter surrounding our suicidal romance.

"We're going to destroy each other! There's no way out because fate is cruel and the future—ha! What future? You'll be the end of me and me the end of you!" I was screaming, my hands coiled into brutal fists.

Logan took several steps towards me.

"I accepted that before I came to you. And I refuse to live whatever remaining time I have on this earth apart from you, do you understand? Such a fate is worse than death!"

"*No.* Don't say that. Use me, damn you! Use me!"

I was right; such powerful things weren't meant for capture, our love would ultimately destroy us and we'd burn, dissolving into nothing more than a mountain of cosmic dust not meant for this world.

The echo of zooming vehicles seemed to pass distantly, and with my eyes wide open, everything was a blur. The snow began to melt through the fabric of my jeans and I realized I was on the ground with Logan kneeling before me.

"I hate you." I whispered.

Logan wrapped me into his warmth and I went willingly.

"I know."

"I hate you so much." My voice was small, my fists no bigger as I pushed and punched at his chest; Logan held me.

"Tell me it's all a lie. *Please*. I need it to all be a lie."

"I can't. I'll never let you go. You've done this to me, Alice. I may be a monster, but even monsters have weaknesses. You're mine."

Our love was destructive, it was reckless and it was the one thing I couldn't give up.

I clung to Logan, causing him pain and enjoying it because that's how sick I was; wanting to hurt him, then heal him the same.

God help me.

Logan carried me back to the Porsche. It had begun to snow again; heavy flakes spiraling from the sky to their death, and I found the display of their demise beautiful. Was it possible for beauty to accompany death? Everyone I'd witnessed die had always been accompanied by terror, yet the snowflakes that melted against the windshield before me appeared so graceful and at peace.

My jeans were soaked so I removed them. Logan watched as I tore the clinging fabric from my skin unceremoniously before pulling out a cashmere throw and placing it over my chilled legs.

"When did you change your plans?" My voice was hoarse, my throat sore.

"The first day I laid eyes on you."

I looked at Logan then, and I believed him. Because whatever this was, I felt it too. I couldn't understand it, but it was there and more powerful than my rational mind.

"I'm lost, Logan. I'm broken."

"On the contrary, my Love. You're my truest North."

I couldn't fathom how that could be.

We parted with the scenic I-70 Interstate; trading it in for a secluded road, entered only via a gate large enough to accommodate a small jet. We rode in a heavy silence as Logan held my hand like an anchor. I needed that; him, and the strength he breathed into me.

Logan pulled to the side and got out to retrieve something from the back. When he returned he held in his hands a new and dry pair of jeans and I wondered if it was possible for him to be any more attentive or detailed. My intuition told me he could, though, I couldn't imagine how.

The private road was smooth and freshly plowed. It wound beautifully for a quarter mile before we approached the heart of the property.

Before me was an infinite mountain landscape, beautifully coated in glistening snow; perfect and untouched. Off to the left stood a shimmering estate that seemed to glow as the light bounced off the snow and dwelling in kind. At some point I'd stepped out of the SUV but still couldn't take my eyes off the almost magical surroundings. Colorado had beauty encased in all its mountain escapes, but it seemed the rarest gems were the ones hidden from the mainstream eyes.

We made our way to the entrance where it became evident how tiny we were within the towering space; how vast the scenes before me spanned and how insignificant I was in the big picture of this world.

"I'm speechless."

"*You're* stunning." Logan whispered the sentiment low in my ear and his warm breath spread healing over me.

We entered through a door that took us directly into what seemed to be a utility room of sorts. The space had lockers and cubbies filled with equipment. The walls housed dozens of snowboards and pairs of skies along with all the body, face, and foot gear you might have needed for any number of sports.

Sports I didn't know the first thing about.

The elevation of the cabin paired with the windows, and the snow covered grounds below gave you the essence of living in the clouds. Evergreens peppered the immediate grounds then grew dense outward, concluding that I'd officially witnessed a real winter wonderland.

"It's spectacular."

"And equally impressive during all the seasons. We'll visit it often enough so you can experience each one."

The fear we may never live that long sat bitter on my tongue so I chose ignorance in its place.

"I'd love that."

Logan brought me flush with his chest, forcing me to look up and meet his gaze. His lips hovered above mine and I stood helplessly lost in his embrace.

His mouth covered mine tentatively before growing confident and aggressive, the edge of each motion bringing me much pleasure and the more I understood why, the more I wanted to make it stop. But I couldn't. I needed it.

Logan pulled away bringing his mouth to my ear, sending a shiver down my spine as his warm breath danced upon my skin.

"You have no idea what it does to me when you shiver like that." His voice was hoarse and daring.

Before I could react Logan had me lifted and pinned against a wall of glass as he stared hungrily into my eyes with the same intensity that always seemed present around us. He ravaged my mouth and left no part of me untouched. Our surroundings were no longer present as I focused only on him and his wicked ministrations.

Logan pulled away suddenly and I whimpered in response.

"I have only so much self-control, Alice. You're stripping me bare."

We entered what Logan referred to as 'The Retreat'. The charcoal, navy blue, and white color scheme set the mood of winter wonderland to a T with an abundance of natural light. I didn't quite catch it at first but once I looked up I realized why: the entire ceiling was made of glass panels.

"In here, the world is a different place."

I felt it. I envied it.

"I can't believe you rent this out."

"I don't."

I didn't have time to inquire further as we heard voices coming from the atrium and followed to find Seth and Marina escorted by the ever-faithful Gabe. My heart tightened at the sight. I wouldn't ruin this day for them with the new revelations of Logan and all that came with him. They deserved the full experience of planning a wedding.

"I missed you so much," Marina said, her voice a mixture of relief and reprimand, which I ignored while crushing her to me, for I had missed her equally.

"Are you all right?"

"I'm good. Really good."

"But the house, everything—"

"I'm okay, Sunshine. I'll survive."

I smiled as brightly as I could.

"How about you? How did your plans go yesterday?"

Marina rolled her eyes.

"The caterers were a no-go. We have yet to find one that produces something that doesn't taste like it came from a frozen dinner tray."

"That bad, huh?"

Marina brought her hands to her face.

"Worse actually, I was being kind."

"And the rest?"

"Yeah, the rest was good. Guest favors: check. Videographer: check. DJ: check."

With each item her hands made the motion of checking it off her list.

With a sudden change of course Marina grabbed my elbow, pulling me farther down the opposite side of the room and speaking not so quietly into my ear.

"This place is incredible. I mean holy cow. Nothing we toured could hold a candle. I mean don't get me wrong but, damn!"

She squealed and I laughed because it was too much not to.

"Wait till you see the master suite."

Marina's eyes went wide with anticipation and she pulled me upstairs without pause.

"Um, we'll be back in a jiffy. Just want to see the view from up here; you know, gauge the space."

Logan nodded politely, Seth smiled at his bride.

"Do you want to see the guest bedrooms too?" I asked.

"Nope."

We both laughed.

The double doors parted and Marina didn't waste a moment.

"Look."

She pointed to the sky visible through the glass roof. I nodded.

"Yeah, I know."

She was grinning from ear to ear and I smiled back, for seeing her so happy helped ease the ache in my heart.

"This is going to make me sound super shallow but I'm going to say it anyways—you totally scored!"

My smile waivered but I forced it back in place before she noticed. It wasn't her fault, she didn't know and I would wait until after the wedding to tell her that not everything was as beautiful as it appeared. It wouldn't be fair to darken her blue skies as she prepared for a life of love with a man hunted.

Like me.

"Oh, by the way how did it go with Jenna?"

Crap! With everything else I nearly forgot about that damn thorn.

"She was creepier than I'd expected— too confident. There's more to it, I just haven't figured out what."

"Have you told Seth or Logan?"

We sat on a pale blue chaise facing the view.

"Not yet, but I will."

Marina grabbed my hand, giving it a squeeze.

"Everything all right with you and Snow?"

I squeezed back.

"It's—everything and so much more."

Marina relaxed at that. Not knowing the full extent of the phrase.

"Have you seen the house since the other night?"

"Nope."

"Well, you'd never have known anything happened at all. Snow's crew had effectively turned back the clock, down to the last detail of paying off witnesses and destroying police records."

Somehow I wasn't surprised. By all measures it was docile compared to what he was capable of. I knew that much.

"How's Seth been?"

"All right I suppose. He's been with me on all the wedding planning but he's not always *present* you know? Like his mind is elsewhere. He tries to hide it, but I'm too in tune with him for it to go unnoticed."

"Is it the case?" I inquired. Marina shrugged in response.

"Perhaps its—"

She began picking at the nonexistent lint peppering her jeans.

"Oh no. Don't you dare try thinking he has the pre-wedding jitters or whatever they call that crap. He's about as committed as you can be before becoming clinically insane."

Marina smiled but her eyes lacked that emerald shine.

"No, not that. I'm too awesome, remember?"

I smiled at that.

"What if it's something worse?"

I didn't want to lie. But telling her the truth was even harder.

"I'm sure he'd tell you. Otherwise I wouldn't worry."

Marina sighed, unconvinced but hopeful.

We sat for a while, content with the quiet and in awe of the view. I wrapped my arm around her shoulder and she clasped my hand with hers to the side. I imagined us just like this, sixty years into the future, reminiscing on a life lived, full of joy and laughter.

The unlikely image brought me to tears and I hoped she wouldn't notice.

"When I was little my mom would put these ridiculous pigtails in my hair. I hated them. I thought they made me look so itty bitty, even though I was, but that's beside the point. She knew I hated them yet every Sunday before church I would sit at her vanity chair while she meticulously parted my hair just so, tied each side with these sparkly rubber bands, and topped it off with a pale pink ribbon to each one, effectively making it that much more childish."

I smiled, imagining Marina's begrudging reflection in her mother's vanity mirror.

"The morning of her funeral my aunt Chloe sat me down at my mother's vanity and for the last time my hair was parted and pulled into pigtails too high on my head and not nearly as perfectly symmetrical as my mom had done just days before; only this time, black ribbons completed the ensemble. All the while I sat as still as a stone trying to understand why my mom was never waking up? My aunt sensed my vacancy and told me about the night she awoke to black smoke, so thick she couldn't see her own hands before her face. An electrical fire, it was later concluded."

I was no longer crying alone.

"My mom hid in a closet. She was four, didn't know any better, and so it took the longest to find her. She sustained third degree burns over sixty percent of her body, and the larger portion of her head. Pigtails were her favorite, copied from her favorite doll which was destroyed by the fire; but after the burns she was never able to have pigtails again."

I tightened my hold of Marina's shoulder.

"I know this might be crazy but I want pigtails on my wedding day. I want my hair parted perfectly, and this time, I want white ribbons. My Mom will be watching and I want to show her how much I loved her and those ridiculous pigtails—I was just too stubborn to realize it then."

Marina's voice caught with anguish and regret for what a little girl could never have known.

"I think she'd love that."

Marina nodded her head for a while before pulling back to look at me.

"Would you do them for me?"

I blinked back the tears but they spilled anyways.

"Of course."

We turned back towards the eagle circling the sky high above the pines and drew each other closer. I held her as she grieved the absence of her mom; the victim of a drunken driver who should've known better but chose to get behind the wheel of his truck anyway. It was late and Gwen was headed home from her ER shift when the truck crossed the divide and collided with her head-on. She was killed on impact. No one had the chance to say goodbye.

The driver's lawyer was able to get him out of serving a prison sentence. Officially it was said the lawyer worked his legal magic but Greg knew it was because the driver was the twenty two year old grandson of the police commissioner, so Greg left the force. He sold the house, packed up Luke and Marina, and moved to Colorado to start anew. He couldn't bear to serve a system that had failed him so tragically.

We'd been sitting a long while, even the snow had stopped its insistent fall; so we headed back downstairs where we found Lex busy in the kitchen.

"Lex. I didn't know you'd be here."

"I'm only staying for a bit. I'm preparing your lunch and I'll be on my way."

I felt so rude.

"Please allow me to help you. I feel terrible."

Lex smiled and I was beginning to understand why Logan cared for her. She made you feel at home somehow. Warm and welcome, not a guest; a member of sorts I guess. I couldn't explain it and yet the emotion was so real.

"All right, why don't you grate that parmesan into the bowl, mix together the Caesar dressing and cut the romaine for the salad."

I appreciated her not turning me away.

"Great."

"And what about me?"

"Oh sorry. Lex, this is Marina. Marina, this is Lex."

"Hi."

Marina waved her hand with that adorable innocent look she was so good at.

"Hello, dear. You may pull the potatoes from the pot, wrap them in foil and pop them into the oven."

To describe what I felt preparing this meal was impossible. In these moments of friendship I felt weightless, I felt invincible, and I felt I was experiencing what life was meant to be. What it should've been.

"Oh my southern love affair, is that banana nut bread?"

Marina's finger pointed accusingly at the double ovens

"Don't forget the ice cream I saw in the freezer." I added.

Lex looked at us both and laughed.

"And don't forget the homemade caramel in that dispenser over there."

"Oh Lex, you're my new best friend."

"Hey!"

"Sorry, Sweets. It's a dog-eat-dog world out there and Lex is playing hard ball."

"Again with the animal references. I need to get you a collar that zaps you or something."

Marina stuck out her tongue in response.

I was loving every moment.

The guys had been absent the entire time. I sensed the reason and chose to lower the veil of ignorance. I wouldn't be robbed of these moments.

"Lex, please join us for lunch. Surely you could stay."

"I would enjoy that. You ladies make me feel so young again, but as it so happens my daughter's birthday is today. And we have a tradition to uphold."

"Oh Lex, that's wonderful. Is she your only child?"

Lex's eyes brightened.

"I have three, all girls. Sydney is the youngest. She turned twenty one today, my baby."

"Lex you must go then. We'll finish up here. Go and enjoy this day, celebrate!"

Lex looked unsure as she glanced towards her apron and back again. I approached her slowly, placing a palm at her shoulder just as she'd done for me earlier that morning.

"Nothing is more important than being with the ones you love. Go Lex, don't worry about Logan. He'd want you to go."

Lex covered my hand with hers and slipped out the door.

I envied Sydney.

Marina bumped my shoulder with a wink before heading to set the table.

"She's a gem. How did such a sweet woman end up with Logan?"

The jab was friendly, though slightly true.

"I don't know actually. But I like her."

"Me too, Sweets, me too. Hey, you better get that banana bread before it burns and *that* my dear…" Marina's index finger was now pointed at me.

"…would be an utter crime."

"All right, all right. I get it already. Marina need banana bread, banana bread need to be in Marina's stomach, if Marina's mouth doesn't get some banana bread then people will suffer. Sheesh I got it." I spoke each word in mock caveman with hand gestures to match.

"Well there's no need to be all snobbish about it. You're like a blood hound—"

I threw a wooden spoon in her direction with a bit more force than I had intended.

"Don't you dare! If you mention another animal you'll never see that banana bread ever again!"

I barely finished before we broke into hysterics.

Everything felt so good here, so right. I was living my illusion and loving every second, savoring it. It was my very own Wonderland.

"Are we interrupting something?"

The guys looked towards us amused.

"Not at all. In fact you saved me from having to hunt you down like—"

I gave Marina a look that said consequences would follow before another spurt of laughter escaped.

"—well, never mind. Lunch is ready. Sit down already."

If Logan expected Marina to address him formally, given it was his property after all, then he ought to look elsewhere. Marina wasn't the diplomatic type.

Logan closed in on me, his hands grasping me not nearly tight enough as he brushed my locks to one side.

"Are you enjoying yourself?"

I looked up, suddenly breathless.

"I am."

And as though to reward me, Logan's fingers threaded deep into my hair where he gripped me with the force I so darkly desired. His lips ghosted my ear teasingly, making promises I ached to reap. But he released me instead to grab the bowl of Caesar salad and left me—needing.

"Seth informs me you're still in need of a caterer."

Logan glanced my way before returning his attention to Marina.

"Unfortunately so. Do you have anyone you'd recommend?"

"Indeed. I've taken the liberty to set up a tasting for you. Thursday at noon on the twenty second floor of my building. They have committed to the eighth on the account you choose to move forward."

"Seth?"

Marina looked to her beloved.

"The matter had been discussed earlier, during the tour. All seems in order so long as you enjoy what they present, my love. The decision is yours."

Only it wasn't.

"Thank you, Logan, that's very kind of you. I look forward to meeting them."

"And I take it that you agree to hold your wedding here as well?"

A series of glances passed between the engaged couple, several having little to do with the question at hand.

"We'd be crazy to decline such an offer. It's almost too good to be true—this place."

Marina gestured to the space surrounding us. Logan smiled politely.

"I assure you it is. I'll have my events coordinator Eleanor contact you. I'm certain you'll find her services priceless given your timetable."

"I'm not sure how to thank you, but thank you."

Marina appeared taken aback, shy and uncertain; unlike herself.

"No need to contemplate the matter. You're Alice's dearest friend so it pleases me to be of service on such an occasion, think nothing of it."

"Wait, you mean we're not paying you?"

Marina finally caught on. Only she had yet to grasp the real reason Logan was doing this. Generosity was merely a small part.

"Safety is of vital importance, Marina. Remember that our lives will now forever be connected through Alice. I request that my gifts be seen as nothing more than friendship and all that comes with it." Logan spoke smoothly, collected and somehow unarguably so.

His presence was made for compliance and nothing less, and it became easily clear why he'd become so highly successful. He was a lethal combination of energy, influence, and supremacy to which you happily submitted and still asked for more.

"Your logic is difficult to argue. I concede, something I'm certain you're familiar with." Marina spoke with a smile, though, the message was clear.

"I believe we'll be getting along greatly you and I. Cheers; to Seth and Marina."

Logan held up his glass and we joined him before drinking our sparkling water.

I imagined ninety nine percent of the population would laugh if they saw us, drinking a toast with no liquor in sight. I knew my reasons for avoiding the substance and those of Seth, but I had yet to know Logan's.

We finished up our meals and Marina vocally enjoyed her her thick slice of banana bread beside a dollop of vanilla ice cream drizzled in caramel dessert. I'd tasted banana bread before so her enthusiasm was rather puzzling until it became evident that what I'd tasted previously was mud and this was the real deal.

Upon my first bite Marina's crazed reaction made total sense. It was as though I'd snuggled next to a fire in my favorite over-cushioned chair reading a timeless book while wearing my pajamas: the perfect cocktail of comfort and indulgence.

We began to clear the table and I suddenly didn't want to leave. I'd found happiness within these walls and the world beyond seemed further away somehow. I felt hidden here, safe— unreachable.

"Marina have you seen the courtyard yet?"

"I haven't."

"Allow me to show you then."

Logan led Marina outside, while Seth remained with me. There were few coincidences in life and this was certainly not one of them.

"The house."

"I'm okay, Seth."

"It was no idle threat, Alice. There was rage and passion; an explosive combination, you know that."

"There's more."

"What do you mean more?"

"When I let Jenna go, she said I shouldn't be so sure of myself. She implied the café was soon to become her property. I would've disregarded it entirely but there's more to it. I can feel it. The house is nothing compared to how far Lily's willing to go."

Seth stood motionless, pulling his thoughts together and calculating the probable outcomes.

"Does Logan know?"

"No."

Seth appeared concerned.

"Why?" He asked.

"It's been a bit complicated."

"No runaround, Alice. I deserve better than that." He did.

"I married him."

For the first time since waking up half alive and seeing the face of a man I'd only ever known as a cold-blooded-killer, I saw Seth taken by surprise.

"When?"

"Last night. I signed the documents this morning."

Seth schooled his features.

"He told me about his parents, I know of his vendetta."

Seth nodded.

"How long have *you* known?"

Seth ran a hand through his short hair in frustration.

"The night before Thanksgiving."

It was my turn to nod.

"It wasn't my place. You had to hear it from him."

"I know. I understand."

We stood silent, peering down at Logan and Marina making their way around the snow-covered courtyard.

"Does Marina know?" He asked.

I shook my head.

"It wouldn't be fair. I'll tell her after your wedding. She deserves that, the wedding of her dreams."

Seth placed a palm upon my shoulder, his way of saying thank you.

"I've tried so hard to make my life standard, normal…monotone. Yet I couldn't keep myself from him. I want to say I tried, but deep down I know that's a lie. I wanted Logan more than anything else. Why? Why couldn't I have picked someone different, someone…simple?"

Seth took a deep breath, releasing it slowly as he gazed at the evergreens outside.

"Marina may as well be my opposite. She embodies everything I wish I was, but wasn't." Seth's voice was haunted.

He turned to look at me and I met his stare.

"Despite your history, you've become one of the kindest people I know. I imagine you've found some part of yourself in Logan. A part you get to live out through him. As I get to live out parts of me through Marina."

It was true then. I'd tried so hard to convince myself I wasn't evil, that through it all I'd chosen the path of peace. But Logan's vendetta may as well have been my own. I just never had the courage to pursue it.

"Seth, if it becomes a choice; you must choose yourself. Promise me."

Seth's features hardened and I saw remnants of Konstantine.

"It won't." He spoke the words hastily and that's when I knew with certainty that my suspicions of his dishonesty had merit.

I stepped closer, placing my palm upon his stone-like cheek.

"This is how it must be. Marina needs you, Seth. Choose yourself and run."

Seth pulled me into him, his embrace saying that which he wouldn't speak.

"Are you happy, Alice?"

I couldn't lie.

"Unbearably so."

"There is no room for guilt, Alice. You deserve happiness, this world owes you that much."

*

"Thank you."

I was in my favorite space, warm, cared for—content.

"For what?"

I raised my chin just enough to meet his eyes.

"Today. Seth, Marina, the wedding plans; all your help. I felt more centered today than   ever I think. It meant a lot to mc. Thank you."

Logan placed his lips to my forehead.

"One day, Alice; one day you'll know the depth of my love, how far I would go, and the roads I would cross."

I understood, and so I wished that day would never come.

The view beyond my window was cold and beautiful, bitter yet striking. The sun had set beyond the horizon, lighting the sky in tones of pale pink and grey.

The interstate was nearly empty and the mountains: ever the more mysterious. Gabe was once again our chauffeur and I found an odd comfort in that.

Logan traced patterns upon my skin, patterns I'd come to crave, patterns which glided over my needy flesh illustrating dreams and hopes and desperate wishes.

Logan led me to the dining room where the table stood, fully prepared with dinner. I felt a pang of sadness until I realized the meal was catered, and relaxed with the knowledge that Lex was still celebrating.

"Forgive me, you'll be eating alone tonight."

Logan kissed my lips too briefly for satisfaction before heading for his study.

I sat motionless, in no hurry to reach for the platters of food before my mouth was taken by surprise, assaulted and consumed the way it should always be in his embrace. Logan pressed me into him claiming every part he touched. I moaned in pleasure as he trailed his lips along my neck and to my mouth once more before releasing me.

"What was that?" I spoke breathlessly.

His gaze was greedy—his hand still at my nape.

"That was my appetizer."

With that, Logan strode towards his office. The door closed and I no longer wanted food.

Chapter Twenty Nine

Logan Snow

"Who's been assigned to the case?"

"McCarthy."

I couldn't breathe. I would never forgive Lily for this.

"There's no way Lily could've known this. It was chance."

"You know better than that, Lorenzo. This is the universe playing its perverse game and we're losing."

I ran my hand through my hair, willing myself to think straight. Keep control.

"How much damage?"

"Enough."

"Log everything. I want every last damn detail. I won't let Jenna walk away from this uninjured. Not for this."

Seth stormed into my office without pause. Judging by his cold stare I knew it was bad news.

"We need to talk."

"Then talk."

Seth eyed Gabe.

"You trust him with this?"

I trusted Gabe with my life.

"You're wasting time, Seth. Gabe stays."

"Pyotar, he's dead."

"Who?"

"My safety net. Nothing about that night was planned. It was a split second decision. I couldn't turn to anyone connected to The Brotherhood for help. Pyotar was high level tech for a client. I'd gotten him out of some shit during one of the audits. He owed me. We wouldn't risk contacting one another after that night; but after everything that's happened these past few weeks, the case…you, I decided it was time to take the risk."

"What safety net?"

"Surveillance, ledgers, flash drives, photographs, I kept insurances. Not only on Ily but every damn client I facilitated a deal with. I wasn't naive enough to believe I was irreplaceable. There were a series of safety deposit boxes. I couldn't go to them myself, Nadia was hanging on by a thread and I couldn't show my face anywhere. Pyotar was to empty the boxes and relocate them without a trail."

Seth paused, staring at Gabe, letting him know he was unwelcome in this exchange.

"The confirmation and new location for the contents was encrypted on a drive with a password only Pyotar and I knew, and sent to a safety deposit box via third party messenger in St. Petersburg. I know it's there but never risked retrieving it. I had no way of knowing if the plan was compromised or flawed."

"And now that he's dead? Is the box still intact?"

"I only know it's still registered. All else warrants suspicion."

"Did Pyotar know about the identities you acquired?"

It was taking every bit of restraint to keep calm, level headed; when all I wanted was to take Alice and run.

"No. But he knew our intended location was Colorado."

"Does Alice know?"

"No. But that doesn't make it right."

"And waking her from this Wonderland she's built around herself is? She's hanging onto this fabricated reality with every bit of hope she has left. You want to drag her out from that tree trunk? Well I sure as hell don't!"

"She'll find out eventually."

I knew that.

"And I would change that too if I had the means to do so. I would make her be ignorant of it all!"

I reached past the credenza and into a hidden slot in the side. I pulled out the flash drive containing information Seth would need. Crow owed me a favor and it was time to cash it in.

"Take this. Tell Crow that Moscow treated you well and you wish to visit again. He'll laugh and then you tell him what you need. You get one shot with him, be thorough."

Seth nodded before leaving me to arrange the rest.

Chapter Thirty

Allison Snow

"Sooo, how was it?"

Marina's smile said all I needed to know.

"Wow. Just wow. And the salmon—I can't thank Logan enough; it was amazing."

"Well that's it then. The caterer is confirmed and you're all set, Sunshine. Only ten days to go!"

Her smile was contagious and I contracted it immediately.

"Have you decided if you're inviting the staff?"

"Oh, don't remind me. I'm so torn. What do you think?"

"Uh uh, don't drag me into it. That's all on you, Sunshine."

Marina rolled her eyes dramatically, leaving me certain she glimpsed her brain before the poor things rolled back into place.

"Much help you are."

"And yet you still love me."

I crinkled my nose and walked off before a wadded-up wash cloth hit the back of my shoulder. But I knew just how to retaliate.

"Did I tell you I found the perfect ribbon?"

Her eyes lit up.

"Can I see it?"

"Nope."

"Oh come on! *Please.*"

I almost gave into those puppy eyes, *almost.*

"You're a big girl now. Ten days isn't that long."

She threw another wadded cloth but I ducked and it missed.

"Fine." She whined.

Keeping my nuptials from my best friend had been more difficult a task than I'd anticipated. There were days I thought telling her now was best, only to then realize that long term, it would be the more selfish choice. So I busied my mind with batters and frostings, eager to distract my slipping resolve.

The past several days had been almost surreal to me. Upon leaving the café I arrived at Logan's home where I basked in love and protection. I marveled at his touch and succumbed to his demands.

Our love was far from smiles and flowers for we were consumed by a hurricane of spectacular chaos; forces capable of shattering everything within its path. I loved Logan and I hated him. He manipulated me, used me, punished me; his life was full of anger and deceit; but despite all his darkness, I couldn't ignore the beam of light at his very core.

A beacon which glowed in every vibrant color I couldn't deny myself; for I harbored darkness equal to his own, a force he helped me channel; an entity only he understood. I loved every part of Logan Snow, every damaged and dangerous piece.

Marina had taken off for deliveries and my body now stood before the pantry, though, I couldn't remember why. My mind was somewhere else, a place where Logan's phantom touch was alive and my hunger grew in response. That's what he'd done to me; that's what I'd become.

And then I felt him. That sensation I knew so well and I turned; knowing he'd be standing at the door.

"Logan." My voice waivered.

"That sound…"

I was pinned against the wall.

"…my name upon your lips…"

My arms pulled above my head.

"…it beckons me and I cannot deny you."

I craved him, required him for survival, always running on empty unless captive in his arms.

"What is it you desire, Alice—hmm. Is it this?"

Logan pressed deeper against me and I moaned, openly and unashamed.

"Just you, any part of you. Always you." I spoke breathlessly.

Logan's hold tightened deliciously in reward.

"It does things to me, seeing you lost in the memory of my touch. I'm drunk on it; consumed by you."

His lips connected with my flesh but evaded my mouth— where I needed him most.

"Logan—"

"Shh." Logan pushed us into the pantry and the door sealed us inside. Everything was black with only the coolness of the steel racks to gauge the space. My hands were pinned, my backside bare and all I needed was his touch. I arched my back, my neck open for his trailing mouth.

"Don't make a sound."

*

"To what do I owe your visit?" I asked, now sated.

Logan kissed the back of my neck as he helped straighten my sweater.

"I couldn't help myself."

I closed my eyes and breathed him in.

Logan twirled me to face him; his angular jaw and high cheekbones, his full lips that promised to do unspeakable things. But it was his eyes that went in for the kill. They drew you in hypnotically and you'd go, ever so eagerly chasing the color of endless beauty until you were so far gone, the road back was no longer visible.

Logan Snow was truly a stunning creature, though, it wasn't his polished bone structure I loved; it was the raw man beneath it all which consumed me. The man that wasn't polished, sculpted to perfection or appealing to the eye, and that was the part of him I found the most beautiful.

"Also, I wanted to tell you in person that I spoke with Dr. Williams, Alex's first set of test results are back and she says there's room for optimism. Gabe brought this back, it's for you."

I took the envelope, unsure of what to say. I looked up but Logan's handsome face was blurry.

"Thank you."

Logan brushed his thumb over my lips before placing a kiss to each eyelid.

"You have the most beautiful soul I've ever known. I'm merely along for the ride, my love."

I nodded, unable to say more.

"I'll see you tonight."

"Wait."

Logan paused at the door.

"Any news on Jenna?" I hated to ask, hated that she was on my mind—hated to speak her name at all.

Logan reached for me, his hands cupping my head, his eyes calming me.

"We will. The team is looking at every detail. We know she embedded a false recording into the security system for the time she was in your office. What you saw on surveillance was a duplicate recording from back in August. It will take some time to retrieve the memory that she wrote over. Do you trust me?"

I nodded.

"You're mine, Alice. Nothing will take you, understand?"

"Yes."

Logan kissed me possessively before disappearing just as swiftly as he'd appeared.

Walking into my office I held Alex's letter close to my heart. Almost afraid to read its contents, fearing I may have given the child false hope. I wanted to help him, do everything I could to give him a fighting chance. But the fear of the alternative lingered, and in the end if that's where it all led—

Dear Alice,

Hey! I'm sorry I haven't written in a while. It's been sorta tough the past few months. Everyone's been smothering me with attention and I kinda just wanted to be invisible instead, you know. I was sorta mad that you kept pushing me to go to counseling. I know you weren't pushing-pushing, but it felt that way. Like you didn't want to spend time with me anymore. I know that's not true. I just needed some time to realize it is all.

The last package was awesome. I'm almost done with it. One more component and I'll be finished with my first ever robot. Thanks.

No offence but the orange tart wasn't my favorite. My grandma loved them though so I guess it worked out but next time could you just send me all Gorilla's? Well maybe a couple snails would be nice too.

I couldn't help but laugh.

Phoenix is hot. I guess it would be awesome if there was an ocean but it's just dry here. I like Colorado more. The views are better back home too. Here, there are no mountains. At least they have some weird statues outside to look at.

I met Dr. William's. She's cool. She's into robotics too so it was cool talking to her about the set you gave me.

I finished up my last test today. There's a huge bruise on my left arm from the one yesterday but it's ok, it sorta looks like a mean bear, I took a picture of it. They said that some things are looking better, I dunno. I don't really want to get my hopes up, you know? I guess we'll see. Mom and Dad are smiling though. They're happy about the move. They keep talking about you and I tell them not to but I don't think they get it. And I'm sure I could make them understand if I reeeally talked to them about it but that wasn't our deal so I just remind them when I can.

I met a kid here same age as me. He's been here over eleven months so he's been showing me around, he's cool. His name is Rex. You know like T-Rex the dinosaur. He lets me play his Xbox whenever I want and he has like 50 games! He says they're mostly from his grandma because his mom doesn't want him playing too much but his grandma sneaks him games each time she visits.

Gabe is awesome. I wouldn't mess with him though, he looks like he knows how to handle a rough situation if you know what I mean. When we were packing up and my neighbor was being a jerk and not moving his car so we could pull out of the driveway, Gabe went over to talk to him. I don't know what he did but Jarred came running over saying sorry over and over. He even offered to house sit for my parents, whatever that means. But it was awesome because you could see he was so scared of Gabe which isn't easy to do because Jarred has always been a jerk, like the kind you wish you could send to jail you know, so that was cool.

He said you married that guy you wrote about in your last letter. Congrats. But don't worry I won't tell anyone. Gabe said he trusted me and I don't want him to think I'm a liar, you know.

It's almost dinner time. We're having pizza tonight. It's my favorite because I can choose all my own toppings and they don't say no, no matter what I pick. Last time I even put crackers and caramel popcorn on! But it didn't taste so good so I'll keep searching for the next awesome combination, then maybe I can tell Pizza Hut about it and they could name it after me or something. That would be cool.

So I just wanted to say thanks, you know, for all this. And sorry, you know, for being angry and stuff. I try to work on it, just sometimes it gets hard. But you're like my best friend and I just want you to know that. And I hope this guy is awesome for you. He's lucky you know. I hope one day we can all hang out. That would be really awesome.

Alex

P.S. I decided to give the counseling group a try.

I stared at the letter. Dear God please give this boy a fighting chance.

Chapter Thirty One

Allison Snow

Marina's absence the past several days had been rather bittersweet. The café felt empty without the beam of light that followed her around like an appendage. I would turn to share something only to see a vacant kitchen before turning back to the batter I'd nearly ruined while sulking.

It was past dinner time before I'd left the café tonight and in honor of that trend I showered longer than planned as well. The room was filled with steam and everything appeared to float in the haze, I liked it that way; out of focus. It felt more familiar to me that way.

Such revelations should've alarmed me, or given cause for worry in the least, but it didn't. It was reckless and so I'd chosen to ignore it.

I applied moisturizer over my skin leisurely, knowing Logan was still at his office. He'd been working late every night. Often times I would be asleep before he joined me in bed, not that he'd sleep himself. He was self-destructive in that respect, the same way I was in my own ignorant ways.

"Alice?"

The sound of Lex's voice finally pierced my brain, enough to jolt me back.

"Just a moment."

I grabbed my robe off the hook.

"Hey Lex."

I smiled but it lacked conviction. Lex seemed to notice.

"Will you dine with me?"

Lex looked so hopeful. She'd asked every night and each time I'd declined. I lacked appetite, I lacked anything really other than Logan's arms around me. It was the only place I felt whole—real. It was unhealthy—even destructive, but so was everything else that bound us.

"Thanks Lex, I'm just a bit tired."

Lex reached out, taking my hand in hers and I felt the genuine heart of the woman.

"How about a cup of tea then? Just for a few moments, then you may rest."

I meant to decline but my head nodded yes instead.

"I'll dress and see you downstairs."

Lex smiled before closing the door behind her and I simply stood motionless for some time.

"There you are. The tea's fresh, come sit down."

I took my usual seat while Lex claimed the seat across from mine. I sipped my tea, fresh raspberries floating leisurely; infusing my beverage with all the scents that reminded me of a time I longed for but would never re-live.

"Anything exciting happen at the café today?" Lex asked.

I thought for a moment, filtering out all the negative events, wanting something positive to share.

"A group of teenage girls came in today all dolled up and happy. I think they were waiting for their show time at the theater so they needed a warm place to kick back for a bit."

Lex smiled, she had three girls after all.

"Each girl was polite and friendly, so beautiful and happy with life. They were full of smiles and giggled a lot. But it wasn't obnoxious, more like—joy I think. Like a carefree night out with the girls, nothing more nothing less."

I twirled my china cup of tea smiling as I remembered the scene.

"But it was the last girl who stood out."

"How so?"

"She was sweet and pretty just like the rest but when it came time to pay for her order of under five dollars she handed

Trish a twenty and said 'If it's okay, would you keep the difference and surprise the next customer to a free order?' and she genuinely looked unsure as though we might actually deny her such goodwill. It took me back as I watched her, how simple and generous she was for no other reason or gain than for the sake of kindness itself. And she was a teenager mind you, that seems to be quite rare."

"That is indeed lovely, though, I get a sense that you see this girl's actions as somehow different from your own acts of goodwill and I'm wondering why?"

I wouldn't normally talk about such things. But with Lex I felt somehow smaller, she had a Motherly effect on me and I couldn't deny how much I liked it.

"The girl's goodwill was pure, no alternate intensions, no need for glory or recognition. She did it for the simple reason of spreading kindness."

Lex's brows drew closer.

"I'm not sure I understand? You too don't advertise your acts of kindness, you seek no recognition and avoid others from ever finding out. How is that different?"

Because I wasn't innocent.

"For me—it's a form of penance."

My voice was smaller than I'd wished for. I didn't want to look up.

Lex stood, leaving me alone before returning several moments later with a fresh crepe filled with strawberries and blueberries topped with whipped cream.

The corner of my mouth rose at how well she'd come to know me in such a short amount of time. Sugar was my go to medicine, I knew enough to know it was mostly due to the psychological connection to my mother more than the food itself. It was a rare occasion that we'd get to sneak ourselves something sweet while preparing the meals. But in the end what did it matter? It was my vice and that was a fact.

I lifted the fork in silent acceptance of her offering and Lex rejoined me at the table.

"I'm in the second half of my life, Alice. I've lived happy times and I've had my share of tragedy as well. Yet with all the years I have on you, I couldn't hold a candle to what you've had to endure. To me, your desire for goodwill unto others is not born of guilt but a testament to the woman you've chosen to be despite the great injustice you've suffered from the day of your very birth. To me, you're more beautiful than the teenage girl; for you've seen the world's most wicked and still advocate love and peace. To me, that's the very *definition* of kindness."

*

I awoke to the sound of the door closing. Logan's arms wrapped tightly around me and I nestled into his freshly showered scent; his skin warm and still damp. I laid my head upon his chest where I loved to listen to the rhythm of his heart. It serenaded me, more beautiful than any instrument or voice. It beat with life and hope and all the dreams I dared to dream.

"You okay?" I asked quietly, unsure if he'd answer.

Logan's hand rested at my head, periodically threading through my hair over and over. With each night he seemed more distant—determined.

"I'm sorry to have woken you, but I needed to hear your voice; it calms me."

I let my question go unanswered.

We laid for a long while in silence, and without lifting my head I knew Logan hadn't fallen asleep; his arms holding me protectively—as though I'd slip away.

"How were you able to forgive Seth for what he did?"

The question startled me.

"Because in many ways he too was a victim of my grandfather."

Logan's heart beat quickened.

"What does that mean, Alice? I need to understand."

"Seth was sold to my grandfather as payment for his parents' gambling debt. He was six. Around twelve The Brotherhood let him go, said the debt was paid."

"So he was free and he chose to come back out of free will?"

"My grandfather saw potential in Seth, he had a good head, one my grandfather wished to mold for himself, but he knew so long as Seth was held against his will there would always be a barrier. My grandfather let Seth leave knowing beforehand that Seth's parents had already overdosed on their latest score. Seth searched them out only to find the decomposed bodies of the two people who cared more about their addiction than their own son; so Seth had two options, sell his body for sex or come back to The Brotherhood. For there was no alternative in his circumstances. Ily knew he'd come back and welcomed him with open arms. Seth was but a kid, he was brainwashed with every opportunity at his feet so long as he remained loyal."

"What was different for him that night?" Logan's voice was low and almost tentative, something I hadn't witnessed in him till now.

"You'll have to ask him."

"I'm asking *you*."

That first year was a treacherous journey for Seth and me, one I doubted we'd complete.

"We didn't speak about that night openly. It was a wound too deep for me and after time I'd come to realize it was one for him as well. After several years passed I'd gained the courage and finally confronted him. He said his life never offered him choices, he was a slave and he'd come to terms with that reality and decided he'd make the most of what hand life had dealt him. He never wanted to be there that night, he wouldn't risk interfering but tried to find another to take his place instead. It didn't work. It was his final test, the prize; a permanent seat at Ily's right side." My voice caught as Seth's words rang clearly in my memory.

"Seth said it was the look on my mother's face as the knife pierced her heart. She chose to be a slave to her own father for the sake of the truth within her soul. It cost her everything but it was a choice, and it was hers. Seth realized in that moment he had one too. Be a monster, or die with a conscience."

My eyes burned with the image of Mama on the floor. A knife to the heart wasn't the sole wound she'd endured. Boris had a signature, he enjoyed the feel of his blade cutting through flesh. The heart was the last wound, the one she couldn't survive.

"What does L.S. Trade Co. do—off the record?" I asked.

Logan's hold tightened and I relaxed into it.

"Another time."

"I'm not asking."

A heavy pause moved over us. I realized I was holding my breath, hating that it affected me so.

"Currency mostly, insurance and—weaponry."

"Your—deals, they're not all legitimate."

"If by legitimate you mean ethical, then no."

"Does it bother you?"

I was tense, Logan sensed it. I wish I wasn't but I couldn't stop the hypocritical anxiety when my own alias was funded by stolen money.

Logan blew out a breath, in no rush to respond.

"Before you, none of it mattered. Before you, I never planned to survive this war. Before you, only one thing mattered: killing the King. That meant money, connections, and influence. There are few ways to get where I am, and most take time with a heavy dose of luck. I had neither. Within these circles we all know we're dirty; whether by accepting payoffs, investments based on fixed markets, sending soldiers to their death so long as the weapons factories continue to operate in the name of national safety; take your pick."

"How do you keep it from your staff?"

"The currency trade is as you say, legitimate. That's what they know. The investments made with such gained funds is where the trail stops. I have a small team I trust which handles various stations of the operation, L.S. Trade Co. in truth is simply a shiny sign for the public and government bureaus."

"Gabe is on that team."

"Yes."

"You two seem to have a bond of sorts."

"I suppose."

"Tell me about your parents."

Silence.

"You said until me you didn't care, does that mean you're going to stop the—other operations?"

"No."

I was silent.

"I would give it all up for you, Alice. In a heartbeat I would live in a tiny home with a picket fence and kids swings and toys littering the yard and I would be happier than I've ever been."

There was a but.

"What good does that picket fence and lot of toys do me if you're not there beside me? Without you, I'm bankrupt."

It took money from corrupt deals to fund my safety.

How fitting.

"What did your father do with Sam?"

"Get some rest, my Love. I would like to share breakfast with you in the morning."

I laid a long time, hours it seemed in silence. Logan's mind was somewhere I couldn't reach, a place he wouldn't share, a place he punished himself.

So I took solace in the presence of his heartbeat, beating reliably, for I was desolate without it.

*

We shared breakfast after Logan loved me in the shower. I hadn't realized how much I needed his touch until wrapped within him. It wasn't a physical need, though I never tired to have it, but rather the connection of the heart; the invisible twine which wove beautifully between us providing me nourishment and reassurance that we were real—surviving.

I felt weighted with several cubic tons of unanswered question, inquiries continuously evaded or blatantly ignored; yet despite the opposition, my desire to catch a glimpse at the man he was or the boy he'd been a distant time ago burned steady and strong.

I was bursting with memories of his young life, memories fabricated by my own eager imagination. I pictured his mother reading to a vibrant boy at bedtime, books with colorful animals that the boy pointed to, doing his best to pronounce giraffe in-between giggles. If I closed my eyes I could almost smell the birthday cake his mother baked for his ninth birthday, it was chocolate and the frosting was extra thick; just the way the boy liked. I saw him standing tall and confident with a young girl dressed lovely for prom while his parents insisted on one *last* picture. I craved to share in his memories of happiness, his times of joy in a home full of love. I needed to know if what I saw every time our eyes met was true, or was it too a mere fabrication of my desperate mind?

But as consecutive minutes ticked away during our silent breakfast, my continued hesitation to broach such things only widened the divide, and not long after, Logan departed. Leaving me to do the same.

The café greeted me with its familiar scent of warmth and dough. Today I would begin on Marina's wedding cake. I had four days to complete my ambitious design.

Rachel officially joined the team two days ago. She needed guidance but the regulars warmed to her quickly. I was relieved, grateful, and irritated for not firing Jenna sooner.

"Hey, Alice?"

"Yeah. You need something?"

"Um, there's a guy, Dan I think? He asked to speak with you."

Rachel was still tentative.

My smile was easy and quick to form.

"I'll just be a moment."

Rachel rushed out front as I laid five fresh peony petals to dry before following suit.

"Daniel! It's wonderful to see you."

Daniel opened his arms and I accepted his welcome embrace.

"It's great to see you too. Wait there's something different about you."

"Really?"

I must've looked puzzled as Daniel continued to scrutinize my appearance.

"Hmm, I don't know what it is, you just seem different somehow."

I shrugged indifference. I wasn't about to divulge unnecessary information.

"So what brings you to my neck of the woods? Need a sugar high?"

Daniel's eyes lit kindly, highlighting wrinkles that came with two small children.

"That's a given. But actually I wanted to drop by and tell you that it seems everything's worked out with Sarah."

"How so?"

"About a week ago we'd received an application for financial assistance from a private donor. We never thought we'd qualify but it appears we'd been granted full coverage for Sarah's home care with no time limit on her recovery."

Daniel's eyes glistened as he fought to keep composure.

"I'm so happy for you—for Sarah. Your family deserves it."

And then Daniel *really* looked at me and I knew he'd figured it out, though, he said nothing, and I appreciated his restraint.

We stood in a comfortable silence, sharing a secret no one needed to hear. Sarah deserved to be around her loved ones, even if she wasn't ready to join them herself—yet.

Soon Daniel hugged me goodbye and in thanks; but it was *I* who'd always be thankful to Sarah for that fateful collision.

Chapter Thirty Two

Allison Snow

Everything was in full bloom and I was fairly certain that I was standing on the edge of utter enchantment. Funny thing was—I didn't remember discussing any of it with Mrs. Frank.

"Mrs. Frank!"

I nearly broke out into a run to catch up with the woman.

"Mrs. Frank, hi."

She seemed puzzled.

"It's, Alice."

"Ah, yes, Alice. Of course, how could I forget such a sweet smile?"

"That's very kind. I hope you don't mind me asking, I mean what you've done is just unbelievable, truly, but I don't remember discussing all this."

I waved my hand towards the isles of eight foot columns made of flowers and the canopy of living beauty above the atrium or the floral mural that had to be no less than ten feet by ten feet at the altar. It was all so breathtaking and—unexpected.

"Yes, we discussed all of this."

I didn't want to offend the elderly woman, she clearly worked magic with flowers but I knew for a fact no such conversations took place.

"Here, you look through this while I go teach that thick-fingered colly-wobble of a man how to properly thread an orchid before he destroys any more of my creations!"

Mrs. Frank bolted towards the eye-catching mural where the older man who I assumed was Mr. Frank noticed her coming and ran off in the opposite direction.

Looking through the event file seemed to clarify all my questions. Every form had the signature of Ellanore Brant: Logan's event planner. Was I really surprised?

The Genesee Estate was bustling with activity as tables and chairs were erected with welcoming fabrics, and cushions laced with silk. Lights mimicking the midnight sky had manifested as though from thin air leaving you searching the artificial sky, certain a shooting star was within reach. The courtyard had been transformed into a space both inviting and warm despite all the surrounding snow.

I was taken aback, momentarily lost, but in the most pleasant of ways. I could never have given Seth and Marina this, but Logan spared no expense or resource, and no string of words could ever convey what his generosity towards those dearest to me meant.

"Mrs. Snow"

I gave Gabe my most practiced look of disapproval.

"It's a necessary formality." Gabe quickly replied.

"One I've insisted we drop." I shot back.

I wasn't going to win. I knew Logan enjoyed those he employed addressing me by his name.

"Everything's been arranged upstairs, the itinerary: on your bedside table. Brooks, Parker and King are on duty tonight."

Gabe was a complex individual. His loyalty to Logan was unquestionable and almost chilling, yet with it I found a sense of comfort. The man was intimidating and stone-like, and it wasn't difficult to deduce that for him to be such, was quite coldly—a necessity. Marina had begun to refer to him as Logan's Gargoyle and though she meant it in good humor, I had to admit there was some truth to her comedy.

"Thanks, Gabe. Good night."

I'd become accustomed to his curt nod, so when Gabe placed his palm upon my shoulder more gently than I would've ever imagined him capable of, I was unprepared. Gabe was gone within moments; leaving behind the itching feeling that his uncharacteristic behavior had a cause better left unspoken.

I left the bustling atrium for the privacy of my suite. I'd been working on a special gift for Marina, something I hoped would bring her fulfillment in a part of her heart she was robbed of. I set up my laptop and inserted the flash drive, making certain everything was ready to go.

It was.

I made my way to the windows where the earth was always calling and the sky ever-alluring. I marveled at the high snowcapped peaks, covered by a heavy fog, and the darkness of night. It was a sky that only the bravest of birds would dare take flight; whose wings spanned larger than my own human frame and whose mind was always that of a predator.

"Mrs. Snow, the last of the crew has left and all exits have been secured. The codes have been changed as scheduled. Will you be taking your dinner in the dining area or your rooms?"

"Brooks, right?"

"Yes, Ma'am."

"Please call me, Alice, I insist. At least for tonight." I remained professional while internally begging he give me this request, for he would otherwise reveal to Marina the secret I'd tried so hard to keep hidden.

"As you request."

"Thanks, Brooks. We'll have dinner in here tonight, send her up when she arrives."

"Done."

As though my earlier thoughts had been broadcast across the inky sky a snow owl began to circle an unfortunate prey that was moments from death. I watched the creature: terrifying, yet still beautiful, and wondered how that could be? Despite knowing the inevitable my heart broke as the owl shot down like a missile, quick, precise; before declaring victory with a high pitched call that echoed as it wove in and over the vista of pines.

The sound of rule.

I watched, angry that I found the creature so alluring and magnificent. For the owl was exotic, and its prey—small, grey, and only a rodent after all. For when we saw mice we screamed with horror, set out poison and contraptions to rid ourselves of such pests, then with the same breath purchased high resolution binoculars and elaborate books, only to sit for hours on end in hopes of catching a glimpse of a creature as marvelous as the snow owl. A beautiful and powerful specimen, not dull and overpopulated.

Not prey.

I was prey. I would always be prey, and yet I couldn't help but be wrapped up in all that was the owl. So was it so difficult to see why humans mimicked such rankings even amongst themselves? The exotic and the powerful could get away with murder, and though most wouldn't admit it, we all knew they did. But we watched because watching beautiful things—

"I'm dreaming aren't I?"

I startled, not hearing her approach, though, I doubt she noticed.

"I know, it's beautiful."

"Somehow my small and speedy wedding isn't feeling so small and speedy. The place looks like it'd been meticulously planned for months if not longer. And the mural—I had to touch it or I'd never have believed it was all real."

Marina seemed reserved. Like it was all beginning to sink in, only she was unprepared to react accordingly. I think I understood why. She felt something was missing.

"It's all for you, Sunshine. Accept it, embrace it, because days such as this don't come around often no matter how much we may try to make them. There's something unique in their makeup, some element not accessible to us, controlled only by the mysterious and celestial. But every so often Heaven gifts us days like this, and this one, Sunshine, is all for you."

She embraced me, giddy and even nervous; understandably so.

"Settle in my dearest. Dinner will be up in a bit and we've got all night to do—whatever it is you're supposed to do!"

"It's happening, right Alice? I mean it's really happening?"

"It is."

I smiled at her, saying nothing more.

Marina got settled in, and I could hear her snapping dozens of photos.

"You about done in there?"

How long does it take to put on pajamas?

"Don't rush me! I'm the bride remember?"

I laughed while setting the makeshift table.

"Oh, Brooks, that smells so good!"

"Compliments of Lex Mrs.—Alice."

I silently thanked him for catching himself.

"Well why on earth would she not join us? I'll go call her."

Brooks put his hand out.

"I'm afraid Lex has already left, she felt this was an intimate affair and didn't wish to intrude."

"That's Lex—always thoughtful."

Brooks said nothing.

"Have you eaten?" I asked him and he looked surprised.

"Yes. Thank you for inquiring, Alice."

"Of course. Have a good night, Brooks."

With a final nod he left to resume his post.

The meal never disappointed. Lex was like a wizard, everything she touched hugged you and brought with it only the most pleasant of feelings.

"Oh that smells divine."

Marina had on her rubber ducky pajamas with her curls barely contained in a loose braid. She plopped down on the floor cushion with a thump before rubbing her hands together like you would at the age of five on Christmas morning.

"Sooo it looks like Lex is definitely my new best friend."

After capturing her first morsel of Chicken Alfredo, Marina let out a loud Mmmm.

"Yep. It's confirmed. Lex wins."

"Well, boo hoo for you because your new best friend lives at my boyfriend's house, hence I'll see her way more than you!"

Marina shot me what I could only describe as a crooked stink-eye before shoving a large fork full of Alfredo into her mouth and smacking her lips sarcastically.

"This pasta's homemade."

"The parmesan breadsticks are homemade too." I added.

"Do we know what's for dessert?"

I lifted the remaining two lids to find two servings of apple blossoms still warm from the oven, and two pints of vanilla ice cream nestled snug in an ice bucket.

"Well, since I'm the bride and I get to make the rules, I decide—I want both our deserts."

Marina reached for the tray eagerly.

"Ha! Nice try. I'd love to see what kind of bride you'll be once you're missing hair on half your head!"

"You so much as go near—"

Before she had time to catch on, I snatched one blossom and licked everything my tongue could slither across in those vital seconds.

"I see you've taken up marking your territory now, that's very canine of you."

It was my turn to shoot off a stink-eye before globing on the ice cream and going to town.

Marina wasn't far behind. We savored every bite for it was worth its weight in puppies. The mess of tableware before us seemed excessive, even to my food-gorged vision, but I couldn't bring myself to care. Tonight I would be carefree and lay my obsessive-compulsive-cleaning-complex to rest—well, for a little while.

"You're crazy, you know that."

We were making noises, laughing, groaning; a hiccup snuck in I think. The only certainty was that there was noise and plenty of it.

"Wow, that's news. You threaten to shave off half my hair the night before my wedding, over an apple blossom no less, and *I'm* the crazy one?! That's rich."

The noise level rose, as did the pain in my side from excessive laughter, and before long we laid like overcooked noodles on the floor, releasing an occasional snicker or snort, or perhaps it was something else and I just simply wasn't coherent enough for it to register. None of it mattered. We were happy.

Stupid and happy.

"Are you going to clean up or what?"

A bread chunk bounced off my nose and I smiled; too lazy to retaliate. With unladylike grunting I rose to my feet and began to pile everything as neatly as allowed back onto the tray. Begrudgingly Marina pitched in, her theatrics in full swing as she used the chaise to aid her in standing upright.

Upon my return from the kitchen I found Marina gazing towards the cosmic-coat outside, as I'd done moments before her arrival. No doubt her mind was equally as distant.

"I prepared something for you."

She turned and the smile decorating her lovely features was no longer as carefree as moments ago.

"You mean, on top of basically throwing me the wedding of my dreams and organizing this night for just us when I know for a fact both Logan and Seth gave you hell for it, oh and covering for me while I ditched all my work duties this past week—on top of all that, you got me something?"

"No, I *prepared* something." I corrected.

Her brows drew together with intrigue.

"You have to sit down though."

The atmosphere of the room shifted, tighter; more meaningful. Marina approached the chair in the corner tentatively, nervous and uncertain. I wondered if she sensed it.

I dimmed the lights to near blackness before hitting several strokes on my laptop which was set to the side.

The projector came to life and Marina was suddenly looking at her mother as the first home video clip played over the screen.

It was Luke's birthday, his cake had a giant number two smack in the center, and after several attempts Gwen bent over to assist her son in blowing out his candle; her hand wrapped protectively around her belly where the future Marina was months from entering the world.

Next, a baby girl wrapped in a pink blanket with white flowers laid snug in her mother's arms, Gwen turned to the camera happy and full of wonder before kissing her newborn daughters forehead

Then, there's a monstrosity of an evergreen taking up most of what was supposed to be a family room, a bright star at its peak and two small children running about, believing they're helping decorate the tree. As they ran around, globs of tinsel were transferred from box to tree, tree to pajama bottom, pajama bottom to rug, and soon the culprit with curly locks was snatched up by slim but loving arms before kisses and giggles filled the room. The camera captured it all; a Mother's love, her embrace, her laugh—for all of time.

Two more clips played before my blurred vision, before the final segment began. The screen stilled on a beautiful close up of Gwen, her eyes slightly squinted from laughing, her smile—radiant, her hands—locked tightly around a six year old curly-haired-wiggle-worm, the park swings and slide still visible behind them.

"My most treasured daughter, my joy, my hope, my heart. I've missed you and do so every moment of every day. No words can express the stunning woman you've become both visually, but mostly at heart. I morn each day that's been taken from us and take solace in witnessing your gracious success's and even the bitter failures which have molded and shaped you into someone extraordinary; and every bit the miracle I saw the first time I looked into your baby-green eyes. Tomorrow you will marry the man of your heart, a man I've come to love if only because he's loved by you, and nothing would please me more than to hold you right now, hug you tight, kiss your head, and share with you all the wisdom a Mother would on such an occasion. But I will settle for watching you from afar, when you feel a cool breeze as you walk down that isle, that's me; I'll be with you. No Mother could be prouder than I for there's no other that holds your place in my heart. Smile my love, laugh, dance, and embrace every gift this life offers. Be happy, Marina; be you."

The screen went dark, the room; still. The space was filled with only one thing: grieving. I leaned back as Marina's head laid on my lap soaking my pajamas with tears as I stroked her head with every effort of not breaking down myself. The audio recording was performed by Marina's aunt Chloe, I was told her voice most resembled Gwen's, and the speech—written by my heart.

Perhaps it was terrible of me, but while I watched the video and audio recording I'd created, I imagined my own mama. I imagined she would've said similar things to me, I imagined that in the times when I was alone, it was my mama drifting beside me along the cool breeze.

Marina said nothing before drifting off to sleep as I continued to stroke her head lovingly, hoping I'd done the right thing, before eventually letting my dreams claim me as well.

Chapter Thirty Three

Logan Snow

"You're certain?"

"Intel is good on this. Seems Seth's concerns had merit. If Pyotar knew about Colorado that would explain why a high level blood would be stationed here."

"I want the team on this now. Seth, brief the group on the target. Everything you remember about him. The kind of women he liked, food he ate, liquor he drank. Find out every last detail of his routine. The route he takes to the factory, where he pumps gas—internet activity."

"Done."

"What do we know about how they're finding their victims?"

"High level profiling. Each victim had flags when we ran them through the networks. They're using an algorithm to search factors such as race, age, origin, hair color etc. Like a fingerprint if there is a strong enough match they set up an abduction. Each victim is taken while alone. Either late at night, in route to work...leaving the gym."

Greg recited the information diligently. A good man. Wise to have left the force. His talents were better suited elsewhere.

"They must realize soon enough that the girl isn't Nadia, yet they kill her anyway." Luke seemed to say this almost like a question.

"Because for The Brotherhood, there's no alternative. Have you noticed any difference between the first victim and the fourth?" I asked him.

"Yes. Severity."

Nice to know Luke was paying attention after all. With all the cold-as-stone looks he'd been sending my way I was beginning to wonder if there was anything else on his mind aside from his hands around my neck.

"Exactly. They're growing impatient. What do you think they'll do if they find the real Nadia?" I felt sick as the words left my mouth.

"The paper trail for the identities of Seth and Allison Red originated in America, nationality shows American. This I believe has kept them from finding you through the algorithm. Physical resemblance however—that's an issue."

I appeared calm as I spoke to the group, but it was in appearance only.

"Greg, we need to find out what ports were causing the flags on the victim's files. There will more than likely be more than one tracker. We need to find how they're connected, who the filter is. It will be someone high level. Most likely with reaches into the weaponry niche and more than likely, Politics. The Brotherhood wouldn't have access to such files without a facilitator or a mole. We need to know what we're dealing with first, then draw a new plan."

I was speaking a million miles a minute and yet it wasn't fast enough. Every second that ticked by felt wasted.

Everyone nodded dutifully. Greg moved almost robotically: a Father nearing his breaking point. Luke followed. Seth stayed back. Dutifully waiting until we were alone.

"You make contact?"

Seth schooled his features. He was marrying the woman he loved in less than twenty four hours. His reality was crumbling beneath his feet.

"We'll receive confirmation via messenger. Crow didn't say how."

Seth sounded almost unsure. Untrusting. He ought to know better. If I gave him a contact. He can be damn sure it's a good one.

"He wouldn't. But the message will come. When it's ready. It will come."

Chapter Thirty Four

Allison Snow

"Where is she?!"

The room shook as three outspoken, overbearing, and loving aunts filled the suite.

"Oh darling, aren't you just a sight for sore eyes."

Aunt Chloe led the pack as they hugged and kissed their niece with every bit of love you'd expect from a southern bunch.

Buckets full.

"I'm so glad y'all made it."

"We'd have come sooner if it weren't for them wretched weather delays. Those airplane people had us shuffled here then there for what seemed like days. By four o'clock this morning we were certain we'd never make it and poor Beth was in tears by then."

"So how are you here then?"

"Some fancy looking man approached us. Called us by name and said he was there to rescue us and get us to your weddin. Like an Angel from Heaven he settled us into a jet and before we knew it, we'd arrived!"

Marina looked at me with a knowing smile. Logan saw to every detail.

"Now let us get a good look at you before we go sneaking them hors d'oeuvre's that look so darn tasty downstairs. This place is fancy, how on earth did you secure such a thing on your timeline?"

Aunt Beth 'Mmm Hmmed' in support to Aunt Chloe's question, while Aunt Clair walked the suite, gliding her fingers over the furniture as though shopping.

"I'll tell you all about it later, right now I must get dressed but I'll see you after okay?"

"Oh must we already—"

They looked comically reluctant before complying.

"I suppose we better get ourselves some good seats before they're all gone."

Marina's head was peppered with kisses while I watched from a safe distance, waving politely as they shuffled out the door.

"You ready?"

Marina met my eyes in the mirror and lowered her head. My hands trembled as I parted her hair. I'd studied every childhood photograph of Marina in pigtails; memorized every detail in the hopes that I could complete the request with as much accuracy as possible. With the elastic bands in place I pulled the wooden box where the ribbon awaited. The ivory silk had rhinestones delicately woven into the edges of each ribbon that caught the light with an elaborate effect. With slow movements I tied each ribbon into its proper place before standing back, allowing Marina all the time she needed before raising her head and finally, opening her eyes.

She was perfect.

"I'm ready."

The glass clock agreed with her. This was it.

I handed her a bouquet of delicate white tulips completing her ensemble, and headed for the door where I knew Dad would be waiting.

The dress Marina had chosen for me was not a look I was comfortable with, not that it wasn't stunning with its flowing skirt and low neckline to better compliment the dazzling pendant I was wearing; it was every bit the beautiful she swore it was when she'd placed it before me this morning.

It was alien and even bizarre to glimpse my elegant reflection in the mirror. My attire had created a mirage of splendor and magnificence which didn't belong to me, and to borrow it felt—forbidden.

I said nothing. With a smile I returned my personally chosen pale seashell long-sleeved dress to its hanger and did what any good friend would've done. Sucked it up and went with it, no questions asked.

With our heels nearing the door Marina stopped before me. "I need to say something."

She had my attention.

"I love you."

"I love you too." I responded.

I must've looked a bit perplexed, this wasn't something new and yet she almost said it as though it was supposed to be.

"No, you misunderstood me. I love you, Alice; because you're lovable. I love you because you're beautiful and kind and selfless and I love you because people who've known me my entire life, who are supposed to know me better than anyone else, whom I've shared a dozen more years of friendship with then you; none of them, *not one* would've given me what you've given me. When you love, Alice, you love purely because what you did for me last night, what you prepared for me was a product of genuine and selfless love, and if I could give you even a tenth of what you gave me it would be to demand you abandon your self-hatred and finally take in your true reflection."

"The dress—the gems—" I understood now.

"Logan helped." She added.

Of course.

"I wanted no one else by my side on this day, so as you walk past the crowd, see what they see; what I see."

Marina didn't give me time to respond as her hand swiftly pulled back the door where she hooked her arm through Dad's and headed down the hall.

*

The seventy eight chairs which had been meticulously positioned and fitted with silk now housed bodies of both the eager and anxious. I was surprisingly pleased to see Marina had in fact decided to invite Steph, Trish, Stacey, and Andrew.

Part of me wanted them to celebrate with us while another part couldn't ignore the rationalization that this entire arrangement had to be the most bizarre and flat out asinine affair. I was maid of honor to my best friend who was marrying my ex-husband, even Hollywood would steer clear of such a laughable idea. As such I kept my mouth shut on the matter, and yet seeing their faces warmed me.

With the music cued I began my swayed steps towards the magnificent mural, serving as the altar. The room was full and every guest turned to watch the pretense to the bride, but I, I only saw one man. He stood in the shadows of the west corridor, his tailored tux as dark as his gaze and his hands; obstructed from view, meaning only one thing, and it was a sobering thought.

As I made my way up the steps I turned to face the crowd. The stunning bride was now making her way towards a worthy man, she was smiling and glowing, yet I couldn't take it all in as intended; my heart, my pulse, every thought and every fiber of my being was tuned into the shadow whose possessive stare penetrated my being wholly.

"I, Gregory Meyer, am the proud Father of an angel. A baby girl who's never let her father forget what true love is; a love that transcends tragedy and heartache and still brings joy to my soul. I have entrusted you, Seth. Love my baby girl the way she was meant to be loved."

Tissues were being handed from one guest to another, each wiping away the evidence of emotion.

Seth hugged Dad, an embrace not common for such men—an exchange of bond and promise. Dad kissed his baby girl with all the love a Father could ever contain; a tear slid down his cheek and Dad made no attempt to conceal it.

Seth held out his hand and Dad stepped forever aside as the glowing bride willing placed her hand in Seth's, and approached the Reverend with unconcealed devotion.

While the Reverend began his opening speech, my mind returned to Logan only to notice him looking elsewhere. Training my sights to find his interest landed me upon Andrew's saddened gaze. As our eyes met, his lit instantly and he smiled. He made no attempt to look away or pretend he'd been staring at someone or something behind me; his heart was open and he smiled easily. I had no other reaction but to smile in return, for a gentle spirit like Andrew's was impossible to be impassive to.

Since the day I'd fired Jenna and refused to tell Andrew more than the surface-lie meant to pacify the staff; things had been tense. As he smiled at me now, I hoped it meant he'd found a way to understand that not everything was *understandable*.

"Every little girl dreams of finding true love, at least that's what I thought when I spent hours upon days dreaming of what true love would look like for me."

I was drawn back to the altar as the audience laughed along with the couple.

"To say that I was taken by surprise would be a great injustice to what you so eloquently did to my world from our first hello, to our first kiss, to the first time you said you loved me. I was captivated and the sun no longer warmed my skin unless I knew you'd be there alongside me to share its rays."

The guests waited patiently as Marina pulled herself together.

"Love isn't what I'd pictured it to be as a child or young girl or even a young adult. Love isn't rainbows with unicorns trotting about while glitter floats freely from the open sky in brilliant hues, and love isn't predicable—it's explosive, chaotic, unrelenting, and even all consuming. Love demands you risk it all and hold nothing back, it offers no safe route and no alternative, and as crazy as it sounds, I've never been happier than now. I'm all in Seth Red, for I've surrendered myself to you and seek no escape from this path that's uniquely ours— wherever it may lead."

The Reverend had no understanding of what just transpired. He smiled politely along with the majority of the attendants unable to conceal their looks of oddity regarding Marina's unusual vow. Though, Marina was none the wiser, her eyes were fixed only on Seth and in the end, that's all that mattered.

"From as early as my toddler years I was instructed that love was nothing more than a weakness, a disease that needed curing by any measure. By age nine I'd become certain that this was true. And somewhere around age twelve I'd decided love was but a cruel myth, for the world we lived in wasn't capable of such things to begin with."

Seth stepped closer taking Marina's face in his palms, wiping away her tears with his thumb.

"I don't pretend to understand, to know what this is, how it's made, or why something so wondrous would allow someone like me—to touch it."

Seth kissed Marina's forehead and not a single person in the room took a breath.

"Upon meeting you Marina Katherine Meyer, a new world was born, a new existence, a new beginning, and a new yearning to dream. I will not love you until my last breath for even death couldn't stop me from that which has bound me to you. I'm forever your faithful so let tomorrow come—and pass."

Seth kissed Marina's trembling lips and not a single beating heart within the room was immune to the display before them. The Reverend waited respectfully as the couple finished their exchange. Seth's mouth resumed its post at Marina's forehead while her arms remained wrapped around Seth.

"Over the last two decades I've joined over three hundred couples in the sacramental union that is marriage. And though I've witnessed many things—to see firsthand two individuals who are truly devoted to the other down to the very core of their being with no pretenses, no conditions, and absolutely no limitations; *that*, is a refreshing and memorable first for me. May we please have the rings?"

Luke padded the breast pocket of his crisp black tux before reaching inside and producing two bands made of platinum, but it was the sentiment they represented which made them priceless. Luke clapped Seth's shoulder as he handed him his baby sister's wedding band before stepping back to watch.

My pulse was erratic as my heart beat wildly, though, not from the continued exchange of the bride and groom.
Fifty feet of floor, chairs, people and flowers stood between us, but such things meant nothing. Logan lived within me, his presence was always potent and never second place. Logan didn't make a point of all the resources and countless hours he'd dedicated in ensuring this wedding commenced without a single glitch. He'd screened every attendant, every tradesman and woman that touched the property line. He'd instructed Ellanore to create something spectacular, for the simple reason that it meant so much to me.

Logan never made me chose, though, I knew his relationship with Seth was nothing more than tolerant, on both sides. I was his devoted and yet he never took advantage, not once treating me as property or even making me feel indebted for all he'd done.

As the couple embraced one another in the final kiss to the delight of their audience, the man who created the event or made it safe enough to happen at all stood in the shadows with no demand for glory, when his efforts deserved nothing less.

As Logan's gaze stormed passionately, I let him know I understood. He would've given me the world if I'd asked. But we both knew it wasn't what I wanted. I wanted Marina to have her dream wedding, an event as beautiful as she, and Logan gave me that. Neither diamond nor parcel of land could've carried through his love more clearly.

The crowd erupted in applause as the music cued, and the couple made their way down the aisle. I threaded my arm through Luke's and began down the steps in tempo with the piano.

"Thank you."

Luke looked at me solemnly.

"I'd say you're welcome but I'm not the one to thank. You know that, Luke."

"I know you're married, Alice."

My eyes shot back to his.

"Thank you for letting Marina have this when you deserved it yourself."

My pace slowed, Luke's followed.

"What Logan and I have isn't orthodox—in any form. I wanted Marina to have this and Logan made it happen without reservation. Make peace with him, Luke—because Logan is *my* forever."

I searched Luke's gaze wishing for him to see the depth of my request. He placed a hand over mine and smiled just enough to say he understood before we both set out to mingle with the celebratory crowd.

The room was filled with laughter and merriment. Platters floated throughout with caviar and truffles and too many varieties to count of deliciousness, meticulously prepared for each set of greedy fingers which grabbed at them. And with several memorable photos captured, I was free to step away and catch a breath.

The bar was busy so I waited a moment for an opening before stepping up.

"Sparkling water please, with lemon if you would."

"Yes, Ma'am."

The chill hit my throat with a soothing effect as I stood back to watch from the sidelines. Dad waved at me and I waved back smiling before he excused himself from the clutches of his sister's-in-law and made his way over.

"Have I told you how beautiful you are?"

"Thanks, Dad. It's the dress—and the jewels, they sort of won't let me blend in, you know?"

I joked while swaying my hips as though twirling my dress like a little girl playing dress up.

Dad hugged me before whispering into me ear.

"I wasn't talking about your dress."

He pulled away and placed a sweet kiss to my cheek.

"I love you, Alice, as though you were my own."

"I know, Dad. I know."

I drew Dad back into a hug, willing the tears to retreat. And after dabbing at my face with more effort than should've been necessary I cut our moment short and excused myself to use the powder room.

The faucet ran with cool water to splash over my face, being careful enough not to damage the mascara I applied for the sake of the occasion. As I met my own refection, I paused.

While dressing earlier I avoided the mirror at every turn for a multitude of reasons, the main culprit being that I simply liked it too much; and that hurt. The silk hugged my generous curves almost too well and though I'd searched the length of my body to find something to hate about the gown, I came up empty.

This was the most beautiful I'd ever been and I should've been thrilled and confident, perhaps even a bit conceded. But something that should've brought me happiness brought with it grief instead because I'd mastered the art of being "common", and anything outside that box of standardness was gravely prohibited by the most basic of survival guidelines.

Suddenly the door swung open and within seconds my back was up against the wall, my mouth captured and my pulse racing. I moaned at the sensations trailing down my exposed neck as my hands held tightly onto his broad shoulders.

"Never again." His voice was hoarse.

"Mmm."

Logan's powerful hands placed mine in captivity while his thigh pressed further in between my own.

"You can ask for anything, an island of your own if you so wish, but you will never ask to spend another night apart from me."

His tone was edged too sharp for banter.

"Never again." I agreed before Logan's mouth ravaged my obedient one in hungry approval.

I could say it was the enchantment of the evening or even the way Logan looked in a tux but none of it would be truly to blame. The all-consuming fire was omnipresent between us, insatiable and potent.

I'd found my center of existence in Logan's eyes and I: his anchor. Where he hurt, I hurt, where I dreamed, he'd raise me above the clouds soaring. What Logan experienced, my soul journeyed beside him; for we were bound by a force which was both our deepest weakness and our greatest strength. And try as I had, I couldn't make sense in any of it. We were beautiful and dangerous and irrevocably explosive.

Logan's breath was mint and heat at my ear.

"You're *mine,* Alice. Say it."

His teeth sunk into my skin and I couldn't drown out the sound of pleasure escaping my lips.

"I was never anything else."

The words broke out in breathless syllables. Logan pulled back, his hands cradling my head, his gaze wild.

"I would walk the depths of Hell for you. There are no limits and no rules when it comes to you. Do you know that?"

I'd lost count the times Logan swore such things and I believed him, every time. This was different. The dimness in the room hid little of the darkness blanketing each word. I'd sensed it for some time, small crumbs I'd been collecting over the past week, and I knew there was more.

I caressed the hard line of his jaw, brushing my fingers over the lips that made promises of beauty—and death.

"I know." 'But I'll never allow it', I wanted to add, though, I knew better. Logan needed to believe it; to refuse him would only inflict pain and no other result. I loved him too much, enough to keep such confessions prisoner.

"Did you enjoy your evening?"

"I did, thank you—for everything."

Logan's lips brushed mine, pulling away too soon.

"Your happiness is all I want, Alice. You've given me what money can't buy, this—this is nothing compared to what I plan to do for you."

Our kiss was slow and reverent, speaking where words were no longer enough. I was cherished, I was loved, and I was protected. Logan was my ultimate undoing.

The door handle rattled before a light knock sounded into the lavish lavatory. I smothered a laugh with my own palm as my head hit the wall. Logan fixed the edge of my dress, trailing his lips across my shoulder before reaching my ear

"Ready?"

I nodded, taking his hand as he opened the heavy door.

Logan exited with swagger, the kind I'd read about in novels but never actually imagined was possible to us real people. He moved with confidence and ownership of himself and all that fell within his path He didn't ask; he took.

I fed off of his energy, I watched it in admiration and longed for such conviction in myself. Where Logan was real, I was but an imposter. Every face I wore, I wore well; I'd become a master in deception, a survival instinct I told myself to ease the guilt. Though, at the heart of it all, faces was all they were. At my core I was one thing—a liar.

Logan lead me by the small of my back towards the mingling crowd in the atrium, his skin heating mine thus rendering the thin fabric of my dress as nothing more than a pointless barrier. Within moments Gabe approached, discreetly whispering something into Logan's ear before disappearing into the shadows once again.

"What was that?"

Before turning his attention to me Logan nodded curtly at a guard near the patio doors, milliseconds later the guard slipped outside and into the moonless night.

"The media."

Why would they care about Seth's and Marina's wedding?

"I don't understand."

Turning to me Logan brought me closer as his hand cradled my cheek.

"The media has been circling the property since preparations began a week ago. Two cameras made it past the perimeter tonight; seems they'd managed to capture several payday images."

"Why would pictures of Seth and Marina be worth anything?"

I was missing something.

"They wouldn't."

"The images aren't of the bride and groom are they?"

Logan's grip tightened and I knew I'd guessed correctly.

"I've eluded the media for years, spent countless resources of every form to remain a mystery, though, an occasional shot here and there was enough to feed the vultures. Once the rumors of a mystery woman arose the stakes have risen. Images of you cannot surface, I make damn certain of it."

The Powder Room had windows. I thought the flashing light was simply security running checks on—whatever.

"What happens to those who cross the line?"

I think I already knew.

"They learn the payoff isn't worth the cost."

Countless times I'd awoken before the break of dawn to find Logan absent from our bed. I would grab my robe and go searching, only to find him in his study every time. Sometimes he was conducting a conference call, other times Gabe was in attendance or he'd be typing away at his Mac. I questioned if Logan was ever free? And I was equally to blame for I'd done nothing but add more shackles. I worried, fearing he couldn't go much longer this way.

Voicing such worries would provide no help and no improvement. Logan was a calculated being and as such, emotion was unwelcome. So instead I smiled weakly just as Luke approached.

"The tables are set, they're seating the guests now so I thought I'd find you two."

I sensed more.

"Before we go, I wanted to thank you. What you've done for my sister today, well it's priceless."

Logan nodded politely but said nothing.

"Also, I wanted to congratulate you both. I'm happy for you. Alice is special so you can understand my hesitation, but I can recognize honor and integrity when I see it, and I can admit where I've been wrong."

Luke held out his hand as Logan accepted.

"I could never fault you for caring about Alice's wellbeing. And I can appreciate the balls it takes to admit when you're wrong."

The men shook with a firm grip before Luke led us to the table we would be sharing with the bride and groom.

"There you are. I was beginning to wonder—"

Marina wriggled her brows with a trouble-making grin.

"The only thing you should be wondering is if you packed all you'll need for your honeymoon."

Marina leaned in, though, her voice had failed to dim its volume in support.

"What's there to pack? Three days in a cabin, alone. Hell, I don't even need this dress."

Out of the corner of my eye I could see the grin on Seth's face, though, he was supposed to be listening to whatever Luke was sharing.

"Just don't go trying to graduate the Polar Bear Club." I teased.

"I doubt we'll be going outdoors all that much."

"No shame, huh?"

"None."

I shook my head as a small laugh sang through. It might've been the pigtails, or the vixen gleam in her dazzling green eyes. Whatever it was, it elicited happiness.

"Have you made your rounds yet—spoken to the crew?"

"Yup."

"What, that's it? How'd it go?"

Marina grinned slyly.

"Leave it to Steph to tell you point blank what the others were no doubt thinking."

I gave Marina a look which said—continue or suffer the consequences.

"Steph said it was 'the most cohesive combination of elegance, love, and utter bizarreness'; oh and that 'we had the sweetest yet oddest friendship she'd ever witnessed' though, in a weird way it made her respect us all the more. Trish nearly spit out her drink, Stace laughed uninhibited, and Andrew just grinned and hugged me. It was all very entertaining, you should've been there."

"Does it make me a scaredy cat that I'm glad I wasn't?"

"Look who's making the animal references *now*."

I swatted away the finger she had pointed at me accusingly.

"And yes, it does make you a scaredy cat which is tragic. I'm so much more of a dog person."

"You're ridiculous, you know that?"

Marina shrugged.

"Who cares, I'm happy."

That she was.

We finally turned to face the others just as the food began to appear before us. Logan had ordered me a lemon basil crusted salmon fillet. It looked succulent with a distinct citrus infused scent.

Logan conversed with Seth, often timing his speech in rhythm with Marina asking for my attention. The choreography was smooth and felt entirely natural, perhaps it was, yet I couldn't escape the digging anxiety that it wasn't. There was an underlying current; dark and unwelcome, and I couldn't shake the build-up of fear within me.

The strategic glances between Seth and Logan or the look of dread on Dad's face as he stared at me inconspicuously, unaware that the mirrored candle base atop the table offered me a window into his hidden fears. Add the cryptic texts and bulked up security—the pieces all piled together in neon colors which I could no longer ignore or find ways to excuse. I willed my heart to pump evenly for if I could just get through this night without panic; that would be enough.

Logan's palm slid over my knee, inching higher with greed and ownership. I had no need to look at him to know he'd noticed. His firm grip radiated suspicion.

"Alice? You're racing." He spoke evenly, his posture poised as he always was, but the current refused to relinquish, it rippled through time and space, pulsing with rage.

"It's nothing, memories that snuck up on me. A distraction is all I need."

But as the lies spilled over my lips it was clear he wasn't buying my dressed up mendacity.

Logan's jaw clenched with displeasure, though, I knew well enough he wouldn't press for the sake of being discreet. Still, Logan's concern continued to bother me long after he'd seamlessly woven himself into the conversation between Luke and Trent who'd come up to give Seth a firm clap on the back. I smiled, in mock involvement to the conversation as my emotions ran from the irrational to compulsion.

There were more secrets dancing around this table than sand in the dunes so the only viable option was to play along and bid my time. I felt disrespected and perhaps that's what hurt the most. I was hoping I'd misread the signs yet by the third message from Gabe I'd run out of excuses.

*

I rubbed my arms, attempting to jump start my blood-flow to warm me against the night frost. Several of Marina's college friends, whom I'd known enough about to call acquaintances, were indulging in the heated conversational nooks prepared by the event staff.

Alcoves of furniture fitted with heated cushions, tables topped with hot beverages, rabbit-skin throws and torches emitting enough heat for luxury. The young and lively guests were none the wiser as I half-heartedly listened from behind walls of shadows while they oooh'd and ahhh'd at such opulence. The tall curvaceous beauty openly joked how much she'd like to take Seth home for a night before another voice mentioned some things odd and peculiar, and so their gossiping ensued. All the while I chided myself.

Since the meal I'd failed to focus on this wedding. The first dance and well prepared toasts, and even the cake cutting; with a cake I'd spent dozens of hours on. All of the moments I'd been achingly looking forward to had been cast in a veil of trepidation, and I felt robbed—by my own shortcomings.

It was now the early hours of the ninth, and the guests were fewer and fewer. So when Logan was pulled away for yet another "nothing to concern me with" issue, I'd decided it was time for some air and solitude.

There was something about standing exposed to the elements which awakened my instincts. The bitter cold stung my skin and invigorated my lungs, I felt my eyes dilate and reflexes sharpen. It was automatic—impulsive. Biologically programmed.

"Mrs. Snow, are you alone?"

A lesser person would've startled; I should have, if only to benefit the guards tentative approach, as though afraid I would collapse before his eyes.

"I am."

"Forgive me, Mrs. Snow but per orders you're not to be outdoors unattended. Allow me to escort you back."

He wasn't one of the regular details, though, he seemed nice enough as he held out his suit jacket to me.

I accepted, on both accounts.

"Wait, take me around back."

The guard seemed unsure so I waved towards the loud group.

"I would hate for them to know of the audience they've been entertaining."

He nodded before ushering me towards the south side of the building. Upon reaching the doorway I slid off the leased coat, doing my best to appear indifferent against my chilled bones.

"You certain you're all right, Mrs. Snow?"

Assuming that my lips were the ideal shade of frozen I understood his look of anxiety, though, I had no intention of sharing my insecurities with the older man. He needn't know that my affliction reached far deeper than skin.

"I appreciate your concern, but I assure you I'm fine. Good night."

With a nod I was left to navigate my way back to the event.

While reaching the head of the stairs I spotted a suit, armed with a slim briefcase, and aimed for Logan's study.

There was a sudden hum inside my head, a warning or a calling; both perhaps. The trusting wife inside me would've continued down the hall, found Logan and happily celebrated until physically incapable. The decent part of me would've politely acknowledged the man as he exited the study giving him no reason to suspect I was on to him or his employer. The ignorant woman I desired to be would've smiled with approval when witnessing such discrete and professional conduct by my husband's subjects. An hour's worth of contemplation and consideration raced within my head during those seconds yet in the end, instinct prevailed.

I slipped behind the marble column two heartbeats before the suit emerged, briefcase-less, and none the wiser to my voyeurism and intent.

Chapter Thirty Five

Allison Snow

Stepping into the dimly lit Study, my heart was drumming violently. The room seemed full of trepidation; the atmosphere surrounding me so alive I believed with certainty the library spanning the north wall was roaring with the inscription "RUN" upon the hundreds of spines.

I'd learned life was a culmination of moments; times of happiness or even mundane; And then there were the defining moments, the ones which effectively altered the future, forever closing upon the present, for nothing would remain unaffected. This was that moment, where everything was about to change.

Within the pristine space, nothing was out of place except *me*. Every article of furniture owned its respectful piece of real estate within the room; even the briefcase taunted my intrusion. It glistened despite the darkness which enveloped the leather, smooth and handsome beneath my trembling fingers.

I danced around it as though performing some form of courtship, perhaps on some delusional platform I'd hoped the outcome would've been different. But what possible change in conclusion could there be when the contents within the leather contraption was nothing but venom.

The latch gave way before I slid my hand inside to pull out several files. Each contained what deep within, I'd already known. My head shook in dispute, my hands trembling despite my will to stay strong, and my heart—burned beyond rescue.

I felt sick, physically and emotionally. I was drowning with every picture and coroner's report which slipped through my fingers. What justice was there when the innocent were butchered? How many lives would be destroyed all because I couldn't part with mine?

I felt his approach moments before I heard the echo of footsteps. The door gave way to a man unsurprised by my presence, a storm brewing within him as he ordered his flock of guards to disperse in a tone eerily calm. As ordered, Gabe exited last, leaving me to face the hurricane.

"Find what you were looking for?"

"Seems I have."

Logan's chest rose with momentum, he was angry, and so was I.

"All you had to do was ask and I would've shown you anything you wanted to see."

Bullshit.

"Ask you say? Ask for what? For you to tell me, your *wife*, that I'd been set up? Or for the simple courtesy of being informed that dead bodies were washing up with a striking resemblance to me? Or was I supposed to *ask* for those I hold closest on the entire bloody planet to keep me updated on matters which affect my very life? Silly me, why hadn't I just asked!!!"

Logan stepped forward, fury etched down to his bone.

I refused to back down, my feet planted firmly despite the damn sequined heels.

"You think me too weak?"

"No."

"Stupid?"

"No."

"Incapable? Daft? Naïve? Narrow minded—"

"Enough!"

Logan had me pinned on top of his desk, his hands treaded deep into my hair as his eyes bore into mine.

"How have you been sleeping since our first night together?"

What does that have anything to do with this?

"Answer me!"

"The best since I can remember." My voice caught and I made no attempt to hide it.

"I know. So you've said, countless times. But how can that be when every night my chest is flooded with your tears?"

I searched his eyes, not understanding his question. What the hell was he talking about?

"Every night you tremble, you weep, battling a war so deep within your soul that your conscious mind holds no memory of the carnage I witness helplessly within our bed. You want the truth? If there was a way I could've kept this from you—I would've without an ounce of guilt. With every beat of my tarnished heart I would've done anything within my power to keep even a single rain drop from your head. Not because you lack the strength or wisdom; because I'm too damn weak to watch you be cut, bleed, and die a little more each night."

My anger fizzled, leaving behind confusion and regret. I had no memory of such nightmares; sleeping in Logan's arms was as close to Heaven as I'd ever been, yet the agony within his eyes was palpable. With his head touching mine his pain was my own. I laid still within his hold absorbing his revelation. I had every right to spit fire yet with every ripple of his pulse, genuine and profound, the fire had no choice but to fade away.

"You should've told me about the nightmares, you had no right to keep any of this from me."

His jaw was set hard, his back rippled with tension. I was suddenly left undesirably alone on what was now a too-cold marble desk. Logan reached into a credenza against the back wall producing a stack of documents which he placed beside me.

"We planned to inform you once we'd received confirmation, that's what you saw."

"We—meaning Seth? Who else, Dad?"

I slid off the desk before reaching to flip through the files.

"And Luke."

Of course.

"I'd like to keep it from Marina, at least until her honeymoon is over."

"Too late."

My face fell.

"What did you expect, Alice? You disappeared in the middle of her wedding, she searched. It didn't take long for her to figure out you were in here."

I'd failed.

"I can make something up, we had a fight, something!"

Logan looked at me hard.

"It's done. You lie to her here and she won't forgive you once she finds out. Keeping her in the dark before was honorable, now—"

It would be betrayal. I made a mistake and it was unfixable.

A knock at the door caused me to flinch. Within a moment Logan stood before me, strong, reliable, beautiful— dangerous. Cupping my face Logan's lips traced mine with greed, a roughness I desperately loved whether right or wrong. It no longer mattered to me. With another knock of urgency our lips parted, pulse rapid, breath heavy.

"It's time."

I understood.

The lights suddenly encroached on our space and this insignificant detail bothered me more than I believed it should have. In the dimness things seemed manageable, somehow within my abilities. But the lights made me feel exposed and the task at hand so—impossible. How stupid I thought, though, that changed nothing.

Dad walked in first, followed by Luke, and as though for sheer effect, last walked in Seth hand in hand with Marina. The men showed varying degrees of dread while Marina simply looked—scared.

"I'm sorry." The words were out without thought.

Marina's brows drew together in confusion.

"Someone better tell me something before I lose it."

Seth led Marina to one of the leather armchairs, we followed, each taking a seat.

Dad looked to Logan questioningly.

"So it's confirmed then?"

"Yes, all of it as we'd suspected."

Dad's hands coiled. Luke's gaze connected with mine, though, he was unable to hold it. He looked away, more than likely thinking I should've listened to him from the beginning, maybe then things wouldn't have happened this way.

"Alice will soon be under investigation for child pornography—" Logan began.

"What! Is this a joke?" Marina shrieked at the preposterous statement, but, however farcical—it was happening.

Seth turned to his wife of several hours, a haunted look spilling over for all to see.

"This will all seem too much, just listen for now, and then…then we can talk okay?"

The reality hit her hard. Her eyes glistened with unshed tears while she blinked them back as best she could. It wasn't fair. She still wore her stunning wedding gown; her pigtails gave view of times far happier than now, times I desperately wished could overshadow our current position. But as she twirled and fingered the symbol of union upon her left hand, I knew the dread of what news awaited her was warranted.

"Lily Snow."

Logan paused, looking at me with unconcealed regret.

"Lily blames Alice for what ended our arrangement. Jenna was hired to spy, after I became more involved with Alice the plan was forged to position Alice for scandal. Jenna was finishing her degree in programming and for all her faults, the girl knew her niche. Various damning encryptions had been fed into Alice's laptop at the café. The materials originated at that very laptop, supporting the validity of the tips to the bureau."

"An idiot could see Alice doesn't get off on watching little kids, how can this even be investigated?"

"Alice hasn't been positioned as a customer, she's a facilitator."

Marina's eyes went wide.

"That's insane! Why this? Why not something equally implausible like selling elephant tusks on the black market? Who knows, maybe she has an assembly line of illegal firearms in the basement of a family-friendly café or better yet let's just go all out and say she's an alien who's escaped from Area Fifty One! Each scenario would be just as ludicrous!"

It would. But that wasn't the point.

"Child abuse and pornography were selected because of me. I'm a significant financial donor to a multitude of organizations fighting crimes against children. Lily wanted the shock value, a scandal."

"I don't get how this affects you."

"Because—"

I stopped him. It should be me.

"Because we're married, Sunshine."

Marina went from fear to confusion—to hurt.

"When?"

My hands twisted.

"The night after Thanksgiving."

She wouldn't meet my eyes, looking to the floor or something in that direction. I wanted to explain myself, make her understand my reasons had merit.

"I see. Well, congratulations I suppose. I would've gotten you something but, well, that's irrelevant now. Back to the investigation then, they'll see its all fraud right? That much has to be obvious unless the entire bureau is made up of brains the size of walnuts."

"The investigation is not the breaking point. We've had enough warning to clean up some of Jenna's mess, and have compiled evidence to the contrary to assist in the investigation. We're not concerned about a conviction."

"I don't get it. If we're not worried about the outcome and there's some bad press for you than why the theatrics? Why do I feel like I'm in a room with the Grimm Reaper?"

We sat quiet for a moment before Seth moved to speak, his face expressionless.

"Several months ago we were approached by a man whose wife had gone missing. During our investigation we uncovered three similar cases."

He paused, straining to remain indifferent.

"The four victims all have physical and ethnic similarities: Russian immigrants, petite, mid-twenties, all with a resemblance to Alice."

The images within the files infiltrated my mind and I wanted to vomit. Everything about the bodies, from the wounds to the post mortem positioning echoed The Red Brotherhood. With each victim the brutality of her injuries intensified, they were growing angrier. I felt myself pale despite my efforts to keep calm. I was trembling as I imagined each victim being murdered for no other reason than resembling someone they didn't even know. Where was the justice?

"Alice?"

I looked up to see Logan. I hadn't realized he'd stood and knelt before me, the others looking on with concern.

"I'm sorry."

My body trembled against my will as Logan wrapped me safely within himself. I reveled in the secureness of him, my eyelids closed and I allowed myself to be vulnerable, letting go of the constant need to show fearlessness when I was the exact opposite.

"Give me your fears, Alice, and take my love instead."

I breathed in each word like oxygen.

"Look at me."

I did so willingly and lost myself within him, just like I always did for that was the only place I found peace.

Logan moved to stand behind me, his hands firmly placed upon my shoulders, feeding me the strength to get through this gathering.

"The story will get national coverage simply because of my position, and regardless of its outcome the damage will be done. Lily did this to hurt me, hoping to get Alice incarcerated and promising Jenna the owner's rights to the café after litigations were over. Ultimately without knowing, Lily did far worse. With such exposure Alice will be located within days. Seth won't be far behind. And you Marina will be right beside him."

"So we flee!" Marina eagerly put in.

"We pack up tonight and get the hell away from here. We can go to Scotland and start fresh. You have connections, Logan, you can make this happen."

Marina looked determined, it gave me hope that she'd survive what was to follow.

"Running will only delay the inevitable. Too much has been lived, too many connections, countless sources retaining remnants and trails to follow. Running won't save us."

We all sat in a tension-wound silence so tight it sucked the air directly from my chest. We all had much to lose, our lives included. Nothing prepared you for such moments, decisions that would haunt you; never good enough, clever enough, fast enough—*never* enough.

"What happens now?" Marina's voice was small, wounded, and it pained me to hear it.

"I've spent the better part of my adult life devoted to the collapse of The Red Brotherhood. My fortune was built with one sole purpose, deals and debts too questionable for such an audience so I'll save you the introduction to my ghosts. I have bodies planted throughout the organization, some have lived inside the reigns of The Brotherhood for nearly a decade and some a mere year, while others have lost their lives."

Seth looked at him with contempt. But Logan continued undeterred.

"I have resources, all of which are being utilized to build our defense. We have one way and one way only of coming out of this alive. Ily. We must lure him out. As long as Ily lives, we'll never run far enough."

"How?" Dad's voice almost startled me. Logan didn't pause.

"Alice."

"The hell you will! She wouldn't be in this mess if it weren't for you!"

Luke looked at me, desperation begging for recognition.

"She's the only incentive Ily will take a risk to obtain."

"No! There must be something else, another option."

Seth stood, pacing behind the chair still housing his wife.

"You have moles, we can incentivize the CIA to target him, extradite and convict. The Brotherhood's crimes extend to dozens of countries, we'll approach each of them if we have to. We can extract the insurance within that safety deposit box and that will offer the authorities enough incentive to move on this."

Seth spoke almost as though to himself.

Seth stopped pacing, his hands coiled into fists of fury and sense of guilt. I'd forgiven him for his participation the night of my mama's murder, though, Seth had yet to forgive himself; a guilt which was clouding his judgment.

"This is the only viable—"

"No, we'll start here then contact Interpol—"

"Enough! Get your head out of your ass, Seth! Alice is all I care about, you understand? I would've cut off your head and delivered it to Ily myself if that guaranteed Alice's life, but you're nothing more than a bonus to him! Ily has one hundred times the resources we have and double that in wealth, we're on the losing team, we have one shot so get your shit together! Or have you forgotten why you never turned to the authorities for help from the get-go?"

"We had a deal! I was supposed to be the bait!"

"And Lily destroyed that plan! It's over!"

"If you'd taken care of that land mine like you were supposed to—we wouldn't be here!"

Seth moved like lightning, throwing a punch and then another. The men collided knocking over my chair and me along with it to the side. The volume exploded as I screamed, the shriek of Marina's cries soon mixed with my own, and before long I couldn't decipher who screamed what. Seth's face was bleeding as Logan pinned him to the ground. I wiped at my eyes desperate to confirm they hadn't killed each other as fresh tears continued to blur the vicious sight. My shoulders shook as I sat helpless against the sounds of broken flesh and widening wounds.

"*Please*, stop. I beg you."

I spoke the words as if into a black hole and closed my eyes; unable to stand the sight any longer. I didn't know who was hitting whom, I didn't want to. I just wanted it all to stop, everything to just—STOP.

What seemed like hours passed and I finally looked up to find that Dad and Luke had remained within their respective seats as though nothing had occurred inches in front of them. Seth was still on the floor, and Logan—he stood looking out the wall of windows to a blanket of snow, pristine and glistening; a stark contrast to the current of rage within him I could almost see with the naked eye.

Dad stood, causing me to focus on his features and regretting it instantaneously. His eyes were wet, his expression hopeless. Today was supposed to be beautiful, a day he gave his little girl away in marriage to a man he loved and cared for, only to have it ripped from under him within hours.

Dad approached Logan speaking out of earshot before they both returned. Luke stood and helped Seth up from the floor and into a chair—it seemed as though we were even further behind than when we first sat down. Nothing was predictable and everything was on the line.

"Now listen."

Dad had a hardness I'd never witnessed, a window into someone he'd hidden from me until now.

"Seth, this was going to happen regardless of Lily. The Brotherhood has been sniffing you out and they were damn close before this fiasco emerged. Blaming Snow won't lighten your guilt. Let it go, Son."

Seth had his head in his hands, unbothered by the blood painting his face.

"Logan, make it happen on one condition."

Logan nodded his attention.

"We fight, the girls live. Even if that means they do so without us."

The sounds of Marina's anguish filled the space as she crumbled beneath everything this day should not have become. I went to console her but she reached for Seth instead as he offered her a false reprieve; but even a false one was welcomed here.

Venom washed over me, providing a numbness I welcomed. I no longer felt present in the room; finding myself lost in the matrix of my own purgatory. I felt trapped and everything I cared for was broken. The devastation was too much too soon and such bitterness chilled my already withering soul.

I'd dared, I'd hoped—I'd lost, and all that I loved would suffer the consequences.

Epilogue

Logan Snow

"The golf club has an opening Friday. We should set it up."

That left us three days.

"I've got plans, next week perhaps." My voice was calm, smooth; when I felt anything but.

"Next week then." Robert spoke easily. As if we were actually friends.

"Cynthia will send you the details." I finish, before the line cut out.

I turned to Gabe.

"Friday it goes public. The press will be ready."

"I never knew you were so fond of golf."

I appreciated the sarcasm. Any agent with half a brain could deduce that call had nothing to do with golf. What did it matter when over half the bureau was corrupt. So long as you covered your ass, no one would talk.

"The acquisition is complete." Gabe continued, and my artery jolted with adrenaline.

"Let's go."

We departed rather briskly. Cynthia seemed nervous, more than likely sensing I'd been planning to replace her. If I hadn't been dealing with all the other shit, she'd have been gone by now.

The L.S. Trade Co. building faded into the background as we headed east, trading in the icon of success for a structure less grand and more fitted for the type of business that transpired within its walls.

We passed the café, a routine detour regardless of our destination. I caught a glimpse of Alice through the glass pane and the small reassurance was enough to keep me motivated.

I was losing her. Since Sunday she'd become more vacant by the hour and it was killing me. She played her role without a glitch upon entering her café, yet once she entered our home she no longer had to wear her mask; a ghost was all that remained. I'd lost all perspective, become possessed with a singular mission: destroy The Brotherhood at any cost.

Pulling up to the concrete building left my blood running as cold as the below-zero temperatures inside it, and as we entered the cinderblock cell I abandoned my conscience at the threshold. There was no moral code for what transpired inside these walls.

The bound and bleeding trash before me was different than those before him. I gave Gabe the signal indicating his Intel succeeded, this wasn't just a sworn-in brother, this was a bloodline member with the information and access I needed.

"How much is your life worth?"

The bag of flesh whose documented name was Vitaliy turned to face me, though, I doubted he saw much of anything judging by the state of his face. I had to give him credit for staying silent after enduring such injuries.

He showed no sign of responding so I picked up the gas can and drenched him slowly for sheer effect.

"You have sixty seconds to change your mind and I'll take pity on you, give you a quick death."

Vitaliy was trembling, despite his bravado he didn't want to die any more than I wanted to take his life. I flicked the match and watched as he gave in.

"The politician is Rick Loneburg."

I blew out the match and cocked my .45, setting it to his head.

"The code."

Vitaliy was breathing hard, sensing his last moments. "The code or I can start with your knee caps to jolt your memory."

"Nine, nine, one, four, eight—three—three."

It was a gamble, I had no way to verify the code's validity but it was all we had, and it was better than nothing.

"You're crazier than my dead whore aunt if you think you can stop us. Nadia will die like the trash she is, only now you'll be joining her. Perhaps Slavic will rape her one last time for old time's sake—"

The bullet dug swiftly through his skull before it hit me *exactly* who this piece of shit was. I suddenly wanted to revive him and tear him limb from limb in a slow and agonizing death and it still wouldn't be enough for what he deserved.

"Loneburg."

It was like acid on my tongue. A senator notorious for all that was wrong with the system. The problem was every seat in the Senate had its own agenda, each greatly incentivized to turn a blind eye. I wanted to vomit and the corpse at my feet had nothing to do with it.

I dialed Seth. He answered on the first ring.

"Yeah."

"The acquisition was successful."

"Business is good I take it." His voice rang light but I knew he was on edge.

"Prospects have revealed themselves. We should gather a team, talk tactics. Have you seen the latest news on Loneburg?"

"No, you know better than to believe the media, they're biased and full of shit."

"Probably right. Beers tonight at my place, we can catch the game."

"See you then."

Code, everything was code; but Seth kept up. I understood what Ily saw in him.

Gabe pulled the Polaroid to take the shots.

"Make it detailed. Ily will want to be certain it's his grandson, we need to set his fuse."

"The placeholders are angry, Snow. The change to the plan has set them on edge. They want to stick with the original blueprint."

"They don't make the decisions. It could be years before the pieces would be ready to play!"

"Olli says they could be ready in several months."

I had come to know Gabe better than he'd ever like to admit so as he looked at me, I knew the real issue.

"You tell them if anyone wants to pull out then do it now and I'll still honor the contract. We don't *have* months."

Gabe nodded. He had a connection to the men which I lacked. Gabe facilitated; I funded. Some were mercenaries, others veterans of a system which cast them aside when they were no longer useful.

After dumping the body into the incinerator we departed. My gut churned and my head throbbed with the sound of the bullet piercing his skull, the venom in his laugh as he fantasized the murder of Alice as though it was the most prized event of his filthy life. But I wasn't the same fool I'd been a decade ago; naïve enough to believe negotiations were possible, that by awarding them the option to leave alive it would elicit a sense of morality or duty. That mistake nearly cost me my own life, and my vision was no longer painted with artificial sunlight. The scum deserved what came to him, yet that didn't make taking a life any easier.

I pushed all sympathetic thoughts aside, focusing only on Vitaliy's last words to feed my revenge. In the world of the underground, mercy was a sign of weakness—a stench the ruthless snuffed out like wolves on a hunt. They fed on it ravenously, and I sure as hell wasn't about to become a part of that meal.

Author's Notes

Thank you for partaking in Alice's world, where remaining alive and living, aren't synonymous. As stated in the synopsis, Alice's story is a duet; the conclusion to the terror will be revealed in book two: *Symbol of Redemption*, due for release August 2016.

For updates and more information about the story or about me, the author, please visit my website at www.natalyaorekhov.com. You may also sign up for my email list to have updates sent directly to you.

I look forward to sharing the remainder of Alice's story with the world, a story that won't be bordered in rainbows or singing the happiest tunes, but it is Alice's story, and it must be told.

Author Biography

As a Russian refugee Natalya Orekhov at a very young age learned that life is anything but fair. If her toys and clothing were not donations from a charity or a kind soul then they were acquired by a technique called Dumpster Diving. As the fourth of five children, Natalya was well versed in the dynamics of big families. Yet despite the bickering and slamming of doors, everyone knew that with this family, blood would always be thicker than water; their screams always took second place to their cheers for one another.

Today Natalya lives in a cozy home in South West Littleton, Colorado, with her husband and two young children. She's known in her neighborhood as an excellent baker and enjoys surprising friends with mouthwatering desserts. Though, moderately young, Natalya has earned several degrees in various disciplines of life—in hardship, heartache, and forgiveness when it's the last thing you want to give. Yet in the midst of such a grueling education, Natalya has also had the great privilege to meet countless individuals with hearts larger than life and spirits that rival the best of them. To such individuals she will be eternally grateful.

With the release of Natalya's debut novel *Symbol of Treason* in November, 2015; she quickly realized the depth of her passion for writing and the hunger her readers showed for stories that reached deeper than surface angst, and down to what gripped the soul. Since, Natalya has written *Symbol of Redemption*, with many more to come.

www.ingramcontent.com/pod-product-compliance
Lightning Source LLC
Chambersburg PA
CBHW051428260626
47162CB00001B/4